Also by Jessica Meigs

The Becoming (previous edition)
The Becoming: Ground Zero
The Becoming: Revelations
The Becoming: Under Siege
The Becoming: Redemption
The Becoming: Origins

THE BECOMING

JESSICA MEIGS

A PERMUTED PRESS BOOK

ISBN: 978-1-68261-856-1

The Becoming:
Book One in The Becoming Series
© 2018 by Jessica Meigs
All Rights Reserved

Cover art by Christian Bentulan

PERMUTED
PRESS

Permuted Press, LLC
New York • Nashville
permutedpress.com

Published in the United States of America

PART ONE
FALL

PROLOGUE

Atlanta, GA

Brandt Evans' scuffed black combat boots struck the pavement as he ran down the rain-dampened street, his heart hammering wildly against his ribs, like it was trying to beat free from his chest. His breathing was loud and harsh. His hands sweated and shook uncontrollably. His whole body was on edge.

He'd been running for over half an hour.

Brandt ducked into an alley without slowing his pace and dropped down beside a smelly, overflowing green dumpster to hide. Leaning against the cool brick wall, he felt the solidness of it, the rough stones scraping against his back through his thin t-shirt. He closed his eyes and struggled to breathe. His lungs burned. His eyes hurt.

He was a rabbit trying to outrun a fox. Hunted. Desperate.

He just needed a moment to rest. Just one moment. He could spare a moment, couldn't he?

Brandt leaned forward and peered at the alley's opening, taking in a deep breath of the sharp, cold January air and rubbing his hands over each of his arms in turn to ward off the chill. He desperately wished he had a jacket as he hunched over and shivered. He held his breath until his chest ached, and then he slowly released it. It clouded the air before his face.

He thought he might have lost them, but he didn't want to take any chances. There was no way to know how many had followed him, how many had caught his scent. He had to assume it wasn't just one or two. He had to assume he was being pursued. Always pursued. If he let his guard down...

Brandt wiped his sweating palms down the thighs of his camouflage pants and leaned back against the wall again. He knew what would happen if he were caught. He'd seen too many people—his sister included—succumb to the plague. He knew if he were caught, it'd all end in blood and pain and death. It wasn't the end he'd envisioned for himself, and he refused to let it turn out that way.

He had to get out of the city, as soon as he could, if he expected to survive. He had to run. He had to get ahead of the infection, flee, and find a safe place to hide.

A faint noise echoed from the alleyway's entrance. Brandt's heart jumped into his throat and choked him. He peered around the edge of the dumpster again, and his hand wandered to the Beretta M9 pistol at his hip. He drew it and ejected the magazine to look inside. It was empty, as expected. He pulled back the slide. He already knew what he'd find: a single bullet, the one he'd carefully counted ammunition to save. Just in case.

But he was nothing if not a survivor, even if his survival had been forced out of him on a promise he hadn't wanted to make. He snapped the magazine back into the pistol as quietly as he could. The sound was too loud to his ears, and he worried that the simple action would draw unwanted attention to him.

As if on cue, a shuffling noise came from the other side of the dumpster. A quiet snarl and an odd snuffling sound followed it. Brandt closed his eyes and instinctively pressed back more firmly against the brick. He became the rabbit again, shrinking back among the loose trash that skittered about in the stiff, cold wind; he hoped against hope that he wouldn't be sniffed out. Another jolt of adrenaline pumped into Brandt's veins as an ominous chill ran down his spine and raised the hair on the back of his neck.

His instincts whispered that there wasn't going to be an escape from this one. He wasn't sure how much more of this he could take. The idea of being chased, of being caught, was slowly driving him insane. He had to do *something, anything* to alleviate the awful sensation.

Brandt took a deep, steadying breath and stood abruptly. His head swam at the sudden movement; his vision dimmed, and the alleyway spun around him. His heart lurched in his chest. Shaking his head, he caught his hand against the dumpster to steady himself and lifted the pistol. The weapon felt incredibly heavy, and the barrel trembled. He swallowed and curled his finger to depress the trigger.

Time slowed to a crawl.

The last bullet left the pistol with a bang. The bullet whipped past the blood-covered man who ran down the alleyway toward him. It embedded into the wall with a splatter of brick. Shards of red stone sprayed the man and cut into his cheek. He was unaffected as he continued his mindless pursuit.

Brandt stumbled back, and the emptied Beretta fell from his limp hand to the pavement. He looked left and right frantically, thoughts blazing through his mind in a flurry, faster than he could catch them. His shot had missed? How had it missed when the target was so close? He was an expert marksman, for Christ's sake! He wasn't supposed to miss!

Brandt swore under his breath and mentally inventoried the weapons left on his person. There hadn't been much to begin with: just the sidearm that now lay expended on the pavement and a rifle he'd abandoned once he had run out of ammunition for it, the extra weight of the spent weapon having been a hindrance. He took a couple of steps back and remembered the one weapon he had left.

Brandt knelt and pulled his KA-BAR knife free from the sheath strapped to the outside of his right boot. It wasn't much, and he wasn't sure how much damage the seven-inch blade could actually cause, but it was all he had left. He stood just in time. The man launched himself at Brandt, hands extended, animalistic hatred in his red-rimmed, bloodshot eyes.

Instinct guided him as he lifted the knife sharply upwards and stood from his kneeling position. In one smooth move that should have been deadly, Brandt slammed the knife's blade into the fleshy underside of the man's lower jaw.

To Brandt's dismay, the man's gnarled hands closed in tight fist in his shirt, and he shook his head violently to free the knife from his jaw. Trapped, Brandt struggled to pull himself from the man's grip, but the man was stronger than he looked. So he did the only thing he could: he wrenched the knife from the man's jaw and slammed it into his left temple.

As the blade struck home, the man's forward momentum carried him a few more steps. He leaned heavily against Brandt and then fell to the pavement in a heap.

Brandt backed away from the body, shuddering as nausea welled up in his throat. He shook it off and took his first real look at the man who'd attacked him. He wasn't anyone

Brandt recognized, which was the best news he'd get all day. This man was too old to have been a current member of the military. He was around seventy, thin and bony and wrinkled with age, hair white and sparse on his head. He was clad in dirtied sweatpants and a bloodstained white bathrobe, his feet bare and torn from running without shoes on the cold, unforgiving streets and sidewalks of Atlanta. The elderly man was definitely a civilian, possibly from one of the local nursing homes. Judging by the crusted blood under his lengthening, yellowed fingernails, the man had been ill for at least four days.

Brandt grasped the hilt of the knife and pulled it free from the man's temple. It slid away from the bone and flesh with an indescribable sound that made Brandt shudder in disgust. He took a moment to wipe the blood from the blade onto the edge of the dead man's bathrobe. He had no desire to continue his exam of the body. He looked instead to the Beretta lying on the wet pavement; the weapon was empty and wouldn't do him any further good. The chances he'd find much suitable ammunition for it in a city under siege were slim, and searching for it wasn't worth his time. The general populace had, days before, raided the gun shops and sports stores in the city for anything usable that had been left behind by the military, and all of the ammunition shelves were likely bare. Regardless, he scooped the gun up and jammed it into the holster on his belt.

Brandt looked around the darkening alley. Night had begun to fall, the dusk settling over the alley and making it difficult to see. He tried to center his mind and figure out where to go, what to do. He couldn't stay on the streets in the dark; it increased his chances of being killed tenfold. The city still crumbled around him, so he needed to move fast. His options were severely limited.

He turned in a slow circle and spotted a red ladder hanging at the end of the alley, almost invisible in the dark. A fire escape, he realized. It at least offered an alternative to returning to the street. He glanced over his shoulder to make sure nothing else was coming in his direction, then returned the knife to its sheath and jumped up. He caught the bottom rung of the ladder and hauled himself onto it, his biceps bulging as he dragged himself up. He began climbing as quickly as he dared.

The metal rungs were slick with rain and ice, and they bit into Brandt's palms and fingers as he trekked up the ladder. His boots slipped on the icy rungs more than once and sent his heart faltering in his chest. It was only through his own reflexes that he didn't fall from the ladder and to the pavement below. The thought of breaking bones and leaving himself helpless was enough to keep him on his guard. There'd be no survival for him if he ended up with a broken leg in a dirty alley in downtown Atlanta. In that situation, he could just slap a sign on himself that said "dinner" and lie back to wait for the end.

Brandt reached the roof easily enough and gained his footing on the flat, graveled surface. From there, he took a few moments to look out across the city and plan his next step. Smoke billowed on the horizon, close to the edge of the downtown metro area. A tornado siren blasted its monotonous refrain from somewhere in the city, warning Atlanta residents to get to a safe place. Gunfire rang out too close to his position for comfort. Screams echoed faintly through the streets nearby, but he didn't dare check out the source. An ambulance siren played its part in the symphony of a city falling in on itself.

Brandt dropped to his knees, suddenly overwhelmed by all the trauma he'd experienced that day. He ignored the gravel digging into his skin through his pants and covered his mouth as he fought off the bile that rose in his throat. The horror he'd faced throbbed in his brain even as he closed his eyes. The things he'd seen and experienced that day were worse than anything he'd ever dreamed of. It was all he could do to remain upright as he fought to choke back the sickness in his mouth and soul.

He couldn't hold it back, though, and he hunched over the gravel and vomited. His throat burned and his eyes watered as he gripped the edge of the building and dug his fingers into the stone. His chest heaved as he coughed up the remains of his last sparse meal. He rocked back on his heels, wiping at his mouth with the back of his hand, and cleared his throat. The taste in his mouth was awful, but it was the last thing on his mind. He felt at his face, testing his own temperature as best he could. He couldn't tell if he was running a fever or if it was just heat generated by his climb up the fire escape ladder. He was sure he'd be feeling the symptoms by now if…

Brandt shook his head, clearing his throat once more as he took in the view. "A virus did all this?" he whispered hoarsely. He looked upon the city once more. The city in which he'd grown up. The city he'd loved more than any other city he'd seen in his time in the military. It was like nothing Brandt had ever witnessed before. It was the beginning of the end of civilization, and the thought terrified him. "How can this even be possible?"

Doctor Derek Rivers was wrong. He had to be wrong. The man who'd freed him and given him the chance to get this far was long dead, one of the early victims of the viral outbreak that, even now, swept over Atlanta and beyond with a speed to rival the Black Death itself. Brandt had thought that Derek had exaggerated when he'd told him what was going on in the outside world. But he hadn't exaggerated. Indeed, he hadn't gone far enough in his description of the total devastation that the virus had visited upon the city.

"Which way, which way?" he whispered. He forced himself to his feet once more. It wasn't time to be puking on a roof and reminiscing about men who were likely dead. He slowly surveyed the rooftop, searching for an escape route and a plan. He looked in every direction uncertain which way would be safest. None of them, really. Safety was a foreign concept to Atlanta now.

Before Brandt went anywhere, though, he needed weapons. He needed food. He needed water. And he needed a safe place to hide for the night.

CHAPTER ONE

Three Days Later

Plantersville, MS

Gray Carter leaned halfway under the hood of an older model Honda Civic, up to his elbows in grease and a grimace of concentration on his face, when a hand clapped against his back. Startled, he narrowly avoided striking his head on the underside of the hood before straightening and turning his grimace onto whoever had snuck up on him.

His twenty-five-year-old brother Theo stood beside him, attired in his immaculate paramedic uniform, his blond hair neatly combed and his blue eyes dancing with merriment. He held a takeout drink tray and a bag of what smelled like something fatty and greasy in one hand, and a wicked grin crossed his face. "I didn't scare you, did I?"

"Oh, shut up, asshole," Gray replied, though he couldn't stop a grin from spreading across his own face. He tugged the well-used rag from the back pocket of his coveralls and scrubbed at the filth that had accumulated on his hands. Engine grease had worked its way under his nails and into the creases of his skin, and he had no hope of getting it all out without liberal amounts of dish soap. "What are you doing here?" he asked, stuffing the rag back into his pocket. "I thought you had to work today."

"I go in later this evening," Theo replied. "I'm just covering for Justin while he's in class. I figured I'd grab us some lunch and drop in to see how you're doing." He looked past Gray at the vehicle and asked, "What's wrong with this one?"

"Fubar-ed alternator," he said. He nodded toward the white door that led from the service bays to the garage's administrative office. "There's a sink in the break room. I can wash up in there."

Gray led the way through the noisy garage, trying to tune out the sounds of the other mechanics banging around under the hoods of cars and calling out to each other. Somewhere, music blasted on the radio, R&B that drove Gray crazy day in and day out, but he wasn't allowed to listen to music on headphones while servicing a customer's car, so he had to endure the torture. As he pushed the doors open to enter the building, the music cut out, and an announcer broke in.

"*We interrupt your regular programming to bring you a breaking news announcem—*" The door swung shut behind him and Theo, and Gray didn't hear what was said. It was probably nothing important, anyway. Half of the news cycles were full of "breaking news" lately, and the vast majority of the notices were inconsequential. After an intense scrubbing session with dish detergent and a rag, Gray sat down in the folding metal chair across from his brother to the feast of cheap cheeseburgers and greasy fries that Theo had unpacked from the sack.

"You *did* get mine with no pickles, right?" Gray asked.

Theo blew the paper wrapper off his straw, shooting it across the table at him, and Gray swatted it out of the air. "What do you think I am?" Theo asked. "Some kind of an idiot?"

"Well..." Gray drew the word out and laughed when Theo gave him a mock-offended look. "I'm kidding, okay? I know you got it without pickles. You never *don't* get it without pickles."

"I don't understand your aversion to pickles," Theo said. He unwrapped his burger and took a messy bite and said with his mouth full of meat and bread, "They're awesome."

Gray wrinkled his nose but didn't reply. He bowed his head and recited the brief prayer of thanks he always made before eating. When he finished, he lifted his head to see Theo nibbling at a fry with a patient smile. He returned the smile and dug into his cheeseburger.

"You still do that prayer thing before you eat?" Theo asked once they'd both settled into the groove of their meals. Gray shrugged and finished his mouthful of burger before responding.

"Yeah, of course," he said. "Why? Don't you?"

Theo dabbed a fry in some ketchup. "Occasionally, whenever I think about it. Which isn't often." He took a bite of burger and reclined in his chair. "Hey, I have tomorrow off. After I get some sleep, do you want to go out on the town, do whatever?"

"Yeah, sure. Sounds like fun," Gray agreed. "We can go bar hopping or something. Maybe pick up a couple of chicks, huh?"

Theo snorted. "You're the most unconvincing womanizer ever," he joked. "You're too baby-faced for one-night stands."

Gray threw a fry at him. "Oh, come on. I'm not any more baby-faced than you are." He bit his tongue to keep from bringing up his own suspicions about his brother's sexuality, suspicions that Theo always seemed to go out of his way to deflect.

"Yeah, you keep telling yourself that." The twinkle of mischievousness in Theo's eyes showed that he was joking, but it still rankled Gray's nerves nonetheless. Before he could come up with a good retort, though, Theo said, "Oh, I almost forgot." He leaned back in his chair, dug into the pocket by his right knee, and tossed a box at him. "I got your prescription refilled for you earlier."

Gray caught the box and glanced at the label, then stuffed it into his pocket. "Thanks. I hadn't even thought about it."

"See, this is why I still hang around you," Theo said, waving a fry in his direction. "If I decide to, I don't know, stop coming by to see you, you'd forget to get your meds refilled and end up suffocating to death."

Gray made a face at him and stuffed the last of his cheeseburger into his mouth. "You've got to give me a *little* credit!"

"Why would I want to do that?" Theo laughed. "It takes all the fun out of screwing with you."

Gray sighed. "Don't you have somewhere to be? Like maybe work, saving people's lives, instead of sitting here making mine miserable?"

"I should be offended, but I don't think it's worth the energy, not after last night," Theo said with a chuckle, grimacing. The disparity between the expression on his face and the sound he made was disconcerting. At his questioning look, Theo explained, "Had to work a car accident. There was a kid involved. Those are always hard."

Gray frowned and leaned over the table, resting his elbows on the edge and studying Theo. "You okay?"

"Hey, it's what I signed on for, isn't it? I wouldn't have made it through paramedic training if I couldn't handle it."

He took a sip of soda. "It just gets rough when kids are hurt. Emotions and all that shit try to get in the way."

"I could never do what you do," Gray said. He started cleaning up their trash, shoving the empty wrappers back in the bag. "I'd be entirely too nervous with other people's lives in my hands."

Theo stood to help him wipe down the table. "It keeps roofs over our heads, so I do what I have to do."

"Yeah, I know, and thank you for that," Gray said. "God knows I don't pull in enough here to do much other than keep me in groceries and maybe pay my cell phone bill."

"How's the apartment working out for you?" Theo asked. "Is everything still okay there?"

"Yeah, it's fine," Gray assured him with a sheepish smile. "I don't know. It's okay. It's just...not home, you know?"

"I know." Theo sighed. "I'm sorry about all this. I've been arguing the case with Doctor Taylor every time I see him, but he's not budging. I don't know what to do next."

Gray glanced at the clock above the door. The second hand ticked inexorably toward the twelve. He sighed and headed for the trashcan, jamming the bag into it. "As stimulating as this depressing conversation is, I have to get back to work. I've still got three hours to finish this car and get chewed out by the boss for only getting two cars done today."

"Yeah, I've got to get to work myself soon," Theo said.

Gray headed out the door and back into the service bays, his brother right behind him. Before he went to his car, Theo stopped him. "Hey, be careful going home this evening, okay? Seems like we've been working a lot of wrecks over the past couple of days, and there are rumors of some scary shit going on over in Georgia and Alabama. I don't want to have to come scrape you off the highway."

Gray smiled tightly. While he was touched that Theo was concerned enough to say something, his brother's over-protectiveness had become almost stifling over the past few months. *Maybe I'm just getting used to staying by myself,* he thought. He wasn't sure if that was a good thing or not.

"I'll be fine, Theo," he promised. "It's not like I drive like a bat out of Hell. Besides, I take that route home five days a week. It's nothing new."

"I know, I know," Theo said. "Can't blame me for tossing that out there anyway, right?" He patted Gray on the back. "See you later, man." He started to walk toward his car but didn't make it more than a few steps before turning and adding, "Oh! Boss Man at the base said he'd really appreciate it if you'd come by when you have time and take a look at one of the ambulances. He thinks it's a fuel injector issue again."

Gray waved a hand at him dismissively. "Tell Doug I'll see what I can do. I'll give him a call in the morning to make arrangements." He shook his head. "I don't know why I let myself get roped into constantly fixing those junkers for you guys."

"Because you're just that damn good, Gray," Theo said. "And admit it. You're a total sucker for a big engine." He retreated to his car, slid in, and shut the door. Gray was still laughing when his brother pulled out of the lot.

* * *

New Orleans, LA

"Your parents are *so* going to kill you."

Remy Angellette wrinkled her nose and scoffed at the girl in the driver's seat, turning her arm around to study the design that had been newly inked onto her left bicep. The skin was still tender and sore from the experience of having dozens of needles rapidly jabbed into it, but in Remy's opinion, the pain had been well worth it. It wasn't her first tattoo, not by far. By now, her mother should have expected that sort of thing from her. She wasn't particularly worried about either her mother's or her stepfather's reaction to the newest addition of art on her body.

"Mom will be fine with it," she assured Casey. "She's pretty open minded about stuff like this. And Jason isn't my father, so I don't really care what he thinks."

"Yeah, but what would your real dad think?"

Remy glanced at the newly tattooed dragon on her arm again and looked at Casey with a smile. "I can imagine he'd definitely approve. Did you forget he had, like, eighteen tattoos himself?"

"No, I hadn't forgotten," Casey said. "Your dad *was* only the coolest parent in existence." She reached to turn the radio's volume up a notch when a rock song came on, piped in via Bluetooth from the iPhone in the console between the two black leather seats.

Remy scooped up the phone to see who the song was by and found it wasn't anyone she'd ever heard of. It was rather catchy, though, and she bobbed her head with the music, subconsciously tapping her foot on the floorboard. "So what are your plans for today?" she asked, raising her voice to be heard over the thumping beat from the stereo.

"I have a paper to write," Casey said with a motion of her hand to the messenger bag by Remy's feet. "Emily Browning."

"Could be worse," Remy said thoughtfully. "Her love poems were pretty awesome."

"Yeah, definitely could be worse."

Remy shifted against the leather seat again, trying to make herself comfortable, and realized her bare shoulder had stuck to the leather seat in the warmth of the car. She didn't want to imagine what the seat was doing to her bare thighs. She leaned forward slightly to unstick her shoulder from the seat and pulled her dark hair back with one hand, holding it off her neck in a makeshift ponytail.

"I've been thinking of maybe going to college," Remy piped up. "Maybe majoring in something to do with music."

"Remy, with the way you get tattoos and buy guitars and stuff, you'd never be able to afford it," Casey pointed out matter-of-factly.

"I know. It'd be nice, though." Remy let go of her hair and tucked the locks behind her ears, careful to avoid the still-healing ring that pierced the cartilage of her left ear. "It'd give me something to do besides stare at a computer screen and surf the internet all day."

"I thought you *liked* surfing the internet all day," Casey teased.

"I do. But Facebook only stays entertaining for so long, and Twitter is just starting to get old," Remy complained. "I need something new to happen in my life. I need all this monotony broken, you know?"

"We should go out and do something spontaneous," Casey suggested. "Maybe take a road trip or something. What do you think?"

Remy shrugged halfheartedly and grabbed her water bottle from the pocket in the door. She took a sip and thought it over. "I don't know. Maybe," she said. "I don't know if I'd have the money for something like that."

"Maybe you could get a new job," Casey said. She steered the Mustang off the paved street and onto a dirt road winding back into the trees.

"Yeah, and maybe I could get a lobotomy too," she said, taking another sip from her bottle.

"I heard Mister Carter—you know, the swim coach from high school?—I heard he's looking for somebody to help lifeguard at the pool this spring."

Remy pushed her hair back from her face again. "I don't know. I'll think about it, okay?" she conceded. "Mister Carter is a douche, though, so I doubt I'll even consider working for him."

"Well, just work for *somebody*," Casey pressed. "Then you can buy your own car and quit bumming rides off me all the time."

"Casey, your Mustang is just so *nice*," Remy said as the car bumped to a stop outside her house. *Dodson*, the mailbox read. She glanced at it and rolled her eyes before unlocking the passenger door and sliding to the edge of the seat. "I'll see you later, chick. FaceTime me after dinner when you get the chance."

"Will do!" Casey said cheerfully. She waved her fingers at Remy, and Remy returned the gesture and walked toward the house.

Casey pulled away as Remy reached the bottom of the porch steps, which she was silently thankful for. It didn't matter how many times Casey had been there, Remy was still embarrassed to have her friends see her house. When she climbed the wooden steps leading to the porch, the planks wobbled under her Chucks, but she was used to it. Despite her attempts to repair the broken steps, they'd stayed irreparably shaky for as long as she could remember. The porch wasn't much better. She stepped nimbly around the soft, rotten spots in the wood and took out her keys, unlocking the front door and stepping into the stuffy house.

A soft, repetitive clicking sound was coming from the kitchen, so Remy started in that direction, scooping a stray hair clip off the table by the door and twisting her long hair into a bun, fastening it on top of her head. She found her mother standing at the kitchen counter, knife in hand, chopping a butternut squash into cubes.

"Hi, Mom," she greeted. She dropped a kiss on her cheek, then went to the fridge to get a bottle of tea. "Any mail for me today?"

"Why? Were you expecting some?" her mother asked.

"Nothing in particular," she replied. It was a lie, but she hoped not an obvious one; she'd been hoping for a package she'd ordered the week before from an online adult novelty store. She hopped up onto a stool by the counter and cracked her tea bottle open, taking a swig. "What's for dinner?"

Her mother scooped up a handful of squash cubes with the blade of her knife and dumped it into a bowl. "I thought I asked you to not get any more of those," she said, her voice tinged with disappointment and disapproval.

"Get any more of what?" she asked, playing dumb.

"Tattoos," her mother said. "It's not…ladylike."

"Mama, *I'm* not ladylike," Remy argued. There were chopped carrots in a bowl, and she stole one and popped it into her mouth, crunching it between her teeth. "And I'm over eighteen. I don't see what the big deal is. It's just a tattoo. It's not like I'm doing drugs or anything."

Remy's mother seemed willing to drop the subject at her declaration. Remy smirked triumphantly and reached for another bite of carrot, only to receive a smack on the back of her hand with the flat of her mother's knife. "Dinner will be ready in an hour," her mother said. "Go do something useful. Clean your room." She looked Remy over and added, "And put on something other than that skirt. It's too short, and you know how your stepfather feels about that."

"Yeah, well, I don't really care what he thinks," Remy mumbled. She retreated before her mother could interject, heading straight to her bedroom upstairs. Once inside, she shut and locked the door, grinning in satisfaction. She headed for her closet, unfastening her skirt in mid-walk, to find something a little less revealing to change into. After donning her favorite lounge pants and a t-shirt with an image of an old computer on it that said, "I have a terrible memory," she buzzed over to her computer, jiggled the mouse to wake the screen up, and with a few keystrokes, she was online and checking her email. She had an hour before dinner was ready, and she had every intention of spending it online with her digital friends.

Remy had a routine for her online activities; she always did everything in a certain order, as if she were afraid she'd miss some snippet of news or gossip that would drastically alter her life. Email, Twitter, Facebook, Instagram, and several forums she found interesting, it was always the same. From there, she went wherever the internet took her. As such, that was how it took Remy until well after she'd waded through the flood of emails that had hit her inbox to find out something was going on. The first indication that all wasn't right was a single tweet she spotted on Twitter.

Kelly Rogers @HotInAtlanta • 1h
Something going on here in #Atlanta. Cell
signal spotty. Phones don't work.
Military all over the street outside.

Remy frowned and leaned closer to her screen, scrolling down the timeline, searching for another reference to Atlanta, her brain shuffling through the myriad reasons why the military would be on the streets of Atlanta. She spotted another tweet, halfway down the page, this from an indie band based in Atlanta that she'd met once when they opened for one of her favorite bands at a smaller venue.

Shred the Strings @
ShredTheStringsATL • 56m
Entire town shut down. #Atlanta toast.
Rumor is riots, virus. No idea
what's going on. No in or out.

And then a third:

Jordan K. Miller @emorybaby • 48m
I heard #EmoryU was on lockdown. My
sister heard gunshots outside.
I don't think this is good.

Remy snorted softly. "You're telling me." She refreshed the page, and her frown deepened as the tweets vanished like they'd never existed. She jabbed refresh on her computer a few more times, then spun her chair toward her TV. Maybe she'd find some useful news about Atlanta on there.

* * *

Plantersville, MS

Whenever Theo had to work pick-up shifts like the one he'd agreed to fill in for that evening, he always found himself praying for a quiet time of it. But it was the weekend, and teenagers in Plantersville had little to do besides throw drunken parties and cause problems for the police and EMS crews in the area. Considering the rumors already circulating about a party to be held at one of the houses on the outskirts of town, he had no doubt it'd prove to be a *very* busy shift.

Theo found his driver, Jonathan Kramer, already sitting sideways on the passenger seat of their truck when he arrived at the base a few minutes before the start of his shift. He dropped his bag off in the room in which he'd spend his downtime, punched in, and joined Jonathan outside.

"Hey, Carter, how's it going?" Jonathan greeted.

Theo shrugged and ran a hand through his dark blond hair. "It's going. How was drill last weekend?"

"It was okay," Jonathan replied. "The usual. Sarge was a total dick. Nothing new about that, though." He thrust a sheet of paper toward Theo. "New marching orders from Doug. Some supplies have been disappearing from a few trucks, and he can't figure out if it's because they're not being logged into the computer properly. He wants us to inventory the trucks on paper at the beginning *and* end of every shift, in addition to accounting for supplies on each of the run reports."

Theo took the paper and skimmed it. "Well, that's all fine and dandy, but this all looks like extra work just for *me*."

"Oh, I've got my own." Jonathan held up a sheet with a shorter list. "Crawling in the fucking dirt, checking the PSI on the tires. This is ridiculous."

"Watch your language," Theo said absently, though he felt silly saying that to a man ten years older than him. He looked the list over one more time, then pulled the ambulance's side door open and hauled himself inside. He was greeted by the sight of dirty gloves, used nasal cannulas and nonrebreather masks, and plastic packaging littering the floor. Soiled linens were piled on the bench by the back doors, and the garbage can attached to the side of the bench was overflowing with everything from used supplies to takeout bags.

"Fucking hell!" Theo exploded. "What the fucking fuck is *this*?"

"And you told *me* to watch *my* language," Jonathan joked. "Needless to say, I wasn't pleased to walk into this a few minutes ago. I figured you were going to hit the ceiling."

"Who the hell left it like this?" Theo asked, already freeing his cell phone from his pants pocket to take pictures of the mess for his supervisor's perusal later.

"Probably the same douchebags who ran out of here the minute I showed up so they'd be gone by the time I found it like this." Jonathan dropped out of the passenger seat and stretched, stepping into view of the side door. "Need a hand? I'm not averse to actually helping around here. Unlike *some* people." He cast a glance toward a four-door coupe that flew out of the base's short driveway. Theo recognized one of the aforementioned douchebag coworkers behind the wheel. He snorted and turned his gaze back to the mess before them.

"Get the stretcher out of the way and grab the broom from the backboard cabinet. I'm going to attempt to inventory while I clean." Theo sniffed the air, his head tilted back like he was a hunting dog scenting for prey. He wrinkled his nose. "It smells like stale fries and piss in here. You smell that, or is it just me?"

Jonathan snapped on a blue glove and circled to the ambulance's back doors, flinging them open. He picked something up from the floor of the ambulance and held it up with one finger for Theo to see. "Found your culprit." He frowned at the ambulance's floor. "Looks like it's leaking, too."

"So not only did they leave us with garbage everywhere, but they left us with a biohazard to deal with too?" To say Theo was thoroughly disgusted was an understatement. He forced himself to stop grinding his teeth and slid open a cabinet, pulling out a red plastic bag. "Drop it in here and tie it off. I'll chuck it later."

It took Theo and Jonathan over an hour to scrub and sanitize the interior of the ambulance, replace the supplies that had been used, and inventory everything. By the time they'd finished, Theo felt a headache niggling at the base of his skull. He massaged his temples and heaved a weary sigh before dropping into the airway seat with all the grace of a hippopotamus. "Aw hell, we've still got to wash the outside, don't we?" he grumbled. "Please tell me it looks like rain so we can put it off a little longer?"

Jonathan cast his eyes skyward and shook his head. "Nope, sorry. Crystal-clear evening sky." He smiled. "You know, if you don't want to wash it, I'm certainly not going to bitch. We could probably hold off until closer to the end of your shift."

"Hey, Jonathan!" a voice called from beyond the truck. It was a familiar one, and Theo sat up straighter in anticipation as the voice grew louder on the owner's approach. His heart fluttered nervously. Jonathan leaned around the corner of the truck to get a look at the newcomer.

"I hear Theo's supposed to be on shift tonight. Is he here yet?"

Theo shoved himself out of the airway seat, nearly tripping over the trauma bag by the side door in his haste to get out of the truck. He stuck his head out the door, spotting Dillon Roberts standing beside the truck, his brown hair glossy in the light from the setting sun and a cigarette dangling from the corner of his mouth.

"He's right here," Theo said, clambering down from his perch inside the ambulance. Dillon grinned and stepped forward, giving Theo a one-armed hug, holding his cigarette out with the other so he wouldn't accidentally burn him. Theo returned the embrace with the same enthusiasm.

"Theo! It feels like it's been ages since I've seen you!" Dillon said once he'd stepped back.

"It's been less than a week, Dill," Theo said, grinning. "How was your trip?"

Theo had met Dillon a mere six months prior when, newly arrived from Florida, he'd crossed the street from his house to the ambulance base and introduced himself to Theo while Theo was washing the ambulance. Since then, they'd become close—*too* close, some might have said, for it to be considered a simple friendship. Theo didn't care what other people thought. Dillon had been there for him through the rough patches of the last several months, including the personal upheaval that had ensued when his and Gray's therapist had diagnosed them with codependency and strongly recommended them to get separate living spaces to help quell that problem.

Dillon took a drag of his cigarette and turned his head to blow the smoke away from Theo. "Trip would have been a hell of a lot more fun if you'd taken that week off and come along like I asked you to."

"I couldn't leave," he said. "You know I had to stay here in case Gray needed me."

"Gray's twenty-one," Dillon pointed out, not unkindly. "I think he'd have been fine on his own. He's living by himself now, right?"

"Not totally," Theo admitted. "I'm still paying his rent and everything. It's stretching me fucking thin."

"Why don't you talk to him about it, see if he'll get a second job to help with that?" Dillon asked. He leaned against the side of the ambulance, and Theo joined him, folding his arms. "You can only do so much, Theo, and you're already stressed out. You need a break." He offered his cigarette to Theo, who accepted and took a deep drag. "That's why I wanted you to go to Biloxi with me. We *both* need to get away for a while." He cut his eyes toward the house across the street, and Theo followed his gaze.

"Are you still having problems with...?" He trailed off and looked at Dillon.

"You have no idea," Dillon said. "I'm so tired of everything lately." He sighed. "Let's talk about better things. You busy tomorrow night? I was thinking maybe we could go get some drinks and hang out."

Theo hesitated, glancing toward the ambulance base, trying to think of a gentle way to phrase it. "I...I can't," he said. "I've already got plans with Gray. We're supposed to go bar-hopping tomorrow night."

The look of disappointment on Dillon's face was obvious. "Oh, come on, Theo. He's got his own friends he can go out with. You see him all the time."

Theo sighed. "I know, but—"

"Don't you want to prove Doctor Taylor wrong?" Dillon asked, his voice gentle. His hand pressed lightly against Theo's bare forearm. "Come on. Go out with me. What'll it hurt? You and Gray can make plans for some other time."

Theo sighed and shoved his hands into his pockets. "Yeah, okay, fine. I'll reschedule with Gray. He won't be happy about it, though. You know how he feels about you."

"Yup, can't stand me," Dillon said almost cheerfully. "Not that I care. He can think whatever he wants about me. No skin off my teeth." He took one last drag from his cigarette before dropping it on the pavement and grinding it out with his tennis shoe. "Want breakfast in the morning after work?" he offered. "I'll cook. I always make too much anyway."

"Sounds like a plan," he agreed. "I'll even help."

A burst of static came from the radio in the cab, followed by a loud tone that set Theo's teeth on edge.

"Sounds like you're about to get a call, so I'll get on out of here," Dillon said, patting Theo on the shoulder as the dispatcher started rattling off the address. "Give me a shout when you're freed up in the morning so I know when you're coming over."

"Will do," Theo agreed. Dillon hugged him briefly, then retreated to the house across the street.

Jonathan exited the base then, waving a notepad in Theo's direction. "We've got a call!" he shouted, making a beeline for the driver's door. "Chest pain."

Theo glanced at Dillon's retreating form and nodded, hauling himself into the truck. "Well, then, let's get this show on the road."

CHAPTER TWO

Memphis, TN

Ethan Bennett's green eyes fluttered open slowly and reluctantly as he surfaced to consciousness. A beam of sunlight filtered through the blinds hanging over the window by the bed and insisted on shining directly onto his face. He groaned and rolled onto his side, squeezing his eyes closed again and trying to avoid the painfully bright light. His head hurt, and when he tried to swallow, his throat was rough, like it'd been sandpapered. He had the distinct sensation of having been run over by a truck.

Yes, he'd definitely drunk too much the night before.

Ethan hadn't really meant to. It wasn't his normal M.O. to get so smashingly drunk. But when the police officers from his precinct in Memphis held off-duty get-togethers, things tended to get pretty wild. And it *had* been a celebration. He'd just been promoted, and his coworkers had felt that there was no better way to rejoice over such an event than to virtually kidnap him and drag him to the nearest bar for "a few drinks."

"A few drinks" had culminated in Ethan puking in some poor bastard's bushes and his coworkers laughing and taking pictures to mark the occasion. He hadn't lost his stomach like that since his days of illicit underage drinking in high school. It was more than a little embarrassing.

Ethan rolled over and looked at Anna's side of the bed. It was empty, the pillow gone cold. He squinted at the alarm clock; its red numbers seared a hole in his brain. It was almost noon. His wife had likely been awake and up for hours already. Ethan was usually up with her. The only time he ever slept in was when he'd had to work the graveyard shift at the station. Or when he was drunk.

That wouldn't happen very often anymore, though. He was a major now, the youngest by almost eight years in all the precincts that made up the Memphis Police Department. He was barely thirty-nine, and he'd already risen to one of the highest ranks in the entire precinct. It was a serious accomplishment but one that was hardly unexpected. Ethan had always taken his job seriously, and the rewards had always been plentiful. When the rumors of the position opening up had begun circulating among the officers, it had been a given among the gossipers that Ethan Bennett would be offered the job. And now that he had been, he didn't know how his life could possibly get any better.

He flopped onto his back and grunted, rubbing at his face with both hands. His palms met stubble, and he grimaced. He needed to shave. He'd have to get out of bed to do it. The very idea was incompatible with the temptation to stay firmly ensconced in his blankets all day. He wondered where exactly Anna was. Neither of them had to work that day. Perhaps he would take her out to dinner after his headache had subsided to tolerable levels.

As the thought wandered through his brain, Ethan sat up in bed and looked around blearily. His eyes didn't want to focus. He spotted a note by the alarm clock and grabbed it. His wife's loopy handwriting greeted him.

Eth,

I went next door to Cade's. She's doing barbecue at her place this evening since it's such a nice day, and she invited us over. She says for you to "bring the beer unless you used it all marinating your liver last night." Come over when you're feeling up to getting out of bed. There are two aspirin on the sink in the bathroom and a little breakfast in the fridge if your stomach can handle it. Congrats on your promotion!

Anna

P.S. I love you!

Ethan grinned and slipped the note into his bedside table's drawer. A stack of similar notes was already inside; he didn't think he'd ever thrown a single one away. He climbed out of bed and stood awkwardly as the room swam, grabbing the bedpost to steady himself before making his way to the bathroom. The aspirin were right where the note had said they'd be. He swallowed both pills dry and studied himself in the mirror above the sink. His eyes were bloodshot and red rimmed, and his blond hair, normally combed to look neat and professional, looked like a rat had slept in it all night. He shoved at it ineffectually and then lifted his arm for a sniff.

That had been a mistake. He smelled like sweat, grime, booze, and cigarette smoke, like he'd lived in a heavily used locker room for two weeks without showering. It was probably the worst he'd ever smelled, and he couldn't fathom how Anna had managed to sleep in the same room, the same *bed*, as him. There was no way he was going to Cade's smelling like this. She'd never let him hear the end of it.

After a long, hot shower, Ethan felt almost human again. His hangover was mostly gone, though his stomach still felt queasy at the idea of food. Regardless, he dressed and went to the kitchen, making a quick stop at the fridge to take out two six-packs of beer, and he smiled at the plate of pancakes sitting by the milk. He debated eating them but instead shook his head and went out the back door to cross the yard to Cade's.

Anna sat with Cade Alton at a glass-topped patio table in Cade's backyard, drinking tall glasses of iced tea as Cade kept an eye on the smoking grill nearby. The scent of cooking meat wafted from the grill, and Ethan had an odd shuddery feeling in his gut, like his stomach was trying to turn itself inside out. He gave the two women a halfhearted wave and collapsed into one of the patio chairs. Setting the packs of beer on the ground beside his chair, he leaned forward to rest his forehead against the cool table with a whine that made him sound absolutely pathetic. He was past the point of caring.

"Look who finally graced us with his presence," Cade cooed in her lightly accented voice, ruffling his hair. Ethan didn't bother looking up as he lifted a hand just enough to stick his middle finger into the air. This merely sent Cade into a peal of laughter. Ethan couldn't think of a single time when she'd actually taken offense to an insult or gesture he'd lobbed at her in the entire seven years they'd been friends.

Ethan dropped his hand back to the table with a thump. "Why exactly are we grilling out in January?" he asked Cade.

"Because it's an unseasonably warm sixty-nine degrees, and I'm a shameless carnivore," Cade responded. She took a deep swallow from her tea and set the glass down beside Ethan. He jerked up a few inches as the thud rang through his head.

"Hon," Anna's voice said from Ethan's left, "did you find that aspirin I left you?"

"Yeah, I took it," he mumbled. "And a shower. I still feel like shit, though."

"You look like it too," Cade added gleefully.

Ethan rolled his eyes and turned his head a fraction to look at her. "Don't you have someone else to insult?"

"Yes, but Drew's asleep right now," she said, lifting her tea glass and taking another sip. "He just got back in from a conference or something near Atlanta. I honestly wasn't paying much attention to what he was talking about. Some techy stuff that went over my head." That wasn't an exaggeration, from what Ethan knew; Cade wasn't technologically inclined and could barely operate her smartphone on any given day. She slid out of her chair and went to the grill to turn the meat. "He's been sick, though. Practically hacking his lungs out. I think he's got the flu or something, but he says it's just 'con crud' and won't go to the doctor about it."

"He'll do it if he isn't feeling well by Monday," Anna assured Cade.

Cade shook her head and made a face, directing her next statement to Ethan. "So you missed all the fun parts of our discussion out here."

"What parts?" Ethan asked.

"The parts where we discussed your, *ahem*, indiscretions from last night."

Ethan picked up a lemon slice from the small plate in the center of the table and threw it at the back of Cade's head; it bounced off her dark hair as his aim rang true. "I *had* no indiscretions," he replied.

"Tell that to the poor bushes you desecrated," Cade teased, waggling her smartphone at him before stuffing it back in her pocket. One of his coworkers must have sent her the photos from last night. *Son of a bitch must pay*, his mind grumbled. She set her tongs down and closed the grill's lid, turning back to him and smiling suddenly. "By the way, there's a certain four-year-old someone in the house who's been here for over a week and would probably *love* to see you before her mom gets here to pick her up at the first of the week."

Ethan sat up and rubbed his face as Cade's words sank in. "Josie's here?" he asked with more energy in his voice. Ever since he and Anna had found out they couldn't have children, Ethan had become ridiculously attached to his best friend's niece, and the little girl seemed equally enthusiastic to see her "Uncle Ethan" when she came all the way from Israel to visit Cade.

Anna smiled and motioned to the sliding glass doors leading into the kitchen. "She was in the living room last time I saw her," she said. "Watching TV."

"SpongeBob," Cade added, returning to her chair. "She's obsessed. It drives me nuts. I get that theme song stuck in my head for hours. Nothing will drive you crazier faster than the same damn pirate on TV eighteen dozen times a day."

Ethan laughed and stood, making his way toward the house and leaving the two women in the backyard. After stopping at the fridge to drop off the beer, he headed into the living room. A little girl in a pink sweatshirt and khaki pants, her brown hair plaited, sat on the floor in front of the television, watching, transfixed, as the yellow sponge and his pink friend did Heaven only knew what inside a cardboard box. Ethan grinned as he watched her, reluctant to interrupt her fascination with the show. He waited for a commercial break before sneaking up and grabbing her from behind.

"What do you think you're doing?" he asked in a mock-menacing voice. Josie squealed and laughed, twisting around to see who it was.

"Uncle Ethan!" she squealed, throwing her small arms around his neck in a tight hug.

"Hey, baby girl!" Ethan said, returning the hug before settling her against his hip. "How are you doing today?"

"Good," she said. "Aunt Cade is making me a hot dog."

"A hot dog, huh?" he said. "Your favorite food, right?" He couldn't stand hot dogs. There was just something about that particular bit of meat that made him cringe inside. He was sure the repeated readings of Upton Sinclair's *The Jungle* in high school hadn't helped any; after that, he was surprised he hadn't become vegetarian.

"Yes," Josie answered with an enthusiastic nod. "Is it done yet? I'm hungry."

"I don't know, honey. Let's go outside and find out," Ethan suggested. He carried her to the back patio doors. As he passed the doorway leading to the den, he caught sight of a lump under a blanket on the couch; he assumed it was Cade's boyfriend, Andrew, taking a nap after his week-long trip to Georgia. Ethan left him alone and headed out the back door.

Anna and Cade remained at the table, talking, as Ethan joined them once more. He settled Josie on his lap and rubbed her back as he stole Anna's glass of tea for a sip. "I figured the other lady in the house should join our fun out here," he said as his wife swatted at him and took her drink back.

Cade grinned and got up from her chair to retrieve a covered plate from beside the grill. "Perfect timing, Josie. Your hot dog is ready," she announced dramatically, carrying the plate over to set it in front of Ethan and Josie. "You'll help her if she needs it?" she asked Ethan as she passed behind him.

"Is that even a legitimate question?" Ethan asked. He grinned and pulled Josie's pigtails back, pretending to tie them together into a bow as Cade sat back down.

"I was thinking about having a movie night tonight," Cade said thoughtfully. She swirled her straw through her tea. "Maybe pulling up some of those movies I added to my Netflix list last week and haven't watched yet. The four of us could kick back after Josie goes to bed. What do you think?"

"Are we *required* to be there?" Ethan teased, looking at Anna. She smiled and, as their eyes met, winked.

"Well, of course. That's why I'm telling you about it," Cade replied. Her tone hinted at just what she thought of Ethan's intelligence level—and it wasn't much.

Anna and Ethan looked at each other for a moment. Then Ethan said, "I don't know, Cade. We'll sit it out this time. I was thinking about spending some quality time with my wife this evening." Anna reached over and grabbed his hand, and he returned the smile she gave him at his words.

Cade's grin became mischievous as she raised her eyebrows. "Oh, I see what kind of evening you're going to have," she said knowingly.

"But, Uncle Ethan, there's gonna be popcorn," Josie said. Her voice was muffled, her mouth full of hot dog. "Aunt Cade always makes popcorn when she watches movies with me."

"You shouldn't talk with your mouth full, Jos," Ethan said, fluffing her bangs playfully. "Anna and I haven't gotten to hang out in about a week. We've both been working."

Cade smiled and said, "You two need to make me an aunt already. I don't care how you do it. "You can freaking adopt for all I care."

"But you're already an aunt, Aunt Cade," Josie said, as if it should have been obvious.

Ethan laughed softly and shrugged at Cade as he pressed his nose against the back of Josie's hair. "We'll see," he said. "I'm not exactly in a hurry, and neither is Anna." He'd yet to tell Cade about the last doctor's appointment, six months before, when he and Anna had found out for certain that they couldn't have children. The last thing he wanted right now was to discuss it with someone other than Anna, even if it meant excluding his best friend from the news.

Anna gave Ethan's hand another affectionate squeeze. "You'll be the first to know if something happens," she said. "Right, Eth?"

He nodded. "Oh, definitely. If I ever decided to tell someone something before you, Cade, you'd probably kill me." And he had no doubt she'd be successful at it, too.

Cade's face brightened. "Speaking of killing, you need to check out my new toy."

An ominous feeling settled into Ethan's gut at her words, replacing the queasy, hung-over feeling he'd had all morning. "Your new toy?" he repeated.

Anna held out her arms for Josie and grinned. "Oh, you'll like it," she assured him, shifting the girl to her lap and sliding her plate back in front of her. "She showed it to me earlier. It's something right up your alley."

"Doesn't make me any less scared at the idea of Cade and her *toys*," he replied. Cade's "toys" were infamous. They usually tended toward the extremely sharp, mildly explosive, and always dangerous ends of the spectrum. Given that she had so many assorted guns and knives hidden around the house, Ethan was amazed that Cade's older sister Lindsey let her keep Josephine for extended periods of time.

Cade led him into the house, through the kitchen and living room, and up the stairs to the master bedroom. Ethan shoved his hands into his pockets and rocked on his heels as he looked around. A photo of Cade in her IDF uniform sat on the table by the bed, multicolored ribbon mounted at the bottom of the photograph. He couldn't remember what the award was for.

Cade threw open her closet door and hauled out a large black case, slinging it onto the bed. Then she went to the dresser, yanked a drawer open, and dug through its contents. Ethan smoothed his hand over the case's rough plastic surface and studied it curiously. It was a rifle storage case, and he had a feeling that whatever was inside was going to prove just as deadly as every other interesting item Cade owned.

Cade produced a small silver key from the drawer and slid it into the lock holding the case closed. "This is seriously the best thing I've ever bought," she informed him as she twisted the key in the lock.

Cade slowly opened the case to reveal a deadly looking rifle nestled in its padded innards, and Ethan let out a low whistle. He recognized the weapon vaguely—he'd seen its type before in a movie or a television show—but couldn't exactly place what it was. "What kind of rifle is this?"

"It's an IMI Galil SAR," Cade replied.

Ethan whistled again. *That* was a name he'd heard before. "Impressive. I'm assuming this is legal?" he teased, giving Cade a light jab in the side. She danced aside and lifted the rifle out of its case, holding it in both hands, her grip as sure as if she'd been using it for years. She probably had.

Cade smirked and tore her gaze away from the rifle. "I don't know, Eth. It's a great idea to show my best friend—who just so happens to be a cop—the rifle I illegally own, don't you think?" She put the rifle away as gently as a mother would tuck in her child, locked the case once more, and gave the lid a tug to make sure it was secure. "So how about those burgers and beer?" she offered, motioning for Ethan to follow her out of the room after a quick stop at the dresser to return the key to its hiding place.

As they passed through the kitchen, Ethan noticed a newspaper lying on the table, and he scooped it up as a small sidebar headline caught his attention. "'Mysterious Illness Sweeps Atlanta,'" he read out loud. "What's up with this?"

"With what?" she asked, leaning to glance at the headline and shrugging. "I don't know. Just some flu or something going around. You know, the usual bullshit."

"Damn, are you sure?" Ethan asked, scanning the article. The details were vague. His eyes caught the byline, and he frowned at the unusual name. Avi Geller. He'd heard or read the name before but couldn't place where. With as light as the article was on details, though, he figured it wasn't anything major and set the paper back on the table. If it had been something important, he'd imagine that the article would have a hell of a lot more detail than that. Shaking it loose from his attention, he began gathering plates and utensils. "Come on, let's go eat," he said. "I'm starving."

* * *

New Orleans, LA

"I think there's something going on in Atlanta," Remy said over dinner. Her words broke through the otherwise quiet sounds of dinner, the tapping of forks against plates and the soft thumps of glasses being set on the table. Her family had never been very talkative at the dinner table. Maddie's chatter about school usually filled the space of time while the table was being set, and once the eating began, everyone was largely silent. So when Remy spoke up during dinner, it was unusual enough an event that it shook everyone from their focus on the food before them, and they turned their eyes onto her. She suddenly felt like she'd made a *faux pas*, and she barely refrained from shifting uncomfortably in her chair under their intense, scrutinizing gazes.

"What kind of something?" Remy's stepfather, Jason, asked. He lowered his fork to rest the tines against the edge of his plate and raised an eyebrow.

"Rioting or something," she said. "I saw some tweets about it online, though there wasn't anything about it on the news. What I did see didn't sound too good. Somebody mentioned something about the military."

"I didn't see anything like that last night," Remy's mother said. She was a flight attendant for United Airlines, and she frequently went on the short-haul flights from Atlanta to New Orleans. "Everything seemed fine. The plane wasn't delayed or anything."

"It didn't start until *after* you left there, Mama," Remy said, fighting to keep the annoyance out of her voice. "Not to mention you didn't leave Hartsfield-Jackson the entire time you were there."

"Remy, don't talk to your mother that way," Jason admonished. "Give her the respect you're supposed to."

"You're not my father," Remy muttered under her breath, but she knew the words were loud enough for all of them to hear. "Don't tell me what to do."

"Remy, please," her mother said in a long-suffering tone. This was an argument they'd had before, and Remy was as tired of it as her mother was. "Not at the dinner table. Save it for when we're washing up afterwards, okay?"

Remy grimaced, but she clamped her mouth shut. It wasn't worth it to argue with her mother, especially not after the whole tattoo debate earlier in the evening.

Maddie, however, didn't share Remy's sense of when to shut her mouth. "I heard at school that there are sick people in Atlanta that are causing people to fight," she announced, prodding at her potatoes with a look of boredom. "Michelle's dad lives near Atlanta, and he told her mom that it's bad over there. He said—"

"Now look, you got your sister started," Jason said accusingly to Remy. She fought the irrational urge to stab her fork into the back of his hand. "What happened to having a nice family dinner *without* all the talk of murders and whatever awful stuff you imagine?"

"Who said anything about murders?" she asked. "Shit, you act like I make stuff up all the damn time. Whatever happened to, I don't know, *believing me* when I tell you shit?"

"Watch your language," Remy's mother scolded. "Especially at the dinner table. Lord, I could smack your father for letting you talk like that."

It took everything in Remy to not say something she'd later regret. She set her fork down against the edge of her plate, put her napkin on the table beside both, and stood, intent on retreating to her room, content to allow her mother and stepfather to not only think they'd have the last word but to let them gloat over it in private.

Once she was in her room, the door locked firmly behind her, Remy went to her closet and started ransacking it for a change of clothes. As she'd climbed the stairs to the second floor, she'd been seized by the firm desire to get the hell out of the house. She didn't have a car, which made getting out nearly impossible, so after she dug a pair of jeans and a comfortable t-shirt out of her closet, she grabbed her cell phone, accessed the address book, and selected the listing that said "Adam." She put it on speakerphone while she changed clothes.

"*'Lo?*" Adam answered, his mouth sounding like it was full of food.

"You busy tonight?" she asked.

"*As busy as I always am,*" he said, which basically meant he didn't have a damn thing going on.

"Good," she said. "Then you can play chauffeur for me. I need to go into town."

"*What do you need to go into town for?*"

"Business."

Adam groaned. "*And I get to play chauffeur for that? Come on, man.*"

"Fine. I'll cut you in to make up for the trouble. Twenty percent."

"*Thirty.*"

"Twenty-five."

Adam sighed loudly. "*Fine. Twenty-five. Good enough, I guess.*"

"When you get here, park at the end of the drive. I'll meet you there."

"*Where are we gonna hit this time?*" Adam asked.

"I'm not sure yet. It'll hit me before too long." She found the bag she was looking for—a larger, slouchier one that would hold a lot of stuff—and started gathering the little things to go inside it. "I'll see you in a few, yeah?"

"*Yeah, yeah,*" Adam mumbled before he hung up. Remy tossed her cell phone into the bag with everything else, then shouldered the mostly empty bag, opened one of her bedroom windows, and slunk out onto the porch's roof to make her way to the ground and meet her friend.

* * *

Plantersville, MS

The crack of pool balls drowned out the country music being piped through speakers strategically hidden around the bar. Gray paid the sound no mind, his eyes following the yellow ball Jack Abernathy had struck. It rolled into the pocket for which Jack had aimed. Gray shook his head, taking a deep swallow from his beer. Jack tilted his head to look at him and give him his familiar shit-eating grin.

"Carter, you are going to owe me some *serious* money when I'm done with you," Jack taunted.

Gray tugged a pack of cigarettes from the back pocket of his jeans, pulling one free and lighting it up. "I said I liked playing. I never said I was *good* at it. Besides, you're probably going to give the cash back anyway, like you do pretty much every time we play." He propped the end of his pool cue on the floor and leaned on it, dragging on his cigarette and watching Jack take entirely too long to line up his next shot. "You going to take that shot anytime soon, or are you too busy waggling your ass for the ladies at the bar?"

Jack tapped the cue ball. The green ball for which he'd aimed bounced off the table's side, rolling to a stop in the center of the table.

Gray heaved a sigh of relief and ashed his cigarette into the tray on the edge of the table, then lifted his stick from the floor. "'Bout damned time."

Jack leaned against the edge of the table, and Gray circled it, trying to choose his best line of attack. "I don't think you've noticed, G," he said, "but I'm not the one the ladies at the bar are staring at. That hot brunette near the end has been watching you the entire time we've been in here."

Gray stretched over the table to line up his shot, resting the pool cue against his hand, and cut his eyes in the direction Jack mentioned. He huffed out another impatient breath. "Come on, man, there's like three of them down there," he said, though a jolt of recognition wormed its way down his spine when his eyes met those of the girl in question. He stuck his cigarette between his lips and exhaled a puff of smoke around it, feigning casualness, before taking his shot and missing miserably. It was an easy shot, and Gray could only account his failure to make it as a bad case of sudden nerves brought on by the eyes that, even now, he could have sworn he felt on his back.

"The one in the skirt and red top," Jack replied. He passed behind Gray to get to the other side of the table, slapping him on the back in the process. Gray flinched and sidestepped away from him, gripping the pool cue tighter, barely containing the urge to smack Jack with it. "You should go talk to her, see if you can get laid," Jack suggested. "Then maybe you'll quit being so damned cranky all the time."

Gray cocked his hip against the edge of the table, took his cigarette out of his mouth, and snagged his beer bottle from beside the ashtray. "Do I look that desperate?" He drank a deep swig of beer. "At least let me wait until after the game's over before you start trying to hook me up with random bar chicks."

Jack snorted. "Hell yeah, I've got to hook you up! God knows you can't get the pretty girls on your own," he joked.

"If we weren't in the bar right now, I'd so kick your ass," Gray said. He jabbed his cigarette out in the ashtray with more ferocity than necessary and finished off his beer.

"But you can't, because then Smitty would call the cops and your brother would want to know why you were in the Brass Monkey in the first place *and* why he was bailing you out of jail. He'd probably get all paternal on you, and I'd never get to hang out with you again." Jack sank another ball. "What's with him? He acts like you're twelve or something."

Gray grabbed his empty bottle, setting his pool cue on the edge of the table. "I don't want to talk about my brother. It's his fault I'm here with you anyway, since he cancelled on me. And don't talk about him that way. It's between him and me." He nodded to the bar. "I'm going to get another drink."

Circling the table, he tossed his empty bottle into the trash and headed to the bar. He stopped a few feet away from the girl Jack had pointed out, the girl who'd been staring at him. The girl who'd given him such a rush of feeling the second he'd laid eyes on her that he'd felt the compulsion to sit down in a daze. He flagged down the bartender, the esteemed Smitty himself. "Can I get another beer, please?" He glanced at the girl out of the corner of his eye and added, "Make it two." Once he had the two chilled bottles in his hand, he slid onto the stool beside the girl, cracked the top off one of the bottles, and set it gently on the counter in front of her. "Hey, April. Long time no see."

She looked up at him, a wide smile spreading across her pretty face. The sight of it sent a pang of melancholy through him. "I was hoping you'd take the hint and come over here," she said.

Gray hadn't seen April Linder in nearly three years, not since they'd graduated high school and gone their separate ways. They'd dated throughout their entire junior and senior years, and things had started getting serious between them until his parents had died in an accident two months before graduation. Thinking about that time of his life still made him sad. Two years was a lot of time for a teenager to spend with one girl. He dragged himself out of memory lane and returned April's smile. "You're looking great. What have you been doing?"

April tucked her hair behind her ear in a familiar gesture. She scooped up the beer he'd put in front of her and sipped from the bottle. "Not a whole lot. Just moved back home." She scrunched up her nose, and he noticed the freckles speckling her cheeks and the bridge of her nose. "College sucks, by the way. Don't even bother with it."

"I take it things didn't go well in Seattle?"

"Oh God no." April grimaced. "I spent the whole time being miserable and getting ridiculed for my accent."

"Assholes," he said.

"Tell me about it." April took another sip of beer. Gray felt her eyes running over him during the pause between them, like she was physically running her hands over his skin. "You're not looking all that bad yourself. Not as skinny as the last time I saw you. More muscular, I think."

Gray gulped from his bottle. "I guess that's what happens when you haul car parts around all day. Well, that and the occasional visit to the gym."

"Still doing body work?"

"Naw, got laid off from that garage," he said. "Been working as a regular mechanic for about a year now. Nothing interesting. Helps out with the whole food thing." He fell silent, turning his bottle in slow circles on the bar. He wasn't sure what to say to April. It'd been years since he'd seen her, and all her reappearance had done was dredge up old feelings he'd thought were long gone. He felt a stirring of sadness, longing, and even a little guilt mixed together in his gut in an amalgam of emotion that nauseated him. He swallowed hard and gulped more beer.

"How's your family?" he asked casually. "Everybody doing okay?"

"Oh yeah!" April said brightly, seizing on the new topic. She took a deep breath, as if preparing to launch into a spiel, and the action drew Gray's attention to the collar of her red blouse. The top few buttons were undone, showing cleavage, and he wondered momentarily if she'd dressed up with the hopes of finding a stand at the bar that night. The thought of her with another guy bothered the hell out of him.

"Mom and Dad are doing great," she said. "Still living in the same ol' house. I'm staying with them until I find a place of my own."

"Yeah?" Gray picked at the edge of his bottle's label with his fingernail. "No, ah, no boyfriend to stay with or whatever?" he asked, trying to be casual about it. He suspected he'd failed. Miserably. Thankfully, April didn't seem to notice.

"No," she said, her dark hair swaying, and her cheeks flushed. "No boyfriend. Haven't had one of those in, hell, two years? Something like that." She laughed ruefully. "That makes me sound so pathetic."

"No, it doesn't," Gray said in a rush. He drew in a deep breath to dislodge the nervousness in his throat. "I haven't dated very much in…well, since high school. Not anything serious, just…you know, flings and shit. Believe me, you're doing a lot better than I am."

April smiled, and his stomach knotted. Theo hadn't been kidding when he'd told him once that the first love was always the hardest to get over.

"So, how are things with you? How are your mom and dad?" She looked suddenly awkward at the mention of his parents and nearly knocked over her beer as she reached for it in her haste to cover the slip-up. "Or, I mean, your brother. How is Theo doing?"

Gray tried to let the reference to his deceased parents pass without comment, though he still felt a pang in his chest at her words and the thought of them. He pasted on a smile, though the last thing he wanted to do was talk about Theo, either. "Theo's doing great. He dropped out of police academy, though. He became a paramedic instead."

"That's awesome," April said. "Are you still living with him?"

"I moved out not too long ago," he said. "Our, ah, our therapist said we needed to get some space from each other because we spend too much time together or some bullshit like that. I don't remember the word for it. Co-something or other. Anyway, I got a little apartment a couple of miles from here, and he helps with the rent, since I really can't afford it."

April smiled in a way that made him feel embarrassed. *She must think I'm a total basket case,* he thought. *Why did I mention the damned therapist? Fucking pathetic.*

"Do you maybe want to get out of here?" she asked. She leaned closer and lowered her voice. "Maybe go hang out someplace more…private? For old times' sake?"

Gray downed the rest of his beer and set the bottle on the bar. "Where exactly did you have in mind?"

CHAPTER THREE

New Orleans, LA

Adam was waiting for Remy just where she'd told him to. He sat behind the wheel of his beater VW bug that was as old as her, drumming his fingers on the steering wheel while he waited for her to show up. Smoke laced around his head from the cigarette he had dangling out of the corner of his mouth, and as she approached the car, she could see the glow of the lit end. It made her want a cigarette, and her fingertips practically tingled with the desire. The feeling came out of nowhere: she wasn't a smoker, had only ever taken a puff or two off a cigarette in her life. She knocked on the passenger window, biting back a laugh when Adam nearly jumped out of his skin.

"You really should pay attention to your surroundings," she chided him after opening the door. "Not paying attention when you're doing something you shouldn't be doing is a *great* way to get busted by the cops."

"Nice to see you too, Remy," Adam grumbled.

Remy gave him a perky smile and slid into the passenger seat, shifting to settle comfortably onto the old, torn leather seat. She pulled the door shut and checked her pockets to make sure she had everything she might need for the evening, double-checked that her cell phone was charged, and motioned toward the windshield. "Drive on, fearless leader."

Adam snorted and put the ratty car in gear, pulling away from the end of the driveway and into the highway. "I'm hardly the leader in this. This is *all* on you."

"All on me?" she repeated. "Need I remind you that you're the one who agreed to drive?"

"Only long enough to get my twenty-five percent," Adam said with a smirk.

"That could take all night," she replied. "I actually have to offload the product before you get your cut."

"Stop talking like that. You make yourself sound like a drug dealer."

"Well, I kind of am," Remy pointed out. "Last I checked, nicotine is a drug. Which, in all technicality, *does* make me a drug dealer."

Adam snorted again and steered the car toward their destination: a mini-mart that Remy had chosen because of its large cigarette stock and its lack of a bulletproof cage around the cashier's counter. Not that the bulletproof portion of the equation was important; it wasn't like she had a gun and an intention to shoot at anyone. She preferred working in a decidedly sneakier way, one that would only end up getting her a misdemeanor slap on the wrist if she happened to get caught.

When they reached the mini-mart, Remy pointed to a spot that was a bit more shadowed than the areas around the gas pumps. Adam parked the car there, and they both got out and started toward the brightly lit building. As always, she took the lead and stepped into the gas station first, buzzing toward the candy racks while Adam split off for the beer coolers in the back. It was a well-rehearsed routine they'd practiced on multiple occasions and worked perfectly for their purposes. The clerk was behind the counter, ringing up the gas purchase for the lone customer who was in the store with them. Remy waited impatiently for the man at the counter to leave, passing the minutes studying the nutrition label on a package of M&Ms, and once he left, she gave Adam the signal.

Ten seconds later, there was the sound of shattering glass near the beer coolers.

"Shit," Adam said from the direction of the sound.

Just as Remy had hoped, the clerk went on the alert at the sound, circling from behind the counter to investigate. As the woman cut down an aisle to see about the noise, Adam started making soothing, apologetic, oh-God-I'm-so-sorry sounds. The woman disappeared into a closet, presumably to retrieve a mop to clean up the beer Adam had broken on the floor, and that was Remy's cue. She hurried forward, circled the cashier's counter, and snagged the first box of Marlboro-brand cigarettes she spotted. Stuffing it under her jacket, she circled back around the counter and headed for the door.

"Hey!" the clerk shouted from behind her, and Remy half turned to see the clerk making a beeline toward her, broom in hand.

Remy looked down and noticed that the outline of the carton of cigarettes was very clearly visible through her jacket. "Well, shit," she said, and she slammed the front door open and bolted out, racing to Adam's car. Adam wasn't far behind, and he flung himself into the driver's seat as she whipped around the front of the car and dropped into the passenger's seat. "Go, go, go!" she urged, yanking her door shut behind her.

Adam turned the key in the ignition. The engine sputtered and didn't start, and he cursed and turned the key again. As the engine struggled to turn over, Remy could barely contain her fury.

"Oh my *God*, Adam, why do you have to drive such a fucking junker!" she exploded, throwing her hands up in the air in her frustration.

"Because I can't afford anything better!" he snapped.

"Well, hurry up and get it started or we're going to get arrested!"

Adam gave the key another savage twist. This time, the engine caught and started, the exhaust pipe letting out a heavy puff of black smoke, though the car sounded grouchy at having to actually do something. Adam gunned the engine a few times, revving it with presses on the gas pedal to warm the engine.

"This is the worst getaway attempt ever," she grumbled. "We're going to get busted. I should've called Shaun."

"Shaun's in jail."

"That's where *we're* going to be if you don't *get moving!*"

"You think I don't know that?" Adam said. He slammed the car into gear and mashed his foot on the gas. The rustbucket VW bug lurched forward with such suddenness that Remy's head smacked against the headrest behind her, and the carton of cigarettes that she'd just stolen tumbled to the floorboard. She was tempted to lean down to grab it, but Adam was driving like a maniac to put distance between them and the mini-mart before the cops showed up, and she was afraid that if she leaned down at this point, she'd end up with a concussion.

"Would you *please* drive like a normal human being?" she demanded, bracing a hand against the dash. "You're drawing more attention by driving like an idiot!"

Flashing blue lights reflected in the passenger side mirror, and Remy groaned. *Too late.* She only hoped that whoever was pulling them over was only doing so because Adam didn't know how to drive and not because they knew that she'd just stolen a carton of cigarettes from a convenience store. She sat up straight, rough-combing her hair with her fingers, and hooked a foot around the cigarette carton to nudge it underneath her seat as best she could.

"Pull over," she snapped. "And act normal. They might not realize it's us they're looking for."

"Oh, they probably already know," Adam said. He was going for his wallet, digging it out of his pocket and rifling through it for his driver's license. Remy tried to play it cool, trying to get into the mindset that she was just a girl out on a date with a friend, because who would suspect someone like her of shoplifting a carton of cigarettes?

The officer approached the driver's window, and when Remy caught a glimpse of his face, she struggled to bite back a groan of exasperation as she dredged up his name from somewhere in her memory. Marc something-or-other. DuBois, maybe? She wasn't sure, but either way, if he knew that there'd been a shoplifting at a convenience store and she was in the area, she was probably the one who'd done it. She slouched down in her seat, hoping the cigarettes were sufficiently hidden under the seat.

The officer knocked on the window, and Adam rolled it down, asking the man in a smarmy tone, "Is there a problem, Officer?"

It took everything in Remy to not reach into the driver's seat and punch Adam in the balls.

"We've had a report of a theft at—" Officer DuBois broke off and leaned down further, shining a flashlight into the car. The light caught Remy full in the face, and she put up a hand to block the glare in her eyes. "Well, well, well, Miss Angellette," he said in a casual drawl, "fancy meeting you here."

* * *

Memphis, TN

Cade awoke with a start to the sound of soft, persistent knocking on the closed bathroom door. She blinked and tried to get her bearings, realizing she'd dozed off in the bathtub. Again. She was submerged to her collarbones in water that had grown tepid; her fingers were wrinkled and soft and felt odd when she bent them. She made sure her thick, dark hair was still gathered into its clip at the base of her skull before climbing out of the tub. Quickly toweling off, she pulled on a heavy bathrobe and opened the door.

Cade skimmed her eyes over the disheveled little girl who stood in the doorway, her khaki pants and pale sweatshirt wrinkled and dirty from a day's worth of play. She chuckled softly, not quite missing the wide-eyed look the girl gave her. "Hey, Josie."

Josie tugged at one of her messy brown pigtails and bit her lip. "Aunt Cade, there's a scary movie on the TV."

Cade raised an eyebrow and released her hair from its clip, going to the medicine cabinet to get a comb. "A scary movie?" she questioned, working the comb through her hair as she spoke. "SpongeBob isn't scary."

"It's not," Josie agreed. She nodded and chewed her lip again, twisting from side to side and never taking her wide eyes off Cade. "It's not SpongeBob."

"Well, what is it then?" Cade sent up a prayer that Josie hadn't seen anything that would traumatize her. Cade's older sister would kill her if Josie came back from her latest visit with a new set of nightmares as a parting gift. She was sure Lindsey still hadn't forgiven her for the last batch of nightmares after she took Josie to the circus and the girl had a run-in with a clown.

"There's a lady talking and people running and yelling." The little girl looked worriedly down the hall toward the staircase. If Cade focused hard enough, she could make out a woman talking, her tone urgent, though her words were indistinct.

"Did you tell Andrew?" she asked, looking down the hall with Josie toward the head of the staircase. Her eyes narrowed, like she could will Andrew off the couch in the den to fix the problem downstairs.

"He didn't say anything," Josie replied. "I think he's still sleeping." She shifted her eyes back to Cade and scuffed her bare foot at the hallway carpet.

Cade made a face of annoyance; she'd have to inform Andrew—*again*—that she wouldn't tolerate him lounging around sleeping all day. She was already irritated that Andrew hadn't joined the rest of them for the barbecue. Ignoring Josie when the girl had a problem was another thing altogether, a situation that might have gotten him kicked out if Cade had been in a worse mood.

Cade set the comb on the sink and knelt in front of the girl, brushing Josie's bangs back from her brown eyes and giving her a reassuring smile. "I'll tell you what," she started. She leaned to look at the glowing red numbers on the alarm clock in the bedroom across the hall; it was after nine p.m. "You're going back home tomorrow, right?"

"Yeah."

"Well, it's past your bedtime, and you need plenty of rest for the trip back home, don't you?" Cade suggested. She hoped dearly that she sounded at least slightly persuasive. It would be much easier to talk to Andrew with Josie tucked away in bed and not practically in front of them when things degraded into an argument—as their discussions always seemed to do lately.

"I guess," Josie mumbled with a small shrug. The little girl didn't quite look at her, and Cade knew that she didn't agree. But her droopy eyes told Cade everything she needed to know.

Cade offered Josie a hand as she stood. "Come on, chick. Let's get your teeth brushed and get you all tucked in."

Josie went to sleep easily, for which Cade was thankful. She smiled indulgently as she looked in at her niece from the doorway, watching as she curled onto her side with her cherished stuffed elephant in her arms. Cade turned on the nightlight and slipped out, leaving the door cracked so she could hear if Josie called out in the night.

Cade went downstairs after a quick stop in her bedroom to change into her own pajamas, pausing in the doorway of the den and looking in on Andrew. Surprisingly, he wasn't on the couch where she had left him. She turned her head and spotted him in the kitchen. He stood in front of the open fridge, staring inside listlessly.

"I think Josie's been playing with the remote," she told him. He didn't reply, just nodded. She sighed and went to the couch, digging around the cushions and pillows, searching for the remote as she half-listened to the television.

"...say they have no indications of what the White House plans to do regarding the viral out..."

"Ah, here it is." Cade scooped up the remote triumphantly and shoved the cushions back where they belonged. She aimed the remote behind her and turned off the TV, cutting off the woman's voice with the click of a button. Tossing the remote onto the coffee table, she headed to the kitchen door again to look in on Andrew.

He remained in front of the opened fridge, drinking straight from a carton of orange juice. Cade made a face. *Strike one*, she thought. She'd have to toss out the remainder of the juice before Josie drank any of it and buy a fresh carton. Especially considering how under the weather Andrew had been feeling since he'd gotten back from his trip.

Andrew lowered the carton and wiped at his mouth with the back of his hand. "What was that about Josie and the TV?" he asked. He looked pale and a little sweaty, his cheeks flushed, and his voice hinted at just how tired he actually was.

"She played with the remote again," she said. "Changed the channel onto a horror movie or something."

"Oh, sorry. I didn't even notice," he admitted with a wince. He moved toward Cade and wrapped his arms around her in a loose embrace. "Why don't we relax on the couch, maybe watch a movie or something?"

Cade grinned despite her annoyance. "I think I like that idea. Are you up to it?" She pressed the back of her hand to his forehead and frowned; he felt hotter than he should have. "You feel like you're running a fever."

"I'll be fine. Let me go get us some drinks, okay?" Andrew offered. He turned to go back to the kitchen, and Cade watched with a deeper frown as he wobbled on his feet. She shook her head and went back to the coffee table, scooping up the remote again and turning the TV back on.

The horror movie Josie had found was still on. Cade made a face of disgust and jabbed at a button to change the channel. She couldn't stand horror movies. The senseless violence made her stomach turn. After spending twenty-five years living in Israel and seeing horrible acts of brutality committed in the streets, she no longer found anything awesome about watching people get hacked to death, even if it was fake.

Cade shook free from her thoughts and glanced at the TV, frowning in confusion. She was sure she'd changed the channel, but the same footage still played on the screen. She pressed the channel buttons a few more times, thinking maybe the batteries in the remote had died, before realizing that similar footage played on nearly *every* local channel. Reflexively, she changed the TV to a news station. Her eyes widened, and she bit back a gasp of shock.

"*Rioting in Downtown Memphis!*" the banner across the bottom of the screen proclaimed.

Cade sank onto the couch, her eyes still wide, her knuckles whitening as she gripped the remote almost hard enough to break it, her heart pounding in her chest. She watched as a nearly frantic journalist reported the events. The street behind her was aglow with flames from a tall building, and several people wandered around in shock as emergency personnel swarmed over the scene. A bead of sweat rolled down the journalist's face as she spoke shakily into the microphone, and Cade wondered if the sweat was from stress or from the heat of the fire.

"What's going on?" Andrew asked as he came into the living room. He held two glasses in his hands; condensation ran down their sides to wet his skin. He squinted at the television and cocked his head to the side.

Cade glanced at him long enough to take in the fact that he was standing by the couch before turning her gaze right back to the TV. "There's a riot in Memphis," she replied, her voice betraying her shock at the news.

"Wow," Andrew breathed. He dropped to the couch beside Cade, nearly spilling the drinks all over them both. When he plunked the glasses onto the coffee table, the liquid in one of them sloshed over the rim. "When did this start?" he asked, wiping the condensation off on the thighs of his pants.

"I'm not sure," Cade admitted, glancing back at the staircase before turning up the volume. She didn't want to wake Josie by turning the volume up too much; she and Andrew would never get the preschooler back to sleep if she came downstairs.

Andrew gave an almost imperceptible nod, intent on the screen for several minutes. The silence during that time hung heavily between them, and the feeling of it lying across her chest like a wet blanket made Cade uncomfortable. "That's really not far from here," he said as a map of Memphis came up on the screen. A bright red star marked the location of the riots and fires in question. He grabbed his drink and added, "Barely three miles."

Cade drew in a breath as she realized Andrew was right. Three miles wasn't much at all. It was less than the distance she ran every morning: five miles, religiously, just after sunrise. Andrew abandoned his drink and went to the front window, his steps still unsteady as he crossed the carpet to look out into the darkness. "You don't think it will come over this way, do you?" she asked.

"No, I think we'll be okay here," he said, resting his hand against the cold pane of glass. He spoke in an absent tone, as if he weren't totally focused on what he said. It disturbed Cade enough to draw her attention away from the TV, and she frowned as she rose from her seat to join him, not finding any reassurance in his words. The sound of the reporter's voice on the TV made her stop in mid-step, and she half-turned to look back at the screen. The woman's voice had taken on a heavier, more noticeable sense of urgency.

"We've just received a report...I'm sorry, is this correct?" the reporter asked someone off camera, her voice shaking. Cade couldn't tell if the reporter was excited or terrified, but both options made her nauseous. She dug her nails into her palms as she stepped closer to the TV. *"We've just received an unverified report from one of the county hospitals that numerous victims of the riots appear to be in some sort of delusional state. There are reports of the injured attacking the doctors and nurses trying to assist them..."*

"Jesus, what's going *on*?" Cade snapped. A twinge of genuine fear buzzed down her spine. She grabbed the remote again and flipped through a few channels, settling on another news program, where a somber-looking man sat behind a desk, holding a small sheaf of papers; she could just make out the faint tremble of the sheets as the man's hands shook.

"Once again, the footage you are about to see may not be appropriate for younger viewers. It was taken on the street outside the Southside residential fire by Fox News reporter Veronica Sawyers."

Andrew drifted away from the window and stood behind the sofa to watch. The scene changed to footage of a young, healthy-looking blonde reporter, microphone in hand, her hair coiffed and makeup applied perfectly.

"Police and first responders are asking everyone to please remain indoors at this time. They're recommending that you lock all of your doors and windows and—" She halted her report

and turned in reaction to someone speaking off camera. As she let out a shocked gasp and a muffled, *"Oh my God,"* the camera panned around to the scene near her.

What Cade saw froze the blood in her veins.

Two large men had thrown a young man to the sidewalk. They crouched over him and pawed at his clothes with a frightening degree of franticness. Cade thought at first that they were mugging the man, but it became apparent soon enough that something much more awful was happening. Blood blossomed forth. As one of the men leaned down and *bit* the still-struggling man, tearing a chunk of flesh from his shoulder, Cade let out a choked gasp and turned away from the screen. She clapped her hand over her mouth as bile rose into her throat, turning her eyes away to look at Andrew. He stared at the television, his eyes just as wide as hers, his skin pale.

"Oh my God," Andrew whispered in a weak echo of the reporter. His hands trembled as he held them at his sides; when he saw Cade looking at them, he gripped the back of the sofa.

"What are they *doing*?" Cade asked, risking another cautious glance at the TV. She didn't want to see anything further, but her morbid curiosity won out over her disgust.

"I think…I think they might be *eating* him."

On the screen, Veronica Sawyer let out a shriek of fear as the two men, moving away from their now-dead victim, started in her direction. *"My God, they're coming this way! Run!"* she shouted. The camera thudded to the ground as the cameraman decided that the reporter's advice was worth taking. Blood-spattered sneakers filled the screen as the killers ran by. Then the feed went black and cut back to the studio, where the anchor looked even more shaken than he had before the clip had aired.

Before Cade or Andrew could speak, the shrill sound of the phone ringing cut through the air. Cade stood abruptly from her perch on the couch and moved to answer it. She saw Ethan's name on the caller ID and snatched up the receiver. "Eth?"

"*Did you see the news?*" Ethan asked without preamble. He sounded breathless and upset. Cade didn't like his tone; it made her stomach feel like it was twisted up in knots.

"Yeah, I did. What the hell is going on?"

"*I don't know, but Anna's gone.*"

Her eyes widened as she understood the source of Ethan's agitation. "Gone? What do you mean, gone?"

"*I mean just that. We were getting ready to go out, and she got a call from the hospital asking her to come in. It was on a volunteer basis only, but she insisted on going,*" he explained. "*The PD told me to stay put and said they'd call in two hours to let me know when I'll be deployed, so I wasn't planning to go anywhere, and I wanted her here with me. I tried to stop her. I don't want her out there by herself. We argued about it, and she eventually took the keys to the Lexus and left without saying anything else.*"

"Oh God. Is there anything I can do?" she asked. She shifted her weight onto one leg and rested her hip against the table. She fought the urge to look back at the TV as the news anchor warned of more potential graphic images.

"*I don't know. I need to go after her,*" Ethan said urgently. Cade shook her head, even though Ethan couldn't see the movement.

"No, you don't need to go anywhere. You need to stay put," she said. "If she comes back and you're gone, she won't know where to find you. Have you tried her cell phone yet?"

"*Yes. I think the network is overloaded,*" Ethan said. His voice was taut with thinly veiled frustration. "*None of my calls or texts will go through.*"

"All the more reason to stay right where you are," Cade said. She grabbed her purse and dug through it, locating her own cell phone and flipping it open. Just as Ethan had said, the display read, "*Searching for network.*" She frowned and tried turning it off and back on, but that didn't help. "What should we do?" she asked. She kept her voice low, and she twisted to put her back to Andrew. "Do you think this is bad?"

"*I only know what I see on the news and what I hear on the police scanner,*" he said. Cade bit her bottom lip hard enough to bruise when she heard just how serious he sounded.

"And what *are* you hearing?"

"*I'm hearing a lot of shit that's telling me that* nobody *should be out on the streets and that* everybody *should be getting somewhere safe,*" he said. "*I'm hearing riots and robberies and lootings and muggings and carjackings and murders and everything else illegal you can think of. All of this has happened within the past hour or two. So yeah, I think it's pretty bad.*"

Cade glanced at the TV again as she digested Ethan's words. Thankfully, the screen showed only the news anchor speaking solemnly into the camera. She read the chyron at the bottom of the screen again and asked in a hushed voice, "Do you think this is related to that virus outbreak in Atlanta?" She didn't know what had prompted the question, but it came out before she thought about it.

"*Maybe. I don't know,*" Ethan admitted. "*Anna said she heard that one of the symptoms is a high fever, and that could cause delirium if it was high enough. That's just a theory. I'm not a medical expert.*"

"Eth…" She glanced at the TV again and added hesitantly, "I saw some footage of a couple of guys actually *eating* a man. Does that sound like just a case of bad fever and delirium to you?"

A weighty silence fell on the line between them. "*Eating him?*" Ethan finally said, the incredulity in his voice coming through loud and clear. "*Are you serious?*"

"As a heart attack," she said.

"*Fuck,*" Ethan breathed out. "*This shit is…there are no words. I have no idea what's going on.*"

"I doubt anyone does," Cade admitted. She looked toward the stairs and then back behind her again. Andrew still stood behind the sofa, his eyes locked onto the television. "Eth, I've gotta go. I think Drew's still feeling jetlagged, and I want to check on Josie."

"*Call me back when you get the chance,*" he said.

A smile quirked at the corner of her mouth. "Okay, no problem." She hung up and let out a breath to steady herself, then turned toward the stairs. "Hey, I'm going to check on Josie," she told Andrew. He didn't respond, but she shrugged it off as fascination with the news and began climbing the stairs.

The upstairs level was calm and quiet, dark and soothing compared to the brighter lights and noise downstairs. Cade started toward the guest bedroom where Josie slept but bypassed it to pause in the door to her own bedroom. She stared into the dark room thoughtfully and considered gathering her important documents, just in case. She finally went inside and opened the top right dresser drawer. She took out a flat yellow manila envelope and made sure her military IDs, social security card, birth certificate, and other similar documents were inside it before going to the closet door. She took out the black plastic case she'd stored in the back of the closet and set it on the bed, dropping a medium-sized duffel bag and a pile of clothes and other essentials beside it. She smoothed her hand over the rifle case to reassure herself and left it there for ease of access. Once she'd packed her bag, she turned to the task of checking in on Josie.

Cade knew something was wrong before she even got to the doorway. She'd left the door cracked when she put Josie to bed, but now it stood fully open, the dim glow from the nightlight near the door spilling out into the dark hallway. She was already on edge from the news; anything out of the ordinary, anything other than the way she'd left it, was enough to make her wary. She approached the door, easing up to it cautiously, and peered around the doorframe, fighting a nervous flutter in her stomach.

A dark form leaned over Josie's bed. The little girl still slept, and the form looked nearly motionless as it stood over her. Cade stepped into the room, her fists clenched and ready as her heart leaped. But she relaxed as she realized it was only Andrew.

"Drew? Everything okay?" she asked, keeping her voice low so as not to disturb Josie. She took a slow step toward him. Andrew continued to stand over Josie, his head bowed as he stared at the sleeping girl's form. He didn't acknowledge Cade's approach.

"Drew?" she repeated, moving closer. She frowned and pressed her hand to his shoulder in a gentle gesture, trying to get his attention. "Are you okay?"

Andrew turned his head so suddenly and sharply that Cade took an involuntary step back. The look on his face struck her silent before she could even consider speaking another word. His expression was angry, heavy with hatred and violence, and the lower half of his face was covered in a thick, dark liquid that slowly dripped off his chin to fall to the cream carpet below.

Cade glanced at the bed and saw that Josie hadn't moved. The dark liquid was all over the bedsheets, all over her pajamas. Her small, thin hand hung limply off the edge of the bed, horribly pale and motionless. As the full realization of what she was seeing hit her, Andrew lunged, both of his bloodied hands grasping at her, his fingers closing into the fabric of her pajama shirt, jerking her toward him. Cade let out a shocked cry and backpedaled, ripping free from his grasp and tearing the front of her shirt open.

"Josie!" she yelled, staggering away from Andrew. She collided with the doorframe, the wood digging into her back between her shoulder blades. The little girl on the bed still didn't move, still didn't respond to her cry, bringing home the cold, hard reality Cade hadn't wanted to face.

She fled to her bedroom, slamming the door behind her, fumbling at the doorknob. She swore as she remembered that she'd had it changed out for one without a lock three months before when she'd accidentally locked herself out of her room. Giving up on the knob, she turned her attention instead to finding something with which to barricade the door. As her blue eyes skimmed the room, they landed on the rifle case she'd left on the bed.

It took Cade two brisk steps to cover the distance to the bed. She grabbed the case and yanked on the lid before swearing again; it was still locked. Darting to the dresser, she pulled the drawer completely out in her haste, the contents spilling onto the carpet at her feet. She dropped to her knees and scrabbled through the pile, looking for the silver key that would unlock the case.

Cade saw a shine of silver near the front of the pile and closed her fingers around it, clutching the little key to her chest tightly. She moved on autopilot as she climbed to her feet and raced back to the rifle case, jamming the key home and twisting it in the lock. Before she could get the rifle out, the doorframe splintered and Andrew barreled into the room, heading straight toward her without hesitation.

Cade took a quick step back from him. "Andrew! Stop!" she ordered, putting both hands up in a defensive gesture as she slipped sideways to put the bed between them. Andrew continued moving toward her, slowly, his eyes tracking her. For a terrible moment, Cade was reminded of a predator stalking its prey, and it didn't take a genius to guess which of them was the prey. She glanced at the phone, wondering if she could get to it fast enough to call for help.

Before she could consider making her move, Andrew lunged. She fell to the side, dodging, and her hip banged into the table beside her bed, the pain drawing a gasp from her. A flash of memory flipped through her mind of something she'd shoved into the table's drawer right when Lindsey had been ringing her doorbell the week before. She fumbled blindly for the drawer, pulling it open, and kept her eyes on Andrew as her hand felt for and found the loaded Jericho 941 pistol she'd stashed inside.

"Drew! Stop!" Cade ordered, swinging the pistol up to point it at him. Her mind fell onto thoughts of Josie, lying dead in the next room, and her eyes took in the blood still staining Andrew's hands and face. She gritted her teeth and squeezed the trigger.

CHAPTER FOUR

Plantersville, MS

It was nearly one a.m. when the sound of his phone buzzing against the bedside table woke Theo up from a deep sleep. It vibrated across the wooden table in jolts and starts, and he groaned, pulling the pillow over his head and trying to ignore the sound. It buzzed its way to the edge of the table before the caller hung up. He breathed a sigh of relief and closed his eyes. He was exhausted and sore, and his bed was too warm and comfortable to even consider getting out of it.

He shifted and braced his hand against the mattress, rolling onto his back and draping his arm across the bed. The other side was surprisingly empty—surprisingly because that wasn't how it had been when he'd passed out earlier that evening. He rolled onto the vacated side of the bed to get a look into the master bathroom. He could just make out Dillon standing at the sink in his boxer shorts, brushing his teeth. He caught sight of Theo in the mirror and grinned around the toothbrush, holding up a finger to indicate for him to wait. Once he spat and rinsed, he wandered back into the bedroom, dropping onto the bed beside Theo with a groan.

"Your phone's been ringing while you were sleeping," Dillon said. He lit a cigarette, and the scent of smoke and tobacco reached Theo's nose. "I took the landline off the hook after the last time. You looked like you needed sleep."

"I did," Theo said, rubbing his face. "Any idea who it was?"

"No clue. I didn't bother answering to find out," Dillon said. He stared at Theo for a moment and then added, "I'm sure it wasn't Gray. He's probably out doing his own thing with his own friends."

"Kind of like I'm doing my own thing with my own friends?"

Dillon winked at him and blew out a lungful of smoke in his direction. "I don't know. I doubt Gray does *that* with his friends."

Theo's cell phone buzzed again. He sighed and rolled over, grabbing the phone and checking the display. "It's work," he grumbled. "Fuck, can't they leave me alone on my night off?"

"You're too good a medic, and they can't get enough of you," Dillon said sagely.

Theo rolled his eyes and answered the phone. "Hello?"

"*Theo, I know you're off tonight, but we need you to come in,*" his boss said without preamble.

"Hello to you too, Doug," Theo replied, scooting to the edge of the bed and grabbing his pants from the floor. "What if I tell you I'm busy and can't make it in?"

"*That's the thing. I* really *need you to come in,*" Doug said. "*There's all this shit going on and—*"

"What kind of shit?"

"*A lot of disturbances in town. Traffic's bad too, so there's been a bunch of accidents between here and Tupelo. We're running on empty, we have calls holding, Tupelo's begging for mutual aid, and none of the crews have had any rest. I need to open up the spare truck and need you and Jonathan to give us a hand* just *until everything settles down."*

Theo rested his elbow against his thigh and his head against his hand. "Doug, look, I'd love to. I really would. But I'm exhausted myself. They aren't the only ones running on empty, okay?"

"I understand, Theo. I do. But I don't have much choice. No one else answered their phones. You were seriously my last resort."

There was silence on the line. Theo closed his eyes and let out a long sigh. "Fine. Just until it quiets down, right?"

"Right. Not a minute longer."

Theo hoped he wouldn't regret this. "I'll be there in about thirty minutes."

The moment he hung up, he threw his cell phone across the room. It crashed against the wall and dropped to the carpet, unscathed by the impact thanks to his military-grade phone case. "Son of a *bitch*," he snarled.

"You're such a pushover," Dillon commented from the bed. Theo made a face at him, and he added, "You totally are! You should have told him no."

"I need the money," he replied, going to his closet, pulling out a clean uniform, and starting to change. "Living here is expensive, and I'm not lucky enough to pull checks to stay home and take care of a sick family member."

Dillon sobered at that, finishing his cigarette and putting it out in the ashtray by the bed. "I'm thinking I might have to get him moved into a nursing home," he said. "It's starting to get to be too much for me to handle."

Theo paused in the act of fastening his utility pants and looked at Dillon. "Shit, why didn't you tell me you were having trouble?" he asked. "I would have helped."

"I know, I just…I don't want my friendship with you tainted by *him*." Dillon sighed. "I've had to put up with Dad's alcoholic ass all my life, and you shouldn't have to deal with him by virtue of being friends with me. I want to keep that aspect of my life completely…" He flailed his hands, searching for a word. "…separate," he finally settled on.

Theo abandoned his attempts to get dressed and went to Dillon, wrapping him in a tight hug. "Hey, it's okay. I don't mind. I handle patients like him all the time, so it's not—"

"I don't *want* you to handle him," Dillon insisted, pulling away and brushing his hair out of his eyes. "Really. It's fine. I promise." He turned away and started searching for his shirt. "Get ready for work, Theo. They need you."

Twenty minutes later, Theo arrived at work, still exhausted and still annoyed at having been called there in the first place. He headed toward the time clock and found Jonathan in the kitchen banging around in the fridge, looking as annoyed as he felt. "I *know* I left some Cokes in here this morning," he said, pushing the door shut with more force than necessary. Jars in the door rattled together as it banged shut.

"Somebody probably drank them," Theo said, swiping his badge to clock in. "Figured you'd have learned by now to not leave stuff in the fridge here. People have a habit of taking stuff that isn't theirs."

"Yeah, well, I guess I give people too much credit for honesty sometimes." He looked Theo up and down. "You look as pissed as me. I bet you had company over, didn't you?"

"Maybe," he hedged.

"Who was she?"

"I don't think that's any of your business." Theo didn't bother correcting the incorrect pronoun.

"I'm aware," Jonathan said. "I just know how it is to get dragged kicking and screaming into work. Did Doug play the whole guilt trip game on you too?"

"Doesn't he always?"

The phone rang then, the shrill chime echoing in the high-ceilinged room. Theo groaned and cut a dirty look at the phone. "Can you get that? I hate talking on those damn things."

Jonathan grabbed the phone. After a murmured conversation, he hung up, looking grim. "One patient MVA at Highway 6 and Hillcrest. Guy's got injuries and appears to have altered mental status with violent tendencies. Law enforcement is on the scene now."

Theo grabbed his bag and headed to the front door, Jonathan right ahead of him. As he hauled himself into the passenger seat, the ambulance's engine rumbled to life. The chatter on the radio was full of static and ten-codes, and he had to close his eyes and focus past it to mentally go over everything he'd need to do at the scene. Then the ambulance's sirens started up, chasing any other thoughts from his mind. A surge of adrenaline rocked through his veins as the truck roared out into the street and headed for the site of the accident.

Jonathan pulled the ambulance over at the accident site, parked in front of a police car, and let out a low whistle. "Jesus, that looks bad," he said, taking in the sight of the wrecked car. Theo snagged a pair of gloves from the box between the seats, stuffed a few extra pairs into his pant pocket, and opened his door.

"Looks like a rollover," he said. "Let's see what we can do." Dropping to the pavement, he called, "Grab the stretcher, backboard, and collar. We're probably going to need them."

He retrieved the trauma bag and made his way to the wrecked car below.

Every side of the car was banged up, scratched, dented, and caved in, like a giant fist had reached down and squeezed the car. All the windows were shattered, and the airbags had deployed. An officer headed toward him, sporting a mark on his jaw where he appeared to have been punched. Theo winced in sympathy.

"You okay, man?" he asked the officer, whose name badge said "Greenlee."

"Yeah, I'm fine," Greenlee said. "Be careful with this one. He's out of his mind. We restrained him, but you'll need Poseys for this one."

"Thanks for the tip," Theo said. After calling to Jonathan to add restraints to the supplies, he hurried past the first responders to get to his patient. What he saw made his stomach lurch.

There's no way this man should be alive, was his first thought.

Of the dozens of accidents he'd worked in the three years since he'd become a paramedic, the only patients Theo had seen in such a condition were dead ones. Both of the man's legs were broken, compound fractures with open wounds through which he could see bone. His left arm was deformed, and congealed blood adorned the side of his head. Gaping wounds on the man's biceps and shoulders exposed the underlying muscle and tendons. Despite his injuries, he was oddly alert, his eyes following Theo's every move.

What caught Theo's attention the most was the look on the man's face. It was…animalistic, feral. He'd never seen a look like it, not even on the faces of the most violent drug addicts he'd picked up. He swallowed hard, steeled himself for the upcoming confrontation, and pasted a reassuring smile on his face.

"Hey, my name's Theo," he said to the patient. The man didn't respond; he merely snapped his teeth like a cornered dog. Someone had cuffed the man's hands to the crumpled steering wheel, and all those present were keeping their distance.

The nearest first responder approached then, a man Theo recognized as Chuck Howitz from the fire and rescue service. "Watch this guy," he warned. "He tried to bite Stevens and Brigham."

"Bite?" Theo repeated.

"We're thinking head injury," Chuck said. "Star pattern on the windshield. Possible chest injuries too, judging by the bent steering wheel. No idea how he got the ones on his arms, though. It's not like anything I've seen outside of a wild-animal attack."

Theo looked around. "Was there another car?"

"Near 'bout as I can tell, guy drove himself off the road," Chuck replied. He clapped Theo on the shoulder as Jonathan approached with the supplies. "Good luck, man. Let me know if you guys need help."

Theo snorted. "I don't know where you think you're going," he said, yanking the car's back door open and crawling inside. "You know we need help." He nodded to Jonathan and started giving orders. "I want full spinal packaging. We'll splint the arm and legs once we've got him free of the car and loaded into the truck."

It took Theo, Chuck, and Jonathan nearly twenty minutes of work and copious amounts of swearing before they got the man, who'd begun thrashing and flailing the moment the cuffs were unlocked, out of the car and onto the backboard.

By then, Theo felt like he'd been dunked into a swimming pool, his uniform sticking grossly to his back with sweat. He panted for air as he and Jonathan strapped the man down and restrained him with Poseys before hauling the stretcher to the embankment.

"I've never in my life seen anything like this," Jonathan said as they loaded the stretcher into the ambulance.

"Me either," Theo admitted. They climbed into the back of the ambulance, and he added, "Grab that pulse ox and get a reading on his O2 and heart rates while I get the EKG going. Then get me set up to start an IV." He snagged the leads from the bag on the side of the monitor and attached them to the man's chest. Jonathan slipped the pulse ox sensor onto the man's finger and turned it on.

"I don't get how this man is still alive," Jonathan said. The patient wriggled and thrashed as much as his strapped-down position would allow. "I've never seen someone with these kinds of injuries so…active." He looked at the pulse ox's display and frowned, switching it off and on and checking the cable running from the sensor to the device. "I'm not getting a reading on O2 or heart rate," he said, switching the sensor to a different finger.

"One of the basic truck's been having problems with theirs," Theo said, wrapping the blood pressure cuff around the man's forearm, avoiding the wounds on his biceps. "Maybe they swapped their crappy one for ours when nobody was looking."

"Maybe." Jonathan tried the pulse ox one more time while Theo leaned across the patient and flipped the EKG monitor on. There was a pause as it powered on, then the display lit up, and a straight line began to trail across the screen.

He leaned closer to it, unsure if he was seeing correctly, then sat back, utterly confused.

"Huh," Theo said. He climbed to the other side of the truck and checked the machine over, then double-checked his placement of the leads. "Nothing here, either. This isn't right."

"You're telling me." Jonathan pulled a bright orange bag from a cabinet while Theo dug his stethoscope from his bag and plugged it into his ears, pressing the cup to the man's chest. He swallowed hard when he realized he was, in fact, hearing what he thought he was hearing. Or *not* hearing, in this particular case.

Jonathan was across from him; he'd pulled the monitor's blood pressure cuff from the man's forearm and replaced it with one from the orange bag, his own stethoscope in his ears as he inflated the cuff and then let the air out. His face took on a startled expression, and he looked at Theo, his eyes wide. Theo was sure his own face mirrored Jonathan's.

"I know," Theo said, his voice hoarse and scratchy. A sense of ominous doom settled over him. "He's got the vitals of a dead man, but he's kicking like he's still alive."

"What the hell do we do in a case like this?" Jonathan asked.

"I'm not sure," he said. "They didn't teach anything like this in paramedic school." He looked at the backs of the man's hands, snagging a tourniquet and wrapping it around his forearm to start an IV. After a few tries, he said, "His veins are all collapsed. I can't find a usable one." He checked his watch, looked out the ambulance's back doors where several first responders were watching as if he was putting on a show, and sighed. "Get in front and head for the nearest hospital. I'm going to splint his legs and arm and see what else I can do for him. I doubt it'll be much."

Jonathan stripped off his gloves, tossed them into the biohazard bin, and jumped from the back of the truck. Theo stared at the patient in front of him as Jonathan shut the back doors, wondering what the hell to do. He'd never seen anything like it. Not breathing, no pulse, no BP, nothing. By all logic, he should have been calling in the coroner. But the patient appeared to still be alive. Theo blew out a breath and, as the ambulance began rolling, pulled out trauma dressings, gauze, tape, and splints to shore up the damage he could do something about. It wasn't far to the hospital, and after that, this strange man and his lack of vitals would be someone else's problem.

"Hey, Jon, call ahead to the ER and let them know what we've got," he called, intending to work his way from head to toe to catalogue all the man's injuries. The man glared at him, snapping his teeth again. Theo tried to shrug it off and took out his penlight to check the man's pupils. Fixed and dilated. His corneas were even starting to cloud. Theo shuddered and reached for his stethoscope again.

"Shit! Theo, hold on!" Jonathan yelled from the cab. Theo grabbed the bar on the ceiling, gripping it tightly with one hand and bracing the other against the cabinets across from him as the ambulance swerved sharply one way before weaving back the other direction. The top-heavy vehicle skidded and tilted. The last thing he heard before he fell across the patient's legs and crashed into the IV cabinet was Jonathan crying out, "Oh my God!"

Theo's head struck the metal bar next to the IV cabinet, and his world tumbled into blackness.

* * *

New Orleans, LA

Remy had been slouched on an uncomfortable bench in a holding cell at the New Orleans Police Department for the past hour, examining her chipped black nail polish and wondering when Officer DuBois would get around to doing whatever he was supposed to do to get her out of there when the screaming started in Holding Cell 2.

> *"Get away from me!"*
> *"Get this stupid bitch off of me!"*
> *"What's wrong with this chick?"*
> *"Somebody get a cop in here!"*

"Great," Remy muttered, slouching against the concrete wall, resting her head on a block proclaiming that Kitty had once been there. "Drunk bitch started a fight. Now I get to sit here even longer." She crossed her eyes and tried to not roll her eyes at the sound of the crash next door. She was the only person in Holding Cell 3, so thankfully she didn't have any drunk, obnoxious cellmates to put up with yet.

For now, her thoughts were currently revolving around how badly her stepfather was going to kick the shit out of her for getting arrested. *Again.* It'd be the usual mess: Jason yelling at her; her mother crying and wondering where she'd gone wrong; and Maddie hiding in her room as she'd been instructed to by her parents. There'd be comments about how Remy had *obviously* gotten her rebellious streak from her father, because her mother's side of the family couldn't *possibly* be capable of anything disobedient, and then—as usual—Jason would bail her out and plead her case to the judge about how distraught she was trying to cope with her father's death and her mother's remarriage and how she was only acting out in a misguided attempt to assuage her grief and all that other hokey psychologist bullshit he liked to spout. It'd be added to her criminal record, she'd be assured once more that she could never get a decent job, and then she'd go on the same downward spiral her father had when he'd packed up and left her mother to become a professional musician and had failed miserably.

Another crash echoed out. It sounded for all the world like someone had ripped the bench free from the wall and flung it across the room. Amidst the screaming, she could hear cops repeatedly ordering someone to stand down, to put their hands up and get on the floor. Uneasily, she rose to her feet and, her curiosity piqued, edged to the cell door and peered out through the small window, pressing her palms flat against the cool steel door, eyeing the scene beyond.

Police officers hurried between the desks, disappearing from view toward the sound of the fighting. More than one had a Taser, and a few even had guns or pepper spray. Remy picked out a single oasis of calm in the middle of all the chaos. Officer DuBois sat at a desk, carefully copying information from a driver's license to a form with a ballpoint pen. At his elbow was an unopened carton of cigarettes.

DuBois looked up from the card in his hand, and their eyes met. She waved and called, "Hey, Marc! When do I get my fucking phone call?"

He sighed, set her license on top of the form, and rose from his desk, reappearing with a key and unlocking her door. "Arms out," he ordered. "You know the drill. No trying to be funny."

"Oh, you're such a sweet talker, Marc," she crooned, obediently extending her arms so he could fasten handcuffs on her wrists. "When are you *ever* gonna use that sweet talk to ask me to dinner?"

"I don't go on dates with repeat offenders," Marc replied, leading her out of the cell. "I told you that last time I arrested you."

"So if this was only the first time I'd been arrested, you'd ask me on a date then?" she teased.

He gave her an exasperated look and stopped at the phone mounted to the wall. "Why do you keep letting yourself get arrested anyway?" he asked, lifting the receiver. "This isn't *Raising Arizona*, and you're too smart to repeatedly screw up like you have."

Remy rankled at the comment but, instead of letting it show, she smiled brightly. "Why, it's the easiest way I know of to get to see you!"

Marc punched a code into the phone's keypad. "If you were about five years older and didn't have a rap sheet longer than my arm, I'd consider it. But only one of those things is fixable."

Remy grinned. "Give me five years and I'll have both corrected."

"Very cute, Rem—"

Gunfire rang out, first one shot, then several more. Marc dropped the receiver and pushed Remy against the wall, standing protectively between her and the potential danger. The noise reached a fevered pitch, an echoing crescendo that made Remy stuff her nose into her wrists so she could get her hands up to cover her ears. When the gunshots ended, the shouts continued, this time for a medic. Marc moved toward the noise then, and Remy followed closely; she figured it wouldn't be smart to stray too far from her arresting officer, but she also felt better sticking close to the nearest man with a gun, just in case. *Of what?* her mind persisted. She didn't know.

Marc stopped at Holding Cell 2 and looked inside; his face paled. Remy swallowed hard, wondering what he'd seen in the cell, and eased forward a few inches, contemplating satisfying her morbid curiosity, but the decision was made for her when a couple of medics jostled her. She stumbled forward and got an eyeful of the scene inside the cell.

Blood. There was blood everywhere. Smeared on the walls. Puddled on the floor. The attacker lay in a pool of her own blood, clearly deceased. Another woman sobbed, covered in blood from wounds on her arms and shoulders. Remy's mouth flooded with saliva, bile rising in her throat. She swallowed convulsively and took a step back from the door.

Marc remembered her then, and he took her elbow. "Miss Angellette, we need to get you back in lock up," he said, leading her away. "This isn't something you need to see."

"What happened in there?" Remy asked.

"I don't know." Marc took her back to Holding Cell 3, which was now full of the other arrestees from Holding Cell 2.

After he unlocked her handcuffs and left her in the cell, she slouched into an empty space on a bench, dropping her head into her hands. She felt a headache coming on, pain throbbing at her temples. She'd have killed for a dose of aspirin.

Remy turned her attention to the subdued women now sharing a cell with her. A Hispanic woman wearing too much makeup sat in the corner, mumbling a prayer. Remy wondered if it would be appropriate to ask the question nagging her. For all she knew, it'd set of all sorts of chaos. But she couldn't let it fester in her brain.

"So...what happened in there?" she asked.

Remy's question brought on a flood of women's voices, all trying to talk at the same time, eager to describe what they'd seen now that they realized there was someone in their midst who hadn't witnessed the events in Holding Cell 2.

"Tanisha attacked—"

"There was a crazy bitch—"

"She said she got bit by a hobo—"

"They're not called hobos anymore, Deena."

The Hispanic woman in the corner started praying louder, like she felt the need to compete with all the other voices in the room.

"Shut up!" one of the women shouted. Her voice was loaded with authority, and everyone present obeyed her order to quiet themselves, looking to her expectantly. She was looking at Remy, her eyebrows raised in curiosity.

"You weren't in there, honey?" she asked, and Remy shook her head.

"No, I was already in this cell by myself. When Officer DuBois let me out to make my call, I heard shooting and screaming."

"My name is Trish," she offered. "I was sitting next to the lady that started attacking people. She was…she was crazy, I think." She looked away from Remy, staring at the floor. "She attacked Debra. It was like she just went…crazy," she said again, like she lacked a word for what she'd witnessed.

"She *bit* Debra," one of the other women corrected. "When that woman attacked her, Debra put up her arm to block her, and the woman bit her. She tore out a chunk of her arm!"

"Yeah, with her teeth!" another woman added. "It was disgusting. There was blood *everywhere*."

"Why'd she attack Debra?" Remy asked.

"Don't know," Trish said. "The lady looked sick, like maybe she'd gotten into some bad drugs. She kept hitting herself on the head, banging her head into the wall, that sorta thing. I figured she was on a bad trip or something." Trish shook her head. "It was the damnedest thing I've ever seen."

Remy nodded, her mind churning over the admittedly disjointed description she'd been given. She was glad she hadn't witnessed it, considering the brief glimpse she'd had of the aftereffects of the attack.

At the sound of a key in the cell's lock, Remy sat up straighter. Her eyes widened when she saw Marc, who beckoned to her. "Miss Angellette, please come with me," he requested. "I need some information for your processing paperwork."

Remy rose from the bench, dusting off her pants and glancing at Trish. The woman was no longer paying attention to her; she was back to staring into space while the rest of the women chattered with each other. The Hispanic woman had started praying again.

"What kind of information?" she asked as soon as she stepped out of the cell. She extended her arms to him, expecting him to put handcuffs on her like he was supposed to. He didn't, though; he just shut the cell door, locked it again, and took her elbow.

"Walk with me," he said. "Don't argue and don't question. Don't draw attention to us."

Remy obeyed, though she was itching to ask what was going on. Around them, the station looked busier than before, downright chaotic: officers calling to each other, radios belching out static and ten-codes, and the occasional arrestee adding their own yelling to the racket. Marc guided her through the mess, then right out the back door into the substation's parking garage. It was then that she dared to speak.

"What the hell's going on? Why are we leaving?"

"I'm getting you out while I have the chance," Marc said. "There's…a problem. I'll explain in the car."

"Where the hell are we going?"

"I'm hoping to take you home," he said. "Well, my house to start with, then we're going to your house." He led her to his cruiser and unlocked the passenger door, opening it for her, then circled to the driver's side and got in behind the wheel. Once he had the door shut and the engine started, he twisted in his seat to look at her.

"Have you heard anything about what's been happening in Atlanta?"

"Only some hints," Remy said, thinking back to the few scattered tweets she'd seen—the ones that had disappeared as soon as she'd hit refresh. "Nothing much, just little comments people made on social media."

"I have an uncle that lives in Smyrna," Marc said. "He called me just before the phones went down. He told me there's a virus spreading out of Atlanta. What he described is…not good. I figured he was exaggerating—he's prone to conspiracy theories and sees federal agents behind every bush. It kind of stuck with me, though, and then when the Thompson thing happened—"

"The Thompson thing?"

"There was a call for a woman at a shopping center attacking people. Thompson and his partner showed up, and the lady attacked Thompson. Bit the shit out of him," Marc said. "He started getting sick. So have all the other people who were attacked at the shopping center. And there are reports of even more sick people in the city. When they're sick, they're violent. Just like my uncle said. The military's gotten involved in Atlanta. It's only a matter of time before they show up here. I'd prefer getting you home while I still can."

"Is it really that bad?"

"Yeah, I think it is," he confirmed, starting the engine and signaling for her to fasten her seatbelt.

"So why me?" Remy asked, buckling her seatbelt as he pulled out of his parking spot and steered the cruiser to the exit. "There were plenty of other women in the holding cells back there. "Why just me?"

"Because you were the only one in there whose paperwork hadn't been processed," Marc said. "For all intents and purposes, you weren't even there. If the military were to come in and take over, they'd want a full accounting of who was in our cells. Since you weren't in the system, I had a chance to sneak you out. I guess you can consider the shoplifting charges dropped."

"I just can't believe you were willing to press them over a carton of cigarettes," she said.

"Stealing is stealing," Marc said. "I don't care what you stole or why."

"So you don't care about the circumstances around it?" she asked. "What if it was, say, a lady shoplifting food because she doesn't have the money to feed her kid?"

"That's different," Marc said. "She's stealing based on need. You, on the other hand, stole something you didn't need."

"Who said I didn't need it?" she asked, and when he glanced at her skeptically, she sighed. "I was going to sell them," she admitted. "I need the money."

"For what, more tattoos?"

"*No.* I wanted to start saving up for school. So I can, you know, get a good job and stuff." At Marc's raised eyebrow, she protested, "What? You think I don't want a good job? I just can't afford school. My mom makes next to nothing, and my dad didn't leave much."

"There's financial aid," Marc pointed out. "You don't have to shoplift. You can just apply for—"

Marc slammed his foot on the brake.

Remy lurched forward, but her seatbelt caught her, biting into her chest and abdomen to stop her movement. Regardless, she threw a hand forward to brace it against the edge of the dash and yelped out, "What the hell, Marc!" She looked at him and realized the expression on his face was wide eyed and horrified. He stared out the windshield, both his hands gripping the steering wheel, and his face had gone pale with shock. Remy followed his gaze, and her heart lurched in her chest. "What the hell is that?"

The street ahead of them was flooded with people. Many were running in the opposite direction Marc had been driving, screaming in a chorus that overlapped itself as they ran. They fled from something, but whatever it was, Remy couldn't see it from the passenger seat.

"What are they running from?" she asked, flinching as someone ran into the side mirror on the passenger side, rebounded off it, and continued on.

"I have no idea." Marc shifted the car into park and tried to open his door, but someone ran into it and slammed it shut. Marc jerked his hand away from the door, as if he'd been burned, and didn't try to open it again.

Remy stared through the windshield, past the fleeing, panicked people, trying to see what they were running from. She couldn't make anything out; all she saw was frantic, terrified people running for their lives. Then she got a momentary glimpse beyond the crowd and clutched the armrest on her door tight enough to make her knuckles blanch. "Oh God," she murmured. "Officer—I mean, Marc?"

"Yeah, what is it?"

"Get us the hell out of here," she said. "*Now.*"

"What is it?"

"I think...I think it's fucking *zombies.*"

* * *

Memphis, TN

Ethan paced in front of the cold fireplace in his living room. He'd been checking his watch and looking out the front windows every few minutes for the past hour, ever since Anna had grabbed her go-bag and run out of the house to go to the hospital. Everything about him, emotionally and physically, was on edge. He desperately wanted to go out, track Anna down, and drag her back to the house, her supervisors be damned. It just wasn't safe enough for her to be out alone without protection against the crazies now running the streets.

The sudden sharp, familiar sound of gunshots echoed in the night. Ethan froze and looked up from his contemplation of the floorboards, counting the shots silently, deciding there were four, and trying to guess where they'd come from. He couldn't be positive, but he thought it'd come from somewhere next door.

Frowning, he grabbed his Glock 17 from the coffee table where he'd put it after the reports of riots broke on the news. He wasn't sure what he'd face as he headed to the front door and opened it, but whatever it was, he'd face it armed.

He held the gun in a casual grip at his side and walked out into the dew-dampened grass. He looked around cautiously as he crossed the front yard to Cade's house. His dress shoes slipped on the grass, and he glanced down at his clothes and made a disgusted face. He should have changed before going to investigate the source of the gunshots. Dress shoes, pants, and a nice shirt weren't exactly ideal for a potential confrontation.

A loud thud at the front of Cade's house drew his attention, and he reflexively lifted his pistol, halting halfway across the yard, squinting through the darkness. The silhouette of a person ran toward him, and the sound of sobbing met his ears. He lowered the weapon as he realized who it was.

"Ethan!" Cade cried out as she ran. "Ethan, help!"

Ethan ran to her, struggling to keep from slipping on the damp grass in his ridiculous shoes, and met her in the space between their houses. Cade dropped a pistol on the grass and flung herself into his arms. He realized only after he'd wrapped his arms around her that her arms and torso were stained with blood, the front of her shirt was ripped open, and her feet were bare and wet. She choked back desperate sobs and buried her face against his chest. Her entire body trembled, and he rubbed her back soothingly as he held her.

"What the fuck happened?"

"Andrew killed Josie," Cade said, her voice muffled by his shirt. Ethan's heart dropped into his gut. "He killed her and attacked me, and I shot him."

"Wait, slow down," he urged, putting his hands up in a calming gesture before resting them on her shoulders. "One thing at a time. What's going on?"

"We need to get inside," Cade said, pulling back from his chest and grabbing Ethan's wrist. She pulled it so hard that, for a fleeting moment, he thought she was going to dislocate it. "We need to lock the doors. It's not safe out here."

Ethan allowed her to lead him back into his house. She slammed and deadbolted the door shut and pulled the curtains covering the windows on either side of the door tightly shut. Once done, she let out a slow breath and wiped at her face with the back of her hand. "He killed her," she repeated. "He was acting like…like one of those *things* on TV." She rubbed her face again, leaving a smear of blood across her cheek. Ethan grabbed a tissue from the box on the coffee table and helped her clean blood from her face. "He fucking attacked Josie while she was asleep. He tore her open, Ethan!"

"Jesus," Ethan breathed as Cade started sobbing again. He wrapped his arms around her again and closed his eyes. He wasn't sure what to do. All of his professional training told him he needed to take her into custody, but his friendship with her and the constant chatter over the police scanner suggested otherwise. "I should go check it out," he said.

"No!" she exploded, taking a step back and shaking her head. "No, no, don't go over there. It's not safe."

"Babe, you said you shot him," he pointed out. Cade looked panicked. That fact, more than any other, scared him. She didn't panic over *anything*. She was the most levelheaded person he'd ever met, and nothing fazed her. Until now.

Cade breathed in a slow, shaky breath. "Yeah, I did. Four times." She scrubbed at her left cheek with the tissue. "In the chest."

"Well, that means he's down. So let's go take a look," he persisted, stepping toward the door.

Cade grabbed his wrist again, this time to stop him. "Ethan…he didn't stay down."

Ethan studied her face for even the slightest hint that she was joking. "Didn't stay down?" he repeated. "But...you shot him in the chest."

"Yeah, and I don't miss," she said, her voice trembling as much as she did. She grabbed a fresh tissue from the box and dabbed gently at her reddened eyes. "I don't miss, Ethan. It hit him in the chest. Four times." She touched her own chest, just above her heart.

Ethan shook his head. "There's no way someone should've survived that. It's not possible."

"He did. He's still in the house right now," she said. "God, I don't know what's going on anymore."

The police scanner erupted in another burst of static and coded chatter. Ethan waited until it fell silent, then said, "I was planning on going out after Anna. I want to pack shit up and get the hell out of town before it falls down around our ears." He paused, then added, "You should come with us."

"What about your work?" Cade asked. "And...and Josie?"

"Fuck work. Yours and Anna's safety is more important. As for Josie..." He trailed off, then shook his head, not sure what to say. If what Cade had said was true, the little girl was dead. He couldn't comprehend it. He studied Cade again. She sat on the edge of the couch, holding her pajama shirt closed with one hand. He figured it was best to address the immediate problem first.

"Go upstairs and get cleaned up," he said. "You and Anna are about the same size. I'll get you some of her clothes." Cade didn't react, merely stood and moved toward the stairs. Ethan caught her by the arm as she passed him. "Come here," he said, pulling her into his arms in a tight hug, ignoring the additional blood that transferred from her clothes to stain his own. "You'll be okay, I promise," he said into her hair, giving the top of her head an affectionate kiss.

"God, I hope so," Cade murmured. Ethan rubbed her back as she simply stood still, and he only reluctantly let go of her when she stepped back from him and wiped at her eyes with her wrist. "Upstairs, second on the right?"

"Yeah." Ethan watched her walk up the stairs. Once she was out of sight, he moved briskly to the coffee table and picked up his pistol and holster again. He fastened the holster to his belt and jammed the Glock into it before approaching the front door. He was going to check out Cade's house and see what he could gather about the situation inside, regardless of her discomfort with the idea.

It wasn't that he didn't believe her. Far from it. Cade was the epitome of honesty, and her IDF training had honed her powers of observation to an extreme. He knew too that she had no reason to make up something so strange and horrible. It was just that it was so unbelievable that he couldn't wrap his mind around it. He had to see it with his own eyes to fully understand it.

Ethan slipped out the front door and pulled it shut with a soft click, then stepped off the porch and approached Cade's house for the second time. His hand rested lightly on top of his holstered Glock. After retrieving Cade's dropped pistol from the grass in the front yard, he slunk to the front porch. The door was wide open and seemed to invite him in.

There was no movement in the entryway, so Ethan drew in a breath and stepped inside, setting Cade's pistol on the table by the door and drawing his own pistol, instinctively falling into the police procedures that had been hammered into his head since his days in the academy. He cleared the living room with a quick sweep of his gun, using the dim light from the TV to check out the area, then headed to the kitchen. When he saw nothing there, he decided to move upstairs to look into the bedrooms.

It was late, so it was reasonable to assume that Josie had been killed in or near her bedroom. The thought of the little girl dead was enough to make pain lance through his chest. Ethan forced an exhale to calm himself and made his way to the guest bedroom.

One look inside was enough. He closed his eyes for the barest of moments and backed away, turning toward Cade's bedroom. He wished desperately he hadn't looked in the guest room. The sight of the bloodstained sheets and the child's motionless body was enough for him to know there was no hope for her anymore. Andrew, though…

Ethan found the man slumped on the floor beside Cade's bed. A sense of unease settled in his gut as he stared at the body. Gingerly, he nudged Andrew with the toe of his dress shoe. The man didn't move. Ethan took a knee and pushed Andrew gently onto his back. He felt for the man's carotid artery, searching for a pulse; there didn't appear to be one. He was, as far as Ethan could ascertain, dead. Perhaps left-over adrenaline had kept Andrew moving even after the fatal shots, he guessed. That would explain Cade's perception that he hadn't stayed down after she'd shot him.

Ethan straightened and scanned the room, noticing a black rifle case resting on the bed beside a duffel bag. The key was in the lock, and the lid was cracked open. He lifted the lid to peer inside; the rifle, scope, and magazine were nested in its gray foam confines. Ethan closed the case's lid and locked it before picking it up and tucking the key into his pocket for safekeeping. He didn't want to leave the rifle unsecured in an empty house.

As Ethan carried the case to the door, a glint of steel in the corner of his eye caught his attention. He spotted a wicked-looking hunting knife on the bedside table, tucked behind Cade's IDF portrait. He picked it up and examined it before searching for its sheath. Once he'd found it in the drawer, he sheathed the knife and tucked it into his back pocket. Then he grabbed the duffel bag on the bed and slung it over his shoulder. When he had everything he thought he should get, he headed into the hall.

Ethan was surprised to find Cade standing at the end of the hall, near the head of the stairs. She wore Anna's clothes and stood with her arms folded, a worried look on her face. One of his spare Glock pistols dangled from one of her hands.

"What the fuck are you doing over here?" she hissed as he approached.

"I came over to check things out." He didn't bother to keep his voice down. He set the duffle bag at her feet and held out the rifle case. "And I got your bag and rifle," he added. "You're welcome."

Cade looked at the bag, and her gaze softened. "Thanks," she said, taking the case from him. She picked the bag up slowly and draped the strap over her shoulder, then looked past Ethan, down the dark hallway toward the guest bedroom. Ethan frowned and touched her shoulder.

"Hey, do you need to...?" He trailed off, the rest of the question hanging between them.

Cade hesitated, then nodded and took a step toward Josie's room. She stopped in the doorway, peering into the darkness. "Where is she?" she asked. The question caught Ethan by surprise, and he strode to her, his eyebrows raised.

"She's right there," he replied, moving around Cade and gesturing into the room. "What the fuck," he whispered as he saw for himself. Josie's bed was inexplicably empty. Where the small body of the four year old once lay was just a dark stain on the sheets. There was an additional splotch on the floor near the doorway, one he didn't remember seeing before.

"Where is she, Ethan?" Cade asked, her voice rising in volume, and her accent became thicker in her agitation as she stepped back from the doorway.

"I don't know, Cade! She was just right there!" he said. He tugged her away from the door and a few steps closer to the stairs.

A soft creak of the floorboards behind him was the only warning Ethan had that something was amiss, and he let go of Cade and turned on his heel. A figure ran toward them in the dim hall, its arms outstretched. He let out a shocked cry and twisted away, pulling Cade with him; his back thudded against the wall, and Cade slammed into the sheetrock beside him. He fumbled for his gun.

It took Ethan a moment to register that the darkened figure was a man and that the front of the man's body was stained with a large quantity of blood. It took him an additional instant to realize that he was taking in the sight of Cade's boyfriend, Andrew.

Cade's breath rasped in her throat as she stood frozen beside Ethan, her palms flattened to the wall behind her, fingernails digging into the paint. Ethan took a step away from the wall and positioned himself between her and Andrew, blocking the man's view of her in an instinctive need to protect her.

"Andrew?" Ethan croaked out, focusing on the man's face. Andrew's dark eyes were devoid of any recognition, locked onto Ethan's face. Something in his gaze gave Ethan the distinct feeling of prey in the sights of a hunter. "Andrew, are you okay?" he tried, regardless of the discomfort in his gut. "You're hurt. Let me get you some help."

Andrew didn't respond, merely taking a slow step closer to him. Ethan gripped his pistol tighter, easing it out of its holster, his stomach churning with nerves. He inched along the wall, away from Andrew, trying to nudge Cade toward the stairs.

"Andrew, I think it's a good idea if you stop right there," Ethan warned, lifting his pistol. He pointed it in Andrew's direction, even as he took another step to put more distance between himself and the dangerous man.

Andrew didn't seem to process his request. His expression suggested he was studying a particularly nice-looking piece of meat. Ethan motioned with his gun and ordered, "Sit on the floor. You're hurt. You shouldn't be walking around." *You shouldn't be breathing,* he thought, taking another step back. Cade pressed hard against his back, her trembling hand gripping his shirt. Andrew, watching his actions, slowly tilted his head to the side and took a shuffling, deliberate step toward them.

"Oh God, Eth," Cade whispered. He fought the urge to turn, fought the urge to take his eyes off Andrew as the man advanced on them at the odd, creeping pace he'd adopted. "Behind him," she warned, her voice still hushed, but now it had a tearful hitch in it.

Ethan shifted his gaze from Andrew to a spot past the man, to an area at the level of his waist. A small pigtailed figure shuffled toward them, a stuffed gray elephant clutched in one bloodied hand. "Josie?" he breathed. Cade took in a sharp breath and dodged around Ethan to go to the girl; he lunged forward and hooked his arm around her waist, dragging her back against him, gripping her tightly. "Cade!

No!" he barked, hauling her toward the stairs. "Get back! Something isn't right!" his instincts screamed at him as he watched the little girl. The way she moved, the open wounds she shouldn't have survived, the horrible similarity between hers and Andrew's jerking, lurching walks—whatever was wrong with Andrew was wrong with Josie too.

"Ethan! Help her!" Cade shrieked, fighting against his grip and clawing at his arm. Ethan winced and swung her around and away from Josie, setting her on the top step.

"Get downstairs, now!" he ordered, his voice hard and stern, and he glared at her with as much anger as he could muster.

Cade opened her mouth to argue. The distant, familiar whir of tornado sirens interrupted anything she'd been about to say. Both of them froze, and Cade whipped her head around to look at the large plate-glass window at the front of the house.

Ethan turned back to Andrew and Josie. Neither had stopped or slowed, only sped up, and he backed further away. "Cade, downstairs," he warned again, pointing his gun at Andrew. "Stop," he ordered. "Stop right there or I'll shoot."

The man didn't stop.

Ethan swallowed and slipped his finger past the trigger guard to rest on the trigger. The tornado sirens blasting outside echoed in his head, making it increasingly difficult to think.

"Ethan, shoot him," Cade urged. "Just shoot him, please!"

Ethan shook his head and took another step back. "Get downstairs," he repeated yet again, grabbing Cade's duffel bag from her shoulder. "Go. Now." He nudged her again, and they stumbled down the stairs, leaving Andrew and Josie on the second floor. He didn't know if they could make it down the stairs, but he wasn't going to stick around long enough to find out.

Once on the ground floor, Ethan went to the front window. He couldn't see much, but he could just make out the sound of gunfire somewhere down the street, accompanied by screams. Even as he watched, a man ran down the street, chased by two other men, both as befouled with blood as Andrew and Josie. He took a small step back from the window.

"What is it?" she pressed. "Can you see anything?"

Ethan looked at Cade. She stood beside him in a protective stance, the pistol she'd lifted from his house pointed up the stairs at her boyfriend. *Her* former *boyfriend,* he mentally corrected. He had his doubts whether the man was still alive anymore, though an explanation as to how a dead man could be attempting to stumble down stairs wasn't exactly forthcoming.

"I think we need to get into the basement," Ethan said. He took Cade's elbow and tugged gently. "As soon as possible."

Cade took a few steps back in the direction Ethan guided her. Her eyebrows rose at the uncertainty in his voice. "What is it? What did you see?"

"Just go!" Ethan snapped, pushing her toward the kitchen's entryway. "Do what I said! Get in the basement! I'll catch up in a minute."

Cade looked at him, wide-eyed. In all the time he'd known her, he'd never raised his voice like that. He couldn't imagine what she was thinking as she cut her eyes away and moved toward the kitchen.

Ethan didn't wait for Cade to disappear into the basement before lifting his pistol and aiming it up the stairway, directly at Andrew's head. "Sorry, man," he said softly before depressing the trigger.

The man at the top of the stairs staggered back at the bullet's impact, the top of his head exploding onto the wall behind him in a shower of blood and gore. He fell back, crumpling to the carpet, as the blood oozed over the pain, already partially congealed. Ethan shifted his aim as a small figure appeared at the top of the stairs and stumbled over Andrew's fallen body, but he couldn't bring himself to squeeze the trigger again. He turned on his heel and fled to the kitchen.

Cade waited for him near the basement door, despite his orders for her to get into the basement. He wrinkled his nose and pushed her firmly to the basement door. "I told you to get down there," he said, reaching around her for the doorknob.

"What did you see?" Cade snapped back, meeting his eyes. In that instant, he knew that she knew what he'd just done.

"I'll tell you when we get in the basement," Ethan said. He swallowed hard and cleared his throat; it felt like a vice was slowly closing around it, strangling his words. He pushed the basement door open.

As a cool draft wafted up from the dark stairwell and blew strands of hair back from Cade's face, the sound of glass breaking drew their attention away from the basement entry. Ethan turned, shielding Cade with his body, as the glass patio door slammed open and the glass shattered. "Oh God," he gasped as a pale-skinned, shirtless older man lurched into the kitchen through the broken door. His face and torso were covered in blood—whose blood, Ethan couldn't know—and a large wound in his bicep oozed wetly. Ethan pushed Cade gently back to the basement steps and tried to move away from the man at the same time.

Cade stumbled down a few steps but turned to look back as Ethan joined her. He tried to close the door, but the pale man reached for them, jamming his hand into the gap between the door and doorframe. His fingers stretched and clawed, his mouth open in an angry, hungry snarl. Ethan had never seen such animalistic hatred in a human being's eyes. He braced his shoulder against the door and pushed with all his strength against the heavy man. Despite his attempts to shove the door shut, he felt it give a couple of inches.

"Cade! Help me!" he yelped.

Cade darted to Ethan's side in an instant, lifting her pistol and pointing it into the gap. The sound of the gunshot right next to Ethan's head deafened him. The pressure against the door gave way, and he stumbled forward, slamming the door closed and blanketing them in darkness. Ethan's hand fumbled, seemingly of its own free will, for the lock. He slid the deadbolt home and sagged against the door, struggling to catch the breath adrenaline had snatched away.

Footsteps thudded above them, staggering through the kitchen and living room. Ethan found Cade's hand, and he wrapped his arm around her as they guided each other down the stairs to the dark room below.

CHAPTER FIVE

Plantersville, MS

The temperature outside was already cool and quickly dropping, but Gray paid it no mind. He led April into the parking lot, her hand in his, their fingers laced together.

"Did you have any particular place in mind you wanted to go?" he asked, hoping fervently that the several beers in his system wouldn't interfere with his driving if she decided she wanted to go back to his place.

Theo would kill *me if he knew I was thinking about driving after drinking,* he thought, but he didn't care. April was there, and he was drunk enough to do whatever she asked him to.

"Just the car is fine," she said, her heels clicking and grinding on the parking lot's gravel. Gray glanced down at them. They were tall red heels, strappy things like the ones he remembered her once referring to as her "fuck-me heels." They made her bare legs look long and slender. "I just wanted some privacy so we could talk without me having to yell over that damned music."

Gray grinned and tightened his grip on her hand. "What were you doing in a country bar, anyway? You hate country."

"If I recall your obsession with Nine Inch Nails correctly, so do you," she said, eliciting a laugh from him.

"Hey, Jack likes it, and it's the best place to go play pool and drink," he said. "I can deal with crappy music for a while if I get the benefits for hanging out with a good friend." He stopped beside his car, a beat-up Chevy Cavalier that had been the only thing he could afford at the time, and fumbled his keys out of his pocket. "So where'd you want to go again?" he asked. There was no way she wanted to hang out in his dirty car, of all places. He slid the key in the door, nearly dropping them on the pavement in his drunken clumsiness.

"Right here is fine," April reassured him. She grasped his jacket, pulled him around, and pressed her mouth to his. He grunted faintly at her sudden attack, but once his brain caught up with her actions, he returned the kiss enthusiastically, wrapping his arms around her waist and pulling her tightly against him. Her lips were soft and tasted like watermelon lip gloss, and her waist felt tiny, almost fragile, in his hands. He smoothed his hands up her back to brush over her thick hair, and she smiled against his lips.

"Could've warned me that that was what you had in mind," he mumbled.

"Why would I want to do that?" April replied. Then she kissed him again, sliding her leg up his to rest her knee against the car behind him. He let go of her waist long enough to fumble for the door handle, and once he'd turned the key, he eased April to the back door and tugged it open.

"Get in," he said. He was surprised at how his voice sounded: low and husky, hoarse with tension and suspense. April looked at him, winked, and climbed inside. He crawled in behind her and pulled the door shut, then tugged her back into his arms and grinned. "Now, where were we?"

April giggled and climbed into his lap, resting her knees on either side of his legs. The position made her dark skirt ride up her thighs to show several more inches of her gorgeous legs. He leaned in to kiss her again, smoothing his palms up those legs. Her hands wiggled into his jacket, pushing it off his shoulders and helping him shrug it off.

"Seems like you've got some *really* interesting things in mind," he half-joked as he tossed the jacket into the front seat. He started in on the tiny buttons lining the front of April's blouse.

"Only if you've got a—"

A thud against the outside of the car made Gray jump. April startled against him, looking between him and the window beside them with wide eyes. "What was that?"

"Nothing," Gray said. "Probably some drunk guy falling against the car. Don't worry about it." He nipped the side of her neck, unfastening another button on her shirt.

Another thud against the car. This time, it sounded like a fist slapping the fogging glass near Gray's head. "Fuck," he swore. Someone outside began hammering on the window, beating on it over and over.

"Maybe it's your friend," April said, a twinge of annoyance in her voice. It was a sentiment with which he could agree. "Maybe he thinks he's being funny or something."

Gray grimaced and reached for the door. "I swear to God, if it's Jack trying to pull some stupid bullshit, I'm going to tear him a new one," he said. He slid over the seat and unlocked the door, pushing it open and already speaking as he climbed out. "Jack, you are seriously the most immature—"

Gray only realized it wasn't Jack outside the car when the tall, dark-haired man who was much larger than he grabbed him by the front of his shirt and slammed him against the car with enough force to knock the air from his lungs. Gray struggled, trying to break free. He swung a fist out and struck the side of the man's face, but the blow didn't faze his attacker in the slightest.

The sound of a car door opening drew Gray's attention for only the barest of seconds. Rather than turn to look, he swung another punch at the man still gripping his shirt.

"What the hell is going on?" April's voice rang out behind him.

"April! Get back in the car!" he yelled, hammering his fist into his attacker's throat. It was a move Theo had taught him in middle school to use against the bullies who'd bothered him, and it *should* have put the man down, especially since he didn't pull the punch. But the man wasn't affected. If anything, the look in his eyes grew angrier, more hateful. That, more than the lack of impact his blows had, told him there was something horribly wrong.

April let out an ungodly shriek just then, a sound of fear and pain personified. Gray's stomach tightened, and he slammed his fists down on the man's wrists. The move dislodged the grasping hands, and Gray ran to help April, heedless of what he was walking into. He circled the front of the car, his heart racing, and stopped short as he beheld the scene before him.

For the rest of his life, Gray would remember the events that unfolded beside his beat-up Cavalier that night as a series of snapshots, snippets of memory that flashed into his brain when he least expected it, taking his breath away and leaving him shaking. The sound of April's screams as she fought off her own attacker; the man hanging onto her upper arms with a bruising grip so tight that his knuckles had blanched; the way the man's face was buried against his neck, and the way he shook his head, like a dog worrying at a piece of meat on a bone; the sickening splatter of blood across the hood of the car as the man jerked his head back from April's neck.

Gray froze, the horror rushing over him long enough for the sight to register. Then he leaped forward, colliding with April's attacker, knocking him to the pavement and slamming his fist into his face. He jerked back when the man took a swipe at him, his fingers hooked like claws, like he was trying to gouge them into Gray's face. Someone grabbed Gray from behind, and he nearly fell forward onto the man underneath. In a panic, he threw his arm out, trying to hit whoever was behind him, falling to the side against the car.

Shouts rang out behind him. Then Jack was beside him, swinging a pool cue like a baseball bat against the head of the man underneath him. Gray collapsed fully against the car, panting, as the bar's bouncer pulled the first man who'd attacked him to the ground. In the frantic scramble to help April, he hadn't realized how open he'd left himself to attack from behind. An odd shudder of fear ran through him, and he wondered what would have happened if the first man had gotten his hands on Gray like the second one had April.

The thought of April slammed hard against his brain, spinning him back around, and he scrambled forward on his hands and knees to her side. Blood flowed freely from the wound in the side of her neck, spilling onto the pavement in a rapidly growing puddle and soaking into her red blouse. Gray pressed his hands to the wound and looked up at his friend. "Jack, help," he begged.

Jack slammed the pool cue into the second man's head again. Then he turned to Gray. "Jesus, what happened?" he asked. He knelt to scoop April into his arms while Gray kept both hands against the wound. Despite his efforts to staunch the bleeding, he could feel her blood pulsing out between his fingers with every heartbeat.

"I don't know," Gray said helplessly. He hurried to keep up as Jack led them into the bar, through a small but growing crowd of bar-hoppers clustered at the door trying to see what was going on outside. "These two guys just came out of nowhere and attacked us. One of them bit April."

"*Bit?*" Jack repeated incredulously. "Smitty!" he shouted. "Call 911! We need an ambulance ASAP!"

Smitty rushed for the phone, and Jack carried April to one of the unused pool tables, snagging a towel off a table and pushing it into Gray's hands. "Tell me everything," he said as Gray pressed the towel against April's wound. "Don't leave anything out."

*　*　*

Theo surfaced to consciousness feeling like he was slogging through a viscous pool of molasses. Something sharp jabbed him between his shoulder blades, and he shifted, trying to remember where he was. His first instinct was that he was at home in bed with Dillon. Then the truth of it came back to him. *Ambulance. MVA. Dead patient who wasn't actually dead. Crash.*

Theo forced his eyes open and shifted again. Whatever was underneath him cracked under his weight. He rolled his head from side to side experimentally, trying to figure out if he was injured. After silently inventorying each bone in his body, Theo determined that the only ache was in his head, where he'd struck it during the crash. He raised his head a few inches off the surface beneath him—a cabinet, he realized, the one where the IV supplies were kept.

A nearby shuffling noise reached his ears. He froze, squinting in the darkened ambulance, but the noise didn't come again. How long had they been like this? Theo didn't remember it being so dark before the crash. And why had no one come for them yet? Jonathan had called them en route; had no one noticed they hadn't shown up at the hospital?

Beyond the ambulance, Theo heard shouts and screams, tires swishing on the pavement as cars sped by, and the distinct noise of two cars colliding, the squeal of metal on metal.

Then he heard the gunshots.

Theo tensed, his ears straining to better make out the sound. The shots were sporadic, firing from uncomfortably close to the overturned ambulance. More screaming and shouting accompanied it, a good deal of it.

And there was something clawing at the leg of his uniform pants.

Theo swore and jerked his leg away. His right hand found the metal bar attached to one of the back doors, and he pulled himself to his feet, balancing with one foot on the side of the stretcher and the other on a cabinet door. "Jonathan?" he called, hoping his partner was okay. When there was no answer, he raised his voice. "Jonathan!"

A low groan from the front of the ambulance. "Right here," Jonathan said, sounding hoarse. "You okay? You hurt?"

"I'm fine," Theo assured him. He gingerly touched the back of his head and felt a large bump on his skull. His fingertips came back stained with blood. "Hit my head. I think I'm okay, though."

"And the patient?"

Theo fished his flashlight out of the pocket by his right knee and mashed the button on the bottom. The light flickered on, and he found himself face to face with the patient.

The man stood on his broken legs an arm's length from Theo, his fingers reaching, grabbing for the front of his uniform shirt. He'd broken free from the stretcher and backboard, though he still wore the c-collar immobilizing his neck. His fingers curled into Theo's shirt, and Theo dropped the flashlight, which tumbled down to roll somewhere below the stretcher.

"Back off!" Theo shouted. He put a hand to the man's chest and pushed him firmly enough to show that he meant business. "I said *back off!*" he repeated when the man showed no signs of understanding. The man seized Theo's shirt in both hands and jerked him forward, his mouth open, his bloodied teeth aiming for his throat. Theo noticed, in the flash of a single second, that the man had bitten clean through his own tongue.

Fearing for his life, Theo fumbled for anything resembling a weapon. His fingers wrapped around the regulator attached to the portable O2 tank strapped to the end of the stretcher. He yanked, dragging it free from its Velcro fastenings, and hefted the partially full tank. He pushed the man back again and raised the tank warningly.

"Back off, man. Don't make me use this," he said, his voice shaking with a mix of nervousness and adrenaline. The man snarled at him and lunged again. Theo raised the O2 tank and brought it up against the side of the man's head with all the force he could muster. The man dropped, tumbling like a stone to rest against the overturned stretcher. He tried to rise once more, and Theo slammed the tank against the top of his skull. Something cracked, and the man went limp. Theo stared at his unmoving form, his eyes wide and his breathing erratic. He gripped the oxygen regulator until his fingers hurt, but he didn't loosen his grip.

Another flashlight switched on at the front of the ambulance, and Jonathan came into view.

"Did...did I just kill him?" Theo asked. He looked up at the other man with wide eyes. The tank slipped from his grasp, clanging against the stretcher and joining his dropped flashlight. He was shaking, and he wrapped his fingers around the bar affixed to the back door, using it to steady himself, ground himself, trying in vain to calm the blood coursing through his veins.

"I don't know," Jonathan said. He eased toward Theo, putting out a hand like he was approaching a wild animal. Theo imagined he probably *looked* like one. "I'm not even sure he was still alive in the first place."

Theo looked at the probably dead man again and drew in a slow breath. "I'm *so* losing my license over this," he said.

"It'll be fine," Jonathan said. "I promise. We'll get you through this, okay?"

Theo tore his eyes from the man at his feet and looked at Jonathan. "What happened?" he asked. "What did you yell out about up there? And how long have we been here?"

"Thirty, forty minutes," Jonathan replied. "As for what I saw...I'm not sure how to describe it."

"Try."

Jonathan was silent for several heartbeats, like he was trying to decide on the right words to say. Theo gripped the metal bar tighter, a jolt of fear shooting through him. He was suddenly, irrationally, scared that the man on the stretcher between them was going to get up and attack him again.

"It was like a riot or something," Jonathan said, his voice low. He looked over his shoulder, shining his flashlight in the general direction of the cab. "There were people in the street, dozens of them, all running from something, but I couldn't see what. there were National Guard guys in there too, I think. I saw soldiers in uniform and people with guns." He glanced at the front of the ambulance again, warily, and that time, Theo followed his gaze. He saw nothing on the other side of the windshield but darkness. "People were shooting each other. It looks like a war zone."

Theo crouched, trying to look out the back windows. "We should get out of here. If it's that bad out there, it's probably not safe for us to stay here, right? And I need to find my brother. If that shit's coming out of town…" He shook his head. "Gray can't handle himself against something like that. Hell, he can barely even *run*."

"I doubt Gray's *that* helpless," Jonathan said. The subtle note of condescension in his voice made Theo grit his teeth. "I'm sure he'll manage. Besides, you'll lose your job if you ditch out. We need to report this."

"Considering I probably just *killed a patient*, I'm pretty sure my job's gone," he snapped. "And if it's not, then they can go ahead and fucking fire me. My *brother* is more important to me than this fucking job." He shoved past Jonathan, grabbed the trauma bag that had fallen against the airway seat during the wreck, and unzipped it. He flung open a cabinet, unloading nasal cannulas and non-rebreather masks from it and stuffing them into the bag. Jonathan moved to help.

"You should take the O2 tank out of that," Jonathan said, unzipping the side of the bag and pulling the tank in question out. "It'll make more room for the other supplies."

"You're helping me?" Theo asked, moving to the next cabinet to empty IV supplies into the bag by the handful.

"God help me, yes," Jonathan answered. He was pulling OB kits, burn sheets, and trauma dressings from the cabinet above him, stacking them neatly in his hands. "There's no way you'd make it all the way into town on your own."

Theo gritted his teeth in mild frustration. Jonathan was talking like he thought he wasn't capable of protecting himself, though the body at their feet said otherwise.

"If something happened to you while I was just sitting around waiting for help," Jonathan went on, "I'd feel pretty damn guilty about it."

Still trying to decide if he'd been insulted, Theo slid the next cabinet open. As he reached for the elastic bandages inside, the cell phone in his pocket began ringing. He fumbled at his pocket, ripping the phone free, and when he saw Gray's name on the display, he swiped to answer and put it to his ear. "Gray?"

"*Theo, Theo, where the fuck are you?*" Theo's shoulders stiffened. Something about his brother's voice frightened him: it was hard, tense, heavy with tears. His stomach lurched.

"I'm on the truck," Theo replied, choosing to not mention that the truck was wrecked. "Are you okay?"

"*I need help,*" Gray said in a rush. "*We need help over here. There were these guys. They attacked me and April, and I—*"

"April?" Theo repeated, furrowing his forehead. "April Linder?"

"Yes, *April Linder!*" Gray confirmed impatiently. "*Look, she's dying, and we can't get an ambulance here. We can't even get through to fucking 911, and I need help!*"

"Okay, Gray, calm down and tell me where you are," Theo said.

"*I'm at a bar. The Brass Monkey. It's about two miles east of my apartment.*"

"Yeah, I know the place." He didn't bother questioning why Gray was at a bar; *he*, after all, was the one who'd ditched on their plans earlier that evening.

"*Just hurry, okay?*"

"I'll try," he said grimly. "Stay inside and make sure you keep people around you. Do whatever you can for April. What's her condition?"

"*She's fucking bleeding out, Theo!*" Gray said. "*Her fucking neck—*"

"Put pressure on it," he cut in. "Just put pressure on it and keep it there. I'll be there as soon as I can. I promise."

"*Theo?*" Gray's voice cracked. He sounded incredibly young over the crackling phone line.

"Yeah?"

"*It's crazy out there,*" Gray said. "*It's...there are people with guns and shit everywhere. Me and Jack, we don't know what to do. Everybody else left when all the shooting started. There are four of us left in here, and we've got the doors barricaded, but I'm not sure how long that'll hold.*"

"Stay where you are," Theo repeated. He squeezed his eyes shut, trying to think. "Don't leave the building if you can help it, okay? I'll be there as soon as I can. I'll run the whole way if I have to."

"*Be careful, Theo,*" Gray said. "*It's bad. You have no idea. I want to get out of here. I really, really want to get out of here.*"

"I'm going to get you out," he promised. "Just stay there. And keep me updated." He hung up and shoved the phone into his pocket, wordlessly snatching up supplies again.

"Everything okay?" Jonathan asked, passing him the drug bag from a cabinet, which he began emptying into the trauma bag.

"Gray's ex-girlfriend is hurt badly, and they can't get any help," he answered. "They're at the Brass Monkey. Think you can help me get there?"

"That's almost five miles away."

"I can handle it," Theo said. He stuffed the last of the medications into the bag, added three IV bags of fluid, and then got the overstuffed bag zipped. He scanned his eyes over the rest of the truck's interior and asked, "You see anything else we might need?"

"AED?" Jonathan suggested.

"And O2," he added. He dumped the pediatric bag's contents onto the floor and stuffed two portable oxygen tanks into it, adding the intubation kit to the pile of supplies he was going to carry.

Jonathan rested his hand on the handle of the ambulance's back door. "Look, before we step out, I've got to ask you this," he started. "I have to know how far you're willing to go. How far you're *capable* of going. I've got to know that I can rely on you in something like this."

"Something like what?" Theo asked impatiently. He was itching to get moving, to set out and find his brother, and all this talk was doing nothing but slowing him down.

"Just...listen for a minute," Jonathan said, not sounding the slightest bit impatient with him. He fell silent, and they listened to the sporadic gunfire outside, the shouts and screams from the people beyond. "It sounds bad out there," he said. "Really bad. A war zone, like I said. I've been in one of those before, but you haven't. I need to know, Theo. Would you kill someone if you had to? Are you *capable* of killing someone? Don't answer right away. Think about it."

Theo clutched the straps of one of the bags he'd packed and stared at Jonathan through the darkness in the ambulance, listening to the chaos outside. His heart pounded erratically, and the smallest tendril of adrenaline crept up his spine. Could he kill someone? *Would* he? It was a hard question. Theo had always been the type who helped others. He worked in emergency medicine to do that very thing. Now he was being asked to contemplate something that went against his nature, and he wasn't sure what to say.

Theo shifted his eyes away from his driver and to the floor, staring emptily at the dead patient lying on the stretcher in a haphazard heap. He thought about Gray, about the promise he'd made in his heart the minute he'd been old enough to understand his duties as an older brother. He'd always assured both himself and Gray that he'd protect his brother, that he'd keep the bullies and other people who'd do awful things to him at bay, that he would do everything in his power to make sure he was always safe from harm. Especially after their parents had died. He would do *anything* for Gray. And yes, he'd even kill for him, if that was what it took. There was no doubt in his about that.

Theo lifted his gaze to Jonathan. "Yeah," he said hoarsely, his voice low. "Yeah, I'd kill if I had to. If it meant protecting my brother."

"That's good to hear," Jonathan acknowledged. "Because there's a chance you might have to." He tugged on the door's latch and kicked the door. It fell open, thudding against the pavement beyond, and Jonathan went to work on the second door. "Once I get us clear, I'll take some of that off your shoulders," he promised. "And then we can start running." He swung the door open and locked it into place, then looked back at Theo. "Let's go," he said, taking a cautious step out of the truck.

There was a loud pop. Jonathan jerked to the side and collapsed, lying halfway on the bottom door. Theo stumbled backward, nearly tripping over the tangle of stretcher and dead body under his feet, as his eyes registered the sight of the bullet hole in the side of Jonathan's head.

* * *

Memphis, TN

Several hours slid by with barely a word between Ethan and Cade. Cade had spent most of the time huddled on the bottom step of the staircase, keeping a wary eye on the door above. Ethan, for his part, had done everything he could think of to stay busy, primarily to keep his mind off the night's horrific events. He'd scrounged up a flashlight from a toolbox, and with its aid, he'd begun digging through boxes and crates in search of potential weapons. Something told him they were going to need anything they could find.

"Are we really going to get out of here?" Cade asked, her voice hollow with exhaustion.

"Out of Memphis?" he asked, pulling a hammer free from a tool kit. He studied it before setting it on the floor beside the box. "Yeah, we are. I just need to decide which way."

Cade took two slow, deep breaths and watched Ethan as he dug through the detritus of her time living in the house. Ethan shone his light toward her; her eyes were vacant as she stared at him. She gave a sudden, decisive nod. "So what exactly are we going to do?" she asked. Her voice was oddly calm, and he raised an eyebrow at how collected she suddenly sounded. "Are we just going to get out of here, pick up Anna, and take off?"

"That's the idea," he confirmed. He took a hatchet out of a box and tested the edge of its blade for sharpness, then set it down and joined Cade on the stairs. "How bad do you think all this is?"

Cade raised an eyebrow. "I think you'd know better than me, Eth," she said softly. "You're the one who was listening to the police scanner."

"I know. I just...it's so unbelievable, you know?" Ethan tried to explain. "I mean, how does something like this happen here? In Memphis? In *America*?"

Cade shook her head and looked down at her lap. Ethan followed her gaze and realized she held her cell phone, tapping its display with a slow, careful hand. "What makes you think America is immune to horrible things?" she asked. "What makes America so special that she shouldn't have to deal with tragedy?"

Ethan blew out a breath of frustration and shook his head. "It's not that. I don't think we're special, at least not when it comes to bad things. I just figured there'd have been more warning is all. More talk of something happening, maybe something leading to the riots. We don't know anything about them! Are they political? Social? Economic? What's going on? There hasn't been anything resembling real unrest in Memphis, and now suddenly we're just...completely immersed in it."

Cade pressed her lips together, looking uncertain. "I don't know. I hadn't heard anything, either. But that doesn't necessarily mean anything." She squinted at the phone in her hand before asking, "What's the plan? Where are we going?"

"I'm thinking Gadsden."

"Alabama?"

"Yeah." He wrapped an arm around her shoulders and gave her a gentle, affectionate squeeze. He rested his cheek against the top of her head as she relaxed against him, and it occurred to him that she was shell-shocked. She hadn't been acting like the woman he'd known for seven years, the woman who'd been so confident and assured, never letting anything bother her. He thought perhaps she was traumatized by what she'd seen that day. "My mother lives in Gadsden now, remember? We can hole up at her house for a day or two and then all get out of here. I tried calling her to let her know we're coming, but I think the phone lines are still down."

"I'm not sure your mom will appreciate three visitors showing up at her door without notice," Cade said, disentangling herself from Ethan's grasp and standing. She stretched almost languidly, rolled her shoulders, and moved to the one unblocked window in the basement. She stood on her toes to look out the window, fingers clinging to the edge of the windowsill for balance.

"I think Mom will be fine with it," he replied, keeping his voice low. "You know she likes you, and Anna and I haven't been down to see her since before Halloween."

Cade nodded and stepped away from the window, looking at Ethan through the dim light of the flashlight he held and brushing her hair back from her face. "The sooner we get going, the better," she said, her voice the steadiest he'd heard all night. "I don't want to stay around this house any longer than absolutely necessary."

CHAPTER SIX

New Orleans, LA

Remy had to give Marc credit: he didn't argue with her, question her, or treat her like an idiot for using something as borderline silly as the "Z" word. He merely slammed the gearshift into reverse and jammed his foot on the gas, twisting around to watch behind him as he drove backward down the street.

Remy had to give him a second credit, too: he was amazing at driving backwards. She supposed he'd have to be, considering he was a cop. He couldn't drive very fast, though; there were too many people and too many cars behind them trying to do the same thing. Her heart was in her throat as she watched the mass of people pursuing the fleeing group, the ones covered with blood and gore, wearing looks of rage on their faces. They were utterly horrifying, and she wondered if these were the sick, vicious people that Marc had described to her.

Marc cut the wheel hard, and with a roar, the car spun into a sharp half circle that put the rear toward the oncoming crowd of people. He shifted into drive, then hit the gas again, steering around fleeing people and taking a hard left.

"Where are we going?" she asked, her hands braced against the dashboard; she didn't even remember putting them there.

"We've got to get past those people," Marc said. "I'm trying to get us to my house."

"What's at your house?"

"Guns," he replied. "Lots of guns. I have a feeling we're going to need them."

"What for?" Remy asked. "You don't think we'll have to…*shoot* any of those people, do you?"

"I hope not," Marc said. "But I'd rather have the guns and not need them than need them and not have them."

Remy couldn't deny his logic, so she shut her mouth. The scenery flew past, people running and screaming, attacking others, and breaking store windows to gain access. She pulled her hands from the dash and dug her nails into her palms, stifling a dismayed cry as the city she loved so much was destroyed—again—this time not by Mother Nature but by the hands of its very citizens.

"Are you okay?" Marc asked, weaving around a motorcycle that lay fallen in the street.

"I don't know. I haven't made up my mind yet." She turned on the radio, hoping to find more information about what was going on. Using the scan button, she shuffled through the stations, but all she found were ones playing music or commercials. There wasn't a word on the air about what was happening in New Orleans. She didn't think that boded well for them.

"I doubt you'll find anything on there," Marc said, and she gave up her search. "We'll check on TV once we get to my house. By now, all this should be on the news."

"We hope," she said.

"Yeah," he agreed.

The rest of the ride was silent, Marc expending most of his focus on getting them to his house in one piece and Remy just trying to keep it together. Her hands shook, but they felt like they were detached from the rest of her body, disassociated from her. She curled her hands into fists again, trying to quell the shaking. Now was not the time to break down. She had to maintain her shit, especially if she expected to make it home.

Home. That made her think of her family. She had no idea if they were even aware that she wasn't in the house, considering she'd never gotten the opportunity to place her phone call from the police station. If they'd figured out she wasn't home and had tried calling her cell phone and she wasn't answering, they were probably worried sick. She needed to call them, but her phone was still at the station. She debated asking Marc if she could borrow his phone but decided to hold off for now. He was too focused, and she was worried that if she distracted him now, he'd wreck the car. That was the *last* thing she wanted to risk. So she kept her mouth shut and tried to stay calm as the cruiser darted through traffic that became increasingly erratic and congested. The scowl on Marc's face deepened until, finally, they broke free. The snarl of traffic and panicking pedestrians fell away when they crossed some invisible demarcation. Remy released a breath she hadn't realized she was holding and noticed that Marc had a triumphant smile on his face.

"We made it," she said, for lack of anything else to say.

"For the moment," he replied. "It doesn't mean we're free and clear. It just means we have a reprieve. This shit is going to spread, and obviously we're going to be right in the middle of all of it."

"You think it's going to get that bad?"

"If what my uncle told me on the phone is true, it's going to get *worse*."

"What are you going to do?" she asked.

"First, I'm going to get us to my house," Marc said, his tone confident, assured that he'd make it there. "We've got to have a means of protection. My uncle told me that the sick people are very violent, and I'm not going near any of them with only one pistol. The last thing I want to do is shoot anyone. Just because I'm a cop doesn't mean I'm trigger happy. But if it's our lives or theirs, I'll pick ours every time." He paused, then asked, "Do you know how to shoot?"

"A little bit," Remy said. "My dad started to teach me when I was a kid, but then he left."

"Damn," Marc said. "Well, I suppose some training is better than none. Were you any good at it?"

She shrugged. "I guess I was okay at it. I don't remember my dad having any complaints about how I was doing."

"I guess that will have to do." Marc slowed the car, and it took Remy a second to realize he was making a right turn into a driveway leading to a modest, single-story brick house. The garage door was already open. He pulled the cruiser into the empty garage and turned the engine off, clipped the key to his belt, then opened his door. "Come on in. We'll get something to eat and see if we can't find some information on what's going on out there."

At the mention of food, Remy's stomach growled, and she wondered how she'd managed to not realize she was starving. She let herself out of the cruiser and waited for Marc to close the garage door, standing awkwardly by the door that led into his house. Once he unlocked the door and stepped inside, she followed him in and looked around, curious what a cop's house would look like.

Surprisingly comfortable and cozy, she discovered. The kitchen was all warm cherry wood, granite countertops, and stainless steel appliances, and the walls were painted a smoothing cream color. Nearby was a small dining room with a round dining table that seated four. Several magazines and a stack of books were perched on the edge of the table, like Marc used it as a catch all for random items. Through a nearby open doorway, Remy could just make out half the living room and a large, plush gray couch covered in several orange throw pillows.

"Nice house," she commented, shoving her hands into her pockets and rocking on the heels of her tennis shoes. "It's a heck of a lot nicer than mine."

"Thanks," Marc said agreeably. He went to the fridge and opened it, rooting around inside and pulling out several containers of leftover Chinese food. "Sorry, this is the best I've got," he said apologetically, setting the containers on the island in the center of the kitchen. "I wasn't expecting company."

"It's fine. Leftover Chinese is right up there with leftover pizza," Remy said, though it was a bit of a fib. She accepted one of the cartons Marc offered her, flipping it open to see what appeared to be sesame chicken inside it. *Could be worse,* she thought, taking the fork Marc handed her and digging in, eating it cold. "What now?" she asked around a mouthful of chicken.

Marc hummed thoughtfully, prodding at whatever was inside his own takeout container with his fork. "Well, I figure I'll go scrounge up the other pistols I have," he replied. "While I'm doing that, maybe you can call your family and check on them, make sure everything is okay." He nodded toward the living room. "Phone's in there."

"Yeah, I'll get on that in a minute," Remy said. After he retreated down a nearby hallway, she went into the living room. She stood in the middle of the room for a moment, studying the cushy couch and television. She spotted the phone on an end table beside the couch and hesitated after a glance at the clock on the wall showed it was two in the morning. She decided to hold off calling them until the sun came up; if they *hadn't* realized she was gone and got woken up by a phone call telling them she'd not only been arrested but had been busted out of jail by a cop—and oh, by the way, had they heard there was some sort of viral riot going on in New Orleans?—her stepfather would kick her ass. She plopped down on the soft, squishy couch, picked up the remote, and turned on the TV. She could at least channel surf to gather information about what was going on out there.

Most of the TV stations were showing infomercials, and she even found a news program replaying the five o'clock broadcast from the day before, much to her frustration. She was ready to throw the remote on the floor when she clicked it a few more times and, by chance, landed on a news channel that appeared to be broadcasting live. She found the volume button on the remote and turned the TV up, hoping they were actually reporting on what was going on in the streets of New Orleans.

To her relief, she found it was a report about an apparent riot going on in Jackson Square—something she'd never thought she'd be relieved to hear. The reporter was one of those chipper, overly perky, annoying bimbos that made Remy want to throw things at the TV every time she saw them on there. She debated looking for another channel, but it was two a.m., so she was unlikely to find anything. Besides, this perky little bimbo didn't look quite so perky any longer. Her hair was actually *out of place*. Remy sat back on the couch, setting the remote beside her and settling in to watch.

"*...problems began approximately an hour ago, when several fights erupted in the middle of Jackson Square,*" the reporter was saying. The chyron at the bottom of the screen said, "*Rioting in Jackson Square*" in bold white letters on a red background. For some reason, she found the headline annoying. "*First responders have informed me that more than twenty people have already been taken to area hospitals with injuries sustained during the melee, which is currently ongoing. Police have been dispatched from all over the city to Jackson Square to try to contain the outburst of violence, but with additional reports of violent outbreaks scattered all over the city, they're warning all citizens who are outdoors to get to a safe place and all those who are already indoors to shelter in place.*"

"Well, *that* tells me nothing," Remy muttered. She heard footsteps down the hall and looked up to see Marc stepping into the room, carrying three belts that each had two holstered guns hanging from them.

"What tells you nothing?" he asked. He glanced at the TV and saw the news. "Are they reporting on what's going on?"

"If you can call it reporting," she grumbled. "To say that it conveyed absolutely no useful information would be an understatement."

"Well, what *did* they say?"

"Rioting in Jackson Square," Remy said. "It's starting in other areas of the city, and there wasn't a word mentioned about any virus like your uncle was claiming."

"Doesn't mean he was wrong," Marc said. "It just means that, if he's right, nobody has quite caught on yet." He looked at the phone on the table by the couch. "Did you call your family?"

"No, not yet," she said. "I didn't think my stepdad would appreciate getting woken up this late. Hell, he doesn't even know I was arrested. Do you think we could keep it that way?"

"I don't see why not," Marc said. "According to NOPD, you were never there, since I never finished filing paperwork on your arrest. Well, except for the dispatchers that I called the arrest in to, but that's not a big deal. Considering everything going on, they've probably already forgotten about it."

"What about Adam?" She'd almost forgotten about him in the fracas at the police department after her arrest.

"What about him?" he asked absently. He was contemplating the telephone, like he was trying to decide if he wanted to call someone.

"What happened to him?"

"I have no idea," Marc admitted. "He was taken into custody by a different officer. I didn't have anything to do with his processing. I have no idea where he was even taken, for that matter. Could have been a completely different substation, for all I know."

"You're a lot of help," she said snidely.

Marc threw his hands up helplessly. "I can't keep track of every single arrestee that comes into the custody of the NOPD. Especially when they were never in *my* custody."

Remy scowled but set the topic aside for now. "What do we do now?" she asked.

Marc looked at the belted guns he held and smiled warily. "Well, I suppose it's time for me to pack up some supplies and try to get you home."

* * *

Plantersville, MS

Gray paced impatiently alongside the pool table on which April's body lay, the fingers of his left hand curled so tightly around his cell phone that his knuckles hurt. He ignored the pain, ignored the throbbing in his skull and the deep ache in his chest. It felt like adrenaline had snatched the air from his lungs in the time since he'd called Theo, and he fought to not dial his brother's number again. He'd said he was coming. Redialing his number over and over wouldn't get him there any faster. It was already too late for Gray's immediate need.

April had died five minutes before, shortly after he'd placed his call to Theo. She'd bled out, her blood spilling across the pool table's green felt, soak through the towels he and Jack had kept pressed against the wound. No one had been able to get through on the official emergency lines. There hadn't been anything they could do for her. She'd died, and they hadn't been able to stop it.

Gray set his phone on a table and ran his hands through his hair, ignoring the sticky blood still staining them. He paced to the end of the table, then turned to go the other way, avoiding looking at April's body lying on the table, pale and cooling. He didn't want to think about what had happened. He couldn't wrap his mind around it, so he simply shut it out. His chest felt tight. He knew he needed to sit, take it easy, and force himself to calm down before he worked himself into an asthma attack. But his nerves wouldn't let him do it.

"Gray, please, sit," Jack begged from somewhere behind him. "There's enough going on without you driving me crazy walking all over the place."

Gray abandoned his pacing and moved to the front doors. The shooting had begun outside not long after Gray, Jack, and the bouncer—whose name was Brendon, Gray had learned—had brought April inside after they'd disabled their attackers. A nightmare had broken out beyond the doors, and in light of the violence outside, Brendon had thought it prudent to barricade the doors, to keep the shooters and any people who might have wished to do them harm out of the bar. None of them had any idea what was going on outside. Gray had, more than once, considered calling Theo back to ask him, but considering Theo hadn't mentioned anything earlier, he suspected that his brother didn't know either. It seemed like the entire world had collapsed around them in a very short time.

"Gray, please," Jack said again, sounding exhausted. "Just sit, okay? You're driving me nuts. Besides, we need to figure out what to do."

"Do?" Gray repeated, whirling to face him. "We're going to call the fucking cops, Jack. That's all we *can* do."

"No, we need to get out of here," Jack replied. "It sounds really bad out there. I don't think we should stick around in here and—"

"We *call the police*," Gray said again, more emphatically. "We can't just leave. There's a *dead body* in here! April is *dead*! The cops need to—"

"We can't call the police," Jack interrupted. "We can't get through!"

"We can't just leave her here!" he protested. He sank into a chair, leaning over to rest his elbows on his thighs. He didn't look at Jack, directing his next words to the floorboards. "I can't leave her here. I can't just…I don't know."

"The police aren't going to come," Brendon said. "There's too much going on right now. They don't have time to investigate the attack on you when they've got people running around with guns. Especially since she's already dead."

"And what the hell *is* going on out there?" Gray demanded. He stood and took a few brisk steps to a window to peer into the darkness beyond. Though the parking lot was poorly lit, he could make out people running down the street and the pop of a gun firing. "I've never seen anything like this. Never even *heard* of anything like this. Do you think it's a riot? Some sort of uprising against the government or something?"

"If it was an uprising against the government, it'd make more sense if it was up in Jackson," Jack mused. He moved to join Gray, and they stood staring into the darkness in silence for several long moments.

"Zombies," Gray mumbled.

Jack gave him a weird look. "What?"

"It's zombies," he said. "It's got to be. Hell, that guy bit April. He *bit* her. Think about it, Jack. It's total *Night of the Living Dead* shit. Zombies bite people. They, like, eat them."

"Gray…. Is the lack of oxygen from your asthma starting to affect your brain?" Jack asked. "There's no such thing as zombies."

"How do you *know* that?" he persisted. "Those two guys who attacked April and me, they've got all the hallmarks of a fucking Romero film. They were trying to bite me, they *did* bite April, and they stank to high heaven, like a damned corpse or something. Maybe there's been a lab accident somewhere or something, and a bunch of dead people are going around trying to, I don't know, eat the living or whatever it is that zombies do."

Jack stared at him, clearly incredulous. "Gray, I do believe you've finally cracked."

"I have not!"

Jack leaned against the wall beside the window, crossing his arms. "Okay then, genius. Where are all the zombie hordes like you see in the movies? There's supposed to be massive crowds of them out there, right?"

Gray shrugged. "I don't know. Maybe?"

Jack sighed. "You know what I think? I think it's just a bunch of people rioting, and you've been watching *way* too many horror movies."

Gray huffed out a breath and crossed his own arms, squinting when he noticed movement in the shadows near the edge of the parking lot. "So you still think we should leave?" he asked, trying to ignore the veiled insult to his intelligence that Jack had dropped on him. "You still think we should ditch out of here? Where would we go?"

"I'm pretty sure your brother would appreciate it if I got you home," Jack started. "I know how he is. I have no doubt he's in a panic trying to get over here to make sure you're okay."

"Yeah, probably," Gray acknowledged. He wasn't going to admit that, deep inside, he was in a fair amount of panic himself, stressing over whether *Theo* was okay. Being out in the town with things the way they were, even inside an ambulance, had to be dangerous. Theo was all he had; he didn't want to risk losing him. "My car is right outside," he said. "Maybe we could—" A thud at the front doors cut him off. "What was that?"

"Sounded like someone at the door," Jack said.

"Or some*thing*," Gray added grimly. He stepped away from the window, edging to the door. Another thud echoed through the room, and Brendon and Smitty circled the counter to join them as they backed toward the center of the room.

"Think we should check?" Jack asked.

"No," Gray replied. "No, I don't think so. I think it'd be better if we pretend like nobody's here. There's a reason we barricaded the doors, right?"

"I think I agree with him," Brendon said. "We should stay inside, stay quiet, and wait for them to go away."

The thudding at the door became more insistent, sounding more like fists—a number of them—beating on it in a discordant rhythm that sent chills up Gray's spine. He gripped his cell phone tighter, contemplating calling Theo again. Smitty walked briskly to the door, moving beside it to peer out the window, trying to make out what was outside.

"Anybody got a flashlight?" Smitty asked, his hushed voice sounding even louder than it should have in the otherwise empty bar. When nobody stepped forward to offer him one, he motioned to Brendon. "Get me the one behind the bar. It's near the shotgun."

"You have a shotgun and you didn't mention it?" Jack asked. "You know we could use that, right?"

"Nobody uses my shotgun but me," Smitty snapped. He glanced at Brendon. "Bring the shotgun too while you're at it. Kid's got a point. We might need it."

When Smitty squinted into the darkness again, a hand slammed against the glass, and he staggered back from the window, stumbling over a stool. The beating outside the door became more insistent, more frantic, accompanied by the sound of shouting. No, not shouting, Gray realized. *Growling.* It was animalistic snarling and groaning and moaning. The sounds sent chills up his spine. The thought of zombies no longer seemed quite so absurd, and he bit back the nausea welling in his throat.

The front doors were shoved inward. The tables and chairs blocking the door scraped against the floorboards as they gave a few inches under the onslaught from the other side of the door. Gray took a few steps back, closer to the table where April's body lay. He turned, intending to search out something to use as a weapon, and that was when his eyes landed on the pool table.

April's body was gone.

"April?" he called out, scanning the dark corners of the bar. Maybe they'd made a mistake. Maybe she wasn't really dead. He looked to Jack, who gave him a quizzical look. "April's gone!"

"Gone? What the fuck do you mean, *gone?*" Jack asked, taking a couple of steps toward him.

"Gone! Not here! Away!" Gray snapped. "Should I get you a fucking dictionary? Or would you prefer a thesaurus?"

"She can't be gone! She's dead!"

"Maybe we made a mistake! Either way, her body's *gone!* Who moved it?"

"Nobody moved it," Jack said, his tone wary. He edged toward Gray, trying to get a look around him at the pool table. He was distracted by the sound of the chairs and tables scraping on the floor again, though, and he hurried to join Brendon and Smitty in their efforts to push the furniture back against the doors.

Gray knelt to peer under the table, like April's body had somehow rolled off or magically sunk through it. He straightened and found himself face to face with April. She lunged at him, her hands out, grasping for him as she snarled, sounding similar to the people outside. He staggered back with a shout of alarm, dodging her grasping hands, when the door behind him gave way and the people from outside flooded in.

* * *

Memphis, TN

The faint tinge of smoke was on the air when Cade and Ethan made the decision to leave the basement, a stench that bothered Cade's sinuses and made her eyes water and sting. "You okay?" Ethan asked quietly, coming up behind her as she stood at the foot of the stairs, contemplating the door above.

Cade didn't bother turning around. "I don't know," she admitted. She sniffed, scrubbing at her nose, like she could rub away the scent of burning. She jerked her chin toward the basement door. "Do you think it's safe to go out yet?"

"Honestly, I don't know," he said. He stepped up to the foot of the staircase beside her, studying the door for itself. "But really, there's no way to know unless we try, right?"

"We can't stay down here forever," she acknowledged. An odd, churning rumble started in her gut, born of nervousness and even a small inkling of fear. She hadn't felt fear—*real* fear—in years, not since...

She shook her head to jar her mind away from the thoughts of war and violence and death that threatened to emerge. They'd only distract her from her immediate goal: getting her and Ethan out of this house in one piece.

Ethan watched her, his eyes large and concerned, and took a slow step toward her, making a strange gesture with his hand like he was trying to decide what to do with it. It fell to hang loosely at his side. He asked again, "Are you okay?"

"Yeah, fine," she said. She squared her shoulders to steel herself, then moved past Ethan to the stairs, retrieving her duffel bag and rifle case from beside it. There were no further words between them. There didn't need to be. Cade glanced at Ethan before easing up the stairs, one step at a time, placing her feet with methodical care. Ethan kept a few steps between them as he followed.

Cade paused at the top of the stairs and studied the bolted wooden door at the top. The deadbolt—an old sliding kind, not very useful for security, but it'd come with the house and she hadn't gotten around to changing it—was bent, bowed inward from the force that had pressed against it. She brushed her fingers over the metal. It was hard to imagine one man being able to bend it like this. She looked back to Ethan again, and he gave her a terse nod and slid the gun at his hip out of its holster. She grasped the lock and pushed it aside with more force than would have normally been necessary. The lock disengaged with a loud scrape of metal against metal. She hesitantly pulled the door open.

Cade was sure her nerves were going to crawl out through her skin. She gripped her rifle case more tightly in her left hand as her right found the holstered Jericho pistol Ethan had returned to her. She steeled herself and lifted the pistol as she peered around the edge of the door. There was no one— and *nothing*—in sight. She breathed out a slow sight of relief, though it was tinged with a deep sense of dread. She hesitated, then eased into the kitchen. Her shoes crunched over broken glass, and a cold breeze gusted through the room. The patio door still stood wide open, the glass shattered, letting in the cold evening air, and two chairs at the small breakfast table were overturned and broken. Glass littered the floor, mixed with a large streak of clotted, dark red blood. A crimson handprint stained the front of the refrigerator, and another smear darkened the doorframe leading to the living room. All was quiet and motionless.

Cade moved farther into the chilly kitchen and stepped aside to let Ethan exit the basement behind her. He swept the room with his own pistol, and she let him lead the way as he eased through the battered kitchen and into the living room.

Compared with the disarray they'd just left behind, the living room was the perfect picture of normalcy. The TV was still on, muted, playing the news; the light from the screen flickered over the scene. The drinks Andrew had made for them still sat on the table, the ice long melted. She nearly expected to see Andrew come downstairs with a smile and an offer to make dinner.

The heavy weight of her rifle case was enough to bring her back to reality. Andrew wasn't going to come downstairs. There would be no more dinners in this house. There would be no more quiet evenings of drinks and bad movies on television. Everything was gone.

Cade understood this instinctively as she glanced at the flickering TV screen. She didn't need news reporters to tell her anything. She just knew.

A slight movement fluttered in the corner of Cade's eye. She turned on her heel and lifted her pistol. But the motion had just been a curtain stirred to life by a cold breeze coming in from the open front door.

"We should get out of here," Ethan suggested. Cade tore her attention away from the billowing curtain as Ethan touched her arm gently to get her to look at him. "Come on, Cade. Let's get some supplies and take the Jeep, pick up Anna, and head to Mom's."

An hour later, Cade followed him to his SUV, her rifle case still in her hand and her duffel bag on her shoulder. She'd changed into a pair of jeans, a flannel shirt, a black leather jacket that had once belonged to her father, and a pair of knee-high, sturdy black boots to protect her feet and calves. Cade thanked whatever deity happened to be listening that Ethan had had the forethought to grab her duffel bag from her bed. She and Anna were close to the same size, but Anna's clothes were snugger than Cade normally liked hers, and they made for some uncomfortable wearing.

Wariness bubbled into Cade's gut at the idea of being outside, especially in the dark and especially after what she'd experienced in her own home. She glanced at the building as she swung into the passenger seat of Ethan's Jeep. It was still dark inside the house, though Cade could make out the shine of a lamp somewhere upstairs and the flicker of the TV in the otherwise darkened living room. She thought of Josie again, and tears filled her eyes. She shook them off and turned her attention to Ethan, seeking a distraction from her grief.

"What the hell is going on?" Cade asked, pushing her hair away from her face again. "What happened in there… it's something more than just a riot, isn't it?"

Ethan started the engine and reached to turn on the police scanner he'd installed on the dash. It sprang to life, filled with static and voices yelling urgently into radios. "If I had to guess, I'd say yeah," he replied. He paused to listen to the crackling radio before adding, "Something isn't right about this."

Cade remained silent and listened with him. If she remembered her ten-codes correctly, several fires burned across the city, and the numbers of fights and shootings and lootings had exploded. She shuddered and looked at her house again as Ethan pushed the Jeep into gear and pressed the gas pedal. She closed her eyes as the tears threatened to spill again, then turned her eyes once more to Ethan. His expression was the definition of determined; he gripped the steering wheel with both hands and stared out the windshield.

"They mentioned road blocks," Cade said, motioning to the scanner. "How are we going to get past them if we come across one?"

Without a word, Ethan leaned forward and set his badge and gun on the dashboard.

Cade stayed silent for the rest of the drive to the hospital, her nails scratching the black plastic case that held her rifle. As the Jeep approached the city block occupied by the hospital Ethan's wife worked at, though, she sat forward in her seat and squinted at the building. The sky had an unusual glow that she didn't recognize. She grasped the case in her lap tighter.

"No. No, no, *no*," Ethan gasped. The Jeep lurched forward as he sped up, and Cade pitched forward against the seatbelt, the belt digging into her collarbone. It took her a moment to realize the source of his distress.

The hospital's emergency room was on fire.

Cade jumped out of the vehicle before it stopped moving, leaving her rifle behind, and strode toward the burning building with the authoritarian air of someone who belonged there. Ethan's car door slammed as he, too, got out, and he started running toward the flaming ER. Cade sprinted after him, keeping an eye on their surroundings.

The parking lot was utter chaos. Dozens of people stumbled around the lot in the light of the fire, the wounded being tended to by the few doctors and nurses available to do so. Others tried to haul patients out of other areas of the building. Everyone was avoiding the emergency room.

"Anna!" Ethan shouted as he drew closer to the building. Beads of sweat formed on Cade's forehead and back; the air felt almost too hot to breathe. She nearly ran into a patient pushing his own IV rack beside him. She stumbled around first him and then a couple of nurses pushing a hospital bed with two people on it toward the opposite end of the parking lot. She caught Ethan's shoulder to stop him as she realized he was taking them too close to the inferno. He paused, shading his eyes against the glare from the fire, and shouted again. "Anna Bennett!"

"Ethan!" a voice yelled from their right. Cade twisted to see an unfamiliar blond woman limping in their direction, dressed in dirty, sooty, blood-stained scrubs, an ID hanging from a lanyard around her neck.

"Jesus, Lisa!" Ethan exclaimed, rushing to her and putting his arm around her for support. The woman almost lost her balance at the impact of Ethan's body against hers, and he caught her by the arm to keep her from falling. "Fuck, are you okay?"

Cade relaxed as she realized that Ethan knew the woman. She skimmed her eyes over the blonde's tired face and filthy scrubs; she had a hand clasped tightly to her shoulder, blood oozing from between her fingers and staining the front of her scrubs further. She wondered what had happened, but she didn't get the chance to ask as the woman answered Ethan's question.

"No, not really," Lisa said. She panted, short of breath like she'd run a long distance. "Everything's gone to hell. I'm trying to find somebody to take a look at this so I can get back to work, but they labeled me low priority on the triage list." She pulled her hand away from her shoulder just enough to show them her wound. Cade frowned. It looked like someone had bitten Lisa on the shoulder hard enough to break skin and draw blood.

"That looks bad," Cade agreed, tearing her gaze from the wound to scan their surroundings again. She rested her hand against her holstered pistol and squinted into the flickering darkness. She felt oddly exposed; a creeping sensation of danger worked its way up between her shoulder blades and latched into her brain at the base of her skull. She tried to shake off the instinctual fear. "What happened?" she asked Lisa.

Lisa pressed her hand to her wound again, fingers digging into the fabric of her scrubs hard enough that her fingertips turned white. She opened her mouth to answer Cade's question, but Ethan spoke up before she could say anything.

"Have you seen Anna?"

Lisa shook her head, tears filling her brown eyes. "We were in the ER with a patient," she explained, her voice trembling. "I think he was from one of the riots. He was going absolutely ballistic. Anna was trying to sedate him, and the man attacked her. Shit hit the fan, and a fire broke out. Anna and I got separated. The last time I saw her, she was running for the main oxygen shut-off panel. When I got outside, someone grabbed me, but I fought him off and ran."

The anguish in Ethan's eyes intensified. It nearly broke Cade's heart. "She's…?"

"I never saw her come out. I'm sorry," Lisa said softly.

Cade saw the exact moment Ethan fell apart, and it was one of the worst things she'd ever witnessed. His face crumpled and his shoulders sagged; he lifted a hand to press it to his eyes. Cade put an arm around him, motioning to Lisa as she squeezed him, taking charge of their planned escape as she turned her friend and nudged him toward the SUV. "Come on, come with us," she said to Lisa, trying to force Ethan to move with her. "We'll get you out of here."

"Where are we going?" Lisa asked, limping alongside them, struggling valiantly to keep up with the brisk pace Cade set.

"We're getting out of town. This city is starting to fall apart," Cade explained. "I don't know what you know or what you've seen in that hospital this evening, and I'm not going to pretend I do. But I think Memphis is turning into another Atlanta."

"You mean the riots?" Lisa asked. Cade opened the back passenger door and ushered Lisa in with a gentle push. Then she shoved Ethan toward the front passenger door, grimacing as he tried to resist.

"Yeah," Cade replied once she'd gotten the passenger door open. She glanced at Lisa. The other woman had leaned back against her seat, her face pale and strained with the pain from the wound on her shoulder. "We'll look at your shoulder as soon as we get out of here," she added. "I learned basic medical care in the IDF." Cade turned back to Ethan and thrust out a hand, wiggling her fingers demandingly. "Keys. Now."

"We're not leaving yet!" Ethan protested. He didn't give her the keys; he didn't even look at her. His eyes were focused on the ER. Cade shoved his shoulder to steal back his attention.

"Ethan, *keys*," she persisted. He took them out of his pocket but hesitated in giving them to her, clenching his fist around them. She scowled and reached for his hand. "And yes, we *are* leaving. It's not safe here."

"Not without Anna," Ethan said, moving the keys out of her reach. She snagged his wrist and pulled his arm back to her, then pried his fingers apart. Ethan fought against her painful grip on his wrist, but he couldn't withstand her attack for long. She snatched them from his hand and looped them around her own finger.

"Ethan Bennett, get in the fucking car before I kick your damned ass," she ordered, pointing at the car door. "And we've been down *that* road before. You know I can do it." She grabbed a fistful of his jacket and shoved him inside the Jeep, slamming the door once he was in, then circling to the driver's seat.

"What about Anna?" Ethan demanded as Cade buckled in.

Cade stared at him coldly for a long moment. She *had* to be cold about it, *had* to be focused on what she was doing, because he wasn't going to like the one option she was giving him. Getting emotional alongside him would only make this worse. "What about her?" she asked. "We can't stay here and hope she walks out of that building. Look at it, Ethan!" She pointed through the windshield. The building still crackled and burned almost merrily against the nearly black night sky, the cheerfulness of the blaze like a slap in the face. "She's not coming out of it!"

"*We're not leaving without her!*" Ethan exploded, glaring back at her. She stood her ground, returning the look as she gripped the steering wheel with one hand. Her knuckles turned white with the strength of her grasp as she struggled against the urge to punch him in the head in the hopes of knocking some sense into him.

"Ethan," Lisa said from the backseat. Cade glanced in the rearview mirror. Lisa's face was drawn from the effort of keeping pressure on her wound. "Ethan, based on what I saw in that ER, what was going on and what she was doing and where she was…I think Anna is dead."

CHAPTER SEVEN

Plantersville, MS

The sound of the gunshot hung in the air around Theo as he fell back against the airway seat. He stared at Jonathan's motionless body lying just beyond the edge of the doorway, horror washing over him. His breath was coming out hard and fast, and he felt a twinge of dizziness tickle at his brain. He shuddered and closed his eyes, trying to slow his breathing before he hyperventilated. He had a sudden appreciation for Gray and what he went through when he had asthma attacks.

Theo knew now wasn't the time to get panicky. He had work to do. He had to get out of the ambulance. He had to get moving. He had to find his brother. After that, he was going after Dillon. From there, he had no idea what he was going to do, but once he had both of them with him, he could figure out anything.

Theo wasn't sure where to start, though. He had no idea if the shot that had killed Jonathan had been a stray one that had just chanced to hit him or if it'd been an intentional kill shot. If it'd been an accident, then Theo was reasonably sure it wouldn't happen again and he'd be okay stepping out of the truck from the back. Granted, "reasonably sure" didn't translate to "absolutely sure," and if the shot had been intentional…

Theo edged toward the back doors. The least he could do was pull the top door shut to minimize the risk to himself. The less exposure, the better. He wasn't going to lie, not even to himself: even being within spitting distance of the doors made him nervous. Figuring it was better to do it quickly, he rushed forward, grabbed the metal bar on the door, and yanked it hard, slamming the door closed before backpedaling from it.

Theo stared at the door, his heart hammering against his ribs, waiting to see if any bullets were going to tear into the open space on the lower half of the doorframe and rip into his body. When nothing was forthcoming, much to his relief, he gathered the trauma bags. The best place to exit was the side door above his head. Though he wouldn't be any less exposed climbing out on top of the ambulance, he figured people were less inclined to look *up* when searching for targets to shoot, so it could offer him some semblance of cover from that perspective. Besides, if he remembered correctly, the exterior cabinets next to the door had extrication equipment in them, including a crowbar and a fire axe. If he was going after Gray, he wasn't going to do it unarmed.

He hadn't decided on his plan for when he got to Smitty's. It wasn't an immediate concern. His main priority was getting to Gray, first and foremost, and then seeing if he could help Gray's friend before she died. From what Gray had described and considering the amount of time that had passed since his call, it was highly likely that April was no longer alive.

Theo slung the heavier of the trauma bags over his shoulder, climbed onto the edge of the airway seat, and unlatched the door. With a firm shoulder against it, he swung the door open and out against the side of the truck.

A cool gust of air blew in and ruffled his blond hair as he dropped back down from the seat to grab the other bag and slide them both out onto the top of the ambulance. After collecting his flashlight from under the stretcher, avoiding the body sprawled on top of it, Theo hauled himself over the edge of the door and fell onto his side. He lay there panting for several long heartbeats, pain shooting through his shoulders, then slid across the side of the truck to an exterior cabinet. The chill of the metal leeched through his uniform, and he started shivering, fumbling at the handle. The door popped open with a loud squeak. Theo tensed, instinctively ducking low, flattening against the truck's metal siding. He lay there, listening for anyone approaching, anyone trying to get after him.

Once he was assured of his relative safety, he knelt once more and swung the second door open. He freed the flashlight from his right knee pocket and turned it on, shining it into the cabinet. He discovered he was holding his breath in anticipation only when he let it out on seeing the tools he was hoping for inside.

"Oh, thank Jesus," Theo whispered, reaching in and picking up the axe and crowbar. The sledgehammer would be too heavy for him to carry for any distance. The axe, too, would likely be too heavy in the long run, especially considering he was bringing two trauma bags along for the ride. But he'd bring both tools, as far and as long as he could carry them.

Wielding his newly acquired weapons, Theo slid to the edge of the truck, peering off the side to make sure no one was waiting below. Satisfied that everything was clear, he lowered his bags and weapons off the side, switched off his flashlight, and slid off the truck. He landed in a defensive crouch and scanned the darkness. Gunshots cracked through the night nearby, and his nerves trembled under his skin, but the act of actually *doing* something, of getting out of the ambulance, of facing the mission to get to his brother—and to Dillon—was invigorating. He collected his bags, slipped the crowbar beneath his belt, and hefted the fire axe in his right hand. Then he waded into the darker shadows alongside the road and began walking rapidly toward town, his fingers clenched around the axe's handle, praying he'd make it to Gray before something horrible happened to him.

* * *

Gray threw his arms up instinctively when April's fingers grabbed at the front of his shirt. He stumbled backward, simultaneously trying to block her advance and protect his face. The bloodstained pool table behind him impeded his retreat, and as she reached for him again, he dodged low, ducked under her arms, and cut around the corner of the table. He straightened in time to hear a gunshot blast from the direction of the door but didn't dare take his eyes off April. His instincts told him that if he did, he'd likely end up injured. Or dead.

Or just like her, the niggling suspicion in the back of his brain suggested. Gray reached a hand out to the pool table, hoping to find a potential weapon somewhere on it. His fingers closed around a pool cue. He hefted it, wielding it between them like a sword, hoping to hold her at bay with it. April didn't look fazed by the heavy stick; if anything, she only quickened her advance.

His heart racing, Gray held out a hand to her, hoping she'd stop, that she wouldn't actually *attack* him. All evidence, especially the evidence currently mobbing *en masse* into the bar itself, spoke to the contrary, though. He drew in a deep breath and shifted his grip to hold the pool cue like a baseball bat. His shoulders tense, he readied himself for the next attack, the one he *knew* would come.

April bared her teeth at him, her once beautiful face full of wild fury. Gray took a step back, braced himself, and swung the heavy end of the pool cue. It collided with the side of April's head, sending her careening sideways against the table. She righted herself, struggling to find her feet, and Gray backed up for breathing room. His eyes flickered in Jack's direction.

Jack, Brendon, and Smitty didn't seem to be having much luck holding off the mob; he was surprised they were still standing. Smitty blasted another round from his shotgun into the crowd, but none that were hit were affected. That only assured Gray of the correctness of his "zombie" suspicions. It was the only explanation he could come up with, regardless of how ridiculous it sounded.

Gray didn't have time to dwell on the possibilities. April was back on her feet and coming at him again. Jack was yelling something at him, but with the distraction of the woman in front of him and the mob crushing into the bar, he couldn't make out a word of what he said. His eyes met April's, and he read the intent in hers clearly.

Gray lifted the pool cue and brought it down on top of her skull with all his strength. She fell against the table, and he lifted the cue and slammed it down, again and again, beating her mercilessly until blood flowed. When she finally stopped moving, stopped clawing for him, he sagged against the table, dropping the pool cue on the floor with a clatter. His lungs struggled for air. But, as before, he didn't have time to catch his breath. Jack was yelling at him again, and now he was able to focus enough to decipher what he was saying.

"Gray! Go! Get the fuck out of here!" Jack shouted across the gap between them. He swung a chair leg at a man grabbing for him before looking back at Gray again. "Back door! Head for your place!"

"What about you?" Gray replied.

"I'll meet you there! Now go!"

Jack turned his back on him and swung the chair leg more vigorously. Gray shook loose his frozen muscles, forcing himself to turn and do as Jack instructed. Sucking in a deep breath, pulling much-needed air in his lungs, he sprinted across the bar, dodging stools and tables, aiming for the storage room door behind the bar's long counter. If he remembered right, there was an exit on the back wall of the storage area that would drop him onto the street immediately behind the Brass Monkey.

He burst into the storage area unimpeded and slammed the door closed. The first thing on which his eyes landed was a glowing red sign that proclaimed EXIT, attached to the wall immediately above the door. Breathing out a sigh of relief, he headed for it, skirting boxes of alcohol and bar nuts stored in organized stacks on metal racks. The sign on the door that warned of an alarm sounding gave him only momentary pause, but with a glance over his shoulder back the way he'd come, Gray decided an alarm was the last of his worries. He grasped the bar and shoved the door hard.

The metal door bounced off the brick wall outside, and a shrill alarm cut through the air, startling him with its volume and sending him scrambling through the doorway. His heart stuttered in his chest as he ran for the corner of the building. He figured if he could get to his car, he could get away faster than on foot, especially since he wasn't in any physical shape to run. He smacked at his pants pockets, searching for his keys, then groaned.

His keys were still in his jacket pocket. And his *jacket* was in his *car*.

"Oh, Christ on a cracker," he muttered. He was screwed. Royally, truly screwed.

Gray peeked around the corner to get a look at the parking lot and shuddered. Those crazy people were everywhere; there was no way he'd be able to get to his car without being spotted, and he'd stupidly left the only weapon he'd had on the bar's floor.

Gray took another half step forward, and his car came into view. The moment he saw it, he knew that getting to it would be impossible; there were simply too many people—*zombies*, his brain insisted—gathered around and near it. A couple of them were even leaning over the side of the car, pushing and shoving each other as they fought to lap at the red fluid staining the window and driver's door. April's blood. Gray swallowed bile and inhaled shallowly through his nose so he wouldn't vomit.

He slunk back into the darkness of the side street, trembling. He leaned against the building and breathed in, slowly and deeply, trying to calm himself. He was going to have to run. He wasn't able to get into his own car, and the chances of him getting a ride from a stranger without getting shot were slim to none. He knew *he* wouldn't have given a random person a lift in the middle of this chaos. He'd told Theo to pick him up at the Brass Monkey. He needed to call him back to arrange a meeting elsewhere.

Gray heard a scraping sound, like someone dragging his heels across gritty pavement. He ran for the end of the street, cut left, and raced for his apartment building.

As he ran, Gray felt in his pocket for his cell phone, pulling it out, his fingers gliding over the touchscreen. He dodged a man coming at him from a storefront and directed the phone to call Theo's number. It took six rings for him to answer, six agonizing rings that sent Gray's heart falling into his stomach in the horrible fear that Theo wouldn't answer. Then he did, his voice coming over the earpiece muffled and breathless but blessedly alive. "*Gray?*"

"Oh, thank God," Gray said. His voice was strained even to his own ears as he sucked in another frantic breath and jumped over a trashcan lying abandoned in the middle of the sidewalk.

"*Where are you? Are you okay?*" Theo asked. "*You sound awful.*"

"Running," he said shortly. He glanced at a corner street sign as he passed it, noting where he was and that he had entirely too far left to run. "My place. Heading there. Meet me, okay?"

"*You shouldn't be running—*"

"Had to," he gasped. He felt at his pockets again with his free hand, hoping he'd have his inhaler handy. He didn't. It was probably in his jacket with his keys. "They got in."

"*Fuck,*" Theo said. He didn't question who "they" were; he probably didn't have to.

Gray checked one more time for his inhaler, like it would miraculously turn up in a pocket he'd already searched. His lungs hurt like hell; he'd be surprised if he made it all the way to his apartment. "Just get to my place. Please," he added, fighting to get more air into his lungs. "I'm going to need your help." He hung up, shoved the phone back into his pocket, and tried to speed up his mad dash.

It took far longer than Gray wanted to get to his apartment building. By then, a deep, tight ache had settled into his chest. In the lobby, he jabbed the elevator call button repeatedly, slamming his fist against the button. He scanned the lobby and noted there wasn't a single person anywhere in sight. He was, in a way, relieved; it meant he was less likely to run into some crazy bastard intent on killing him, but if he passed out in the lobby from lack of oxygen, he'd be pretty well up the creek without help.

The elevator arrived, the cool steel doors sliding open. Gray flung himself inside and punched the third-floor button. His heart racing painfully, he squeezed his eyes closed and sagged against the wall as the elevator ascended, praying that Theo would get there soon, that he'd make it there before he collapsed. He was sure there were no more inhalers in his apartment; Theo wouldn't have filled his prescription if there were. He mentally ran through the different home remedies his mom had used when he was a kid and had fought near-constant minor asthma attacks that would hit him without warning. *Coffee, black coffee,* he remembered. *Two cups.* Something about hot water too. And breathing out heavily through his mouth to try to push out carbon dioxide. He wasn't sure if that part was true, but he vaguely recalled reading it somewhere. Regardless of its validity, he started trying it, taking in short breaths and letting out long, heavy ones as the elevator dragged to a stop with a squeak and groan of the cables. The doors slid open noisily.

Before Gray could step out of the elevator, a man darted inside, pushing him against the back wall with enough force to drive what little breath he had left in his lungs right out of them. He put his hands out defensively as the man grabbed at his throat. Gray let out a weak cry of alarm and shoved hard, managing to get enough precious space between them to work his leg up and put his knee into the man's gut. The impact sent the man stumbling wildly backward to the edge of the elevator. Gray took another fast step forward and kicked him again. He caught the man's head in his hands and drove his knee hard into the man's face. The sound of cartilage and bone snapping met his ears, and sharp pain darted through his knee. The man collapsed onto the floor, and Gray started stomping, slamming the heel of his shoe as hard as he could onto the man's face. When the man stopped moving, Gray stepped over him, heading for his apartment. He recovered the spare key taped to the top edge of the doorframe, and then he was inside, slamming the door and throwing the locks home.

Gray slumped against the closed door for only a moment before forcing himself forward. He leaned heavily on the wall and pushed himself along it toward the bathroom, hoping he had a spare inhaler in the medicine cabinet. But his world began spinning sickeningly around him, and he knew he wasn't going to make it that far. He managed a few more steps before he sank to his knees, panic invading his mind as he struggled desperately to breathe.

* * *

Outside Memphis, TN

Cade drove the SUV well out of the city before pulling over to consult a map. She eased the vehicle off into the grass at the side of the road and pushed the gearshift into park, then turned to look back at Lisa. The woman lay slumped sideways across both seats, her eyes closed. Earlier, Cade had stopped the car in a strip mall parking lot to help Lisa bandage her shoulder and give her painkillers from a bottle of Advil in the console. Sleep was probably good for Lisa right now. The woman was shaken up from her experience at the hospital; Cade didn't begrudge her whatever rest she could get.

Cade leaned across Ethan and hit the switch on the glove box with her thumb. The door swung open and banged Ethan on the knees; he didn't react to the impact. Cade scowled and retrieved the map book from inside, flipping open to the T section. "You know, you're not the only person who's lost someone tonight," she said softly, her voice thick with emotion. She didn't look at Ethan, instead skimming the map of Tennessee as she searched for the SUV's general location.

"I know," Ethan said, continuing to stare out the window. Cade trailed her finger over the paper, found their location, and studied it carefully, trying to decide the next move. "We should get off this road," he added, finally tearing his eyes from the window to glance at Cade.

"Yeah, I think so too," she agreed. She set the book on her thigh and took his hand, giving it a gentle squeeze. "We're going to be okay, right?" she asked.

"I sincerely hope so."

Cade closed her eyes as a surge of emotion welled up and nearly choked her. The only thing she could think of was Josie and Anna and Andrew, and it was almost too much for her to handle. But she *had* to stop thinking about them, because those thoughts would do nothing but distract her from the task of getting the three of them to Ethan's mother's house in one piece. She took several deep breaths and pushed everything to the back of her mind with a mighty shove, burying it all there deeply, where it wouldn't suddenly surface at an inconvenient time.

Cade opened her blue eyes and dropped her gaze back to the map book in her lap. She mentally centered herself the same way she used to when she was assigned a task in her time in the IDF. It was about focusing herself, keeping her mind on the task at hand, and avoiding distractions. She passed the map to Ethan and asked, "So what do you think?" It was a poor attempt to draw him away from his sadness, but thankfully, it worked.

Ethan bowed his head and looked over the map thoughtfully. Cade could practically see gears turning in his head. "How about here?" he asked, pointing to one of the highways crossing the state. "I think we should stick with highways instead of interstates to avoid as much traffic as possible."

Cade leaned across the seats to look at the route to which he pointed. "That's a long drive. I hope you're ready to help out," she said. She checked the rearview and side mirrors before shifting the SUV back into drive and easing onto the road once more. "Is Lisa okay back there?"

Ethan twisted in his seat to look. He reached back and pressed his fingers against Lisa's cheek, holding them there for a moment. "Yeah, she's breathing, if that's what you mean," he answered. "She's running a bit of a fever, though." He sighed with exhaustion and rubbed his face once he'd pulled his arm back into the front seat. "She could probably use the sleep. Hell, *I* could use the sleep."

Cade tilted the rearview mirror down for a moment to get a better look at the sleeping woman. "You don't think she's getting an infection or something from that wound, do you?"

"I'm not sure. I think it's too soon for an infection."
He unbuckled his seatbelt. "Pull over again. Let me get in
the back."

Cade sighed in annoyance and eased the Jeep back onto
the shoulder, barely resisting flipping the bird at another
vehicle that blared its horn as it passed. Ethan was out the
passenger door and into the backseat within seconds. She
started driving again as he woke Lisa, pushed the shoulder
of her scrubs aside, and gently probed her wound through
the bandage.

"Maybe we should find a doctor," Cade suggested.
Apparently not satisfied with his cursory examination, Ethan
removed the bandage she and Lisa had taped over the wound
earlier. Even as Lisa looked on the verge of drifting off again,
he peeled the gauze back from the wound—the bandage
stuck sickly to the injury—and gasped as it finally pulled free.

"Fuck," he said. "I think maybe you need to take a look
at this."

"Why me?"

"Because you're the closest thing we've got to a doctor
right now."

Cade slowed and adjusted the rearview mirror once again
to see Lisa's shoulder. As she caught a glimpse of the wound,
her foot slipped off the gas pedal. She shifted her foot to the
brake to slow down further as she gaped.

"There's no way that's possible," she said. She hated the
way her voice shook and tried to steady it. What she'd seen
made that exceptionally difficult. "Ethan, it looks like it's…
festering."

"I know," he said.

"But…that's not possible," she added. "I mean, so soon after the injury? It should take *days* to get that bad. Maybe even weeks!"

"I know," he repeated.

The wound looked like nothing Cade had ever seen, and she'd seen a lot of injuries in her life. In a rapid succession of glances in the mirror, she saw indentations and punctures from teeth that were the perfect size for an adult human being. The wound didn't look fresh anymore, either. Instead, it was beginning to blacken; the skin around it had become inflamed, strange red streaks radiating out from it into the uninjured tissue nearby.

Cade looked out the windshield again, attempting to keep her attention on the road ahead. "What do we do, Eth?" she asked. "That's bad enough to need a doctor. There's no way I can handle it on my own. She needs antibiotics before it kills her. Do we find her a doctor in the next town, or should we continue to Gadsden and find one there?"

Ethan covered Lisa's wound with fresh gauze before speaking again. "I think we should take her to the ER in the next city," he said. "Especially since she keeps dropping in and out on us. I'm not sure she's even totally conscious at the moment. Pass me the map?" Cade found it on the passenger seat and passed it back to him. He scooted forward on the seat to lean closer to her as he studied the map. "Think she can hold out until Holly Springs, Mississippi?"

Cade tried to get another glimpse of Lisa in the mirror, but Ethan blocked her view. "She'll have to. Is she definitely running a fever?"

He sat back again and touched Lisa's forehead and cheek in turn with his wrist before nodding. "Yeah, she's burning up. It's over a hundred for sure."

Cade swore and pressed harder on the gas pedal. "I'll try to hurry," she said. "The sooner we get her help, the better."

Thirty minutes passed without further comment, though Cade constantly glanced in the rearview mirror to make sure Lisa was still alive. She didn't know why she was so convinced she'd find the woman dead; perhaps it was the way she seemed to fall in and out of consciousness, bordering on sleep one moment and blinking half-awake the next. Perhaps it was the nature of her injury, the way it seemed to be rotting out, eating into her skin and sliding into her bloodstream. Cade had no idea how long it would take for something like that to kill a person, especially at the speed it seemed to be spreading.

Ethan had moved back to the front passenger seat to help her navigate once they'd settled on a temporary destination. They listened to the police scanner, trying to find out anything they could about the situation in Memphis. Cade was surprised to discover that the outbreak of riots wasn't confined to Memphis and Atlanta. On the radio, stations had begun reporting similar outbreaks in cities like Birmingham, New Orleans, Mobile, and Biloxi. The interstates were jammed with vehicles as the populations of the Southeast's major cities tried in vain to flee the chaos. It seemed as if, in one single night, the entire world had gone to hell.

Ethan changed the station to check for updates from other DJs every few minutes. After the millionth time he'd twisted the dial, Cade let out an exasperated sigh. "Eth, you're driving me nuts."

He threw the map book on the floorboard in frustration and let go of the radio's tuner. "*Fuck*," he snapped. "What the hell's going on? I can barely keep up with all this shit."

"It's not just around here," Cade said. "It sounds like it's almost everywhere. Like it's...I don't know." She rubbed her eyes with the heel of her hand and sighed, then dropped it as a thought occurred to her. "You don't think that virus has something to do with it, do you?" She vaguely remembered asking Ethan the question the last time they'd been on the phone, but in the hectic events that had followed, she'd forgotten until this moment that she'd never gotten more than an "I don't know" from him.

"Virus?" he repeated vacantly, scooping the map book off the floor. "What virus?"

"The illness that was going around Atlanta," she clarified. "You remember? The one the hospitals are having so many problems treating."

Ethan sat quiet in thought for a moment before saying, "It sort of makes sense. But at the same time, it doesn't. I mean, what kind of virus makes people act like *that*?" He jabbed his finger at the in-dash radio. Cade couldn't help but agree with him.

"I've never heard of one," she admitted. "I don't think a virus like that exists."

"But *something* does," he pointed out. "*Something* is making these people crazy. *Something* is causing all these riots and murders. And I don't think that it's something we've seen before."

"I don't think so either," she said. She looked in the rearview mirror to check on Lisa again and saw, to her surprise, that the woman was sitting up, her dark eyes watching Cade with a steady, unblinking gaze. "Hey, Lisa. You feel any better?"

Lisa didn't respond, simply continuing to sit oddly upright and stare at Cade with a blank, empty look. "Lisa?" Cade asked.

Ethan twisted in his seat to look at the silent woman. As Cade cut her eyes back to the windshield again, Lisa lunged forward, a horribly familiar almost-snarl erupting from her throat. An image of Andrew flashed through her mind. She started to turn her head, but Lisa's arm hooked around her throat, stopping the motion, and she let out a strangled cry as her head was jerked back hard against the headrest. Lisa's forearm pressed down against her throat, cutting off her breath.

Cade instinctively grabbed Lisa's arm with both hands, pulling at it desperately as Lisa's fingernails dug into the back of her neck. The Jeep swerved violently, and she was forced to let go of Lisa's arm with one hand to grab the steering wheel and get the car back in control. She wedged her fingers between her throat and Lisa's arm and pushed the limb away enough to gasp out, "Ethan, stop her."

Ethan sat in the passenger seat, eyes wide, in shock at the sudden attack. Cade's words were all he needed to prompt him into action. He grabbed Lisa's arm and tried to pull her away from Cade, prying at her elbow and wrist with both hands and pulling with nearly all his strength. But he was unable to dislodge her grip. Cade opened her mouth and tried to suck air into her lungs as her head swam. She clawed Lisa's skin as her nails dug more firmly into the back of her neck; her skin broke with a sharp stab of pain.

Cade took her foot off the gas as Ethan hauled on Lisa's arm again. The pressure on her throat eased slightly. Taking the opportunity, she slammed both feet on the brake pedal. Everyone in the car lurched forward. Lisa slammed into the back of Cade's seat, and her grip loosened enough for Cade to take a single deep, precious breath. Ethan yanked on Lisa's arm again as her grip loosened, and her arm came away from

Cade's neck with the awful sound of bone snapping. He growled and shoved Lisa into the backseat once more.

Lisa lunged toward her again as soon as her back hit the seat. Cade grabbed the steering wheel again and punched the gas pedal hard to throw Lisa against the backseat more firmly. Lisa caught her balance almost immediately at the faster speed, grabbing a fistful of Cade's dark hair and pulling hard. Cade's head hit the headrest again, her eyes watering in pain, and she yelped.

"Get her the hell off me!" Cade yelled. Her head tilted back with the force of the pressure Lisa put on her neck. She fumbled blindly between the seats, trying to locate the pistol she'd stashed in the console earlier. When she located it, she pointed it awkwardly in Lisa's general direction. "Get this bitch off me before I shoot her!"

Ethan grabbed Lisa's hands and tried to pull them from Cade's hair while Cade waved the gun in her face in an attempt to scare her off her. It didn't work, though, and Cade gasped as Lisa hooked her arm around her neck again and squeezed her throat. The broken bones in Lisa's arm dug into her throat. Somewhere in the back of her mind, she wondered how Lisa could continue to attack her with what would under normal circumstances be an agonizing injury. Ethan snatched the pistol from Cade's hand and pointed it at Lisa, firing a shot into her right shoulder.

Cade was deafened by the gunshot. She barely heard Lisa's snarl as the shot loosened her grip on Cade's throat and threw her back against the seat. Lisa turned her eyes to Ethan and bared her teeth at him, and he recoiled against the dashboard. Cade finally got the SUV onto the side of the road, and the Jeep sprayed gravel as she slammed on the brakes. Lisa lurched toward Ethan, and Cade shoved the gearshift into park and unfastened her seatbelt. She turned to face Lisa, fumbling for anything she could get her hands on that resembled a weapon.

Before Cade could find anything, Ethan raised the pistol and pointed it at Lisa. "Back off!" he barked. "Sit the fuck down now! That's an order!"

Lisa dove toward them once more. Ethan grimaced, adjusted his aim, and squeezed the trigger. The bullet slammed into her forehead and threw her back against the seats. She sprawled there limply and didn't move.

Cade covered her ears belatedly as the second gunshot in the enclosed space of the Jeep made her ears ring. Ethan muttered something under his breath that she couldn't hear, and she leaned back against the steering wheel, panting. She felt dizzy, and as Ethan watched Lisa's body guardedly for any sign of movement, she leaned forward to rest her head against the back of her seat.

"Oh my God, what the fuck?" Cade said breathlessly, hoarsely. "I've got to get out of this fucking car." She pulled on the door handle, bile rising in her throat, and cursed as she found the door locked. She slapped at the unlock button before throwing the door open and staggering into the fresh air outside.

Cade's stomach roiled as she stumbled away from the Jeep. She leaned over and vomited into the tall grass at the side of the road. A car door shut, and a moment later, Ethan was at her side, rubbing her back soothingly as she coughed and wiped at her eyes.

"Here," Ethan said, holding one of his clean t-shirts out to her. She accepted it gratefully and used the hem to wipe her lips, then shoved the stick of gum he handed her into her mouth. "You okay?"

"I don't know," Cade admitted. She chewed the peppermint gum furiously to get the acrid taste of bile out of her mouth and refused to look at the car; the thought of getting back in it made her cringe. "Did we just kill her?"

"Yeah, we did. But I don't think it was really Lisa in there. You know what I mean?" He smoothed his hand over her dark hair. "That woman wasn't acting anything like Lisa. Lisa wouldn't have tried to kill you, and she wouldn't have pulled that bullshit and gotten herself shot." He paused and turned back to her, his face serious. She knew by his expression that he was about to suggest something she wouldn't like. "We need to get the body out of the car."

"Should we call the police?" Cade asked, knowing the answer to the question before she'd even really asked it. They hadn't called the police in Memphis after what had happened with Andrew, had they? And they wouldn't this time, either.

She finally stole a reluctant look back at the vehicle. She was surprised at how normal it appeared sitting at a slant on the side of the road. She'd expected it to look dark and sinister, to bear some evidence of the events that had transpired inside of it on its outsides. As she stared at the Jeep, a van sped by on the highway with a roar of its engines, but it made no move to slow or stop.

Ethan had been silent as he'd thought her question over. Finally, he shook his head slowly and said, "No. They have enough to worry about right now. Just…trust me, okay?" he urged, putting his hand gently against her back. "We need to get her out of the car, and then we need to get to Gadsden and make sure my mother is okay."

CHAPTER EIGHT

Plantersville, MS

Theo was shaking with overexertion when he reached Gray's apartment building. It had thankfully not been *too* hard to get from the ambulance to the apartment; he'd spent most of his time practicing the simple avoidance of everyone and everything he'd seen, animals included. He didn't know if whatever was causing people to act insane was affecting animals too, so he'd decided to play it safe and take no chances.

The lobby was empty when he stepped inside, his shoulders and back aching from the weight of the trauma bags. He stood in the doorway of the main entrance, examining every visible nook and cranny and dark-shaded corner in sight, making sure nothing lurked, waiting for him to pass. He cast a glance at the ceiling. The lights were still on. For some reason, he'd expected the electricity to be out. He figured if the chaos outside escalated, it would only be a matter of time until that happened. Heaving a sigh, he headed to the elevator at his right.

Theo pressed the elevator's call button and shifted the bag on his right shoulder, trying to balance it better against his back and squeezing the axe's handle. While he waited impatiently for the elevator to arrive, his eyes repeatedly flickering to the display above the doors, his worries over his brother made his stomach churn.

"Come on, you fucking elevator," he muttered. He slapped his hand hard against the call button and looked at the display again. The red LED number still said "3." Clearly, the elevator was stuck on the third floor. Gray's floor.

Turning away, he resigned himself to climbing the stairs. He shoved the stairwell door open and stepped inside, squinting in the flickering light from the light bar above him. Several moths buzzed around the light fixture, slamming against the plastic covering. He let the stairwell door fall shut and listened past the buzz of the lights for any noise. The stairwell appeared to be empty of everything but him and the bugs.

Theo grasped the railing and started to climb the steps, taking them two at a time, his heart racing by the time he reached the third-floor landing. After a bout of uncertainty over what he'd find, he kicked the door open and burst through it, the axe ready to swing at whatever came at him. He stepped into the dim hallway and made straight for Gray's apartment.

Theo slowed as he approached the elevator; there was a body lying half inside the car, blocking the doors from closing. His pounding heart jammed into his throat. He swallowed hard, trying to stuff it back down, and took another step closer. When he got a clear look at the body, a surge of relief ripped through him so powerfully that it nearly sent him to his knees.

The man was much older than Gray, in his late thirties or early forties, his dark hair going salt and pepper. His face was bashed in, his nose shattered, and the bones around his eyes and forehead crushed. It was clear the man wasn't alive. He forced himself away and moved to Gray's door, knocking hard, then digging his keys out of his pocket and thumbing the right one free. He slipped it into the lock and turned the key. The lock snapped, and he pushed the door open; the hinges squeaked softly, and the door brushed against the carpeted entryway with a soft shushing sound.

The darkness inside the apartment was the first thing Theo registered. He fleetingly wondered if Gray had made it there or if he was, God forbid, lying somewhere outside on the pavement, dead or dying. The thought sent a lightning bolt of fear through him. He closed his eyes to listen carefully, then called out, "Gray?"

Gray knelt on the floor at the end of the hallway, slumped sideways with his head resting against the wall. Even from where he stood, Theo could see him struggling to breathe, his shoulders tight and tense, his hand pressed against the wall, fingers curled and blanched like he was trying to claw his way into the sheetrock. Theo rushed forward and dropped to his knees in front of him, offloading the heavy bags from his shoulders. He took his brother's face in his hands and forced him to look up at him.

"Where's your inhaler?" Gray merely shook his head and closed his eyes, pressing his faintly blue-tinted lips together.

Theo swore and unzipped one of his bags, sorting through supplies and cursing himself for not taking the time to get *some* semblance of organization inside the bag. When he finally found a nebulizer and the medications he needed, he blew out a breath of relief. "You drive me fucking crazy sometimes, you know that?" he said as he prepared the nebu-lizer, hooked it to one of the pilfered O2 tanks, and cranked the tank to six liters. A soft hiss greeted his ears as the oxygen flooded into the mask. Once a white mist started to come from it, Theo shoved the mask against Gray's face. "Breathe, you stupid fucker."

Gray gave him a dirty look even as he pushed the mask closer to his face and breathed in deeply. Despite his irritation at Gray for doing something he should have known would make him ill, Theo smoothed his hand over his hair before crushing him into a tight hug. Gray returned it, digging his fingers into Theo's back.

"Jesus Christ, you scared the *hell* out of me," Theo said. "Don't you *ever* do that again."

"Couldn't help it," Gray replied hoarsely. The mask muffled his words, and Theo had to lean closer to make out what he said. "They got in."

"Where's your friend?" Theo asked. The mask fogged over with one of Gray's exhalations, obscuring the lower half of his face. "What's his name? Jack?"

"He told me to go," Gray said. "He's supposed to meet me here."

"Think he will?"

A moment's hesitation. "Honestly? No."

"And…April?" Even before Gray said anything, Theo could see the answer—and the hurt—in his eyes.

"Didn't make it." Another several breaths fell in the silence between them. "She…she died. Bled out. I think it hit her…" He tapped the side of his neck, where all the important veins and arteries would have been.

"I'm so sorry, Gray," Theo said sincerely. He caught his brother's wrist and pressed two fingers to the inside of it, seeking out his pulse and starting to count. He lost track of where he was when Gray spoke again.

"She didn't stay dead, Theo."

He looked up from his watch, wrinkling his forehead in confusion, and leaned closer. "What? What do you mean?"

Gray pulled the mask away from his face so he could speak more clearly. "I mean just that," he said. "She died, and then she came back and attacked me."

Theo thought of the patient he'd picked up at the accident site earlier that night. "You know what the scary thing is?" He pushed the mask firmly against Gray's face and looped the elastic strap around his head. "That's not the craziest thing I've heard all day. Or seen, for that matter."

"What happened?" Gray asked, trying to pull the mask back down.

Theo kept his hand on it, preventing him from moving it. "Breathe the meds in, damn it," he snapped. "Jon and I had an MVA to work. The patient kept trying to attack us. We tied him down to the stretcher, but he still kept coming, and..." He shook his head. "I killed the guy." His voice cracked, much to his disgust, and he turned away from Gray, focusing on the trauma bag. He started idly pushing supplies around.

"I'm sorry." Gray shifted to sit with his back against the wall and pulled his knees to his chest, reclining his head back on the sheetrock. "What the hell's going on? It's like the whole fucking world's gone crazy tonight."

Theo pressed his lips together and studied his brother closely for any further signs of distress while thinking over what he'd said. "Maybe it has," he said. "I'm thinking maybe...I don't know. A biological attack? Maybe nuclear?"

"Maybe," Gray said, his voice heavy with doubt, and Theo silently agreed. It was a ridiculous idea. Nuclear accidents wouldn't make people behave that way. It'd just kill them.

"Damn, I wish you had a TV," Theo said. He pulled a pulse ox from his bag and took Gray's hand, slipping the sensor on a finger and turning it on to measure Gray's blood-oxygen levels and heart rate. "You got any idea what the hell might be going on?"

"Zombies," Gray said. "It's got to be zombies."

"Zombies?" he asked incredulously. "I think you've been watching too many horror movies."

"Jack said the same thing," Gray said. "But what if I'm right? I mean, April. She was dead. Stone cold fucking *dead*. You taught me how to check for that kind of thing. She was dead. No way someone could've survived that kind of blood loss. She *got back up* and attacked me. No way that's possible unless it's zombies."

"We're not living in a Romero movie," he said, his thoughts flickering back to his patient and what he'd said to Jonathan at the time: "*He's got the vitals of a dead man, but he's kicking like he's still alive.*" "Zombies don't exist," he said, despite his internal misgivings. "No way. It's not physically, humanly possible."

"They're *in*human and *un*natural," Gray countered. "That's why they're called the *un*dead."

"Just sit back and breathe, okay?" Theo said. "I'm going to find a radio, get some idea of what's going on out there. When you're feeling better, we're going to head for Mom and Dad's house." *After a couple of stops, that is,* he added silently.

"We need weapons," Gray said. "Guns or something. A headshot is supposed to kill zombies, right?"

"I thought I told you to shut up and breathe," Theo retorted. He noted Gray's oxygen saturation and turned the pulse ox off, shoving it back into his bag. He stood and stretched, then gathered the discarded plastic packaging from the supplies he'd used. He looked Gray over one more time, noting how much better he already looked. The blue tinge to his lips was gone, and he didn't look so pale and desperate anymore. "I'm going to see what food you've got," he said. "We should get supplies together while we can. You stay here and relax and let the drugs do the work."

Once the kitchen door was shut behind him, Theo slumped against the wall beside it, burying his face in his hands and letting out a slow, shuddering breath. The horror of what he'd done in the ambulance, what he'd seen happen to Jonathan, and what he'd encountered on his race to Gray's apartment pounded at his temples, and he struggled to block the images from his mind. He couldn't protect his younger brother and couldn't go after Dillon if he was too focused on the hellish thoughts rattling through his brain. Because ultimately, Gray and Dillon were his priorities, and he was going to do whatever it took to keep them alive.

Even if it meant committing murder.

Thoughts of Dillon prompted Theo to reach for his cell phone, and he pulled it free from his pocket, scrolling to Dillon's name in his contacts list and selecting it. He put the phone to his ear, his nerves fluttering as it rang, stirring up fear at what he'd do if Dillon didn't answer.

"*Theo?*" Dillon's voice came through the line, and Theo felt the tension in his shoulders immediately begin to melt away.

"Dillon, are you okay?"

"*Yeah, I'm okay,*" he replied. "*What's going on out there? Things are getting crazy as shit out there, and it's only gotten worse since I got home.*"

"I don't know, but things have been bad," he said. He glanced at the kitchen door and lowered his voice. "We wrecked the ambulance. Jonathan's dead. And my patient tried to kill me."

"*Jesus, are you okay?*" Dillon asked, and Theo could hear the rising panic in his voice.

"I'm fine," he assured him. "I'm not hurt, other than a bump on the head. I'm with my brother at his place." He paused, contemplating all of their options, and settled on his best course of action. "Look, do me a favor, Dill."

"*Anything.*"

"Close up and lock down," he instructed. "Bolt your doors, barricade them, do whatever it takes for you to stay safe. Get yourself a weapon and hole up."

"*And then?*"

"Wait. Stay there," he said. "And stay safe. I'll be there as soon as I can. How's your father?"

"*Not good,*" Dillon replied. "*The power went out an hour ago, and his oxygen...*" He didn't need to say anymore.

"Okay," he said. "We'll worry about that later." He didn't say what he was thinking: *You're more important to me than he is.* He ran a hand through his hair, tousling it. "Just stay safe, okay? Don't leave the house for anything. I'll be there soon."

"*Theo, be careful,*" Dillon said hurriedly, like he was afraid he'd not get them out before Theo hung up.

"Of course," he said. "I'll see you in a while." He hung up then, tucking the phone into his pocket. He shoved away from the wall and went to the nearest cabinet, looking inside without really seeing what was in front of him. His mind spun, going over everything he knew about survival, considering everything he'd require to keep the three of them alive. They'd definitely need better weapons; he wasn't sure the fire axe and crowbar would continue to be a reliable means of protection.

Theo wanted a gun.

The thought was foreign to him. He'd certainly never shot a person before. He didn't have much experience with firearms beyond the instruction his father had given him as a teenager. He'd never been interested in instruments that could cause injury or death. Gray, on the other hand, had gone out hunting with their father on more than one occasion. While shooting deer was a world apart from shooting a human, he thought maybe Gray could do it if necessary.

Gray'll be a far better shot than me, that's for sure, he thought wryly.

Theo grabbed a couple of packages of ramen noodles and a pan and got the noodles boiling on the stove. While he emptied the cabinets of all the nonperishable food he could find, the kitchen door squeaked behind him. He looked over his shoulder to see Gray standing in the kitchen doorway, the mask still on his face and the oxygen tank in his hand. He noted how much better his color looked.

"You okay?" he asked. Gray nodded and set the tank on the counter. "I think you'll be okay to take the mask off now. You look a hell of a lot better than you did a while ago. I still want you to take it easy, though."

Gray pulled the mask off, dropping it onto the counter by the tank with a sigh. "What are you doing?" he asked, his voice still hoarse.

"Making us something to eat." Theo snagged a fork from the dish drainer by the sink and stirred the noodles. "Figure it won't do any good for us to starve to death while waiting on everything to calm down. Besides, I didn't get the chance to eat my dinner before the...before the whole mess with the ambulance."

Gray took a chair at the two-seater dining table, spinning it around to sit in it backwards. He looked at Theo, the reluctance in his eyes obvious. "Didn't you have a partner?" he asked. "Like, the guy who drove your ambulance for you?"

"Yeah," he said. He didn't want to talk about this. Not even with Gray. The snap of the gunshot was still audible in his ears. He turned his back on Gray and stirred the noodles again, lifting some with his fork to see how done they were.

"Where did he go?"

Theo sighed and turned off the stove, reaching for the flavoring packets. "He's dead," he said. "Got shot in the head."

"Jesus, I'm sorry," Gray said. "What...what's the plan? What are we gonna do?"

"I want to get us to Mom and Dad's," Theo said, "and I don't want to wait too long. Things might get worse the more time passes. We've got the TV and Internet and those generators Dad bought after the hurricanes. A heck of a lot more supplies, too." He stirred the flavor packets in. "I've also got a couple of stops I need to make before we get out there, too."

Gray seemed more animated at the prospect of doing something proactive. "So when do we leave?"

Theo spooned the hot noodles into two bowls before answering. "As soon as possible."

* * *

En Route to Gadsden, AL

It didn't take Ethan long to move Lisa's body out of the Jeep's backseat. He laid her body out on the passenger side of the vehicle so she couldn't be seen from the highway until after they'd left, covering her with a blanket before moving back to the car to scrub blood out of the seat. Cade waited on the side of the road, her back to the blanket-covered body. Her shoulders were so tense that he could see her stiffness from where he stood.

Ethan ran his hand through his hair, pushing blond strands away from his eyes and scrutinizing the darkened interior of the Jeep. It looked like he'd gotten as much blood as would be possible out of the seat, but the faint scent of metal hung in the air. He wrinkled his nose and took a step back from the open door. He and Cade were probably going to end up driving to Gadsden with the windows rolled down, despite the chill biting into the air around them.

"How's it coming?" Cade called. She didn't look at him, just kept her eyes on the traffic passing along the highway. He felt another pang of worry. He knew this wasn't the first time the Israeli woman had been involved in a killing. It wasn't his first time, either. Their histories had put them in the occasional situation where it'd been necessary to pull the trigger. Somehow, though, this time felt different. This time felt more like murder, despite the threat Lisa had posed to them. Maybe it was the fact he'd known her in life that made her death so different for him.

Abandoning the car, he walked to Cade, standing beside her in companionable silence and watching the traffic. He wondered where all the people were going, where they thought they could escape to. North? East? West? He knew it was only a matter of time before whatever caused all this chaos spread to other cities—and possibly even other countries.

Ethan let out a weighty sigh and shook free from his thoughts. He hooked an arm around Cade's shoulder, pulled her close, and squeezed her gently. "I think the car is about as clean as it's going to get," he told her.

She leaned into his side and asked, "What are we going to do?"

"Ideally, we'll get to Gadsden, like we planned," he said, leaning his head against hers. "And when we get there, we're going to meet up with Mom and then hole up and not think about anything for a while. A long while, if I can help it."

"And after that?"

"We'll cross that bridge when we get to it, okay?" he said. He took a step away from her and tugged at her arm. "Come on. We need to get moving. I'll drive for a while."

Ethan could sense the gratitude in the look she gave him, even in the darkness around them. She pulled away and circled the Jeep to the passenger side, stepping delicately around Lisa's body to climb in. He considered not moving on until the highway was clear of cars. But that could take hours, and he didn't think they had hours. Resigned to the likelihood that someone would see Lisa's body on the side of the road at some point, he climbed in the Jeep, put it in gear, and headed down the highway once more.

Cade and Ethan traveled in silence for over two hours, the radio the only sound between them. As they listened to the frantic reports on the airwaves, Ethan dialed his mother's number repeatedly, but he kept getting the operator informing him that his call could not be completed. He swore as the operator's mechanical voice spoke into his ear, slamming the phone down into the console between the seats. "Fucking phones are down," he grumbled.

Cade pushed her windblown hair out of her face and rolled up her window halfway. She pulled her leather jacket tighter around herself. "Can't get in touch with your mom?"

"No, and I'm worried," he admitted, slowing the Jeep as he approached a very long line of glowing tail-lights. "The radio's mentioned—"

"Birmingham," Cade finished. Gadsden wasn't far from Birmingham in the grand scheme of things. It wasn't beyond the realm of possibility that the escalating violence had reached Gadsden, and they were both fully aware of it. "I know. I heard."

Ethan fell silent as nightmarish thoughts swirled in his head. He had no idea what he was going to find once he and Cade reached Gadsden, but he had a suspicion that it'd be something he wouldn't like. He tightened his grip on the steering wheel and glanced at Cade. She'd picked up his phone and had begun scrolling through his contacts list.

"Have you tried sending a text message?" she asked, starting to type with her thumbs on the touchscreen. "Sometimes if the network is overloaded with voice calls, it's easier to get a text to slip through."

Ethan's cheeks flushed with heat as he shook his head. He was honestly embarrassed that he hadn't thought of that. "No, I haven't," he said. "My mother doesn't text. I'm kind of in the habit of not sending them to her."

Cade continued pecking out her message on his phone. "Well, I'm sending her one anyway." She finished the message and hit the send button, then set the phone back in the console before looking out the windshield at the cars ahead. "Is there any way we can get around this damned traffic? I don't feel comfortable getting stuck in it. God only knows what'll happen with so many people around."

Ethan grabbed the map book and flipped back through it to examine the map of Alabama. "We're over the state line now, aren't we?" he asked. He squinted through the windshield, searching for a road sign to give him a hint of their location.

"I think I saw a sign back there that said something about Jasper," she suggested. He found Jasper on the map and started measuring the distance between it and Gadsden with his fingers.

"We want to avoid Birmingham itself," he said, walking his fingers over the paper. "And the way I normally go to Mom's takes us right through Birmingham. We should get off on Highway 69 up ahead and cut up above Birmingham."

"Sounds like a plan," Cade said. She twisted around to retrieve her heavy black rifle case from the backseat, setting it across her knees reverently and nearly hitting him with it in the process. "Can I have the key, please?"

"Key?" he repeated. "What are you doing?"

She shrugged innocently. "Doesn't hurt to be prepared, does it? Now, key please."

He sighed and shoved his hand in his pocket, pulling out the silver key. He didn't hand it to her right away; instead, he closed his fist over it and stared at her as the Jeep idled in the stalled traffic. "You're not going to get us in trouble, are you?"

"No, I'm not," she said. "I barely even have any ammo for it. It's just a precaution, Eth. Always be prepared and all that shit."

Ethan snorted and shook his head ruefully. "You weren't even in the Girl Scouts, Cade," he pointed out, surrendering the key.

"And you weren't exactly a Boy Scout, but the idea still holds true, doesn't it?" she said. She took the key with a look of almost unholy glee on her face.

"Why do I get this horrible feeling I'm going to regret handing you that key?"

"Probably because you know me *entirely* too well."

* * *

New Orleans, LA

Remy saw her first sick person up close and personal when she and Marc walked out of his house just after dawn. Marc had spent most of the time gathering supplies from around his house while she'd finished her meal and taken a nap on the couch. She felt groggy despite the sleep, and she suspected it hadn't been enough. Then again, she was used to getting about twelve hours of sleep whenever she crashed, staying in bed until the afternoon sun cast light across her pillow. She'd stretched, yawned, accepted the bowl of cereal Mark had offered her, and ate it while she trawled through the news stations that broadcast information not only for the city of New Orleans, but for the nation at large. More of the stations had begun broadcasting while she'd napped, tossing aside pre-recorded broadcasts from the evening before and the talk shows filled with bitter, shrill-voiced women and the infomercials advertising the latest fad in cooking and weight loss to focus on the problems that had invaded their normally lively city overnight.

"Anything new?" Marc asked, crossing the doorway that separated the living room from the kitchen, carrying a case of bottled water.

"Not much," Remy called as he disappeared from view. She heard him kick the garage door open, followed by the thuds of his feet as he descended into the garage. A moment later, she heard the sound of one of the cruiser's doors opening and closing, and then he rejoined her in the house.

"They've confirmed that it *is* a virus," she continued, "and that it appears to have originated in Atlanta. A lot of commentators think the CDC is to blame."

"Of course," Marc said snidely. He disappeared again, and Remy heard him opening cabinets, pulling objects out, setting them onto the counter. "The world is probably ending, and the news networks drag on experts and commentators."

Remy finished off her bowl of cereal and set the dish on the coffee table, then put her shoes back on and joined Marc in the kitchen, taking the dish with her. "Just set it in the sink," Marc said distractedly. He was organizing canned food in neat rows. A cardboard box with the Amazon logo printed on the side sat on the counter nearby, the handles of a couple of cooking pots sticking up from inside it.

"What are you doing?" she asked.

"Getting food together to take with us," he answered.

"You think we're going to need all that?"

"I'm running on the assumption that I won't be coming back here," he said. "Worst thing that could happen is I have to unload a bunch of groceries out of my patrol car once this is over."

"But you think we'll need it," she said. For some reason, looking at the rows of canned food and boxes of dehydrated potato flakes gave her an unsettled feeling, and the sight of it hammered home the reality of what they faced.

"Yeah, I think we're going to need it," Marc said. "Considering the speed this appears to be spreading, things are going to get a hell of a lot worse before they get better."

"That doesn't make *me* feel any better."

"It's the unfortunate reality," Marc said. He stared at the canned food, studying the label on a can of English peas. "You said you know how to shoot, right?"

"A rifle," Remy said. "But not very well." She glanced at the pistol he wore, which was in a holster on a belt wrapped around his hips. "I could adjust if I have to use a handgun."

"Good, because you'll have to," he said. "I don't own a rifle, only small arms."

"Fine. I can handle it."

Marc reached into the cardboard box and withdrew a belt with a single holstered revolver hanging from it, offering it to her wordlessly. She wrapped the slightly oversized belt around her waist, fastening it with the Velcro closure. "Be careful with it," he said. "I don't want you accidentally shooting yourself with it."

"Aye, aye, *el capitan*," Remy said with thinly veiled sarcasm. She fiddled with the strap holding the revolver in its holster, unsnapping it a few times, trying to adapt to the weight of a pistol belt around her waist. It felt absurdly heavy, like it would throw her off balance the moment she attempted to take a few steps in any direction. She imagined running from a horde of sick people and falling because of the unaccustomed weight of the weapon. She didn't want to imagine what would come after that.

The idea was a bit absurd, she knew, but it didn't change that niggling worry lurking in the back of her brain. She squared her shoulders, trying to toughen up, and pasted a smile on her face. "When are we leaving?"

"Ten minutes," he replied. "If you need to go to the bathroom, now's a good time."

Ten minutes later, they stepped out of the house into the early morning air, and that was when Remy first saw the woman.

She stood in the middle of the street, looking oddly forlorn, like she was lost. Her long blonde hair fell in a knotted, tangled mess past her shoulders, leaves and twigs entwined in the strands. Her blue jeans were ripped and torn, and her t-shirt was half off, hanging limply on her right side, exposing her multi-colored polka-dot bra. She looked like she'd been assaulted, and if it weren't for the blood all over her clothes and face and the manic look in her eyes, Remy would have gone forward to help her. However, some animal part of her brain warned her not to go near the woman; she looked dangerous, like she wanted to take a chunk out of Remy's throat.

"Marc…" Remy said warningly, keeping her voice low. He looked up and past her, spotting the woman.

"Stay away from her," he murmured. "She might be dangerous."

Feeling sick to her stomach, she nodded. Her hand shaking, she reached for the passenger door handle, curled her fingers around it, and tugged. At the same moment, the woman in the street raced forward with a look of fury on her face. Remy gasped and pulled on her revolver; the strap was still buckled over it, though, and when she yanked, the belt merely slid a couple of inches up her hip. Marc was much faster on the draw, and he had his pistol out and pointed at the woman before Remy could unsnap the strap on her holster.

"Remy, get in the car!"

"Are you—" she started.

"In the car!" he repeated, his voice stern but not angry, just hard enough to show he meant business. She opened the door and slid inside, and once she was in her seat, she turned, trying to watch what was happening outside. The sound of a single gunshot outside rocked through the silence, and Remy jumped, banging her head against the passenger window. The driver's door opened, and Remy rocked back in her seat reflexively, alarmed, thinking maybe it was that woman climbing into the car, but her brain calmed from its tizzy the moment she saw it was Marc.

"What happened out there?"

He turned the key in the ignition, and the engine roared to life. "I don't want to talk about it," he said, not looking at her as he shifted the car into reverse.

"But I heard...did you..."

"You didn't hear anything." He gunned the engine, and the car roared backwards, thudding over something that felt like a speed bump but at the same time was distinctly *not*. Remy squeezed her eyes shut and clutched her armrest, deciding resolutely to not look at the reality in front of her in favor of studying the insides of her eyelids. Things were much more pleasant in the darkness.

"You okay?" Marc asked after a long silence, and Remy startled again. She hadn't realized it, but she'd started dozing a bit, despite her fitful sleep the night before. She blinked her eyes open and rubbed them, then raked her messy, tangled hair out of her face. "You look rattled."

"Yeah?" she said. "You don't, and I think that's what surprises me."

"I'm just telling myself it's part of my job," he said. "As a cop, you always expect that one of the times you pull your weapon, you'll be forced to squeeze the trigger. I've been lucky enough to never have to do it before." The unspoken "*until now*" was heard loud and clear in the space between them.

Remy looked out the window. Marc's statement was a tacit admission of what he'd done. She tried to picture it, the way his wrist would have kicked back when he squeezed the trigger, the flight of the bullet closing the distance between him and the woman, the back of her skull as it blew out and sprayed brain matter and blood on the road behind her. She didn't know if he'd shot her in the head. Intellectually, she knew that police officers were taught to fire at center mass, but her brain couldn't let go of the idea of him taking a head shot.

Marc slammed on brakes, sending her sliding forward on her leather seat. She caught herself against the dash. "What the hell?" she yelped, and she looked through the windshield and saw exactly what had made him hit the brakes.

"Oh hell." She pressed back in her seat like she could melt right through it, clutching her armrest and trying not to scream, though she could feel one attempting to bubble up. "Marc..."

"I see it," he said.

There was no way he could have *missed* it, not with the way the entire street was blocked. They were on a narrow side road that was a bit off the beaten path, one less subject to the tourist traffic clogging many other roadways; however, that hadn't stopped a large number of sick people from finding it. There were dozens of them, packing the street from sidewalk to sidewalk, spilling back down the road for several blocks. The crowd was made of all manner of people: men, women, young, old, black, white.... There was even a priest near the head of the pack, his once-white collar stained red with blood. Even though the windows were closed, Remy could smell the pure, animalistic stench of them, that odd scent of old blood and other bodily fluids she didn't want to think about, hovering over the street like a miasma.

Remy had just registered these sights, rapid fire, her brain barely processing the images, when they started moving toward the cruiser. "Get us out of here, Marc!"

"Working on it!"

Marc shifted gears, the tires squealed on the pavement, and the car raced backwards. Remy grabbed the armrest with both hands as he drove the car backwards the way they'd come, unable to take her eyes off the scene in front of them. The sick people—*infected*—broke into a run, slow at first, then gaining speed and momentum, and started chasing them down the street.

"Oh God, Marc, they're coming this way," she squeaked, her voice barely loud enough to be heard over the roar of the engine.

"I'm aware, Remy!" Marc growled.

Remy looked at him. He was turned around in his seat, looking back behind the car, squinting through the cage separating the front and back seats. He steered the car relatively straight, considering he was driving backwards. The sick people were gaining on them because Marc just couldn't drive *fast enough* this way, and as the leading edge of the crowd thudded into the car's grill and grabbed ahold of it, she knew in that second that she was going to die.

"No, no, nonono," she chanted, the repetitions running together in her panic. She jammed her feet against the floorboard, pressing her shoulders back into the seat, like those couple of inches might mean the difference between life and death.

"Hang on!" Marc yelled and whipped the car around, tires squealing as they skidded, coming to a stop in a near-

180 degree turn. Two of the sick people clutching the grill tumbled away with the momentum of the turn, falling out of sight. Then he shifted gears and slammed his foot on the gas. The car shot forward, pressing her back into her seat, and she gasped and threw her hands into the air like she was on a roller coaster.

"Yes!" she cried. "You did it!"

"Not in the clear yet," Marc warned her.

He had his eyes fixed on the windshield, his hands fastened to the wheel like he was a drowning man and it was his life preserver. He cut the wheel to the right, barely avoiding two cars fender-bendered in the middle of the road, and swerved onto a side street. It was blessedly clear of sick people, but several cars were parked along the sidewalk on either side, abandoned by their owners.

"Where are we?" she asked. "I've lost track."

"I think I have too," Marc admitted. He was leaned forward in his seat, squinting out the windshield, his eyes scanning every inch of the road ahead, presumably looking for a street sign. "Look for anything you recognize."

"You're a cop," Remy said. "I thought you guys were supposed to know your territory better than this."

"This isn't my territory," he told her. "I patrol the area where that convenience store you knocked over happens to be located."

"I did *not* knock over that store," she protested. "I think what I did was technically shoplifting. A misdemeanor, I'll have you know."

"I'm aware," he said. "Consider the charges dropped."

Remy laughed. The absurdity of having *this* conversation with her arresting officer at *this* point in time wasn't lost on her. "So how come you don't know the city that well?" she asked. "I mean, I've lived here all my life, and I usually can get around pretty easily if I'm paying attention."

"Because I'm not from here," he said. "I'm originally from Baton Rouge. I only moved here three years ago." He tapped the brakes and steered around another vehicle, this one sticking out a bit too far into the street, and on the sidewalk nearby, Remy spotted what looked like two men hunched over the body of a woman. There was blood, so much blood. She shuddered and looked away, not wanting to know where that blood was coming from.

"Well, that explains a lot," she said. She shifted her eyes forward, determined not to look back at the men on the side-walk again as the cruiser rolled past. "What made you move to NOLA?"

"Think we can talk about this later?" he asked. "Like, maybe when we're not in the shit and I'm not trying to keep us from getting killed?"

Remy flopped back in her seat with a huff. "Fine. Geez. Sorry. I was just trying to keep my mind off shit."

Marc's expression softened. "Yeah, I just need to focus. I don't want to wreck." He turned his head from side to side, like he was studying the lay of the land, and a smile flickered across his face. "I think I know where we are."

Remy blew out a breath of relief. "Oh thank God."

"I should be able to get us out of h—"

The thud of the body bouncing against the hood interrupted the rest of what he'd been about to say. Remy gasped, and Marc slammed on the brakes instinctively, the tires squealing on the pavement.

"No, no, don't stop!" Remy screeched. The horrible mental image of the two men bending over the corpse of that woman flickered through her mind, and she banged a fist against the dash. "Go, Marc, go!"

It was too late. A flood of people emerged from alleys, doorways, and the shelter of cars and poured across the street toward them.

"Oh shit!" Marc exclaimed. He shifted into reverse, intending to back down the street like before, but the route behind them was blocked, so there was no escape that way. More sick people were coming down the street from the direction they'd been heading.

Remy whipped her head in either direction, searching for a gap they could flee through, but there wasn't one. They were trapped. Solidly and irrevocably trapped.

"Oh God, Marc, we're going to die here," Remy moaned as the crowd converged on the cruiser. "We can't get out of here, and we're going to die here."

"No, you're not," Marc said, his voice strong, his jaw set with determination. He stared at the mess beyond the car, unblinkingly. "You're not going to die here." He shifted the car into park, unbuckled his seatbelt, and reached for his gun. "Get in the driver's seat," he said, not looking at her. "When you see an opening, take it."

"Wait, where are *you* going?" Remy demanded, grabbing his arm to keep him from moving.

"We need a distraction," Marc said. He had to raise his voice to be heard over the sick and violent; the crowd had begun slapping their fists and palms against the car in a discordant, disorienting rhythm. "I'm going to create one."

"But...how will you get back to the car?" Remy asked, her voice weak.

"I won't be able to," Marc said. "I have to draw them away while you get out of here." He gave her a tight smile.

"Don't worry. I'll be fine. I know where you live. I'll catch up with you there."

That was a lie. She knew it, and he knew it. Nevertheless, it didn't stop him from reaching for the door's handle. He popped the lock on the door, then she grabbed his arm again and tugged it. "Come here," she said, and she dragged him halfway across the console between them and pressed her mouth to his.

It wasn't a spectacular kiss, not by any means, most certainly not the best she'd ever given. But the meaning behind it was more important, and she hoped Marc realized what it was.

A goodbye.

He gave her a somewhat mournful look when he pulled away, his eyes searching her face, like he was committing every inch of her to memory. "Be careful," he said, and then he was gone, shoving his way out of the car into the crowd outside without a backwards glance. As he did so, a sick man grasped the door and wrenched at it, trying to get to Remy. She heard gunfire outside the car, and she added her own to it, ripping the revolver from its holster and pointing it at the man, squeezing the trigger twice in rapid succession. The man staggered backward, and Marc kicked the door, slamming it shut.

He was out of the vehicle for several moments before Remy climbed into the driver's seat. Her heart felt as if it was rattling in her chest like a castanet, and her lungs heaved, struggling to take in enough air past her terror. She shifted in the leather driver's seat, clutching the steering wheel with one hand and the gearshift in the other, waiting for her moment as she struggled to see past the tears swimming in her eyes.

"Damn it, Marc," she whispered. She didn't understand why he'd been so quick to run off. He could have stayed with her. They could have made a different plan. Now he was gone, bailed.

There was nothing she could do. He was already out of the car and out of sight, the people attacking the car had followed, and the crowd behind the car was thinning. She hesitated, wondering if she should try to follow him, but his instructions had been clear. She shifted into reverse and let the car roll backward under its own power.

Driving backward was more difficult than Marc had made it look, and she clipped more than a few vehicles until she reached a point where she could turn around. Then she slammed her foot against the gas and raced away, not daring to look back.

She was too scared that, if she did, she'd see Marc on the ground, splayed out and bloodied, people hunched over him.

CHAPTER NINE

Plantersville, MS

Shivering, Gray followed Theo out of his apartment early the next morning. He'd found another jacket before they left, and he wrapped it tighter around himself, looking down the street warily. Morning still hadn't fully dawned yet, and the street was cast in a haze that left a bluish tint over everything. The air smelled damp and smoky. Gray gripped the crowbar Theo had given him tightly. He didn't like being outside, not even with his brother. It felt too dangerous, like someone was watching every move they made; he could practically feel eyes on his back. He shivered again and hurried to catch up with Theo, who'd begun walking down the street at a brisk pace.

"Where are we heading again?" he asked, matching his pace to Theo's.

"Did you not listen to a word I said this morning?" Theo asked with thinly veiled annoyance.

"Well, no. I was eating."

"We're heading for the ambulance base," Theo said. His eyes darted around in a manner that, at any other time, would have struck Gray as paranoid. As it was, he was sure his own eyes were doing the same thing. "My car is parked there. We need to get it so we can make it to the house." He seemed like he was leaving something out, his tone hinting at an evasiveness that meant he was up to something. Gray chose not to say anything about it. Yet.

"We could walk to the house," he suggested. He wasn't keen on the idea of going deeper into the hostile city to pick up Theo's car. Especially since there were so many other options around them. "I can make it."

"I'd rather we not risk it," Theo replied. "I only have so much albuterol and O2, and I want to save it for an emergency." He cast a sidelong glance at Gray, and he shifted uncomfortably under his brother's scrutiny. "That said, we do need to get you some inhalers, don't we?"

"Where do you propose we get some?" Gray asked. "It's not like we can just walk into a pharmacy and get a prescription filled."

"True, but we *can* just walk into a pharmacy," Theo said. "Nobody said a pharmacist has to be there."

"Isn't that breaking and entering?" Gray asked, looking Theo over. He'd never struck him as the type to advocate illegal activities, and now there he was, proposing they break into a pharmacy to steal asthma inhalers. Wonders never ceased.

"Oh, come off it, Gray," Theo said. "You should know by now that I'd do whatever it took to keep you breathing. Besides, it's not like we'll get *arrested* for it. The police, I imagine, have more important things to deal with right now. *If* they're even still functioning."

"If that's the case, why don't we just take one of these cars?" Gray asked, waving his hand at the street around them. "It'd be better than walking all the way to the base for yours. I could hotwire one and get us moving a hell of a lot faster."

Theo looked at him with undisguised curiosity. "You know how to hotwire a car?"

"Damn straight," Gray said. "It's one of the first things I learned how to do to a car."

They walked silently while Theo thought his suggestion over. Gray glanced between his brother and the street. He felt antsy; he wished Theo would make up his mind so they could get out of there. Finally, Theo asked, "You haven't ever actually, you know, *stolen* a car before or anything, have you?"

"No, of course not!" he protested. "Do I *look* like the type of person who'd run around stealing—" He caught sight of movement in the corner of his eye and tensed, grabbing Theo's arm to stop him. "Did you see that?"

"See what?" Theo asked, tugging his arm free and moving in front of him protectively, much to Gray's annoyance. If he didn't know better, he'd think Theo believed he couldn't take care of himself.

"I saw something moving over there," Gray answered. He pointed to the coffee shop across the street; the shop itself was dark, the front windows broken and glass littering the sidewalk and street. "I don't know what it was, though. But I'm not sure I liked the way it was moving."

"What do you mean?"

"I don't know how to describe it," he said. "He was moving sort of…I don't know, jerky? Like he couldn't walk right. Like he was hurt or something."

Theo suddenly looked more alert. "Hurt? Think they need help?"

"I vote we keep moving," Gray said. Something about the whole situation, something about the way the figure had moved…it made him uneasy. He pulled at Theo's arm again.

"Come on, let's just go. Don't worry about it. Every man for himself and all that shit, you know?"

Theo visibly wavered between moving on like Gray suggested and tracking down a possibly injured man and helping him. Then he nodded. "Okay, fine, you're right. We should just get moving. We don't have time to worry about anyone else right now."

No sooner had the words left his mouth than something darted across the street and slammed into him, driving him to the sidewalk. He grunted when he impacted with the concrete, his bag crunching under him, and he instinctively put his hands out to block the attack. Gray grabbed the back of the man's jacket and dragged him off his brother, swinging him around and against the side of a parked car.

The man regained his balance awkwardly, standing on an obviously broken leg. He turned to face Gray, and Gray recoiled at the look on his face, a mix of hate and hunger, a predatory look. Just like the look April had given him. He sucked in a breath and lifted the crowbar, holding it like it was a baseball bat.

"Stay back!" Theo commanded, regaining his feet and joining Gray, axe in hand. "Stay back, you hear me?"

Gray eyed their attacker. "He's not listening. I'm not sure he's *capable* of listening."

"Yeah, I know your zombie theory," Theo said. "Should we run?"

"He'll just follow us." The man stepped toward them, and he shoved him back again with the crowbar. "You know what we have to do, right?"

"I'm trying to not think about it."

The man took another shuffling step forward, and Gray adjusted his stance before swinging the crowbar, slamming the curved side of the hook into the man's head. The man's temple gave with a crunch, and he collapsed against the car. Despite the deep indentation in the side of his head, a blow that would have killed or at least incapacitated anyone else, he was up and coming after them again immediately.

"Jesus," Theo gasped. He grabbed Gray's jacket and dragged him back. "Jesus, why didn't that kill him? That should have killed him!"

"I *told* you!" Gray crowed, waving the crowbar at their attacker. "I *told* you they were fucking zombies!"

Theo shoved him aside, and Gray watched in horrified fascination as he swung the axe into their attacker's forehead. The crunch of bone sent a chill of disgust up his spine. The man still stood, held up only by the axe embedded in his skull, still gripped in Theo's hands. Theo stood in wide-eyed shock, staring at the man in front of him like he couldn't believe what he'd just done. Gray could see fine tremors running through his shoulders.

"We need to go," he told Theo, trying to shake him out of it. "We've got to find a car. The ambulance base and the pharmacy, remember?"

Theo tightened his grip on the axe and wrenched it from the man's skull. Blood splattered onto one of his boots as the man collapsed to the pavement. Gray gingerly nudged the body with the toe of his shoe, testing to see if he was, in fact, dead. Once he was satisfied that the man would remain motionless, he looked at Theo again.

"Let's go," Theo said. "I think we should definitely use your hotwiring plan. I suddenly don't feel like walking all the way to the base anymore."

* * *

Gadsden, AL

Ethan pulled the SUV to a slow stop in front of his mother's house. It was just after dawn, and in the dim light, it was difficult to see the house. No light came from it or any other house nearby, and the street was dark. The lack of light made Cade nervous, and she gritted her teeth and leaned forward in her seat, clutching her rifle for comfort. She flipped the glove box and console open and asked, "You got a light, Eth?"

Ethan nodded and opened his door. "Yeah, there's one in my bag in the back," he said, getting out. Cade opened her own door and eased slowly out of the Jeep, lifting her rifle to her shoulder and sweeping the street. Her instincts screamed for her to get back in the Jeep, but she wasn't letting Ethan get out alone.

"What's with the gun?" Ethan asked, offering Cade the flashlight. She took it and turned it on, shining it over the front lawn of Ethan's mother's house as far as the beam would reach. She didn't see anything out of the ordinary—other than the oppressive darkness in the street.

"Rifle," she corrected automatically. "And I'm just taking adequate precautions." She spoke casually, but her tone didn't do much to mask the nerves kicking in her stomach. She kept the flashlight beam ahead of her as she made her way to the front door. "Your mom can yell at me for waving a rifle in her face later. I'm just trying to keep us from getting killed right now."

"Getting killed?" he repeated, following Cade up the concrete walkway. "You think it's that serious?"

"That's what my instincts are telling me," she said as she reached the front porch. "And I learned very quickly to listen to them in the IDF. They never failed me then, and I'm sure they won't now. Open the door."

Ethan followed her lead, drawing his Glock from its holster, pulling his keys out of his pocket, and thumbing through them to find the right one. Once he unlocked the door, he nudged it with his foot, swinging open with barely a sound and revealing an interior that was just as dark as the street outside. "Who's first?" he asked.

"I'll go," she volunteered. She pulled the keys from the lock and tossed them to him before slipping inside, scanning the dark entryway as she shone her flashlight across it. "Where would your mother most likely be?"

"Probably upstairs in her room," Ethan guessed. Cade frowned as she moved farther into the foyer to make room for him to enter behind her.

"Leave the door open," she said, dropping her voice to a hushed murmur, more out of an abundance of caution than anything else.

"Why?"

"Just in case we need to get out quick. Because I actually have a sense of self-preservation." She nodded toward the living room. "I'll check out the living room and kitchen. You hit the other rooms on this floor, then we'll go upstairs." She caught his forearm as he started to move past her. "Keep your eyes open and stay on guard. You never know what we'll find here. It's best to be prepared for the worst."

Cade closed her eyes for a moment as Ethan disappeared into the darkness, his footsteps echoing faintly against the walls. She suddenly felt horribly alone. In the absence of the one distracting element she'd had since their flight from Memphis, she found her mind sliding back to thoughts of Josie and Andrew. Tears pricked at her eyes, and she bit down hard on her lip, struggling to quell them and get back on the task at hand. Shouldering her rifle again, she moved on cats' feet toward the living room, barely making a sound.

Cade had been to Ethan's mother's house before, when Ethan had dragged her along to visit his mother after his father's death. The room looked almost exactly the same, though there were a few new pictures of Ethan and Anna lining the mantelpiece. She pointedly didn't look at the photos as she swept the rifle quickly over the room before easing along the wall to the kitchen.

Cade stopped short as she took in her initial sweep of the kitchen. Her eyes widened in surprise. The kitchen had been the scene of a tremendous fight. Canisters of flour and sugar had been knocked over and their contents spilled across the counter and onto the floor. A bowl of cereal lay broken and clotted on the breakfast table in the corner. Chairs were overturned. The open back door let in the frigid air from outside. The knife block in the center of the island counter lay on its side, the largest knife missing from its slot. Cade shone her light around to look for it and spotted a pool of partially congealed blood near the fridge, splashed across the wooden floorboards, and splattered on the bottom half of the refrigerator. She was unsure if it was enough blood to indicate that someone had died there, but it was enough for her to call for assistance.

"Ethan!" she yelled. "Kitchen, quick!"

It took Ethan only moments to meet her in the kitchen. She shone her flashlight beam around to show him the scene, and he stopped short two steps into the room and sucked in a sharp breath. "Jesus, what happened?" he asked.

"Your guess is as good as mine," she said. "It looks like there was a serious fight in here. You find your mom?"

"She isn't here," he confirmed. "I finished up downstairs quicker than I thought and checked out the second floor. No sign."

Cade went to the open back door and looked out across the backyard. A cold wind blew through her dark hair and inched underneath her jacket and flannel shirt. She shivered violently. "Maybe she got out of here," she suggested. "Think she might be at a neighbor's or somewhere nearby?"

"Maybe," Ethan said doubtfully. "We should check it out."

"Wait," Cade said. She stepped out onto the back deck, her boots thumping hollowly on the treated wooden planks. She studied the shadows of the backyard for anything unusual, her instincts still yammering at the back of her skull, clamoring for attention. She drew in a breath and stepped back inside, shutting the door and locking it behind her. "We should wait until the sun comes up. I want to be able to see everything around us."

"But my mom—"

"If your mom is at a neighbor's house, she'll be fine for another thirty minutes," Cade insisted, going to the front door to close and lock it too. "And if she's not at the neighbor's house..." She trailed off and let the implication hang in the air.

"Then there's nothing we can do for her," Ethan finished.

She nodded and retrieved a kitchen chair, setting it by the front door and sitting, studying the street outside in silence. Finally, she asked, "Are you okay?"

Ethan crouched on the floor beside her, balancing on the balls of his feet and dropping his forearms onto his thighs. "I don't know," he admitted, focusing on the floor. "I'm still trying to cope with Anna—" He broke off and shook his head. "And now maybe my mom too," he added.

Cade caught his hand and squeezed it gently. "And Josie," she said. She turned away and tried to look at the street outside the window again. The thought of the little girl hurt, so once again, she shoved it to the back of her mind where she could deal with it later.

Nearly an hour passed before Cade felt it was light enough outside. She rose to her feet and unlocked the front door, opening it cautiously. "I'm going to check out the neighbor's house," she said. "If you want, you can stay here in case your mom shows up."

Ethan hesitated before shaking his head and standing, drawing his pistol from its holster. "No, I'm going with you," he said. "Just in case you need some backup, you know? You're a good shot, but someone can still get the jump on you."

Cade smirked and raised an eyebrow, resting her rifle against her shoulder, barrel pointed toward the ceiling. "You say that like you have no confidence in my abilities," she said, stepping onto the front porch. Her mood lifted as she had something to focus on, a mission to accomplish.

"I just don't want you getting overconfident," he said, following her out the door. He lowered his voice as they left the safety of the house and moved toward the dawn-lit street.

"Eth, I was in the IDF for seven years," she pointed out. "I worked as a sniper for most of that time. I'm pretty sure I have a lock on not getting overconfident at this point."

Ethan chuckled, and she gave him a smile before descending the front steps. Her brain settled into its old military mindset, and she eased to the street with all her senses on high alert. There was no movement on the street, not a bird or a cat or a dog or a person, unusual for a residential neighborhood like this, and the lack of movement nagged at her like nothing else. She turned in a half-circle to sweep the yards on either side of them with her rifle as she walked toward the street.

"Where would she be most likely to go?" she asked, stopping to wait for Ethan to catch up.

"Probably Miss Jemison's house," Ethan said. "They've always been pretty close. Mom might have thought to go there for safety in numbers or to see if Miss Jemison needed any help."

"Where's that at?" Cade asked.

"About three houses down on the left." He pointed to the house. It was a stately brick affair, reasonably new, with a neatly landscaped front yard and a short fence surrounding the entire lot. It wasn't a fence designed for any level of serious protection, more decoration than anything else.

Before Cade and Ethan had passed even one house, Cade saw movement in the corner of her right eye. She froze, her shoulders tensing in a moment of indecision. Then she turned on her heel and moved to stand between Ethan and the threat presenting itself. It was a man, and he crossed the yard of the house across the street and headed directly toward them.

"Hey!" the man shouted. His eyes flicked to the rifle aimed directly at his head, and he skidded to a halt at the edge of the sidewalk. He lifted a gun of his own and pointed it at her. Ethan sidestepped from behind her to aim his own weapon at the man, prompting him to visibly tense, but he didn't change his stance.

"Who are you?" she demanded.

"Are you one of them?" the man countered.

"I asked you a question," she snapped.

The man ignored her, saying again, slowly and carefully, "Are you one of them?" His voice was strained.

"Are we one of *what*?" Cade asked, glaring at him. She'd never appreciated having a gun in her face, and it was only serving to piss her off.

"Are you infected?" the man asked impatiently.

It was as the man uttered those words that Cade noticed the way he stood. Despite the tenseness underlying his words, he wasn't physically tense at all. Indeed, he was nearly relaxed, his stance speaking of professionalism and expertise with the weapon he held. The idea of him being military or law enforcement flitted through her mind, even as she narrowed her eyes.

"Infected?" she repeated. "What the hell are you talking about?" She didn't dare look away as the man met her gaze. His eyes were warm and brown, flecked with hints of gold, and drew her in like a moth to flame. He hesitated, then removed a hand from his pistol and put it up in surrender, lowering the weapon to hang at his side.

"Put it down," Ethan ordered, speaking for the first time. "On the ground. Now."

The man sighed, the noise touched with a tinge of exasperation. He set the weapon on the ground at his feet; Cade noted the camouflage pants and scraped, dirty black combat boots the man wore. He straightened and held both hands out to his sides, like he was showing Cade and Ethan that they were both empty.

"Who are you?" Cade asked again now that they had the man unarmed. She suspected, though, that despite his weaponless state, he was far from defenseless.

The man made a cautious gesture at their surroundings and said, "It's not safe out here. We need to get inside."

"What's going on?" Ethan demanded as Cade lowered her rifle. He didn't put his own weapon away.

"I'll explain in a minute," the man said, heading back toward the house from which he'd come. "Once we're inside."

Cade lifted her rifle again as the man put his back to them. "Not until you tell us who the hell you are," she said to his back. He stopped and turned slowly to look at her. His dark eyes were curious as they skimmed over her entire body. Cade stiffened self-consciously but held her ground and kept her rifle steady.

"Interesting accent you have there," the man observed. "What is it, Middle Eastern? Israeli, maybe?" He stepped forward and held out a hand. "Lieutenant Brandt Evans, United States Marines."

Cade hesitated before lowering her rifle and offering her hand in return. "Cade Alton, former Israel Defense Forces," she replied.

"Enough with the fucking pleasantries," Ethan snapped. "Tell us what's going on."

"Like I said, we need to get inside first," Brandt said. He glanced down the street and at the pistol at his feet. He didn't try to pick it up. "Is that your SUV over there?" he asked Cade.

"It's Ethan's," she replied, gesturing to the man in question.

"Move it over here," Brandt said, pointing to the house behind him. "My base is inside. I'm assuming you've got supplies in that SUV? At the very least, it'll make a good escape vehicle in case we need it."

"Escape from *what*?" Ethan pressed.

"Eth, put the gun down," Cade ordered. She waited until he'd complied before adding, "Go get the Jeep. I'll deal with him."

"Cade, you don't know—"

"If it's safe?" she interrupted. "I can take care of myself. Now *go*."

Ethan gave Cade one more look that told her just how much he didn't like leaving her alone with a stranger. Then he nodded and headed to the Jeep. "So, Marines?" she questioned.

"Yeah, Marines," Brandt affirmed. "We're both military people, huh?" He paused and motioned to the house again. "Come on. Let's get inside. Ethan can take care of himself, right?" She nodded and followed him up the walkway after he'd retrieved his weapon from the sidewalk. "So where are you two from?"

"Memphis, Tennessee," Cade said. She raised an eyebrow as Brandt winced.

"Jesus, and you guys made it out of there alive?" Brandt asked. Disturbed by his incredulity, Cade grabbed his shoulder to stop him.

"What do you mean? What the hell are you talking about?"

"The virus," Brandt said as he gave her a strange look. "The one they're talking about on TV? It's almost completely wiped out Memphis overnight."

Cade raised her eyebrows and shook her head. "A virus?" she repeated as Ethan jogged up to them. "So it's true? A virus is actually causing all this? It's not just…rioting and shit?"

"The virus that's been spreading out from Atlanta, yeah," Brandt said, looking at Cade as if she'd lost her mind. "The one that's causing all these people to go crazy." He nodded toward the door. "Get inside. I'll explain."

"What about my mother?" Ethan asked softly as Cade started to step into the house.

Cade studied his face, trying to get a read on his emotions. Before she could speak, Brandt piped up to say, "If your mother lived on this street, she isn't here anymore. I've already been through the houses. You're the first person I've seen since yesterday afternoon."

"So where is everyone?" Cade asked, stepping inside and pulling Ethan after her.

"They were picked up throughout the day yesterday," Brandt said. "By the military for screening and possible quarantine. They're trying to contain the virus, but that'll never happen. It's out of their control. Out of *anyone's* control."

Ethan swore softly under his breath and shut the door behind them. He locked it and faced Brandt, crossing his arms. "And were you the one who spilled blood in my mother's kitchen?" he asked, fixing his cold eyes on Brandt.

Brandt raised an eyebrow in confusion. "What?"

"Ethan, stop it," Cade snapped, stepping between the two men. "You're not helping anything at all." She turned back to Brandt and resisted the urge to cross her own arms. "Now tell us what's going on," she said. "All we really know is what we've heard on the radio, and that isn't much. Just riots and murders."

"Sit down and relax," Brandt said, motioning to the floral-printed couch in the living room. Cade thought it looked hideous, but she sank onto the cushions nonetheless, setting her rifle on the seat beside her. Ethan took the spot to her left, sitting straight-backed and tense, watching every move Brandt made. "You two look like hell," Brandt commented. "I take it you haven't had any sleep."

"I take it you didn't either," Cade said. She'd noticed the dark circles under his brown eyes and the tightness of his face as soon as she'd seen him up close. He'd had at least one recent sleepless night.

"I haven't slept much in days," Brandt admitted. "Not since, well, not since all this shit started."

"But it only broke out in Memphis yesterday," Cade said, sitting straighter.

"It only broke out in *Memphis* yesterday," he corrected. "It's been going on in Atlanta to some degree for about a week."

Silence fell. Ethan and Cade stared at Brandt as he crossed his arms and leaned against the doorframe; Cade noticed he positioned himself where he could see both the living room and front door, like he was standing guard. He looked as if he were about to say something but didn't speak, instead waiting for one of them to break the silence.

"What's going on?" Cade asked.

Brandt rubbed his face with a hand. "I know some of what's going on, but I don't know everything," he said carefully. "And I don't know if what I know is very accurate. This is all being caused by some type of virus."

Ethan abandoned his quiet contemplation of his hands and looked up at Brandt like he was trying to gauge if he was serious.

"Its official name—at least, so I've heard—is RPV, or Regenerative Psychotic Virus," Brandt continued. "But it's becoming more commonly known as the Michaluk Virus."

"Why the Michaluk Virus?"

"Because as far as we know, the first guy who died from it was named Kevin Michaluk," he explained. "It started last week, as far as I know. An employee at the CDC got infected with it, and he passed it to everyone he came into contact with shortly after, and they passed it to everyone *they* came in contact with, and so on."

"How does that have anything to do with the riots in Memphis and, apparently, Alabama and Atlanta?" Cade asked.

"It's what the virus does to your mind," Brandt said, his expression hard and serious. "I can't say I completely understand how it works. I'm a military man, not a scientist. It's like it gets into your mind somehow, and it...it mutates whatever's there. It attacks the areas where anger and hatred are kept. The victims of the virus become, well, homicidal. They develop a taste for violence, for blood and...and flesh."

Ethan and Cade stared at Brandt. "For...flesh," she repeated slowly, raising her eyebrows. "Like zombies or some shit?"

"Something like that," Brandt said.

"Treatment?" Ethan questioned.

"As far as I know, there isn't one."

"Well, that's fucking great," Cade muttered, frowning and flopping back against the couch. "How does it spread?"

"I'm not a hundred percent sure," Brandt admitted. "Initially, the virus was airborne, but that variant died pretty quickly. I haven't seen an airborne case of Michaluk in a few days. Now it seems to be spread by contact with bodily fluids. Saliva, blood, whatever. If it comes into contact with your own blood or has a way of getting into your bloodstream, then you've got it."

"Shit," Cade breathed, glancing at Ethan. "Do you think that's what happened to Lisa?"

"Lisa?" Brandt repeated. "Who is Lisa?"

"She was one of An—one of Ethan's wife's coworkers," Cade explained. "She was at work in one of Memphis hospitals. She got attacked by some man after there was a fire in the emergency room. She...she didn't make it."

"Is that where the blood in the backseat came from?" Cade nodded, and Brandt stepped back quickly, pulling his pistol out from its holster and pointing it at them. "Are either of you injured? Did any of her blood or saliva come into contact with your eyes or mouth or any cuts or scrapes you have?"

Ethan leaped up and pulled his own pistol. Cade swung her rifle from the couch cushion beside her to point it at Brandt.

"By your own admission, if we were infected, you'd damn well know it by now," Ethan said in a tight, barely controlled voice that Cade had never heard from him before. He stood by her, finger positioned along the trigger guard, teeth clenched as he glared daggers at the tall man in the doorway.

A wave of frustration and exhaustion suddenly washed over her. "Can we all just calm down already?" she asked, lowering her weapon. "Things are bad enough without all of us constantly pointing guns at each other."

"You know, she's right," Brandt said, though he didn't lower his pistol. "You really should put your gun down."

"Put yours down first," Ethan ordered.

"No thanks, Mister Policeman," Brandt said sarcastically. "I think I'm fine like this."

"How did you know I was a cop?"

"Badge on the dashboard."

Cade groaned in annoyance and waved the barrel of her rifle at Brandt. "*Both* of you put your damn guns down now before I just shoot you both and get the hell out of here," she snapped, resisting the urge to kick the wooden coffee table at her knees.

"The lady's right," Brandt said. "We really should be focusing on getting out of here."

Cade made a face as neither man lowered his gun. She set her rifle on the couch, stormed to Brandt, and shoved his arm down to his side. "I said put your damn gun down," she repeated, just loud enough for him to hear.

"Fine, but only because you asked so nicely," Brandt replied just as quietly. She waited until he put the gun away before stepping back and nodding to Ethan.

Ethan slowly lowered his pistol and slid it back into its holster. Brandt leaned against the doorframe once more as if nothing untoward had happened. "So what do you propose we do?" Ethan asked.

Brandt pulled a small notebook out of his back pocket and tossed it onto the coffee table. "My observations," he said. "We start by getting you two educated. We can't deal with this shit without knowing what it is we're dealing with."

CHAPTER TEN

Plantersville, MS

Gray got a Camry's engine running in short order, and watching him work was like magic to Theo. He kept forgetting how skilled Gray was at everything related to cars. Sometimes, it was scary how much he knew.

"Ready to roll?" Gray asked.

"Yeah, but you're driving," Theo said. "I don't think I can focus enough right now." He slung his bag onto the backseat and set the bloody axe on the floorboard, then slid into his seat, buckled his seatbelt, and hit the power-lock button. When Gray gave him an odd look, he added, "Can't be too careful, can you?"

"True," Gray conceded. He put the car in drive and tapped the gas, rolling off the curb.

"Head for the base," Theo instructed. "I've got to pick up a few things." *Like Dillon.*

Gray coasted into the street, his eyes flickering over their surroundings. "Thank God we live in such a small town, you know? Lower population, which means fewer crazy people and less chance we'll end up getting killed. Theoretically."

"Yeah," Theo said softly. He watched the downtown area roll by, propping his elbow against the edge of the door and resting his head on his hand. He wasn't thinking about the rest of Plantersville. Truth be told, he didn't *care* about the rest of Plantersville. He only cared about two people in it: Dillon Roberts and Gray Carter. And, of course, himself. He was aware how incredibly selfish that sounded, but he didn't care about that, either. His brother and Dillon were all he had left that he cared about, and he refused to allow anything to happen to either of them.

Beside him, Gray chattered about road congestion and what they were going to do when they got to the ambulance base. Theo nodded noncommittally whenever it seemed appropriate, but he didn't focus on Gray's words. He *couldn't*. There was too much weighing heavily on his conscience for him to worry about whatever Gray was nattering on about.

In the past twenty-four hours, he'd committed murder not just once, but *twice*. It was an action so against his nature, so against his impulse to *help* people, not *hurt* them, that he couldn't reconcile it with what he knew of himself. He kept trying to tell himself that it had been necessary, that it might continue to be necessary to protect himself, Gray, and Dillon. But he couldn't get past the mental horror. He could still smell the metallic tang of blood from the latest victim.

"Hey, are you even listening to me?" Gray's voice broke into the haze of his thoughts. He glanced at him, but when he didn't answer right away, his brain still trying to catch back up with reality, Gray asked, "Theo? You okay?"

Theo cleared his throat. "Yeah. Yeah, I'm fine. Just... thinking is all." He shook his head, then focused on his brother. "What's up?"

Gray glanced at him several more times, and he was sure if they weren't in a moving vehicle, Gray would have been staring at him like he could read his mind. The thought of Gray being able to do so was, frankly, terrifying, especially considering all that his brother didn't know about him and his personal life.

"I was just asking," Gray began, "do you think this craziness is just in Plantersville? Or do you think it's everywhere?"

Theo studied the horizon. He wasn't sure for what he was searching. Smoke? Explosions? A red haze in the air to indicate some form of biological attack? Alien invasion? He had no idea.

"Theo?"

"Sorry, thinking again." He rubbed a hand over his hair and sighed, letting the breath out slowly. "Honestly, I don't want to speculate," he said. "Best case scenario, it's just here. Then the National Guard can come in and help evaluate people who haven't gotten sick or whatever is causing all this… crazy shit."

"But what if it's, like, worldwide or something?" Gray asked.

"I don't know," he said. "I'm not sure what would happen then. Probably a total breakdown of civilization."

"What do you mean by breakdown?"

"Sort of what we're already seeing." He turned to face Gray, resting his back against the door. "Do you remember all that stuff we saw on TV back when Katrina hit New Orleans? All the lootings and shootings and lack of food and water and power?" Gray nodded. "It'd be a lot like that. Maybe even worse, since it'd be everywhere and not just confined to one city."

"I can't imagine that," Gray said. "New Orleans was bad enough. Worldwide sounds like something out of a horror movie."

"This coming from the guy who suggested everybody out here is turning into zombies," Theo said. "Zombies are a physical impossibility."

"Last week, I'd have said that all this was a physical impossibility," Gray said. "I think the world's pretty much proven us wrong on that." He slowed and eased around a wrecked vehicle jutting into the roadway. "If it *has* affected places outside Plantersville, what are we going to do?"

"What we have to do," he said. "Whatever it takes to survive."

The ambulance base came into view, a white building sitting at the curve of its street in all its single-story glory. Theo drew in a breath of relief, noticing there wasn't an ambulance in sight. "Fuck."

"What?"

"There aren't any ambulances here," he said. "That means nobody else made it back."

"Oh," Gray said, realizing the implications of Theo's words. He eased the car to the front of the building and pushed the gearshift into park. "Theo...I'm sorry."

"Don't start," Theo said. "Not right now." He got out of the car and retrieved his axe and bag from the back. "Stay here."

"What? Why?" Gray scrambled out of the car before Theo could stop him, grabbing his own bag and crowbar and glaring at him across the roof of the car. "I'm not letting you go anywhere by yourself."

He gritted his teeth. "Gray, get back in the car."

"No!" Gray snarled. "You might need backup. You never know what might be in there! None of the ambulances are here, but that doesn't mean the building is empty."

"Which is *exactly* why I want you to stay *here*," Theo said, jabbing his finger at the ground to emphasize his point. "If there's anything in there, you'll only risk getting in my way."

"Getting in your way," Gray repeated, the cold fury in his voice palpable, even with the car between them. Theo read the anger and desperation in his eyes, the determination in the muscles jumping in his jaw as he clenched his teeth.

"*Fine*," he said. "Just stick close and stay behind me. And whatever you do, *don't* wander out of sight."

Gray slammed the car door hard enough to make the entire vehicle shake. "I'm not a kid, you know," he snapped, moving to the front of the car. "I can take care of myself."

"Humor me," Theo begged. "Please?"

Gray rolled his eyes and followed him to the base's front door, trying to be quiet even though by slamming the car door he'd probably alerted everything living and dead in a half-mile radius that they were there.

Theo cast a glance at the white and green house across the street. It was shut up tight, no signs of movement. He hoped that meant Dillon had done what he'd asked him to do. He didn't want to think of his friend going crazy like the people on the street. Or of him being a victim of the same.

He pushed the thoughts aside and tried the doorknob. Surprisingly, it was unlocked, and he eased the door open. He paused there, studying the entryway for oncoming dangers. He tried the light switch just inside the door; the power was out. He grimaced and fished out his flashlight, shining it around the interior.

A quick check of every room revealed that the building was empty. Theo couldn't say that didn't relieve him. He motioned for Gray to follow and led him to the supply closet, keying the combination into the lock on the door and pulling it open. "Use whatever you need to pack up as many supplies as you can. Leave the monitor batteries and things like that. We don't need them. Grab every type of gauze in there, elastic bandages, oxygen masks, everything like that. I'm going to hit the drug cabinet."

"How am I supposed to *see* to do this?" Gray asked. "You have the only flashlight."

Theo held it out to him. "Here, take it," he said. "I know my way around base well enough to get to the supervisor's office without it."

Gray took the flashlight from him and disappeared into the supply closet. Theo called after him, "Don't forget to keep an eye on your back!"

"Yeah, yeah," his voice replied from the darkness.

Theo made his way to the supervisor's office at the back of the building. The drug cabinet sat directly behind the desk, tall, imposing, and very firmly bolted shut. A clipboard hung from a nail on the side of the cabinet with forms clipped to it. The key to the lock would be on the supervisor's keyring, which was likely in the pocket of the supervisor on duty. He hefted the axe and made short work of the lock, delivering a single blow to shatter it. One of the doors swung open, and he set the axe on the desk and threw the door open, grabbing the tiny drug vials by the handful and stuffing them into the bag he wore over his shoulder.

After collecting his personal belongings and keys from one of the bunk rooms, he headed back out to find his brother. Gray was just emerging from the supply closet with a bulging blue canvas bag. He shined his flashlight right in Theo's face, prompting him to put up a hand to block it and say, "Watch it, you spaz."

The light skirted away. "Shit, sorry," Gray said. "I didn't know it was you. You scared the hell out of me."

Theo took the flashlight from him and shined it into the supply room to make sure he'd gotten everything useful. "Go wait by the front door," he said, handing him the bags of supplies he wore. "I'll bring the car around for us to load up. Then we've got one more stop besides the pharmacy to make before heading to the house."

"One more stop?" Gray repeated. "Where?" Theo didn't answer him, just pointed toward the entryway. Gray huffed in exasperation but, thankfully, complied. Theo slipped out the back door; his Hyundai Santa Fe was still parked near the storage shed, untouched by the chaos. He unlocked it, jumped into the driver's seat, and pulled the vehicle around to the front of the base. Within minutes, they had everything loaded into the Santa Fe, leaving Theo to focus on the next task. He squared his shoulders, preparing for a fight.

"Get in the car, lock the doors, and stay here," Theo said.

"What? Why?"

"I've got something I need to do," he said. "And I don't want you getting hurt, because I don't know what I'm walking into."

"If you think you're walking into something bad, why the *hell* are you doing alone?" Gray looked ready to hit him with his crowbar.

"Because I don't want you getting hurt," Theo repeated.

"Where are you going?"

"In there," he said, pointing to the house across the street. "I won't be long."

"You hope," Gray grumbled.

Theo rubbed his temple with the heel of his hand; he could feel a massive headache coming on. "Fine, come with me," he conceded. "Move the car to the house's driveway. I'll walk over. Then come in and shut the door. Stay in the foyer so I don't accidentally attack you." Without waiting for a response, he started across the street, intent on finding Dillon before something else did.

* * *

In a foul mood, Gray moved the Santa Fe to the green and white house that sat on a hill overlooking the street. He'd never really understood his brother. At times, he was an enigma wrapped in a mystery, and it was times like this that his lack of understanding was painfully obvious. He'd watched Theo cross the street, climb the hill, and produce a key to unlock the door, stepping inside as if he owned the place.

Maybe he had a girlfriend, he considered. Maybe she lived there, and he needed to pick her up and take her back to the house with them. That would explain his constant canceling of their nights out over the past several months. But why wouldn't he have told him about a girlfriend? It didn't make sense.

He retrieved his crowbar and climbed out of the car, checking to make sure the street was clear before starting toward the house itself. He remembered Theo's orders about staying in the foyer, but when he heard voices deeper in the house, he couldn't resist disobeying. He eased across the foyer and down a short hall leading to an even darker interior. There was a strange, musty odor to the air, like the house had been shut up for a long time. It was distinctly medical, like the hospital ER that their parents had been taken to after their accident. The smell brought back unpleasant memories, and he shuddered.

He followed Theo's voice to a bedroom near the end of the hall. He hesitated, peering into the room, curiosity eating at his insides. The first thing he saw was a hospital bed, a thin, skeletal form lying on it beneath heavy blankets, unmoving, its head tilted back and its mouth open in a final rictus. An electronic oxygen system sat beside the bed, silent, its panel dark. The oxygen tubing connected to it ran to the still figure in the bed.

Theo was speaking on the other side of the bed, his voice low and soothing but at the same time choked, like he was struggling to contain emotion while comforting someone else. Gray eased further into the room, and Theo came into view.

Theo knelt on the floor facing a man who was crammed against the wall, his knees to his chest and a sofa pillow gripped in his hands. Gray didn't know him, but he looked somewhere between his own age and Theo's, thin and dark-haired, pale and shell-shocked. His hands shook so badly that Gray could see the tremors even with him gripping the pillow, and his brown eyes swam with tears. Theo made a gentle, shushing sound, gripping the man's biceps.

"It's okay, Dillon," Theo was saying. "I promise, it's okay. You did what you had to. There weren't many other options."

"Yeah, but he was my *father*," the man protested. He sounded stuffy, like he'd been crying for a while.

"And he was dying," Theo said. He pried the pillow from the man's hands and set it aside before wrapping him in a tight hug. The man clung to him, and Gray had the sudden feeling he was intruding on something highly personal. The scene before him just seemed so...familiar.

Gray swallowed and, though he was reluctant to interrupt, cleared his throat. Theo jumped and released the man, whirling to glare at Gray. Despite the anger on his face, Gray saw a flash of guilt and embarrassment in his brother's eyes. "What the hell are you doing?" Theo demanded, rising from the floor. "I thought I told you to stay in the foyer!"

"I thought you needed help," Gray replied. He glanced at the other man, who was getting up from the floor. "Who is that?"

"A friend of mine," Theo said. When Gray continued staring, he said, "Gray, this is my friend Dillon Roberts. Dillon, Gray."

Dillon wiped his eye with the heel of his hand and gave him a weak smile. Gray didn't bother returning it. "We should get moving," Gray said, turning his attention back to Theo. "You said we were going to the house. We're still a good bit away from it."

He strode out of the bedroom, intending to head for the foyer and the front door. He felt a cool draft of air gust down the hall from the open front door but barely paid it any attention. Gray wasn't an idiot. He'd known for a long time that his older brother had harbored bisexual tendencies. Though Theo had never told him that, it was an open secret that hung heavily between them, unspoken but there. It didn't bother him, not really. What Theo did on Theo's time was Theo's business. But the fact he obviously didn't feel he could introduce Gray to the person he clearly cared about was what pissed him off.

Even now, he could hear them, their footsteps moving toward the door. Theo's friend—*Dillon*, he reminded himself—was murmuring something about getting some clothes. Gray wasn't focused on them, and with a glance out the front door, he wasn't focused on his own thoughts anymore, either.

One of those zombie things was in the front yard.

Gray froze. He didn't know how he knew the woman in the yard was a zombie. He just *knew*. Maybe it was the way she stood, like a newborn colt trying to find its legs. Maybe it was the vacant expression on her face. Maybe it was the blood smeared down the front of her white shirt and gathered at the ends of her sleeves. Whatever it was, his instincts told him to avoid her at all costs.

Theo had seen her too. His hand closed around Gray's bicep, tugging him back from the door. "*Stay here,*" he mouthed, pointing at the floor emphatically. Then he started toward the door.

Gray grabbed his arm to stop him. "You are *not* going out there!" he hissed.

"Of *course* I'm not," Theo breathed back. "I'm just going to shut the damned door."

Gray took a step back, bumping into Dillon, while Theo crept toward the door. Theo stopped in the opening, looking out at the lawn beyond, and the blood drained from his face until he was white as a sheet. He eased the door shut with a soft click, then slammed the lock and deadbolt into place and scrambled away from it.

"There are more than just one out there," Theo said, his voice still hushed, like he was afraid it'd carry outdoors.

"How many?" Dillon asked.

Gray could see Theo steel himself, could see the fear in his eyes and the worry in his stance. "Maybe ten?"

"Ten?" Dillon repeated. "That's not so bad."

"You haven't seen what those bastards can do," Gray replied. "What do we do, Theo?"

Theo looked around the foyer like he was lost, rubbing the back of his neck, then stared at the ceiling like he could see through it. "We should go to the second floor and wait them out. They can't stay out there forever. Once they're gone, we'll run for the car and get out of here."

"Where to?" Dillon asked. "And what's going on? There was all this shit going down outside, and then you called me up and told me to lock down and hide. I heard shooting for *hours* last night."

"We're going to our house," Gray said. "There are supplies and a generator there, along with more weapons."

"What kind of weapons?" Dillon asked.

Theo's look was grim. "Guns. Hunting rifles. Not many handguns, and I'm not sure what sort of ammunition we have, but we can manage with rifles, I think. It's better than what we've got now." He held up his axe to illustrate his point.

Something banged against the door then, and Gray jumped. The three of them looked at the door at the same time, and he waved his hand at the stairs. "I think that's our cue to get up there."

* * *

New Orleans, LA

It took Remy three hours to make it out of metro New Orleans. Compared to the usual forty-five minutes or less it typically took, it was an eternity. She was forced to avoid the interstates and the major throughways, sticking to roads that were mostly uncongested. Of the cars she did see, none of their occupants made a move to stop her. Everyone was too focused on their personal goals to pay attention to a random police car in their midst.

When Remy got close to home, approaching the last stretch slowly and cautiously, she smiled slightly at the sight of the mailbox at the end of the road. Even if it did say

Dodson, it still represented *home.* She steered the cruiser up the driveway, her stomach churning with anticipation.

The house looked the same as always, as broken down and well lived-in as usual. But there was something *off* about it at the same time, though she couldn't put her finger on what. She pulled the cruiser to a stop at the head of the driveway, cringing when the brakes squealed, and shifted into park. She sat there, listening to the engine idle, waiting. For what, she didn't know.

Remy studied the tree line curving from the edge of the road around to the back of the house. There was no movement she could see. To the right was an open field, formerly a pasture before the farm it had been part of was sold at foreclosure and the land divvied up for individual houses. She felt her heart skip a beat.

There was a crowd of people making its way across the field toward her house.

Remy had no idea if these were sick people or not. Ultimately, it didn't matter. They were heading toward her family, and she had to get in there and warn them.

She cut the engine off and scrambled out of the car, leaving the keys behind and running across the half-dead front lawn. The front door was locked, and she didn't have her keys, so she began beating on the door, hoping they hadn't packed up and gotten the hell out of Dodge and left her behind.

She'd just begun wondering if anyone was home when the locks disengaged. When the door swung open, she found herself staring down the barrel of a shotgun. She reflexively took a step back before realizing it was her stepfather. Jason apparently recognized her at the same time, because he lowered the rifle with an exasperated sigh and stepped aside.

"I don't want to know where you've been, who you've been with, or what you've been doing with them," Jason said. "Get your ass in here."

Remy obediently stepped inside. Though at any other time she might have argued with him, she figured it probably wasn't time for her ridiculous, petty bullshit. "Have you heard about what's going on?"

"Of course I have," Jason replied, shutting and bolting the door. "Why the hell do you think I answered the door with a shotgun?"

"Then you should know that there are a bunch of sick people coming across the field," she said.

Jason's eyes widened comically. "How many?"

Remy rolled her eyes. "Hell, I don't know," she said, exasperated. "I didn't stop to count. Suffice to say, 'enough' should be a good answer."

Jason swore under his breath.

"What? What is it?"

"It's your mother," he said. "She's sick."

"Sick?" Remy repeated. "How sick?"

"Pretty damn sick," he said. "If we have to go anywhere, I'm not sure we'll be able to move her."

"How the fuck did *that* happen?" Remy screeched. "She was fine last night!"

"Keep your voice down!" Jason barked. "She's resting, and you will *not* wake her up." He paused, then said, "She got sick overnight. When it hit her, it hit hard and fast." He shook his head. "She must have caught it on the plane."

"How bad is it?"

"It…I'm not sure, but it looks like that stuff they're showing on TV."

Remy's insides turned to ice. "No," she breathed. "Where is she?"

"Asleep on the couch," he said. "Don't wake her up, okay? She needs to rest."

Remy nodded absently and moved toward the living room, pausing in the doorway to stare into the dim room. There was a lump on the couch, covered with a blanket, a tangled mop of highlighted, dark brown hair in the vicinity of the lump's head. Curled in the nearby recliner, a thin paperback in hand, was Maddie. She was rhythmically flicking her fingers over the edges of the book's pages, though she wasn't actually reading the book. She was too busy staring at the lump that was her mother. Remy stepped into the room, and Maddie looked up from her book and smiled brightly.

"You're home," Maddie said, sitting up straighter. "Daddy got really mad about you sneaking out last night."

Remy moved closer to the couch. "How's Mama?"

"Sick," Maddie said. "She's been on the couch all morning. Daddy keeps watching the news. He looks really worried."

As he should be, Remy thought, though she didn't dare say it out loud. There was no sense in scaring the crap out of her sister. She knelt beside it to brush her mother's hair out of her face. "Mama?" Her mother didn't reply.

A bang from the kitchen drew Remy's attention away. She stiffened and looked toward the kitchen, and when the bang came again, she jumped up. "Stay here," she told Maddie. She pushed to her feet and started out of the living room, hoping the noise had just been caused by her stepfather doing something in the kitchen.

No such luck. When she stepped into the kitchen, she realized there were several people on the dilapidated back deck behind the house. She bit back a swear and backed away from the door, watching the shadowy figures as they moved from one end of the deck to the other, presumably searching for a way in. She fumbled at her waist, searching for the revolver Marc had given her. "Jason!" she hissed into the house.

Jason appeared from the upstairs level, his face creased with concern. "What is it?" he asked, his voice too loud for her comfort.

"Keep it down!" she hissed. She jerked her head toward the back door. "We've got company." His eyes widened at the sight of the shadowy figures. "They moved a lot faster than I expected them to."

Jason crossed the kitchen to look out the window over the sink. "There are more coming too," he said, still too loudly.

She rubbed one of her temples with a hand. "We need to get out of here."

"We can't. Your mom is too sick to move," Jason reminded her.

"We don't have a choice," she retorted. "I've seen first-hand what these people do, and it's not something I want to experience personally."

"Is that where you were last night?" Jason asked. "Experiencing things *personally?*" His voice was neutral and calm, casual, like he didn't care about the answer. Maybe he didn't; maybe he was just making small talk out of sheer nervousness.

"I was actually with a cop," Remy said with equal neutrality.

There was a loud bang against the back door. Both of them jumped, and Jason lifted his shotgun and pointed it at the door. "You get arrested again?" he asked.

"You act like it's a regular occurrence," she grumbled.

"It is."

Any further discussion was interrupted by the sound of breaking glass and the sight of an arm thrusting through the space where the glass had been. At the same time, Maddie's piercing scream rent the air, and the blood in Remy's veins froze.

"Oh God, Maddie!" she gasped.

The scream brought on a renewed frenzy from the people outside, and the door started shaking on its hinges.

"Go!" Jason snapped, raising his voice loud enough to be heard over the commotion. "Go to Maddie. I've got this."

Remy bolted to the living room, yanking the revolver out of its holster and raising it defensively. A short, dark figure ran out of the room and nearly plowed headlong into her, and she raised the revolver at an angle so it wasn't pointed at her sister. "What's wrong?" she asked, grabbing Maddie and shoving her behind her.

"Mama," Maddie said, crying so hard it was difficult to understand what she was saying. "She tried to hurt me!"

"Hurt you how?"

Maddie didn't get the opportunity to explain. She didn't have to. Their mother stumbled into view, her hair a tangled mess, her face slack with something that made Remy think of delirium, though that wasn't quite the word to describe it. She looked confused, out of it, but at the same time, she was with it enough to focus on Maddie with a single-minded intensity, baring her teeth and staggering forward, her arms outstretched like a zombie in an old black-and-white horror movie. Remy grabbed Maddie's hand and nudged her backward, not taking her eyes off her mother. Instinctively, she knew something wasn't right with her mother; some animal part of her brain flinched away from the woman, screaming at her to either destroy the danger in front of her or run and hide.

A crash from the kitchen heralded further danger, and a blast of her stepfather's shotgun punctuated the noise. Then Jason's voice boomed out, rising over the escalating sounds in the kitchen. "Remy! Take your sister and run! Get upstairs and hide!"

Remy snorted. Upstairs was the *last* place you were supposed to go in the unlikely event you found yourself in a real-life horror movie. But this was no movie. She grabbed Maddie's arm and propelled her toward the stairs. "Go! Move!"

Maddie charged upstairs, her bare feet making soft, thudding sounds on the steps that Remy could barely hear over the ruckus. Remy backed away from her mother, intending to make sure no one came near Maddie. As soon as she was sure her sister was upstairs, she broke away, following.

When she started up the stairs, a hand closed around her ankle, and she crashed down hard. All the air in her body rushed from her lungs. The hand that had grabbed her clawed up the back of her jeans, and she kicked out, thrashing. She spun around, trying to roll over, and saw it was her mother. She didn't look like her mother anymore; she looked evil, a being filled with hatred and hunger as she tried to drag herself up Remy's body. Remy's mind skittered to the sight she'd witnessed on the street, the two men leaning over a bloody body, and she tensed, kicking out again. Her foot connected with her mother's hip, throwing her off balance but not stopping her progress. Desperate, she fumbled for her revolver, but to her dismay, she couldn't find it. She looked back and realized it'd fallen from her hand when she'd been tripped, and it lay a few steps above her, out of reach, balanced precariously on the edge of the step.

The shotgun blasts in the kitchen went ominously silent.

As her mother clawed at her more desperately, Remy got her legs under her and thrust upward, sending her mother crashing into the wall, jarring the revolver off the edge of the step and sending it toppling to the floor alongside the staircase. Remy stood, looking around frantically for another weapon she could use. There was nothing, so she scrambled over the bannister, landing heavily on the floor two feet away from the weapon. She snatched it up and aimed it at her mother.

It took three shots to put her down. Two impacted with her chest, splattering blood on the wall like punctuation marks. The third struck her in the head, and she dropped to the stairs, her arm outstretched above her like she was reaching for something. Remy didn't have time to mourn, though; more invaders had flooded the kitchen, and with no more sounds of defense from Jason, she had to assume he was out of action. Stuffing the revolver into the holster so she wouldn't lose it this time, she bolted up the stairs, leaping over her mother's body.

She paused on the landing between the first and second floors; her eyes landed on an item that looked like a cross between a very long knife and a machete, mounted on display hooks inside a shadowbox screwed to the wall. The hilt was wooden, worn shiny by hands that had used it in the past, and despite the fact it had hung on the wall for as long as she could remember, the blade still looked sharp. It was called a bolo knife, and it had belonged to her paternal grandmother, who'd brought it from the Philippines when she'd immigrated to America. It would be the perfect silent weapon to protect her and her sister. She snatched it off the wall, along with the thin sheath that hung below it, and slid the blade inside the sheath before charging the rest of the way upstairs.

Maddie was screaming and crying so loudly their distant neighbors could probably hear it. Remy ran toward her bedroom near the end of the hall, where Maddie was probably hiding in her closet again, like she did whenever she had bad nightmares. Still holding her revolver in one hand and her newly acquired bolo knife in the other, she entered her bedroom and went straight to the closet.

Maddie huddled on the closet floor, her arms folded over her head, like she was doing tornado drills at school. Her sobs were even louder now that the door was open. Remy nudged her with her foot. "Hey, shut up," she said. Maddie made no effort to obey; the floodgates had opened, and there was no one left to shut them. Holstering her revolver and propping her knife against the wall, she dropped to a knee, grasped the girl by the shoulders, and shook her to get her attention. "Maddie, you have *got* to shut up!" she hissed. "If you don't, they'll find us!"

Maddie only cried harder.

There was a thud on the stairs, and Remy crawled into the closet with Maddie, though she knew it was a terrible idea. Crawling in the closet was a surefire way to get trapped. But she had no choice; she could hear the distinct thump of someone making it to the second floor. She pulled her revolver again and tried to remember how many shots she'd already fired. She was sure it had been five. She fiddled with the revolver, trying to figure out how to open the chamber, and when she did so, she shook the ammunition out. Five empty cartridges and one bullet fell into her palm. She tossed the empties on the floor, jammed the one bullet into the pistol, snapped the barrel back in place, and spun it so it was ready to fire with the next trigger pull.

In the hall, she heard multiple sets of feet. She tensed and crawled deeper into the closet, dragging Maddie with her. Maddie squealed, and she clamped a hand hard over her mouth, trying to muffle the noise. The girl was officially hysterical, her fear overriding any good sense she might have had, and Remy had no idea how to get her quiet.

"Shut up, Maddie! Shut up!" Remy hissed, hooking an arm around the girl's head to better anchor the hand she held over her mouth. "You're gonna get us killed!"

Her warnings didn't make any difference; Maddie was too far gone. Remy couldn't help thinking of the sight of those men tearing into that woman again, and she tried dragging Maddie further into the closet, looking desperately for a way to shut her up. There was nothing, of course. She thought longingly of the ammunition she'd left in the cruiser in her panic to get to her family, but it wasn't going to do her any good now.

She and Maddie were going to die in her closet at the hands of a bunch of crazy, sick people.

"Maddie, Maddie, Maddie, you've got to be quiet," Remy said into her ear, lowering her voice and struggling to calm her, though she knew it was too late for that. There were already footsteps in the bedroom. She could hear at least three sets of feet against the carpet. She almost whimpered as her own fear started overcoming her, the horrible images she'd seen on the streets pounding in her brain. She'd do anything to save her sister from that gruesome fate. Anything else would be better than that.

Before she even truly registered what she was doing, she tugged her sister to her, pressed a kiss to her temple, and murmured, "Maddie, I love you. I'm sorry." She put the revolver to the place she'd kissed and squeezed the trigger.

Maddie slumped over, tumbling to the carpeted closet floor, her sobs finally silent.

Remy dropped the now-empty, useless revolver to the carpet and grabbed the bolo knife. Her hands shook, but her mind settled into a resolute determination. She'd protected her sister, saved her from the brutality of death at the hands of these sick, murderous people. As for her, she'd go down fighting.

The closet's doorknob rattled. She pushed to her feet, careful not to step on her sister, and pulled the bolo knife from its sheath. She braced herself, then kicked the closet door open as hard as she could.

The impact of the door sent the figure pulling at the knob flailing backward, and like a bowling pin, it fell against its companions, sending all three tumbling to the floor. She dodged a hand grasping at her ankle and started for the bedroom door, stopping short when she heard more of them in the hall. Backpedaling, she raced across the room and slammed into the window on the other side. Though it was the last thing she wanted to do, she put the bolo knife away, needing both hands free, and unlatched the window. As her attackers staggered to their feet, she shoved the window open and looked at the ground below.

It was, thankfully, clear.

Seeing that sent a surge of need through her: the need to survive, the need to *get away*.

With one last glance to gauge how much time she had left to escape, Remy slung one leg over the sill and ducked low. This was a climb she'd made before, multiple times. She could do it again, piece of cake.

Hands grasped the hem of her shirt as she scrambled over the windowsill, but she punched them away with one hand. Another hand grabbed at her, throwing her off balance, and she fell out the window, tumbling to the ground below and landing in the grass with a hard thud. For the second time in the past twenty minutes, the air left her lungs, and she lay spread-eagled in the grass, struggling to breathe, staring at the window she'd just fallen from. Her attackers crowded at the window, as if they were attempting to launch themselves out at her.

Remy rolled over, grimacing at the pain darting through her left side. She was pretty sure she'd cracked a rib but knew it wasn't time to whine over it. Clutching at her side with one hand and clinging to the bolo knife with the other, she started back around to the front of the house where she'd parked the cruiser. It was unmolested and, thankfully, not surrounded. She supposed they had no interest in an unoccupied vehicle. She raced forward, yanked open the door, and threw herself in.

In seconds, she had the engine started and swung the car around, speeding down the driveway with a spray of dirt and rocks and a sob of desperation as she fled her childhood home forever.

CHAPTER ELEVEN

Gadsden, AL

Brandt dropped into the armchair across from the couch and rubbed both hands over his face and through his short dark hair. He slumped over to rest his elbows on his knees, yawned widely, and felt the muscles in his jaw stretch.

"Tired?" a voice asked.

He tilted his head up from his contemplation of the floor enough to see Cade standing in the doorway between the living room and kitchen. Ethan banged around in the kitchen, hopefully making something for them to eat. He hadn't been eating well or as much as he should have since fleeing Atlanta, and he'd begun to feel it. It'd been difficult to keep food down, though, so he hadn't wanted to put anything in his mouth.

Brandt discreetly trailed his eyes over the woman in the doorway as she crossed her arms. She was stunning; he'd thought so the minute he'd laid eyes on her on the street. He found the combination of dark hair and blue eyes intriguing, and the fact she was a military woman drew his interest even more. IDF babe, indeed.

"Yeah, I'm absolutely wiped," he admitted. Cade didn't move from the doorway, just continued watching him as she cocked a hip to lean against the doorframe. He tried to decipher the expression in her eyes but found the task impossible; the woman was a closed book.

"You should rest," she suggested. "You look like you're ready to fall over."

"I feel like it too," he said, rubbing his face again and shaking free of his sly stare. He leaned back and rested his head against the chair's backrest. "I've been by myself for the past several days, just trying to stay ahead of the infection. I haven't had much time for sleep."

Cade finally moved farther into the living room, sitting on the edge of the coffee table in front of him and resting her elbows on her knees. Brandt's eyes drifted to the neckline of her slightly too large flannel shirt; the top few buttons were undone, and it sagged open enough that he could make out the edge of her bra. He forced his eyes back to her face; she smirked and adjusted her shirt so nothing showed.

"Where exactly are you from?" Cade asked. "We've told you some about us, but I still don't know anything about you."

Brandt shrugged and slumped down in his seat, enjoying the muscles in his back relaxing. He felt a bit sheepish at the fact he'd practically grilled Cade and Ethan for information but hadn't said anything about himself in return. "I'm from Atlanta."

Cade sat forward. "Atlanta?" she repeated. "You lived there, or you were just on active duty there?"

"Both," he answered. "I grew up in the Peachtree area, and my parents lived there." He brushed his hands through his hair again and grimaced at how dirty it felt. Now that he had companions with whom to share watch duty, he really needed to take a shower, pronto. "I…volunteered for duty when they needed soldiers at the CDC, and I was there when the infected—" He stopped midsentence and closed his eyes, shaking his head. "It's been rough," he finished simply.

Cade didn't push the issue further. If she'd tried, he would have bluntly refused to tell her more. There were things he couldn't tell her and Ethan—things he *wouldn't* tell them. They'd never understand.

"All the more reason for you to rest," Cade said. "I can handle watch for now, since you say we need it. You should sleep." He glanced at the kitchen door, and she added, "I'll make sure Ethan gets some sleep too." She leaned forward and winked conspiratorially. "He gets seriously cranky when he hasn't had sleep."

"I noticed," he said, chuckling. He sat up straighter and stretched to work the kinks out of his stiff back. "Is he always so trigger happy when he's tired?"

"I don't know," she admitted, shrugging. "I've never really seen him in a situation involving exhaustion and guns."

"So are you two…?" He trailed off meaningfully and raised his eyebrows in silent suggestion.

"What?" Cade looked back at the kitchen door, then laughed as comprehension dawned on her. "Oh, no! We've just been friends for the past seven years," she said, shaking her head, even as a sad look crossed her face. "He's married," she said. "*Was*. And I had a boyfriend."

"What happened to them?" Brandt asked gently, though he didn't really have to. He knew the answer.

Cade didn't look at him, just waved her hand vaguely. "All of this. Anna was an RN on duty at the hospital. It burned. And I…I had to shoot Andrew."

"I'm sorry," he said. "That had to have been hard."

A silence fell between them, but it was a companionable silence in which they spent their time lost in thought. When Brandt spoke again, it was lighthearted. "Damn, I could use a drink," he admitted, dropping both arms to the chair's armrests. "But I've decided no drinking while this shit's going on, am I right?"

Cade nodded and stood. "I'll at least get you some water," she offered, heading to the kitchen again.

He watched Cade go, his eyes drifting to her jeans as she walked by, then shook himself and tried to relax. He'd been so tense over the past week that he couldn't imagine ever being relaxed again. He hadn't been kidding when he'd told Cade it had been a long week. He'd spent it running from Atlanta and the virus spreading out from it, only to find another outbreak in Birmingham. He'd done things of which he wasn't proud. He'd stolen cars and motorcycles and even some kid's bike right out of a front yard. He'd bought supplies from stores until he ran out of money and his credit cards maxed out. But it would all be worth it if he could just survive the initial outbreak.

"Here," Cade said, her voice breaking through the haze of his thoughts. She tapped him on the arm with a mostly cold bottle of water, and he opened his eyes.

"Hey, thanks," he said, accepting the bottle and cracking it open. He took a long swallow of water as Ethan came in and sat on the coffee table, offering Brandt a plate that held a baked potato and meat that he was pretty sure was hamburger. He accepted it gratefully. "Man, you went all out with the food, huh?" he said, digging in.

"Just because the world's going to shit doesn't mean I'm going to start eating a bunch of garbage," Ethan said. He offered Cade a second plate and started in on his own. He waited until they were halfway through their meals before asking, "Are we going to make a plan or anything?" He picked up the small notepad Brandt had tossed onto the coffee table, then rifled through the pages and skimmed the contents.

"Yeah. You got a map?" Brandt asked around a mouthful of potato. He swallowed and took another drink of water before continuing. "We need to pick a place to go and plan how to get there."

Ethan got up, leaving his food on the table, and headed to the front door. "Yeah, map's out in the car," he said, unlocking the front door and starting to open it.

Brandt shook his head and stood, setting down his own plate and grabbing his pistol. "Wait, let me go with you," he offered. "Never hurts to have backup."

Ethan didn't respond either way, so Brandt let him lead the way outside. He stepped onto the porch in the chilly, late afternoon air and was surprised at how much cooler it'd become in just a few hours. Earlier in the day, it had been abnormally warm for the time of year, and now it had dropped into the fifties, maybe even lower. As he exhaled slowly, the air clouded faintly in front of him. He paused and looked back at Cade; she'd followed them to the doorway and had her rifle in hand. He smiled as he saw how prepared she was for anything; it was a good trait to have, considering what they faced.

"You stay here," Brandt suggested. "For backup. There's no sense in all three of us going to the car if we don't need to."

Cade nodded, though she didn't look pleased at being left at the house while Ethan and Brandt headed to the Jeep. Brandt nodded in return and followed Ethan to the SUV, keeping his pistol out as he scanned their surroundings closely. Ethan opened the passenger door and began rifling through the interior, searching for and locating a road atlas from between the front seats.

As Ethan straightened and tucked the book under his arm, Brandt saw movement a block down the street. Though he couldn't make out finer details, it appeared to be three people coming in their direction; squinting revealed that two of the figures were teenagers—one of them a cheerleader still in her uniform and the other in dark clothes. The third seemed to be a housewife in sweats. Their clothes were all stained with blood. Brandt frowned and aimed his gun in their direction. They weren't close enough to shoot, and he didn't want to fire his weapon until he was sure they were the enemy. He didn't want to risk killing uninfected people, and if these three *were* infected, the sound of gunfire would only draw more infected to them.

Ethan started to push the passenger door shut, but Brandt caught it in his hand and made a shushing gesture. "Hey, Bennett, check that out down the street," he murmured.

Ethan followed Brandt's instructions and dropped his hand to his own pistol. "Who are they?"

"I don't know, but I think they're infected," he admitted. Two more figures joined the three already in the street, and he stiffened. "Don't ask me how I know this," he continued. "I've seen too many of them. They have this...distinctive way of moving, almost like they're not in control of their bodies. They walk funny. They *move* funny. When you've seen as many as I have, you just know." He took a slow step toward the house. "Don't make any sudden movements or sounds," he warned, stepping onto the sidewalk. "We need to get to Cade. It's time we moved out of here."

Ethan nodded and eased the door shut before following Brandt onto the sidewalk. Brandt motioned for Cade to stay silent as the two men mounted the porch steps.

"What is it?" she asked, her voice low. She backed into the entryway to give them space to come inside.

"We've got five people—"

"Make that seven," Ethan reported. He joined them just inside the door and leaned to look down the street again.

"*Seven* people," Brandt corrected. "And they're coming this way. There's a high chance they're infected. I'd just about stake my *life* on it. I don't want to take risks by sticking around, so I think it's a good idea if we roll the hell out of here."

Cade shouldered her rifle and asked, "What do you need me to do?" She slid into a calm, unperturbed demeanor, the hallmark of her military professionalism and skill. He found the ease with which she did it highly impressive.

There was an odd silence as Brandt tried to connect the dots in his mind to form a plan. But the presence of the infected approaching their position was enough to rattle him back into the hours immediately after the fall of Atlanta and the pursuit he'd faced as he attempted to flee the city.

Ethan noticed his indecision and stepped up, taking charge in the absence of any suggestions from Brandt. "Cade, get our bags," he ordered. "I'll get the car started. Brandt?"

Brandt snapped out of the memories clouding his head. "I've got something I need to get," he said, moving to the staircase that led to the second floor. He went straight to the master bedroom and grabbed the large duffel bag sitting on the bed, slinging it over his shoulder and rejoining the others. Ethan was about to step out the front door when he made it downstairs. "Bennett, wait."

"What is it?"

"I have a better idea," Brandt said. He turned to Cade. "You said you were IDF, right?"

"Yeah, I was a marksman," Cade confirmed.

"Guard us while we get to the Jeep," he instructed. "You're probably a far better shot than either of us." Then he turned to the older man. "Ethan, *you* are going to help me get the bags to the Jeep."

Ethan hesitated, either unwilling to take orders from him or unwilling to allow Cade to take on the more dangerous tasks. But he nodded and took the bag the woman held, slung it over his shoulder, and adjusted the strap. Cade slid toward the door almost silently, her rifle up against her shoulder as she eased out the door. Brandt motioned to Ethan and followed her out, drawing his own pistol and pausing at the top of the porch steps. Cade stayed on the porch, lurking at the railing to his right, her rifle aimed down the street. Brandt assessed the situation and saw the group of seven making their way toward them in their disjoined walk. They were only two houses away. He frowned and aimed his pistol at them.

"Bennett, you first," he ordered. He waited until the older man got to the street before adding to Cade, "Wait until I'm at the sidewalk before following."

"No problem."

"And I suppose it goes without saying that if they make any aggressive movements toward us—"

"Take them out," Cade interrupted in a clipped tone. "Got it. Now go."

Brandt headed for the street, trying to keep his movements slow and steady to reduce the risk he'd be noticed. But his effort was for naught. The seven infected people began moving more quickly. He swore and gave up stealth, stopping in the middle of the street and lifting his pistol to aim it at the group once more.

"Cade! Get moving to the car! Now!" he yelled.

Cade ran, passing behind him and throwing herself into the Jeep's backseat. Ethan was already in the driver's seat. He started the vehicle's engine as the infected people reached Brandt's position in the street.

Brandt cursed and aimed his weapon at the nearest one, the blonde cheerleader. Her blue-and-white uniform was covered in enough blood to suggest a recent kill. She had the familiar look of hunger and hatred on her face that he'd seen so many times in his escape from Atlanta. He squeezed the trigger. A bullet slammed into her forehead and threw her back onto the road.

His focus on the cheerleader drew his attention away from the other six for only moments, but it was enough. A tall man in a brown jacket got behind him, grabbing Brandt's gun arm and wrenching it backward. Brandt turned into the attack and planted his foot in the man's stomach, pushing him away and jerking his arm free. He followed with an additional kick to put extra distance between them.

The housewife in sweatpants had insinuated herself between Brandt and his route to the Jeep's passenger door. He lifted his pistol and squeezed the trigger, but the teenage girl in dark clothes jumped him from behind, and his shot went wild. She wrapped her arms around his neck and shoulders and knocked his weapon from his hand. He ducked beneath her arms and hooked his foot around her knee, pulling hard and knocking her to the ground as he knelt and drew his knife from its sheath on his boot. He turned to put the housewife down with the knife, trying to step away from a hand clutching the back of his jacket.

The familiar sharp snap of a gunshot rang out before he reached the woman. The woman jerked backward as her head exploded in a spray of blood, and she fell to the ground by the Jeep.

"Brandt! Stop playing around and get in the fucking car!" Cade yelled. He glanced back and saw her standing on the backseat, her upper body hanging out of the Jeep's sunroof. She had her rifle in hand, and as Brandt looked at her, she policed her brass, gave him an unreadable look, and adjusted her aim to point the barrel at the next infected attacker.

Brandt took the opportunity Cade's cover fire offered him to retrieve his pistol before yanking the passenger door open and falling inside. "Go, go, *go*," he urged. He pulled the door shut and tugged Cade down inside the car.

Ethan slammed his foot on the gas, and the SUV leaped forward with a squeal of rubber on pavement. One of the infected was in the car's path, and the thud as they ran the woman over made Brandt's heart lurch.

Brandt dropped his head against the seat and exhaled in relief, raking his hands through his hair and looking at his companions. The looked whole and healthy and reasonably together, despite the circumstances. He couldn't have asked for more.

"Which way are we going?" Ethan asked, breaking his thoughts.

"Go west. Toward Mississippi," Brandt instructed. He took two deep breaths to steady his nerves before continuing. "Let's try Tupelo. Michaluk's caught up to us, and we need to get ahead of it again."

* * *

Plantersville, MS

Theo had spent an entire hour pacing in Dillon's bedroom while he, Gray, and Dillon waited for the danger in the front yard to pass so they could get out of there. His stomach burned with indigestion and stress, and his neck and shoulders felt stiff and sore. He rubbed the back of his neck and rolled his shoulders, trying to loosen them.

Gray had been crouched by the window facing the street the entire time, watching the activity below for the break they needed. He'd barely looked at Theo during that hour. Theo wondered what was wrong, why his brother was avoiding him. Clearly, something bothered him.

Dillon was on the other side of the room, half inside his closet, searching through his abundant clothing to find the most useful items to pack into the duffel bag on the bed. Theo wasn't sure how much he'd find. Dillon had always been the type who went more for stylish than functional, and Theo was willing to bet that Dillon didn't even own a suitable pair of tennis shoes.

His hands shaking, Dillon pulled a shirt from its hanger and started folding it, fumbling the fabric. He went to Dillon, touching his shoulder lightly. Despite the noise he'd made to warn of his approach, Dillon jumped and whirled around, shirt in hand, eyes wide. Theo took the shirt from him and folded it. "You okay?" he asked, pitching his voice low so Gray couldn't hear him.

Dillon's shoulders slumped, and he reached for another shirt while Theo tucked the folded one into the bag. "I don't know," he said. "It's...a lot to take in, you know?"

"Yeah, I know," Theo said. Dillon folded the shirt he held, his hands moving more confidently than before. Theo steadied himself before murmuring, "Jonathan's dead."

"Dead?" Dillon repeated. "How? Are you sure?"

"He got shot in the head. Right in front of me," Theo said, his voice cracking as he forced the words past the tightness in his throat. To his disgust, he realized he was shaking, and he shoved his hands into his uniform pant pockets. Dillon's eyes flickered over his face, and he stepped forward and wrapped his arms around him in a tight embrace, returning the one Theo had given him an hour earlier, when he'd found him huddled against the wall in his father's sick room. Dillon's fingers feathered through the hair at the back of his head, and he buried his face into Dillon's shoulder, silently praying Gray wouldn't turn from the window and see him in his moment of weakness.

When he straightened, Theo wiped his eyes discreetly. Dillon clasped his shoulder before turning back to the closet. Theo watched him pick through his clothes and forced deep breaths into his lungs, then turned away and looked at Gray.

Gray hadn't moved an inch in the intervening moments Theo had spent with Dillon, still staring out the window, his fingers tapping impatiently on his thigh. Theo knelt beside him and asked, "How's it looking out there?"

"They're almost gone," Gray said. "Something down the street caught their attention, so they've been drifting that way." He indicated the direction opposite the ambulance base. "A few more minutes and it might be clear enough to get out of here."

"I still want to stop by a pharmacy," Theo said. "CVS isn't far from here. We could be in and out, quick and easy."

"I think we should go home first and wait a few more days for some of the chaos to die down before even *thinking* about going someplace public," Gray said.

"Gray, what are you going to do if we get separated and you have an asthma attack?" Theo asked. "What will you do if something happens to me? If I'm not around to help you? You don't have an inhaler."

"I've got an inhaler," Gray protested. "It's…" He trailed off, remembering the loss of his inhaler at the Brass Monkey.

"There are three of us now," Theo stated. "Three is better than two. We can all go in, grab as much as we can, and get out before anything gets ahold of us. I know I'll sleep better if I know you have what you need to take care of yourself."

Gray heaved a sigh, running his hand through his hair to push it back from his forehead. He squinted out the window, and Theo followed his gaze, examining the yard below for himself. Where before there'd been ten zombie-people in the yard, now there were only two. One milled near the sidewalk, close to the end of the driveway; the other lurked near Theo's car. Though the man by the car looked easy enough to take down, the woman at the end of the driveway was larger than he was, and while he was used to hauling around and occasionally manhandling heavier patients in his line of work, there was only so much he could do.

The sound of a zipper sliding closed let Theo know that Dillon had finished packing. Perfect timing, too, since he didn't want to wait any longer to get moving now that most of the danger below had passed. He pushed to his feet and shouldered his pilfered axe.

"Come on, let's get to the car while we've got the chance," he said. "Both of you stay behind me and don't make any sudden movements that might get their attention. Got it?"

"Got it," Dillon said, and Gray nodded. Theo moved to the door, leading the way into the hall and downstairs. As they descended, single file, Dillon said quietly, "What about my father?"

"What about him?" Theo asked, his voice hushed. His palms were sweating against the handle of his axe, and he wiped them on his uniform pants.

"Shouldn't we do something about...about his body?"

"We don't have time," Theo said, feeling a pang of sorrow. "I'm sorry, Dill. We'll have to come back in a day or two and deal with it then."

He glanced at Dillon and saw his eyes shining with tears, but he was nodding understandingly. "Yeah. Okay. You're right. The living are more important now, right?"

"Right," he confirmed. They reached the first floor, and he paused, checking their surroundings. Everything still looked secure. Dillon looked uncertain but willing to go along with whatever Theo planned. Gray, on the other hand, looked determined, his jaw set, his crowbar gripped in his right hand like he was ready to swing at the first thing that pissed him off.

"You two ready?" Theo asked. They both nodded, and he unlocked the door and pulled it open.

CHAPTER TWELVE

Plantersville, MS

Gray drummed his fingers nervously against the steering wheel of Theo's Hyundai, studying the building in front of them. The CVS was the only major chain pharmacy in town, and he'd expected them to walk into a mess. Oddly, the beige-painted concrete façade, red awnings, and plate glass windows were untouched. There were no other vehicles in the parking lot, and everything was still, though that didn't do much to erase his nagging worry.

"What are you thinking?" Gray asked the silent figure in the passenger seat.

Theo barely moved, intently studying the building. Finally, he said, "I don't like it."

"Why not? It's untouched," he pointed out.

"It's untouched, yes," Theo repeated. "I've seen several stores that have been looted. Even a coffee shop. But a *pharmacy* hasn't been touched? I want to know why."

"Maybe they just haven't gotten this far yet," he suggested. Theo wordlessly pointed to a hardware store across the street; its windows were broken, and the front door was smeared with a streak of blood.

Dillon sat forward from the backseat. He'd been so quiet that Gray had nearly forgotten he was there. "All this shit started overnight," he said. "The rioting and violence and stuff. And it all started on the east end of town, judging by what I gathered on the news before the power went out. CVS closed at, what, eight last night? Maybe Gray's sort of right."

"Sort of?" he repeated, trying to decide if he should be indignant or not.

"With everything starting on the other side of town, maybe nobody has made it down here yet," Dillon said.

"Maybe there isn't anyone else alive to loot it," Theo said.

"Because *that* isn't morbid or anything," Gray retorted.

"Turn the engine off but leave the doors unlocked," Theo said. "Just in case we need to get back in quickly. Nobody comes out to the car alone, and inside, we stay within earshot of each other, no matter what. Once inside, Gray, I want you to grab as much canned food as you can, and Dillon, you hit up the OTC meds and bandages and all that stuff. If either of you happens to see anything particularly useful, go ahead and grab it."

"What are you going to be doing?" Gray asked, already visualizing the interior of the store and everything inside.

"I'm going to hit the pharmacy for the prescription drugs," Theo said. "I'll know better than you two which meds are essential and which we can live without."

"You should grab any painkillers for sure," Dillon said. "If not for our use than for trade. I have a feeling if things get worse, the barter system will make a comeback."

"Good point," Theo agreed. "Shall we?"

Gray flung his door open and slid out. After picking up the crowbar he'd tucked between the driver's seat and console, he waited impatiently for the other two to join him and followed Theo to the front doors. After they jimmied the doors open with the crowbar and shoved them wide, all three of them stood inside the entryway, staring into the darkened store, trying to see if any dangers lurked in the aisles. When nothing emerged, Theo turned on his flashlight. "Wait here," he instructed and ventured into the store, cutting left toward the cash registers. As he disappeared from sight, Gray took a few steps forward, not liking him going out of sight.

A hand closed around his bicep, and he whirled to hit whoever had grabbed him before checking himself when he realized it was just Dillon. "*What?*"

"Theo said to wait here," Dillon said. "We should do what he says."

He scoffed. "You always do what you're told?"

"Not usually, but considering this could be a matter of life or death, I figure it's smart to listen for once," Dillon said.

"Life or death is precisely why I'm going after him," he replied. "And if he was really your friend, you'd agree."

Before Dillon responded, Theo reappeared, carrying two plastic-wrapped flashlights and a package of batteries. They cracked the plastic open and inserted batteries into the flashlights. They turned on easily, their yellowish beams illuminating endcaps of candy and shampoo, and Gray grabbed a shopping cart.

They split up then, heading in different directions, Theo beelining for the back of the store, Dillon heading in the same general direction for the OTC medications, and Gray moving left to the grocery items. There wasn't much in the way of food in a pharmacy store like this, but Gray filled up a shopping cart with several twelve-packs of bottled water and quite a few shopping bags stuffed to bursting with canned goods. Once he'd cleared everything usable off the shelves, he shoved the heavily laden cart toward the front doors; by the time he made it there, he had begun feeling a little winded. He sagged against the shopping cart, taking a moment to breathe, and remembered Theo's orders to not go to the car alone. He pushed off from the cart and headed into the store to sweep each of the aisles for anything else useful.

* * *

Theo went straight to the pharmacy counter at the back of the store, walking with Dillon for most of the way since their destinations were close. They spent most of the walk silent, and it wasn't until they reached the end of the cold medicine aisle that Theo broke the silence.

"I want you to take this," he said, holding the axe out to Dillon.

Dillon looked at him with wide-eyed surprise.

"Just while I'm at the pharmacy counter," he insisted. "You can give it back when I'm done."

Dillon stared at him and then asked, "Why did you do this?"

"Do what?"

"Come after me," Dillon said. "Bring me with you."

"You're my friend," he said.

"You have other friends," Dillon pointed out. "I don't hear you making plans to go after them."

"That's true," Theo conceded. He idly picked up a package of cold and flu medicine and dropped it into the cart Dillon had brought with him. "But I'm not sleeping with my other friends either, am I?"

"I don't know," Dillon replied. "Are you?"

"You're really going to ask me something like that?"

"It's a simple yes or no question, Theo," Dillon pressed.

"Fine, then. No, I'm not. You're the only person who even knows I lean that way, *and* you're the only one I care about like that," Theo said, his exasperation overcoming any reticence he might have had at the admission.

Dillon looked flattered. "Really?"

Oh God, Theo thought. "Dill, I don't think this is a good place or time to have this talk. Can we save it for when we get to my house? We can explore it in depth then."

"Among other things," Dillon joked, and when Theo rolled his eyes, he held his hands up defensively. "I'm sorry, okay? I'm trying to distract myself from the crappiness of this situation."

"Well, keep trying," Theo said. "And take the axe, for my piece of mind?"

Dillon set the axe on his cart. "Fine," he grumbled. "Only because you asked nicely. But you're getting it back the minute you finish in the pharmacy." He surged forward and caught Theo's shirt, hauling him in for a scorching kiss. Breaking away, cheeks flushed, he said, "For luck."

Theo laughed. "Best lucky charm ever," he commented. "I'll be right back." He turned away from Dillon and headed to the pharmacy counter, climbing over to get into the employees-only area and setting about the task of gathering as much medicine as he could stuff into the canvas shopping bags he'd pilfered from the front of the store. Starting at one end of the drug racks, he began picking out the useful drugs, leaving ones he had no use for or wasn't sure about, and dumped his selections into the bags he carried.

Theo was nearly done when he heard the shout of alarm, followed by a crash of metal shelving. He dropped his bags and ran to the counter, vaulting over, half-sliding on his hip across it and dropping to the carpet on the other side. "Gray?

Dillon?" he called. He heard a moan from the general direction he'd left Dillon. There was another crash, this time like metal on metal, and Dillon's cry of pain.

"Dillon!" he shouted, racing along one of the aisles, searching for his friend. "Dillon, where are you?"

"Theo!" Gray's voice yelled, and Theo skidded to a halt, disoriented, trying to figure out which aisle it'd come from. Another clang, then Gray added, "Aisle seven! Seven!"

Theo altered his course, halting at the end of the family planning aisle for a few seconds to assess what was going on before charging into the melee. Gray stood over Dillon, swinging his crowbar at an unknown man grabbing at him with a manic-ness that suggested he was one of the crazy people like his patient from the night before. Dillon lay on the carpeted floor behind Gray, making soft, choked moaning sounds. Several shelves were collapsed, the merchandise from them scattered on the floor and on top of Dillon, the metal shelves bent like something had been flung against them. The axe lay beside Dillon, and Theo lunged forward and scooped it up.

"Gray, down!" he shouted, and Gray dropped without hesitation, falling to his knees. Both of them struck simultaneously. Theo swung his axe sideways as Gray thrust upward with the pointed end of his crowbar. The crowbar embedded into their attacker's stomach at the same time Theo's axe sliced into its neck. The force of the axe blow took the man's head half off, and he pulled the weapon free, hefted it, and swung again, slicing the man's head the rest of the way from his neck. The head banged against a shelf of lubricants and tumbled to the floor. The body followed close behind.

"You okay?" Theo asked Gray, looking him over for injuries.

Gray looked pale, shaken. He motioned behind him. "Dillon," he said, and Theo's brain focused enough to hear the other man's choking, gurgling gasps for air. He whirled around and dropped to his knees beside him. Dillon lay on his back, both hands clasped to his throat, and Theo didn't have to move his hands for him to know what was wrong; judging by the rate of blood flow from the wound, he had only moments to act. His brain skidded right into paramedic mode without a second's hesitation. "Gray, get me bandages, fast! Better yet, grab my medic bag from the car. And run!" Gray scooped up his crowbar and took off.

The entire time Theo was giving orders, he'd stared at Dillon, and Dillon had stared back, his gaze beseeching, pleading with Theo to help him. But under the plea, he could see resignation, like Dillon knew he was going to die and was, in the last moments of his life, accepting it. It was the look of impending doom that Theo had been taught to recognize when he'd been in paramedic school, and seeing it on Dillon's face was nothing short of horrifying.

"No, no, no, don't give up!" Theo said, tears pricking at his eyes. He pressed his hands on top of Dillon's. "Please, don't give up, Dill, please."

By the time Gray returned with Theo's medic bag, staggering under its weight, Dillon had slipped into unconsciousness. Theo worked feverishly, slapping on bandages, layering on more as they became soaked through. Kneeling on Dillon's other side, Gray pushed Theo's hands away from the wounded man's neck.

"I'll work on controlling the bleeding," he said. "You deal with the other stuff."

Theo dug into his bag and pulled out supplies. He lashed a tourniquet around Dillon's arm, slapping his skin, trying to get a vein to rise enough to start an IV. Once he had one, he pulled out an IV catheter, saline bag, and tubing and rapidly started a line. He'd barely finished taping down the IV catheter when Gray said, "Theo, I don't think he's breathing anymore."

Theo whipped around, looking at Dillon's motionless body with wide eyes, watching for movement. When he didn't see any, he pushed Dillon's jacket out of the way and braced both hands against his chest, starting compressions, hard and fast. "AED, now!" he snapped breathlessly to Gray. When Gray didn't move, he snarled, "Go get the fucking AED!"

"I don't think it's going to help," Gray said quietly. "You're not going to get him back."

"Shut up!" Theo yelled, pausing the compressions long enough to blow two breaths of air into Dillon's lungs before resuming compressions again.

"What will happen if you *do* get him back?" Gray asked. "He's just going to bleed out, and then you'll be right back where you are right now." He grabbed Theo's wrist, disrupting his rhythm. "Theo, stop." Theo glared at him, and he added, "You're torturing him. And yourself. Stop and think for a second. What would he want?"

Theo wrestled his arm from Gray's hand and started compressions again, but his mind spun with his brother's words. He knew Gray was right—he *knew* that. He'd told patients' families the same thing on multiple occasions when he'd been called to their homes for unresponsive patients and had to explain that nothing could be done. A lot of families would be in denial, demanding he do something, *anything* to save their loved ones. He'd always felt a touch of exasperation at their reticence to believe what he was saying, but now that he was faced with the same decision, he found he couldn't blame them for their determination to keep fighting, even in the face of hopelessness.

He looked at Dillon's face and tried to decide what to do. *What would Dillon want?* he wondered, contemplating his face. Dillon's skin was unnaturally pale, his lips blue from lack of oxygen, his eyes closed, his jaw lax. He slowly stopped compressions and sat back on his heels, panting from the exertion as tears flooded his eyes again. A sob burst from him, and he hung his head. Dillon was dead. There wasn't anything he could do, even if he *could* somehow get him back from cardiac arrest. His best friend and sometimes lover was dead, and there wasn't anything he could do about it.

Gray took his arm and gently hauled him to his feet, pushing him toward the front doors. "You should step outside, get some air," he suggested, leading him to the front of the store. He shoved his crowbar into Theo's hands and motioned to the car. "Go sit in there. I'll get the stuff and be out in a minute."

Theo hesitated, looking at him worriedly. "What are you about to do?"

"I'm going to get your medical bag and axe," Gray said. "Trust me, okay? And get in the car."

Theo slowly started toward the car. He felt numb inside, his stomach churning as if he was going to throw up. He slouched against the side of his car, sucking in deep, steadying breaths of cool air. He was unsteady, like his world was swimming, and his lungs felt like they were full of water. His hands shook, and he nearly dropped the crowbar. Pulling open the rear car door, he set the crowbar onto the floorboard, and he'd just shut the door when he heard a heavy thud inside the pharmacy.

"Gray?" he said, calling out loud enough to be heard, but there was no response other than another thud. He was about to go back inside when Gray appeared from the darkness, carrying his medical bag, the two sacks of prescription medications, a bloodied axe, and a towel. His jeans were stained with fresh blood. "What did you do?"

"What?" Gray asked with clearly feigned innocence.

"What. Did. You. Do?" Theo asked again, more emphatically. "What's with the blood on your clothes? What did you do, Gray?"

"I did what needed to be done," Gray said, using the towel to clean the blood off the axe's blade.

"What's that supposed to mean?"

"It *means* he was going to turn into a zombie, like April did, and I did what needed to be done to keep that from happening."

Then the pieces fell into place—the axe, the blood on Gray's pants, the thuds he'd heard—and a hard fury flooded into him. He grabbed Gray's shirt and slammed him against the side of the car. "What did you do?" he snarled. "What did you do to Dillon?"

"He got bitten by one of them," Gray replied, unfazed by his anger. "Just like April! He was going to turn into one of them. I doubt you wanted him to be like that, and while I didn't know him, I'm pretty sure he wouldn't want to be one either! I was trying to spare him from a fate I personally consider worse than death!" He squirmed a little and tried to pull out of his grasp. "Let go of me, Theo. We've got to get out of here. Now isn't the time for this."

Theo stared for a moment more, then pulled him off the car just enough to slam him back against it again. "Don't think this is over," he snarled, letting go of his brother and stepping back. He got into the passenger seat and slammed the door.

* * *

Gordo, AL

Brandt, Cade, and Ethan drove through the late afternoon and part of the evening, taking whatever back roads and dirt roads it took to get around the ever-growing traffic jams lining almost every highway and interstate outside every city considered even somewhat major in the state. They were approaching the Mississippi state line, traveling through a small Alabama town called Gordo, when Brandt gave Ethan's arm a gentle punch to get his attention.

"Hey, Bennett, stop at that gun shop," Brandt said, pointing to the short, squat white building off the road. The gravel parking lot in which it rested was well lit. A liquor store sat beside it, sharing both building space and parking space. Ethan gave him a questioning glance and pulled the Jeep into the tiny lot.

"What are we here for?" he asked.

Brandt unfastened his seatbelt and looked back at Cade. Her rifle rested across her knees, and she looked absently out the side window, pointedly avoiding looking at the still-dark splotch on the backseat. "We need supplies. You're a cop, right, Bennett?"

"It's Ethan," he said irritably. "Not Bennett. And yes, I am."

"Got your badge?"

Ethan looked into the rearview mirror and made a worried sound as he saw the expression on Cade's face. A slow smirk spread across her lips, and she shook her head back and adjusted her ponytail. Her expression of understanding and borderline mischievousness made Ethan nervous, and he grimaced and turned back to Brandt.

"You already know I do. What do you need it for?" he demanded, snatching the badge off the dashboard. He closed his hand around it; the dull metal edge dug into his palm. He used the faint pain to ground himself and focus on not getting angry at the sneaking suspicion that crept over him.

"We're going to commandeer some guns and ammo from this shop," Brandt explained.

Ethan gaped. Despite his attempt to remain calm, he nearly exploded. "That's not even fucking—" he started, then jabbed his finger at Brandt. "That's *robbery!*"

Cade unbuckled her seatbelt and slid to the back passenger door. "Eth, we need the weapons," she said. "And they declared martial law an hour ago. We can do this and it's not *completely* illegal. Just in that hazy gray area." She waved her hand in a motion to indicate that haziness and nodded to Brandt. "Hell, Brandt's military, so he's been given ultimate authority to do what's necessary to maintain the peace. That, of course, won't happen, and I think we all know it. But my point still stands." She opened the door and exited into the cool, late evening air, then leaned back in and added, "We're doing this with or without you, Ethan. We just need you and your badge because civvies tend to react to police badges better than camo."

Ethan sighed and turned the Jeep's engine off. He grabbed his Glock from the console between the seats and slid it into its holster before climbing out of the Jeep. "I sincerely hope you two know what you're doing," he said, circling the vehicle to join them.

Brandt gave him a wide grin that only served to make him feel like the acid in his gut was trying to crawl up his throat. "After you?" Brandt offered pleasantly, even as he moved toward the gun shop's entrance.

Cade passed Ethan, her own pistol in hand. He noticed that, thankfully, she'd left her rifle in the car; he was sure the sight of it wouldn't do much to keep people inside the shop calm. She patted his shoulder. "Don't look so nervous. We'll be fine."

He was far from reassured. "You're enjoying this entirely too much," he grumbled. Brandt opened the shop's door and strode inside; Cade winked almost playfully and entered behind him.

As they stepped inside, the old man behind the register grabbed a pistol from underneath the counter and brandished it, moving to stand protectively by the cash register. Ethan raised his own weapon and held up his badge. "Police," he announced in a calm voice. "Put down your weapon."

The old man hesitated and squinted myopically at Ethan's badge. Ethan hoped the man wouldn't notice it was a Tennessee badge and not an Alabama one. To his relief, the old man set the gun on the counter and looked the three of them over doubtfully. "What do you want?"

"The state of Alabama declared martial law," Brandt said, moving to the counter and picking up the old man's gun. After a moment's study of the weapon, he tucked it into the waistband of his camouflage pants for safekeeping. "We're here to commandeer weapons and ammunition."

"You can't do that!" The old man glared at them and crossed his arms, looking ready to fight them off if they so much as stepped closer to him.

"We can, and we are," Brandt said. He moved around the counter and held his hand out. "I need your keys to the cases, please."

"You can't do this," the man tried again weakly. He clutched the keys tightly, not looking inclined to hand them over.

"Sir, I don't think you want to be arrested right now," Cade warned. "Just do what the man says." She eyed the array of hunting knives in the locked case serving as the front counter.

"Sir, we need your keys," Ethan said, using the soothing yet stern voice he employed in the line of duty. The old man hesitated and then set the keys in Ethan's outstretched hand. Ethan tossed the keys to Brandt; the lieutenant caught them and started unlocking cases and pulling out rifles, shotguns, and pistols. He lined them up on the counter as if putting them on display. "We're very sorry about this...what's your name?"

"Ralph Mackenzie," the old man said grumpily. He crossed his arms again as Cade and Brandt grabbed duffel bags from the shelves and selected pistols and rifles, loading them into the bags.

"I'm sorry we have to do this, Mister Mackenzie," Ethan said. To Brandt and Cade, he warned, "Don't take everything. Only what we need. Leave him the rest to protect himself and any family he has."

Cade nodded and offered Ralph several of his pistols. When he didn't take them, she set them on the counter, the appropriate ammunition next to them. After she watched Ralph for a moment, expecting a response that didn't come, she addressed Brandt instead. "I want to get some of those knives," she said. "Never know when you'll need a quiet weapon."

Brandt looked at Ralph. The old man still stood by the counter, almost sulking, as they raided his merchandise. "Hey, do you know if that liquor store next door is open?"

Ethan turned sharply. "No drinking," he ordered.

"I'm not planning on fucking drinking."

Ralph nodded at Brandt. "It's open. Opened three hours ago," he said in the surliest tone Ethan had ever heard from a person.

"Thanks, man." Brandt grabbed two duffel bags and slung them onto his shoulders, securing them against his back before walking out the front door. Ethan watched through the windows as Brandt loaded the bags into the Jeep before heading to the liquor store. Then he gave Cade a quizzical look.

"Hey, don't ask me," Cade said defensively, studying one of the knives she'd taken from the glass case. "He's doing his own thing. I'm just following along if it looks like something that won't get us killed. Surviving this is more important to me than anything else."

Ethan sighed and holstered his pistol. "Do you see anything else in here we'll need?" he asked. He squinted at a rack of camouflage hunting shirts hanging nearby and wondered if they should take any of them.

"I only got what I know how to use," Cade said. She fastened a knife sheath to her belt, slid the knife she held into it, and grabbed another one. "I need to get a boot knife," she mused. "A nice sturdy one like Brandt's got." She dropped the knife into the bag left on the counter and looked to Ralph. He still lurked behind the counter, watching them.

"You look like you're preparing for war," Ralph commented uneasily.

Ethan studied the man and considered his options. Then he pushed one of the pistols on the counter toward Ralph. "I think we are," he admitted. "It'll probably do you good to shut up shop and barricade yourself and your family in your home with enough food and water to last as long as possible until everything's cleared up."

The front door banged open, and Ethan drew his pistol as he spun to face the danger, instinctively pointing the weapon at the door, ready to defend them against anything that walked in. But it was only Brandt returning from his field trip to the liquor store. Ethan sighed, exasperated, and started to put his weapon away again.

"No, don't," Brandt warned. "The guy who runs the liquor store," he started to explain.

"Tom," Ralph interrupted.

"Yeah, Tom," Brandt said, waving a dismissive hand at Ralph. "He's down."

"What did you do to Tom?" Ralph demanded, his voice rising in pitch and volume. He moved forward suddenly, his hands out like he was ready to come around the counter and throttle Brandt. Cade snatched a pistol from the counter and pointed it at the man's head in one smooth movement. Ralph froze and put his hands up defensively as he faced down the barrel of the gun.

"Back up, you old coot, or I'll put you down too," Cade warned, her eyes hard and cold again. She flexed her finger over the trigger and clenched her jaw.

"Cade," Ethan barked a sharp warning, pushing her arm down to force her to lower the weapon. "Now's not time for that." He looked to Brandt once more and asked, "Did you get whatever you needed from the liquor store?"

"Yeah, I got enough to last," Brandt replied vaguely. "We need to move."

"We do," Ethan agreed. He gently removed the pistol from Cade's hand and set it back down on the glass-topped counter. "Once again, we do apologize, Mister Mackenzie. If we all make it out of this shit alive, we'll see what we can do to fix this."

Ralph looked even more alarmed at his words but didn't speak. He simply nodded and backed up another step to press against the empty gun cases lining the wall behind the counter. He remained there with his eyes wide and his hands clenched into fists.

Brandt walked out the door without another word and made a beeline for the back of the SUV. Ethan waited until Cade left the gun shop before following her out, not looking back at the old man standing forlornly against his empty gun cases. Cade slid into the backseat of the Jeep, and Ethan joined Brandt at the rear of the vehicle. He tilted his head curiously as he saw four opened cardboard boxes full of assorted types of liquor. "You planning on having a party or something?"

Brandt smirked and picked up a box. The bottles inside jingled together as he hefted it and nodded at the Jeep's cargo door. "Or something," he answered. "Open that up and help me load these, would you?"

Ethan rolled his eyes and opened the back door, reluctantly picking up another box. "What are you going to use all this alcohol for?" he asked, shoving the box inside.

"You probably don't want to know," Cade spoke up. Ethan looked up and saw her perched on the Jeep's roof, her legs hanging down into the car through the opened sunroof.

She had her rifle in hand again. "It's almost definitely illegal. I'd bet a hundred dollars on it."

"You bet right," Brandt confirmed. He gave the woman a mischievous grin that made Ethan's stomach turn, then pulled out his wallet. He removed his last dollar bill, wadded it up, and threw it in Cade's direction. "You'll get the other ninety-nine later, darlin'," he drawled with a playful wink.

Cade laughed and caught the bill with an easy motion of her hand. She kissed her closed fist before lifting her hips off the car to shove it in her pocket. "I'm going to hold you to that, Evans," she warned, grinning.

Ethan resisted the urge to glare at Brandt as the man eyed Cade, and he shoved the last box of liquor into the back with more force than was strictly necessary. It was like watching his little sister get hit on by the worst kind of guy, and it was, quite frankly, nauseating.

The faint sound of a police siren brushed the late evening air, and the three of them looked up simultaneously. Ethan squinted down the highway in the direction of the noise.

"What the hell is that?" Cade asked.

Brandt swore and slammed his hand against the Jeep. "That fucking bastard called the damned cops!"

"Wouldn't you call the cops if three people with guns walked into your business and stole your shit?" Ethan asked. He shut the cargo door hard enough to jar the entire vehicle. "Get in the fucking car. Cade, get off the roof. I want to get to Tupelo and locked into someplace safe before dawn."

PART TWO
SURVIVAL

CHAPTER THIRTEEN

Three Weeks Later

Tupelo, MS
Brandt's Journal
March 8th

I'm following Cade's lead and keeping a journal. I can guarantee this won't last. I've never been good at this kind of thing, and I've never been the type to spill out everything I'm feeling, on paper or otherwise. This will probably end up being one of those bald-facts affairs that just tells things the way they are. And the way things are isn't exactly the way I want them to be.

    We are, figuratively, in the shit.

    We made it to Tupelo as safely as I expected. We've been in this little house for over a month now, unmolested for the most part. There's been a few incidents involving an infected or two getting close to where we're hiding, but they were taken care of quickly and quietly. It's scary how efficient we've gotten at this.

Cade spends most of her days either keeping watch on the roof or sitting in the living room while we try to find reports on the radio. Ethan spends most of his time being the dickish guy he was when I first met him. I suspect that's his normal personality, despite Cade's assurances to the contrary. But I'm getting off topic. I said I'd write down what happened, and that's what I'm going to do.

So here's where we stand now:

By the fourteenth day after Atlanta's fall (one week after I met Cade and Ethan), the entirety of the southeast was ravaged by the Michaluk Virus. There were some holdouts, mostly in small towns and cities that weren't close to the larger metro areas, but even those have since fallen. Now, as far as we understand, it's just isolated pockets of survivors scattered across the southeastern states, struggling to live.

By the sixteenth day, the last TV news station went off air, presumably permanently. We're not sure what happened, but my theories tend to involve the infected, so it doesn't do to ask me about it. Cade thinks the news reporter gave up and decided to find his own hideout. Two days after he *stopped reporting, the power in our safe house went out for good.*

By the twenty-fifth day, we lost the last of the radio stations that we could pick up. The final DJ went off the air with screams of terror. I don't think I'll ever forget the sound.

On top of all this, none of us have seen another breathing, uninfected soul since we stopped in Gordo, Alabama. This fact on its own is disturbing enough. The additional fact that we've been forced to move further away from Tupelo's main center twice in order to get away from the hordes of infected is downright frighte

Cade gasped. The sound broke through Brandt's train of thought, and he dropped his pen; it rolled halfway down the sloped roof before slowing to a stop. Narrowing his dark eyes, he looked at Cade accusingly, wondering what in the world she was freaking out about. But he was more irritated at the fact he'd now have to get up to retrieve his pen before a gust of wind took it the rest of the way off the roof.

It was early in the morning of their third day at their newest safe house. Cade had been on the roof since sunrise, and he'd joined her soon after—partly to keep her company, but mostly to get away from Ethan. The older man had become surly and withdrawn the longer they'd been in Mississippi. Well, *more* surly and withdrawn, he amended silently. Ethan had struck him as a grouchy bastard when they'd met, and nothing he'd done had dislodged his initial impression. Besides, it was much more pleasant on the roof with Cade, despite the air that still clung tenaciously to its early spring chill. As he breathed out, the air fogged before his face in the same way it had in a dark alley in Atlanta....

He shook free from the dark thoughts threatening to surface and turned his attention fully to Cade. "What is it?" he asked, impatient despite his determination to keep his cool.

"I thought I saw people down there," she said, pointing down the street.

Brandt sat up straighter, suddenly attentive, and moved to one knee, following her finger to see what she thought she'd seen. He couldn't deny the way his heart pounded at the thought of other uninfected people; he longed for company outside of Cade's and Ethan's. Even though he liked both of them just fine, especially Cade, he preferred an ever-changing environment, and the last month had offered nothing like that. But no matter how much he squinted into the distance, he couldn't see anything.

"I think if you actually saw something, it was just one of the infected," he said, his shoulders sagging. He set his notebook onto the roof beside him and slid down the slope to grab his pen, hissing through his teeth as a knuckle scraped roughly against the shingles. He stopped halfway down the roof to study his injured knuckle as Cade replied.

"I don't know, Brandt," she said, her voice heavy with doubt. He looked up at her; she frowned, keeping her eyes on the street below. "I could've sworn that whoever I saw was running."

Brandt scooped up his pen and crawled back up to his spot beside her. "Yeah, I hear the infected can run too, you know," he pointed out, picking up his ragged notebook, resting it on a knee, and smoothing a hand over its battered cover. "Relax, okay? Nothing's gonna happen around here. And if something *does* happen, it's not like the infected can get up onto the roof."

Cade sighed and shook her hair back from her face, then whipped out her ever-present hair elastic—he still wondered where she kept those things—and pulled her dark locks back into a tight ponytail, which made her face appear hard, her jaw strong and more angled than before. He realized, as his eyes traced her features, that Cade's own eyes were locked onto a distant point on the street. He jammed his pen into the spirals of his notebook for safekeeping before looking at her full-on.

"There's nothing down there," Brandt said. "If there was, I'm pretty sure we'd know it by now."

A slow, know-it-all smirk spread across Cade's face as he finished speaking. She gently elbowed him and stood up. "Oh, there's nothing down there?" she asked. "Then what's that?" She pointed down the street again. He followed her gesture reluctantly, wholly convinced he wouldn't see anything of significance down there.

Brandt was proven wrong when he saw two figures running down the street. One hunched under the weight of a large bag, supporting the other with one arm even as he stumbled along beside him. They were too far away for him to make out finer details. He stood beside Cade and picked up her rifle, aiming it in the direction of the two figures below.

Cade grabbed his arm and yanked it hard, nearly dragging the weapon out of his grip. "Brandt!" she protested, horrified.

"I'm not going to fucking shoot them," Brandt snapped, wresting the rifle away from Cade. "I just need your damn scope." He squinted through the scope in question and studied the two figures, watching their movements, the way they walked and gestured and helped each other along.

It was two men, as far as his scope-assisted eyesight could discern. The dark-haired one appeared to be younger and was dressed in jeans and a mid-length dark coat; the older one was blond and had on some sort of uniform with patches on the sleeves. A dark blue bag was slung over his shoulders, resting on his back. The way it bulged coupled with the way the man was bent over indicated that it was quite heavy. He tried to make out further details, such as words or logos printed on the man's uniform patches, but they were too far away and the patches too indistinct at this distance.

"They don't have Michaluk," Brandt concluded. "We should get them inside. There might be infected nearby."

"Are you sure?" Cade demanded. She took the rifle from him and gave him an offended look, like she was disgusted that he'd dared to lay hands on her precious weapon. He had a mental image of her stroking the rifle lovingly, like someone would a dog, complete with the sweet crooning of "*Who's a good boy?*" He bit back a snigger as she continued. "What if you're wrong and they *are* infected?"

"Well, that's what the rifle is for, isn't it?" Brandt suggested. He climbed the steep slope of the roof, slipped through the window, and leaned out to help Cade inside. "All I know is that neither of them appears to be infected," he continued. He grasped her hand and assisted her inside. "And I can't in good conscience leave them to fend for themselves when I have the ability to help them."

Cade hesitated and looked back at the street. The two men were coming into view, and Brandt could see more details without the aid of the rifle scope. "Damn, Alton, you must have the eyes of a hawk," he commented, realizing she'd spotted them from a great distance without binoculars or a scope. "Come on, let's get downstairs and get them in the house."

Without another word, Brandt headed through the dark bedroom he and Cade had climbed into and stepped into the equally dim hallway. He debated taking out the flashlight he kept in his jacket pocket, but he'd become familiar enough with the house that he thought he could make it to the front door without it. As he descended the stairs, his boots thudding heavily on each step on the way down, he could hear Ethan in the living room, doing exactly what he'd left him doing earlier: pacing restlessly in front of the unlit fireplace. His arms were crossed, and he grumbled to himself, though the words were drowned out by the sound of creaking floorboards and Brandt's hurried footsteps.

Ethan jerked his head up as Brandt darted into the room and snatched the steel crowbar from the coffee table. "What are you doing?" he demanded. The other answer was the sound of Cade running downstairs. Ethan's expression was a perfect picture of bewilderment as he shifted his eyes from Brandt to Cade. "What's going on?"

"There are people outside," Cade explained, reaching the bottom of the stairs and circling to the living room. Brandt strode to the front door and began prying away the boards with which they'd reinforced it. The boards came away with a loud creak of nails tearing from wood as she continued. "We're trying to get them inside."

"What?" Something in Ethan's tone made Brandt pause, and he half-turned to look at the other man. "Absolutely *not*. You're not opening that door," he said with a shake of his head.

Brandt ground his teeth together in frustration and wordlessly turned his back to the man, attacking the boards again as Cade debated with Ethan. It was better to let her handle the verbal part of the argument; if Ethan pushed the matter with *him*, he might not be able to resist the urge to hit him across the jaw with his crowbar.

It was never good for Brandt to get pissed off when he had a potentially deadly weapon in his hands. Things never turned out well.

"Ethan, we can't leave them out there!" Cade protested as Brandt ripped a board from the doorframe viciously. He glanced back again and saw Cade sling her rifle's strap over her shoulder, resting the weapon against her back. He wondered if she too was trying to resist the urge to inflict bodily harm on Ethan. "It's not right!" she continued. "They need help, and we can give it to them!"

"What kind of help can we offer them?" Ethan demanded. "*None.* We're not in control of anything here! Our supplies are limited. We're barely hanging on as it is. It's just too fucking dangerous to open that door!"

"Ethan Bennett, I *cannot* believe you're suggesting we leave people out there when we can offer them shelter and survival!" Cade snapped. "If we leave them to die, we're just as bad as those fucking infected *things* out there!"

A heavy silence fell between them, and Brandt could feel the weight of it resting on his shoulders. The final board came free, effectively removing the only major barricade to the outside. He dropped the board onto the floor and unlocked the deadbolt, grabbing the doorknob with one hand and the crowbar in the other to serve as a weapon before looking over his shoulder at the two friends. They stood less than a foot away from each other, Ethan's arms still crossed and Cade's hands on her hips, their eyes locked on each other's faces and expressions set in hard determination and anger.

"Debate's over," Brandt said. "Are either of you going to give me some backup, or am I handling this alone?"

The question was enough to drag them away from their tense scowls. Cade pulled her rifle from her shoulder, shaking her head. "I've got it, since Ethan's being a jerk," she muttered, striding to the door. She gave Brandt a small smile and added, "I'll stand guard on the porch while you get 'em. You run faster than me."

"Oh, is that the only reason for me to be saddled with the harder job?" Brandt joked. He hefted his crowbar and made his way to the porch, Cade close behind, and scanned their surroundings. He didn't see any immediate dangers, but that didn't mean they were safe, not by a long shot.

"Yes," she answered with a little laugh. "Go get 'em, tiger." She punched him playfully on his bicep, and he couldn't resist grinning. She looked more relaxed and less angry than she had when she'd faced off with Ethan, and he was grateful. The last thing he wanted to deal with was an angry Cade.

The porch steps creaked under his boots as only old wooden steps could, sending a chill down his spine and making him think of ghosts and haunted houses. As if he needed anything else to creep him out nowadays. He looked around the dead street as he crossed the yard, and his frown deepened considerably. He couldn't see the men they'd spotted from the roof; he was going to have to go into the street to find them, and he didn't relish the idea.

Brandt glanced back at Cade; it was a bit reassuring seeing her standing at attention on the porch, her eyes on the street, constantly scanning for dangers. Still, her presence didn't do much to reduce the sense of exposure that settled on his skin as he moved into the center of the street. There was movement far in the distance to his right, and he wondered if the infected were massing nearby. The idea didn't settle his nerves.

The two men were nowhere to be seen. Maybe they'd found shelter in a nearby house in the time it'd taken Brandt to get the front door open. Or perhaps they'd been grabbed by an infected person while Brandt had pried at the boards nailed to the doorframe.

"Brandt!" Cade called softly. He turned, and she pointed to his left. In the direction she indicated, there were the two men, still limping away as fast as their obvious exhaustion would allow. In the time it had taken him to get outside, the men had made it half a block down and into the yard of a house across the street.

Without further thought, Brandt darted after them, calling out just loudly enough to get their attention. "Hey! Hey, stop!"

The men halted mid-step, and the older of the two let go of the thinner one and pointed an old revolver right in Brandt's face, standing protectively between Brandt and the smaller man. Brandt stopped short and held up both hands defensively. The crowbar dangled, useless, by the hook over the fingers of one hand.

"Who are you? What do you want?" the blond man demanded. His grip on the revolver was so tight his knuckles had paled.

"I am *so* tired of having guns pointed at me," Brandt remarked casually. He forced his gaze away from the barrel and looked behind him, though the training that had been hammered into his head over the years screamed at him that he shouldn't take his eyes off the dangers in front of him. He tried to ignore the little voice. "Look, I have a hideout over there," he said, pointing to the house. Cade was just visible on the porch, and he knew she must be tense as she watched the exchange. "Me and two friends. We're trying to offer you shelter."

"Why? What's in it for you?" the man asked, his voice hard, a steely glint in his blue eyes. Brandt glanced at the revolver again; the barrel shook noticeably. Focusing past the gun, he took in his first *real* look of the man. His outfit was, indeed, a uniform. He wore a dark button-up uniform shirt and dark pants, and sturdy boots adorned his feet. A gold nameplate on the right side of his chest said "Carter." Brandt lit onto the patches on his sleeves, and a slow smile spread across his face.

"Nothing. Just the idea of additional security and helping other people," he finally answered. "And perhaps your skills as a paramedic would come in handy too."

The man hesitated, looking torn between the decision to go with Brandt and the decision for him and his friend to find their own hiding place. As he debated, Cade called out from the porch again.

"Brandt, there're infected coming this way!"

Brandt swore and turned away from Carter, lifting the crowbar defensively. He scanned the street in every direction, but he couldn't see any infected coming toward them from anywhere. "Where? Where are they?"

Cade didn't answer, just lifted her rifle and pointed it down the yard toward the empty house next door to theirs, in the opposite direction from Brandt's position. She aimed at something he couldn't see, but the fact she aimed her rifle at all was a solid indicator that something was about to go horribly wrong.

"Shit, if she's actually about to fire that thing, it's fucking serious," Brandt said. He grabbed Carter by the arm without a moment's consideration for the fact he had a gun pointed at him. "Come on, we've got to go!"

Thankfully, the two men didn't question his order. As he moved toward the house, his boots hurrying over the pavement and sidewalk, the men followed him to the front porch.

Cade waited at the top of the steps, her rifle still aimed down the street, lining up a shot.

"No, don't!" he gasped, storming up the steps to stop her. He motioned with the crowbar for the two men to enter the house; they bolted into the dark interior without question. "The sound of the gunshot will only draw them here."

Cade tensed and removed her finger from the trigger she'd already begun squeezing. "They're moving between the trees," she reported. "Hiding behind them and cars, fences, bushes, trash cans, whatever. They're working to keep me from seeing them. They might even be working together. Strategizing or some shit."

Brandt caught Cade's arm and propelled her toward the front door. "Let's discuss this inside," he said as he followed her into the house.

The younger of the two men had sat down on the edge of the coffee table, and Carter had dumped the heavy bag onto the floor and knelt in front of him by the time they'd entered. Brandt registered the sound of the younger man's breathing: hard and fast, his inhalations deep and wheezy; it was obvious the man was in respiratory distress. He wondered if he should offer to help, but the open front door suggested otherwise. He shut and bolted the door, grabbed the nail gun, and set to work reapplying the boards he'd pried loose. He'd leave the medical problems to those who knew better than he how to handle them.

"Who are you?" Ethan demanded over the loud thump of the nail gun slamming the last nail home. Brandt set the tool by the door and moved back toward where the action was. He was sure if Ethan maintained the same attitude he'd had before the door opened, there would be trouble.

Ethan stood in the center of the living room, his arms still folded in that familiar pose he'd taken every time he got irritated. There was a hard look on his face as he stared at Carter, who still knelt on the floor by the coffee table. Cade lurked by the darkened fireplace, her rifle in her hands, her shoulders straight as her wary gaze shifted between Ethan and the two men. It was obvious Cade didn't know how to handle the tension in the air between the men. Truth be told, neither did Brandt.

"My name's Theo Carter," the older of the strangers said as he rubbed his companion's back soothingly. "This is my brother, Gray." He didn't add anything further as he started to unzip the bulging blue bag at his feet.

Ethan pulled his pistol from its holster and pointed it at Theo. The man froze and looked at Ethan with narrowed eyes. "Is he infected?" he asked sternly, motioning toward Gray with the gun.

"What the hell?" Theo said in exasperation. "*No*, he's not infected! He's got fucking asthma, and he needs his damned inhaler before he suffocates!"

Brandt had to take control of this situation before things spiraled out of hand. "Ethan, cut it out," he ordered. Ethan's bad mood had gone on long enough, and it was time either he or Cade reined it in. He grabbed Theo's bag before the paramedic could get into it and dumped its contents onto the coffee table beside Gray. "You'll excuse me if I search this, won't you?" he asked. "Just as a precaution."

Brandt didn't wait for a reply as he began pushing around the objects on the table. The bag had been packed with an assortment of first aid supplies, both basic bandages and medical tape and more advanced syringes and medications, as well as a strange metal contraption in a blue canvas roll. It resembled some sort of medieval torture device; it was definitely not something he'd want used on him. "What's this?"

"It's a laryngoscope," Theo said shortly. He snatched the inhaler to which he'd referred out of the pile and passed it to Gray without further elaboration.

"Ah." He set the roll back inside the bag, still completely lost as to what exactly a laryngoscope was, and looked up at Ethan. The man still glared at Theo; it was obvious he was far from happy about having additional people in their safe house. Brandt wasn't exactly thrilled with the idea, either; however, he was far from willing to abandon others to the dangerous streets when he could offer help. He stood and moved closer to Ethan in case he did something stupid. Considering how unstable the man had acted over the past few weeks, he wouldn't have put it past him.

"My name is Brandt Evans," he began, taking charge of the introductions. He paused, debating telling them his rank and where he was from. But then he shook his head and added, "I'm military. Marines. The cranky bastard to my right is Ethan Bennett from the Memphis PD." He dodged the swipe Ethan made at him and continued. "And the lovely but deadly lady over by the fireplace is Cade Alton, formerly of the Israel Defense Forces."

Theo nodded a short greeting to Cade, who'd remained wordless throughout the entire discussion. She nodded back at Theo solemnly, then crossed the room to join Brandt and Ethan. "We should quarantine them," she suggested, her voice low. "Just as a precaution, in case they've gotten infected and aren't showing symptoms yet."

"How would we go about doing that?" Brandt asked. As he spoke, he watched Ethan carefully and tried to guess what was going through the man's mind. He couldn't be sure, but given the way Ethan's eyes narrowed as he stared at Theo and Gray, it wasn't good.

"I say we kick them out the front door and send them back where they came from," Ethan grumbled. The man was moody, and the only thing the hardness in his voice made Brandt want to do was punch him in the mouth.

"*That* isn't an option," Cade snapped. Brandt was glad to see her dishing Ethan's attitude back to him. He knew Ethan still didn't trust him much, regardless of the time they'd spent around each other and the effort he'd put into trying to prove himself to Ethan. As a result, the other man had been reluctant to listen to much that Brandt had to say; maybe Cade could get through to him.

"Maybe we can shut them into one of the bedrooms and keep an eye on them or something," she suggested.

Brandt saw one glaring problem with her idea. "None of the bedrooms upstairs have locks on the doors," he pointed out. "How are we going to shut them up in a room if we can't lock the door?"

Cade didn't speak, but her eyes slid sideways, past Brandt. He followed her gaze to the nail gun he'd left by the door. "Wait, you want to *nail the door shut?*" he asked incredulously. "I mean…seriously? What if the house gets attacked while they're stuck in there? We'd never get that door open in time to get them out."

She rolled her eyes. "In this house? If the infected attack we're done for anyway, because you sealed off *all* the entrances when we got here. Nailing them into a bedroom upstairs would make them a hell of a lot safer than we'd be in an attack. It's our only option right now. I personally don't want them wandering around the house if one of them is hiding an injury."

A hoarse voice interrupted them. "We're not hiding anything." Cade stopped talking, and all three of them turned to look at the two men. Gray stared at them steadily, his face set in a look of determination. "We're not injured *or* infected. If we were, we wouldn't be here. We're not bad people, and we wouldn't bring that virus around people who aren't sick."

Brandt looked back at Ethan and Cade pointedly. "See?" he said. "I think they're okay."

Cade made a disgusted face. "You're too trusting," she commented.

"What can I say? It's part of my charm," Brandt joked with a helpless shrug.

Despite his attempts to lighten the mood, Ethan still looked ready to punch a hole in the nearest solid object. Brandt preferred it not be him. "I still don't like this," Ethan muttered. "I still think we should just put them out."

"Tough shit," Brandt bit back. "I think we could use them, especially Theo. He's a paramedic. That *could* come in handy, you know. Because between the three of us, all we know is basic first aid and CPR."

"Precisely," Cade agreed. She wrapped her fingers around Ethan's wrist and squeezed. "And on that note, we need to talk," she said, directing her statement at Ethan. "Because you've been acting like a royal pain in the ass, and frankly, I'm sick of it." She waved her hand at the two men sitting in the room and added to Brandt, "You…I don't know. Deal with them or something."

She stormed out of the room, hauling Ethan toward the kitchen, leaving Brandt standing in the living room watching the two newcomers and trying to figure out what in the world to do next.

* * *

Cade fumed as she stormed into the darkened kitchen, her hand still in a vice-like grip around Ethan's wrist. Her teeth were clenched, and her face was set in an unattractive scowl, but she was past the point of caring. The last month had been the ultimate test of her patience as she and Brandt had watched Ethan pace and mutter and snap if they dared disturb whatever he had going on in his head. Her patience had certainly failed the test; she was only moments away from punching him in the face as hard as she could. She'd have already done it if it weren't for the very real concern that she would break something in the process. In her hand, not in his face.

Cade goaded Ethan into the center of the kitchen and let go of his wrist. Her hand had been curled around his wrist tightly enough that, when she released him, her fingers ached. She flexed them a few times before crossing her arms. Once the kitchen door had swung shut, she finally spoke.

"*What* is wrong with you?" she asked. Her throat felt tight; the words almost hurt as they choked their way up from her vocal cords. She dug her fingers into the undersides of her arms, scraping the nails over her skin and struggling to maintain control. She wanted more than anything to wipe the ugly look Ethan was giving her right off his face. Preferably with her fist. *Resist, resist,* she chanted silently.

"*Nothing* is wrong with me," Ethan shot back, his tone mimicking Cade's as he glared at her in return. They faced off for several more silent, tense minutes. It didn't take Ethan long to shift his eyes away. Cade allowed a small, triumphant smirk to spread across her face before stamping it back down.

"Don't give me that bullshit," Cade warned. She looked him over, from his face down to his feet and back up. She wasn't happy with what she saw. He'd dropped weight and looked too tired and thin. "Don't tell me 'nothing' when I know damn well you're not acting like the man I've been friends with for the past seven years," she continued. "You're not acting like yourself *at all*. You're fucking…cold. Hell, I'd even go so far as to say you've become cruel."

"I have not!" Ethan protested.

She held up a hand to stop Ethan before he could say more and jabbed her finger at the closed kitchen door behind her. "Then what the *hell* was that?" she demanded. "The Ethan I know would *never* have suggested leaving others to suffer before this virus struck! Not when he had the means to do something about it! *What* is your problem?"

"Nothing, Ca—"

"Do *not* make me repeat myself," she barked. "You *know* how much that pisses me off."

A weighty silence fell between them. It sat on Cade's shoulders, and she wasn't sure she could shake it off. Especially not as she watched the way Ethan's face crumpled. His shoulders sagged, and he looked away from her, almost like he was ashamed of something. She hoped it was his behavior. She studied him for a moment more and felt her anger begin to ooze away.

"Ethan?" she questioned.

He didn't look at her. "I want…no, I *need* to go back to Memphis."

Cade stared at him, raising an eyebrow, then took an involuntary step back. "You need to go back to Memphis *why*, exactly?"

Ethan hesitated and looked at the floor. Cade was oddly reminded of a schoolboy on the brink of facing down a punishment for something he'd done wrong, and the impression left a sour taste in her mouth. She didn't like how...reduced Ethan seemed to have become. When she finally spoke, her voice was as soft and gentle as she could make it in the face of her remaining irritation.

"You want to go back to look for Anna, don't you?"

Ethan blew out a slow, heavy breath and nodded with a reluctance so obvious that Cade had to resist the urge to slap him for being borderline pathetic. He finally looked at her, and his eyes were shiny, enough so that for the horrifying moment that passed before he answered her, Cade wondered if he'd been fighting tears. "I just have to know. I can't deal with not knowing."

"Well, you're going to *have* to," she snapped. It came out more harshly than she intended, but she didn't regret the tone she'd taken with him. Far from it. She was past the point of losing patience with him, and she hoped the hard stance she took would knock sense into his obviously scrambled brain. "You *have* to deal with it, Ethan! You don't have a choice!"

"Yes I do!" Ethan growled. For the first time in the conversation—and only the second time in their friendship that she could remember—he raised his voice at her in anger. "I can go back and look for her!"

"She's dead, Ethan!" Cade said, struggling to maintain her own cool. "You heard Lisa. She was in the hospital when it burned. She's dead!"

"What if she's not?" he shot back. "We don't know for sure! We didn't see her at all! We just *left*. How do I know she was actually *in* that damned place? She could have been... hell, I don't know, hiding somewhere or something!"

"You're grasping at straws, Ethan! *She's dead!*" Cade hadn't meant to raise her voice, but the last words came out in a shout. Silence dropped between them. She realized she was panting in anger, and she struggled to control her breathing before she hyperventilated. She clenched her fists and dug her nails into her palms, fighting to rein in her emotions. She never lost it, not like that. She'd spent years honing the ability to keep tight control over every twinge of fear and anger and hopelessness she felt. She didn't know what had come over her, but she wasn't going to back down. And she wasn't going to let Ethan ruin every fragment of control she'd ever had.

Ethan, for his part, looked stunned and hurt by her words. Before he could speak again, Cade tried once more, this time keeping her voice quieter, steadier. "Eth, you can't go back, okay?" When he opened his mouth to interrupt, she held up her hand. "Wait, let me finish." She paused to gather her thoughts, then continued. "You haven't acted like yourself all month. Yeah, you were okay when we were initially getting the hell out of Dodge and trying to find your mother, though you acted like an ass to Brandt, and I doubt even *you* would argue that. But since we settled here in Tupelo, you've been driving both of us insane. You're cold, distant, and careless, you have your ass eternally on your shoulders, and whether you want to hear it or not, you've become almost *cruel*." She used the word again, though it pained her to do so. "You're *not* the Ethan I know. The Ethan I know would never have considered sending two people back out into danger when he had the means to help them. I'd ask what the hell has happened to you, but I'm pretty sure I already know the answer."

They stared at each other after she finished her spiel. She could tell he didn't like what she'd said at all; he fought back a scowl and crossed his arms again, and when he finally spoke, there was a frigidity to his voice that almost made her shiver.

"I don't trust them," he admitted. "You can hardly blame me for that. I don't trust *anyone* out there. Look at the situation we're living in! I barely tolerate Brandt being here, but at least he has a useful skillset, and he's not incapable of helping keep the three of us alive. Those two? I don't know a thing about them, and I don't trust them any further than I could throw them." He shook his head and ran a hand through his hair, looking away. "I don't want them here," he continued. "With two more people to deal with, the length of time our supplies will last is cut in half."

Cade stared at him, eyes wide with surprise. "You can't be serious," she said. "You think like that?"

"Of course I'm serious," he argued. "I'm looking at this from a *practical* standpoint. We can't afford to take in every single survivor that comes in our general direction. I won't risk us dying because of some stranger interjecting himself into our situation and taking up our supplies." He blew out a breath and added, "They need to go."

She shook her head. "Not just no, but *hell* no," she said. "We're *not* forcing those men back onto the street."

"Then I'm going back to Memphis," he said, his tone hinting at a finality that she sensed she'd never argue out of him. "And I'm going to look for Anna. You can come with me if you want, or you can stay here and take your chances with Brandt and those other two men."

"You can't *possibly* make me choose—"

Ethan cut her off before she could finish her sentence. "Cade. Which is it going to be?"

Cade looked at him and bit her lip nearly hard enough to break the skin. She shook her head and tried to wrap her mind around the choice he'd asked her to make.

* * *

Theo knelt on the floor beside the coffee table, mechanically repacking his medical supplies into his blue canvas bag. He wasn't sure what to think of his new companions. The man who'd identified himself as Brandt seemed friendly enough; after all, he'd been the one who had gotten them inside, seemingly against his friends' wishes. Cade was distant, and Ethan appeared to be an absolute bastard. He made a mental note to not engage with Ethan if it could be helped.

Theo shook his shaggy blond hair back from his eyes and looked around the room curiously. Brandt stood several feet away, halfway between the coffee table and the kitchen door, his arms crossed. Brandt eyed the closed kitchen door, and Theo could make out the sound of raised voices. He should have been making conversation with the man responsible for his and Gray's rescue, but Brandt didn't seem interested in talking at the moment.

The living room was much dimmer than the brightening day outside, and it took Theo a moment to realize it was because the windows were covered up and, in some cases, boarded over. There wasn't much furniture left in the room; most of it had been used as makeshift boards for the windows. There was a plaid couch pushed against the wall behind Theo, and the coffee table on which Gray sat was shoved against it, leaving no space between the furniture and hinting that the couch was little used. The room was sparsely lit by a battery-operated camping lantern on the end of the coffee table; its light cast strange shadows in the corners, making the room look dingy and creepy. But it was nowhere near as scary as being outside with the infected.

Theo glanced at Brandt and saw he still stared intently at the kitchen door, though the voices on the other side had fallen silent. He wondered what was going on; this obviously wasn't a cohesive group, as it had appeared to be on first glance. He cleared his throat, and Brandt looked at him. He couldn't get a read on the tall man's eyes in the dim light. "Ah, is there a problem?" he asked delicately, nodding toward the kitchen door.

"Maybe," Brandt said evasively. "Ethan has been acting like an idiot. I think Cade's trying to straighten him out." He sighed heavily, suddenly sounding weary. "He's not normally like...well, that, according to Cade. She's always said he's really into helping people, so I'm not going to claim I get why he's acting that way." He glanced at the door once more, then stepped closer to Theo and Gray. "You two are the first uninfected people we've seen in nearly a month."

Theo nodded understandingly as Gray offered him the inhaler back. He clipped the red plastic cap back onto the mouthpiece and returned it to the trauma bag.

"You're the first people we've seen too, besides each other." Gray's voice was still strained. Theo put a hand on his shoulder and squeezed reassuringly. "We've been hiding in our parents' house, but we were running low on everything. Food, gasoline for the generators, all that. So we made a run for it. That's how we ended up here."

"Where are you two originally from?" Brandt asked, drawn into a conversation despite his obvious interest in the argument that had restarted in the kitchen.

"Plantersville," Theo answered. "It's about five miles southeast of here. It was a suburb of Tupelo, but the fires..." He trailed off as he remembered the sights he'd seen from a distance while fleeing his parents' house, and he tried to swallow the awful feeling creeping up from his gut.

"The downtown area burned," Gray clarified. He looked at his lap and clenched his fists, knuckles turning white. "It was some sort of accident. There wasn't a fire department left to put the fires out. A lot of the buildings were too close together, and they just all went up in flames. Me and Theo, we got lucky. We lived on the outskirts."

Brandt picked up a dining chair pushed against one of the walls and carried it to a spot near them. He set it down and eased onto it as if he were tired and sore, resting his elbows on his thighs. When he finally spoke, it was to ask a question that Theo had been anticipating but hadn't looked forward to answering. "So what were you two doing when the Michaluk Virus got to you?"

Theo blew out a breath to steady his nerves. "I was at work when I realized something was wrong," he said. "We'd gotten a call for an MVA out on Highway 6, and the patient we picked up was acting out of his mind. He kept trying to attack me, and my partner and I secured him to the stretcher with restraints. We were running lights to the hospital when we wrecked, and he broke loose and attacked me. If it weren't for my driver…well, I probably wouldn't be sitting here today."

"What happened to your driver?"

"Jonathan…he didn't make it," Theo murmured.

It was a statement that required no elaboration. Everyone had lost someone at some point, whether it was a friend, family member, or lover, and "didn't make it" had become a catch-all for the bad things that could happen to a person after the world went to hell. And Theo was personally acquainted with several of the bad things that could happen.

The silence following Theo's words wasn't uncomfortable for Theo, but Gray started getting fidgety. Theo wasn't the only one who noticed him shifting his weight on the coffee table. Brandt studied Gray for a moment before asking, "So what's your story?"

"Almost the same as Theo's," Gray said, his voice still hoarse. He cleared his throat. "Except mine involves a bar and a really long run that gave me an asthma attack. Theo showed up at my apartment with a load of stolen medical supplies in a bag, looking like he'd been run over by a truck. Ever since, we've just been trying to stay alive."

The renewed silence wasn't as heavy as the previous one had been. Brandt stared at Theo intently, but before he could ask any more questions, the kitchen door slammed open. Cade stormed out and made a beeline for the staircase, her dark hair bouncing off her shoulders as she charged up the stairs, the scowl on her face making her unapproachable. Theo recoiled when he caught a glimpse of the look in her eyes; he wasn't stupid enough to say anything to her.

Brandt, it seemed, wasn't quite as smart. He stood up abruptly and took two steps toward her as her feet struck the stairs. "Cade, what is it? What's happened?"

She stopped halfway up the stairs and held out a hand, palm out, signaling for him to stop. She shook her head and braced a foot against the next step up the stairs. "No, Brandt. Not now."

Brandt looked lost as he held both hands out in a cross between a defensive gesture and a bewildered one. But he didn't speak as Cade climbed the stairs. The three men watched in silence as she climbed, and moments after she disappeared into the darker second level, a door slammed. Gray and Theo winced as the sound echoed through the house, and they frowned at each other.

"I'm not sure I'm comfortable with how...*loud* these people are," Theo muttered to Gray. He was reluctant to let

Brandt hear, as if he might offend him and get them thrown back out onto the street. He supposed social niceties died hard, but he really wouldn't have put it past anyone to kick out people considered unnecessary. It was something he'd have thought about doing if someone became a drag on his or Gray's potential survival.

"I don't like it either, but what choice do we have at this point?" Gray said in an equally hushed voice. "If we don't stick with them, I don't think we're gonna make it. We don't have the supplies or knowledge, not like they do."

Theo fell quiet and contemplated his brother's words. Gray was right, of course. He was right about so much lately, so deep and thoughtful compared to the way he'd been before the outbreak. He'd matured a lot—acting at least ten years older than his twenty-two—and Theo often wondered where his brother had gone. Sometimes, he suspected Gray's new-found seriousness was the only thing keeping him grounded throughout everything that had happened.

But as he watched Brandt start pacing in time with the footsteps above and shoot worried, nervous glances at the closed kitchen door, doubts began to surface. He wasn't sure if staying with them was the right thing to do; he wasn't sure if what he and Gray had to offer would be enough for these people in the face of the skills they themselves must possess.

Most of all, Theo worried that this seemingly dysfunctional group of warriors might lead to his and his brother's deaths faster than if they stuck it out on their own.

CHAPTER FOURTEEN

Tupelo, MS

Ethan sat at the wooden table in the dark kitchen, fists clenched on the surface before him. His eyes stared vacantly across the room as he tried to contain his anger. It was irrational, really, how enraged he was at Cade. He'd thought that *Cade*, of all people, would have understood. He'd thought she would push the issue, that she wouldn't let him go alone. He had thought he could rely on her to do what he needed her to do.

Instead, when he'd pushed, she had only pushed back. And then she'd chosen three virtual *strangers* over the man who had been her best friend for seven years. It had blown his mind when Cade stood there with her arms crossed, when she stared him down and said, her voice calm but edged with anger, a simple "No."

But her refusal hadn't changed Ethan's mind. Not in the slightest. Now, more than ever, he was determined to go back to Memphis, to search for his wife and find out, once and for all, exactly what had happened to her. He owed her that much.

Ethan was still mulling this over when the kitchen door swung open and Brandt strode into the room. He fought the urge to roll his eyes as Brandt walked up to him and braced the knuckles of both hands on the table's scratched surface, leaning close to Ethan. "What do you want, Brandt?" he asked impatiently. He didn't have time for Brandt's show of machismo. He had more important things to do now that his nerves were easing off their anger. He didn't have space in his day planner for Brandt's temper.

"What did you do to Cade?" Brandt asked. He kept his voice level and quiet, though Ethan could tell it took effort for him to do so. Ethan glanced at the kitchen door, behind which the two men—the two *strangers*—still remained.

"Did you leave them alone out there?" he demanded.

"So what if I did?"

"They could be, I don't know, robbing us fucking blind of all our supplies while you're in here picking a fight!" he snapped, rising half out of his chair, bracing his hands against the table between them.

"And what purpose would it serve them to take weapons and gear they can't even use or carry?" Brandt replied, shaking his head. "They want to stay, and they're staying if I have anything to say about it. They could be useful, especially Theo. He's a paramedic, for Christ's sake. And you never answered my question."

"What question?" Ethan asked, sitting back down in his chair and balling his hands into fists again. He was stalling and was well aware of it. But he didn't want to explain himself again, especially not to Brandt. Talking to Cade about his plans was one thing, but Brandt? That was another issue altogether, and his plans were none of Brandt's business anyway.

"What did you do to Cade?" Brandt repeated in a measured tone. It was obvious that it was taking everything in Brandt to not reach across the table and throttle him.

"I didn't do anything to Cade," he said defensively. Brandt leaned forward suddenly, and he edged his chair back a few inches from the table, not caring that the action made him look cowardly; Brandt was larger than him, and he wasn't stupid enough to put himself in reach of Brandt's muscular arms if he could help it.

"Do *not* fucking lie to me, Bennett," Brandt snapped. Anger flared in his eyes like a fire burning too hotly, and Ethan swallowed hard. He'd never seen Brandt angry. It wasn't a pleasant sight. "I *know* you did or said something to piss her off. I might have only known you two for a month, but I figured out pretty quick what Cade looks like when you've done something that makes her want to kill you. And she was more pissed off than I've seen her in the past month. What did you do?"

Ethan, unable to meet Brandt's eyes, shifted his gaze back down to the kitchen table. The men sat in silence as Ethan studied the scratches on the surface, tracing one idly with his finger and wondering how it had gotten there. The family that once inhabited the house in which they now hid had been long gone by the time they'd gotten there, and Ethan still wondered what happened to them. Just like he wondered what happened to Anna. He wondered if she'd made it out of the hospital, if Lisa had been wrong. He wondered if she'd returned to their home and found him gone, if she was even now hiding out in their house waiting to see if he'd return.

Or if she was nowhere to be found.

Brandt's eyes were still on him. He was waiting patiently on his answer, and it didn't seem like he was going to give up anytime soon. Despite his reluctance to tell Brandt anything, he sighed again and started talking.

"I want to go back to Memphis," Ethan started. "I need to find my wife. I have to know what happened, because I can't just…sit here with the idea that she could be out there alone somewhere."

Brandt nodded, and Ethan was grateful that he didn't seem judgmental at the idea *and* that he didn't seem to be about to bring up the probability that Anna was dead. "So when are you wanting us to go?" he asked gamely, catching Ethan by surprise.

"Us?" he repeated. "No, Brandt, there's no 'us.' I'm not taking either of you into that…that *cesspool* so I can look for Anna. It's too dangerous, and I'm not risking anyone else's lives because of what I need to do. It's better that I go alone."

Brandt studied him for a few silent minutes. "You're going to need a lot to get you there. Food, water, weapons. We've got some to spare to start you off with, but you should collect what you can on the road."

Ethan breathed out slowly and stood, heading toward the kitchen door. He paused halfway across the room and turned to look at Brandt. "I'm glad you understand," he said. "Cade didn't take the idea too well. She doesn't want me to go."

"Truth be told, I don't want you to either," Brandt admitted. "We need you here. But I understand why you feel you need to go. Cade will come around, I think, especially if you explain to her that you're coming back. Which you will be, or I'll track your ass down and kick it across the state of Tennessee." He said it matter-of-factly, and Ethan didn't doubt he would do it.

Ethan stifled a laugh, then pushed the kitchen door open to return to the living room, Brandt right on his heels. Theo and Gray still sat in the dim room; Theo had moved to sit on the table beside his brother, and Gray remained hunched on the edge of it. The latter looked better; he didn't appear as pale and distressed as when he'd first come in, and his breathing looked easier.

As Ethan took a moment to look at both men, he realized his initial gut reaction when confronted with their presences had been completely unwarranted. Brandt was right. They could be useful to them, especially Theo. He knew he'd feel better about leaving Cade if he left her in the presence of medical personnel.

"So," Ethan started casually. He shoved his hands into his pockets. "What can you two do for me?"

"I'd think it would be obvious," Theo said, motioning to the blue bag at his feet.

"Yeah, for you," Ethan said. "What about him?" He nodded to Gray.

"I'm more useful than you think," Gray said testily, reaching for Theo's bag. Ethan tensed as Gray plunged a hand inside, but when the man only pulled out a book with a soft leather cover, he relaxed. It took him a moment to realize the book was a Bible, and it was stuffed to overflowing with computer printouts. Ethan took a step closer as Gray began pulling the sheaves of paper out of the book.

"What are those?" Ethan asked, kneeling beside Gray as his curiosity overcame his standoffish façade.

"Maps," Gray said. He stood and spread the papers out on the coffee table. "I printed it all out from the Internet before it went down. Basically, each sheet is roughly five square miles of the city of Tupelo and the surrounding areas." He took a red marker out of his back pocket and held it up. "According to the people I talked to on the ham radio at my parents' house, there are quite a few of the areas that are totally congested," Gray explained. He dropped his finger onto a paper, pointing to a street that had been colored in with the red marker; there were some notes scribbled beside it in small print. "Perfect example. This street. It's a no-go. There's a pile-up of wrecked cars blocking most of it, so it bottlenecks halfway down. Perfect place to get ambushed. On top of that, it's crawling with infected. You go through there, you're almost guaranteed a death sentence."

Ethan sighed and addressed Brandt. "Go get these guys some food, okay? We've obviously got some talking to do here, and both of them look half starved."

Theo and Gray both gave Ethan grateful looks, and Gray continued as Brandt left the room. "Most of this comes from the ham radio Theo found. There are still a few people out there exchanging some useful information over them. I'd just turn on the radio and sit and listen and write it all down." He took another book from Theo's bag, this one a thick, journal-like tome, and handed it to Ethan. Ethan flipped it open and discovered it was full of tight, carefully printed handwriting; it outlined every area where travel difficulties and high concentrations of infected could be found from Tupelo to as far west as the Louisiana-Texas border and as far east as North Carolina. Ethan was impressed at the thoroughness of the information collected.

As Ethan browsed through the book, Brandt came back into the living room with two wrapped sandwiches and a couple of bottles of water. "I hope neither of you is vegetarian," he said as he passed the food out.

Gray tore the wrapper off his sandwich and took a big bite. Theo was more reserved, twisting the cap off his bottle and taking a swallow before giving Brandt and Ethan both a nod of thanks.

"It's fine," Theo assured them, neatly unwrapping his sandwich and taking a cautious bite.

As Ethan turned back to Gray's papers and maps, Gray spoke again, his mouth still full of sandwich. "Have you seen those things?" he asked. "I mean, have you really *watched* them?"

"I have, some," Brandt spoke up. He sat heavily in the dining chair he'd vacated earlier and ran a hand over his face. "But our policy has been more 'avoid at all costs,' so we haven't studied them in detail."

"You're not going to be able to avoid them forever," Gray said. He paused to swallow a mouthful of food before continuing. "How many times have you guys had to move now? Three? Four?"

Ethan looked up from the notes he'd been reading on the margins of a nap. "This is our third place in Mississippi."

"I figured as much," Gray said, his voice confident. "How many times have you had to move because one of you went out for supplies, got spotted by one, and next thing you knew, you had an entire horde coming down on you?"

Brandt and Ethan fell silent. Ethan looked at Brandt, only to discover Brandt was already looking at him. Every one of Gray's suppositions had been spot on. Every time they'd had to move in the past month, it was because of a scenario exactly like the one Gray had described.

"It's because they're *hunters*," Gray continued. "They don't just wander around, see an uninfected person by chance, and think, 'Mmm, lunch.' They have *scouts*. And those scouts go out and look for signs of you. And when they see them, they *hunt* you down. And when they find you, they don't attack. They just disappear. Because they go back to the other infected and lead them to your location, and that's when you end up with a horde knocking on your door."

"I don't see how that's possible!" Ethan protested. "I mean, I've never seen—"

"You just admitted a few minutes ago that you've spent the past month not seeing," Theo interrupted. "I'm not surprised you haven't noticed. But trust us, that's exactly what we're doing. Too many people have seen them do it too many times for it to be a coincidence. They *strategize*."

"They plan their attacks," Gray elaborated. "I'm not sure how. I don't even know how they communicate, because I've never heard any of the bastards talk. But they do communicate somehow, and then they find you and surrounding the house you're in. They coordinate and concentrate their efforts at every exit and window so you can't get out. And then they just…" He trailed off and waved his hand, at a loss. "Come in," he finished lamely.

The four men fell silent at Gray's words. Ethan stood from his spot by the coffee table and bowed his head in thought. The information was a lot for him to take in, to process. And the thought of the infected being capable of hunting, of tracking and coordinating and attacking together…frankly, it was terrifying. He'd never considered the infected intelligent enough to do that; to him, they'd always seemed to be mindless killing machines. To learn otherwise went against everything of which he'd convinced himself over the past month.

He didn't think he was going to get much sleep tonight.

"It makes sense," Brandt acknowledged. He shifted uncomfortably on his chair and refused to look at them. "The whole idea of scouts. Especially after what Cade…" He trailed off, much to Ethan's annoyance.

"After Cade *what?*" he demanded.

"After what Cade started to tell me when we were getting these two inside." He motioned to Theo and Gray. "I didn't have time to dig for details, but she started to say something about how she only saw one of the infected, that it was hiding from her so she couldn't take it out. It didn't make much sense to me, but..." He shrugged. "There you have it."

Ethan looked at the ceiling as Brandt's words settled in. A soft thump sounded from somewhere upstairs, and he hummed thoughtfully and shifted his eyes to the staircase. "Should we go get her?" he asked Brandt. "She might need to know this."

"No, leave her," Brandt replied. "She'll come down when she's ready. As pissed as she was, we might not see her for the rest of the day."

The silence descended again, lasting for several minutes before someone broke it. "So what's the plan?" Theo asked.

Ethan looked at him, startled from his thoughts. "Plan?"

"Well, you've been spotted by one of the infected," Gray said. "You can't expect to stay here much longer. Hell, I'd say you best get out of here no later than tomorrow morning. So what's the plan? What are we going to do?"

Ethan hesitated and looked to Brandt for guidance. The question was one he hadn't expected, and he was far from prepared to answer it. Brandt shrugged, holding his hands out to his sides again. Ethan shoved his own hands back into his pockets. "I'm not sure," he finally admitted. "I mean, I know what *my* plans are, but as for you four...I don't know."

Theo's eyebrow rose in question. "Your plans?"

Ethan wasn't sure he wanted to tell them his plan, but there was no sense hiding it—they'd find out soon enough. "I...have to go back to Memphis," he said. "Personal business." The words came out feebly, like he hadn't convinced himself of their importance yet.

He shifted from one foot to the other as Theo and Gray exchanged looks, their expressions clearly stating they believed Ethan was insane. He tried to brush it off as the sound of pacing began again upstairs, the floorboards in the old house creaking under Cade's boots. The sound was followed moments later by a noise that sounded suspiciously like something crashing against a wall. All four of them looked at the ceiling once more in concern.

"She's getting mad again," Brandt said.

"*And* making too much noise," Gray added.

Brandt stood, moving his chair back against the wall where they usually kept it. "I'll go up and tell her to keep it down."

"Shouldn't I go?" Ethan asked, taking a step toward the stairs.

Brandt caught him by the arm. "No, she'll probably shoot you if you show your face upstairs right now. Better for me to go instead of you." He dropped his voice and added, "Besides, don't you have some packing to do?"

Ethan had half a mind to object, but deep inside, he knew Brandt was right. Cade was angry enough that there was no telling what she'd do if he knocked on her door. Brandt must have seen the acknowledgment in his face, because he headed upstairs, taking the steps two at a time. Once he was gone, Ethan turned back to Theo and Gray.

"Sorry," he said with an apologetic frown. "Things have been a little…tense here lately."

"That's not an understatement or anything," Gray muttered, beginning to tuck his printed maps back into his Bible.

* * *

Cade didn't care how much noise she was making. She'd become the very definition of angry. She wasn't sure who she was angrier at: Ethan for proposing such an idiotic idea as to go back to Memphis *alone* or herself for not having the backbone to either stand up to him or to go with him.

It was an asinine idea. Going back to Memphis was bad enough. After their arrival in Mississippi, the three of them had witnessed the footage of the city's fall on the limited TV that had still been available. At the time, Brandt had even gone so far as to say he'd have ranked it just behind Atlanta in how badly it had caved to the infected. And Ethan wanted to go *back* there? Just to try to find someone who was most likely not even alive anymore?

Cade wouldn't lie to herself: she had no desire to go back to Memphis, with or without Ethan. Nothing would drag her there, no matter how hard it pulled; the thought of going back into the city, the neighborhood, the *house* where Andrew and Josie had died was enough to deter her from ever stepping foot in the area again.

Cade still had no idea if the virus had gone worldwide, if her sister was still breathing—wherever she was—and if she was still waiting for word on where Cade and Josie were. She hadn't been able to get in touch with Lindsey before the phone lines went down. She'd been forced to resign herself to the fact that Lindsey was permanently unreachable.

A thump on the closed bedroom door startled her from her thoughts and drew her attention back to the present. She moved toward the door, casting a baleful glance at the shattered drinking glass resting at the baseboard. It didn't take more than a second to unlock the door, and when she opened it, the expectant scowl on her face melted away in surprise when she realized it was Brandt.

"What do you want?" she bit out, managing not to cringe at how angry her words sounded.

Brandt showed no surprise at her blatant display of rudeness. "Uh, hi? The guys downstairs think you're being a bit too loud up here, and honestly, I agree. So could you please drop the noise level to about a four?"

Cade sighed and turned away, leaving the door open so Brandt could come inside if he so desired. "He's just so *stupid!*" she exclaimed, clenching her fists for a moment. She didn't bother turning to see if Brandt still stood there. "What in the hell does he think it's going to accomplish?"

"Peace of mind. Closure. Whatever they call it." Brandt came into the room, and he paused to look at the broken glass. "It's just something he feels like he has to do."

"Doesn't mean I have to like it," Cade muttered. She pushed her ponytail off her neck and plopped onto the edge of the bed. "I thought he'd change his mind if I told him I wouldn't go with him," she admitted. "Turned out he didn't want me to go anyway."

"Yeah," Brandt said, his voice hoarse. He walked across the room to look out the window.

"You don't actually condone him going, do you?"

"No, but there's really nothing I can do to stop him either, is there?" he said. "He's a grown man. He makes his own decisions."

"Doesn't mean I have to like those decisions," she repeated.

"Hey, I'm not saying I like it," he said. "From a practical standpoint, it's going to put a crimp in our security. But from a personal standpoint, well, I've kind of started to like the cranky bastard, and I don't really want him to leave. I mean, who's going to help me keep you in line when he's gone?"

Cade nearly laughed despite her annoyance. "Hey, who said I needed to be kept in line? I can handle myself just fine, thank you."

Brandt finally turned to Cade, concern in his dark eyes. "Are you okay with this? With sticking with me and a couple of guys you barely know?"

She mulled over his question. She had several options: she could stay with the men for the protection they offered, if nothing else; she could follow Ethan and maybe offer him additional support and backup; or she could strike out on her own, though she knew instinctually that that would likely lead to her own death. Deep in her heart, though, she knew it was no contest. She'd stick with her personal plan of safety in numbers, even if it meant allowing her best friend to leave for untold dangers alone.

"Yeah, I think I can handle it," she said with a confidence she didn't feel.

"Hey," Brandt said, kneeling in front of her and patting her knee in an awkward attempt to comfort her. "Ethan's going to be okay. He's tough, you know? I'm sure he can take care of himself just fine."

"And if he gets to Memphis and doesn't find what he's looking for?" she asked. "What if he just…falls apart? No one will be there with him to make sure he gets through that. He's not as strong as you think he is, Brandt."

He studied her face, and though she was dying to look away, she kept her gaze on his warm brown eyes, which were full of concern and compassion. It made her feel embarrassed, a little like the helpless female she knew she wasn't.

Brandt cleared his throat and broke their shared gaze. "So it's looking like we're going to have to move again," he said conversationally, rising to his feet and stretching. "Gray has this theory that actually makes sense, and I think you should hear it."

Cade sat up straighter. "What kind of theory?"

Brandt began talking in a hushed voice, explaining Gray's theory, his eyes locked onto the window by which he'd stood for most of their conversation. And Cade's heart sank as the implication of his words hit her full force.

* * *

Gray was surprised at how much noise such a small group of people could make. It sounded like a herd of monkeys trampled through the rooms, talking and throwing supplies around. He supposed the noise levels were a matter of perspective; it'd been so long since he and Theo had dared to raise their voices above a murmur that the activity in the house seemed louder than it actually was.

Gray leaned against the couch cushions and watched Theo and their new companions sort and pack food, water, and ammunition into different bags. Theo had relegated him to the couch because of his earlier asthma attack, though Ethan was less than pleased by Theo's insistence that Gray rest. Gray had done his best to be useful, despite his forced perch on the couch. Instead of watching the others work, he'd taken his maps back out and, with the help of Ethan's road atlas, had begun plotting ideal routes from the city and marking potential locations for setting up a new safe house. One option was particularly good, and he noted it in his journal.

Gray looked up from his tight, careful handwriting and watched Ethan study a pistol Cade had given him. He thought that what the man planned to do was one of the stupidest things he'd ever heard; no one should have been going into *any* of the larger cities, especially not alone. He didn't know Ethan, but something told him he would remain undeterred by the danger.

Sighing, he waited for Brandt to pass with a case of bottled water before standing and approaching Ethan, a small bunch of papers clutched in his hand. A nervous twinge shivered through his stomach as he stopped in front of the older man. Ethan didn't look up as he shoved the pistol into his bag, and when he spoke, he sounded impatient.

"Yeah, what do you need?"

A bit taken aback by Ethan's attitude, Gray shook it off and forged ahead. "I, uh…here," he said, thrusting the papers toward Ethan.

Ethan finally looked up as the papers invaded his line of sight. "What's this?"

"You said you wanted to go back to Memphis to look for your wife, right?" he asked. "Well, I figured out the fastest, safest route you can take."

Ethan looked up from the papers, surprised. "You did this?"

"Well, yeah," Gray answered with a little shrug. "I mean, you said you were planning on coming back, so I figured it could be helpful for your trip."

Ethan gave him the barest of smiles and folded the papers, carefully tucking them into the front pocket of his bag. "Well, thanks. Really. Thank you," he said. He glanced around before dropping his voice and adding, "I'm sure they'll help. Cade'll track me down and kick my ass if I don't come back in one piece."

"So, uh, you got everything you need?" Gray asked. "Like, supplies and stuff?"

"I believe so," Ethan said, giving the interior of his bag another probing look. "I could use more ammo, but I'm going to try to collect more on the road. You guys will need it more than me. There are four of you to cover."

Gray nodded again and watched Theo and Cade set a box of canned food and a heavy black bag on the floor by the front door. Cade had her rifle slung over her shoulder to rest on her back; the woman never seemed to allow it to stray far from her. "She really knows how to use that thing?" he asked.

"Oh yeah, total crack shot," Ethan acknowledged. "Fucking amazing. She can shoot almost anything exactly where she wants to hit it. It's almost scary how good she is. I've never seen someone shoot that well."

Gray smiled and tucked a lock of dark hair behind his ear. His hair had gotten too long; it'd begun to get that way before the world went to hell, and he'd had to listen to Theo constantly tell him to cut it. In the past month, though, a haircut had been low on his priority list, faced as he was with the continued challenges of not getting his face eaten off.

"What's the plan for you four?" Ethan asked. When he gave Ethan a quizzical look, he clarified. "I mean, you had the time to come up with a plan for me. Did you come up with one for you guys?"

"Oh! Uh, yeah, I did." Gray retreated to the couch to get the appropriate papers, shuffling through them to find what he was looking for. When he took them back to Ethan, the older man studied them curiously.

"Biloxi?" Ethan queried. "I thought we were trying to *avoid* larger cities."

"Well, yeah. But I heard on the radio that the areas closer to the coast aren't as heavily infected as those more inland," Gray explained. "Not anymore, anyway." He sat on the edge of the coffee table and retrieved his journal; it didn't take long to find the pages he searched for, and he offered the book to Ethan and grabbed a state map. "See, the guys on the radio said that once the infected cleared out most of the larger cities in the coastal areas, most of them began migrating further inland in search of, well, food, I guess you could call us. The best chances of survival are closer to the coast, because the infected are moving *up* the state, not down." He smoothed his hands in a northerly direction up the map of Mississippi. "Once they hit water, there wasn't anywhere else to go, so they turned around and came back up."

"How reliable is this information?" Ethan asked. "These guys on the radio, where do they get all this?"

Gray shrugged and folded the cover of the map book so Mississippi stayed on top. He hadn't considered that; he didn't know where the information relayed over the ham radios had come from. "I don't know," he confessed. "I think most of it came from other radio operators, people who actually live down there."

Ethan hummed thoughtfully and tapped his fingers on the page as he thought the information over. "I have to admit, I'm impressed," he said, offering the book back to Gray. "To be honest, I'd doubted how useful you would be. I mean, Theo's usefulness is pretty obvious. He's a paramedic, and that could come in handy in any number of situations. But I had no idea what to think of you."

"Hey, I'm not good at *just* this," he protested. "I'm a mechanic, and I can handle a hunting rifle pretty damned good. My dad used to take me out deer hunting all the time. I've been shooting a rifle since I was eight."

"Where exactly is your father?" Ethan asked. Gray glanced up at him and then back to the floor, unable to meet Ethan's eyes as the question brought back painful memories with which he hadn't quite coped.

"They're...my parents, they died in a car accident," he explained. "Theo and I have been taking care of each other since then." He blew out a breath. "Thank God neither of them is alive today to see all this."

Ethan dropped the subject, and Gray saw a fleeting look of sorrow cross his face. Theo approached and paused in mid-step as he, too, got a look at Ethan's expression. He frowned in concern before speaking.

"So we've got everything together and ready to go," Theo said. "Now it's just a matter of deciding *when* to hit the road." Glancing between the two of them, he added, "Everything okay over here?"

"Yeah, fine," Gray answered, wiping both hands down the thighs of his jeans. "What do you need me to do?"

"Absolutely nothing," Theo said. "Except sit and rest, because I think Brandt and Cade have decided you're going to be the driver for the first leg of the trip, wherever that may take us."

"Biloxi," Gray said. Passing the roadmaps to Theo for safekeeping and packing up the other papers. "I figure the closer we get to the coast, the better."

"Good thinking," Theo said. "Now we need to decide when to leave."

"I vote now," Ethan said. Gray looked at him in disbelief, and the low tones of Brandt and Cade's conversation halted as they too looked over.

"Now?" Cade repeated. "Are we even ready to leave right this minute?"

"Hey, you're the ones who said everything is packed and ready to go," Ethan pointed out.

"Just because the *shit* is ready doesn't mean *we're* ready," Cade shot back.

"You just don't want to leave yet because you know I'm going a different direction than you," Ethan snapped.

"Of *course* it's *always* about *you*, isn't it?" Cade snarled.

"You're only delaying the fucking inevitable, Cade!" Ethan said, almost yelling by that point. Theo took a careful step away from him.

"Okay, lady, cool it," Brandt said, putting a gentle hand on Cade's arm and tugging as if pulling her back from a fight. Gray exchanged an uncomfortable glance with Theo; he hadn't expected these seemingly capable people to end up coming apart at the seams. Not for the first time, he wondered just how capable these people were and how they were going to manage to keep their hides alive.

CHAPTER FIFTEEN

Tupelo, MS

The next morning found three of the five survivors outside
the safe house, gathered around Ethan's SUV, loading water
and food and weapons into the back. The early hour was a
good time to leave, Brandt realized as he muscled a case of
bottled water into the cargo area. He'd noticed the month
before that the infected were always slower and sparser in the
mornings, maybe because of the early morning chill, so it was
the perfect time to slip out mostly unnoticed.

Cade stood guard on the roof of the Jeep, her ever-present rifle in her hands as she knelt on a knee and studied their
surroundings. Brandt glanced at her and smiled as the sound
of bottles rattling together in a box caught her attention. She
returned the smile before focusing her eyes back on the horizon. She was all business when it came to keeping watch; he
admired her focus.

"All clear?" Brandt asked, pushing the Jeep's back door
closed as quietly as he could.

"Yeah, I don't see anything," she confirmed, looking at
Gray, who lurked by the driver's door, a battered hunting rifle
in his hands. "You?"

"Nothing," Gray said. "It's practically dead out here."

"Horrible choice of words," Cade said, barely suppressing a laugh. Even Brandt had to crack a smile at that.

A thump at the front of the house drew Brandt's attention. Ethan and Theo came out of the house, pulling the door shut behind them, and Ethan took a can of bright orange spray paint from his bag and aimed it at the front door. When he was done, the word "SAFE" was scrawled on the wood, and he and Theo joined the rest of them at the Jeep.

"What's with the spray paint?" Brandt asked.

"We left food and water on the coffee table in case someone who is uninfected comes by and needs a safe house," Ethan explained, looking sheepish. The expression confused Brandt. "We figured it may come in handy for someone who might need it, you know?"

Brandt nodded understandingly. Ethan had been a reticent bastard in the past month, reluctant to share supplies or weapons with anyone else. His assistance to potential unknown survivors, however minor, was a major concession on his part. Perhaps her angry words in the kitchen had actually made an impact.

Her words hadn't changed Ethan's mind about setting out on his own, though. The evening before, Ethan had snuck out and, after a two-block journey in the dark, had located a motorcycle in good condition that he planned to drive back to Memphis. After that revelation, Cade had been reduced to giving Ethan the silent treatment, and no matter how hard Brandt tried to convince her to talk to Ethan, she'd refused to the last.

As Ethan approached the motorcycle parked at the end of the driveway, Brandt thought it was worth it to try again. He moved around the side of the Jeep and tapped Cade on the leg. She broke her study of the street to give Brandt an unreadable expression.

"What?"

Brandt nodded toward Ethan and tried to shake off the uncomfortable feeling the feigned indifference on Cade's face gave him. "You really should talk to him."

Cade shifted her eyes away as soon as the words left Brandt's mouth. "Why?"

"Because he's your best friend and because he's leaving," he answered, rolling his eyes, exasperation creeping over him. He still couldn't believe Cade and Ethan were behaving this way. They were *adults*, not teenagers having a tiff. "I'm sure he'd appreciate it if you said goodbye to him, maybe if you wished him luck."

"I don't really care what he'd appreciate," she said.

"Cade," he said firmly, and he didn't continue until she looked at him. "Don't be a bitch. You know there's a chance he might not make it back."

Cade's head jerked up at his words, and the look in her eyes was hard and cold and frightening. For just a moment, he couldn't see Cade. All he could see was a hardened soldier, a dead-eyed machine. The unsettled feeling it stirred in his gut made him swallow hard and take a step back from the Jeep.

"Don't you say that," Cade snarled. Her eyes burned with a fresh bout of anger; she clenched her fists and nearly stood up on the roof of the vehicle. "Don't you fucking say that!"

Brandt squared his shoulders and forced himself forward again. "Why not?" he demanded. "It's true, isn't it? There's always a chance he won't come back!"

To his surprise, Cade dropped down from the Jeep's roof, landing on the driveway in the narrow space between him and the vehicle, her boots crunching on the gravel. He took another involuntary step back to make space between them. Her eyes were still hard and angry as they locked onto his, and she held her rifle in a white-knuckled grip. In that moment, more than any other in the previous month, he truly believed she was capable of killing him.

"Say it again. I dare you," she said, her tone steady and cold and dangerously low.

"I said, there's always the chance he won't come back," Brandt repeated. He did his best to keep his voice steady, but a faint tremor snuck in.

Cade stepped forward, studying his face. His shoulders relaxed as she simply stood there. Maybe she wouldn't do anything to him after all.

But then out of the corner of his eye, he caught a glimpse of a fist swinging toward his face. Before he could dodge, it connected with his jaw, and he staggered backward in surprise. Theo lunged forward and dove between them to push them apart.

"Don't you fucking say that!" Cade shouted, trying to get around Theo to reach Brandt. Brandt held both hands up defensively, even as pain throbbed through his jaw and radiated to the entire side of his face. Ethan abandoned his motorcycle to sprint into the commotion, grabbing Cade from behind, using his arms to trap hers against her sides, hauling her away from Brandt. He pinned her to his chest as she struggled to break free. "Don't you ever fucking say that!" she yelled again, trying to jerk away from Ethan.

"Cade!" Ethan said sternly. His grip on her tightened, and he twisted, hauling her farther away from Brandt and pinning her against the Jeep. "Keep your voice down before you bring the damned infected down on all of us!"

The woman sobered at Ethan's words, her shoulders slumping and her head dipping as she looked down. Ethan let her go, and she stepped away from the Jeep, slinging her rifle over her shoulder with a short nod. "Yeah," she said, her voice hoarse. "Sorry."

"Brandt. *Brandt*," a voice said to his left. He realized Theo was looking at him in concern. He blinked stupidly at the other man and flinched as Theo grabbed his head and turned it to get a look at his jaw. "You're going to have a serious bruise there," Theo observed, prodding at the spot. Brandt swatted his hand away as a sharp jab of pain shot through his jaw. "Does it hurt?"

"Fuck no. It was like getting brushed by the wings of a fucking butterfly," he snapped. "Cut it out. I'm fine." He gingerly poked at his own jaw, wiggling and shifting it uncomfortably, and glanced at Cade again. She and Ethan still stood by the Jeep, engaged in a low, intense conversation. Cade still appeared upset, which meant she was attempting to change Ethan's mind again and he was resisting. "Damn, that woman can hit," he marveled. "Don't ever get on her bad side."

"Oh, believe me, I don't plan to," Theo said. He picked up his blue medical bag from where he'd dropped it and slung it over his shoulder again. "You should've seen it from the outside. Definitely one of the coolest punches I've ever seen. That was the kind of shit you only see in action movies." He gave Theo a dirty look, and Theo put his hands up defensively. "No offense, man. Just an observation."

"Observe this," Brandt said, and he raised his middle finger at Theo. Theo laughed, but before he could retaliate, Gray spoke up from the other side of the Jeep.

"Uh, guys?" Gray said.

Brandt turned as he registered the urgency in Gray's voice. Gray pointed his rifle down the street in the direction from which he and Theo had come the day before.

"They're coming," Gray finished. He yanked the driver's door open and nearly dove into the Jeep. Moments later, the engine ground to a start, the sound drawing Ethan and Cade from their conversation.

"What's going on?" Ethan asked, stepping away from Cade. Brandt didn't answer, instead moving to the rear of the vehicle to look down the street.

A heart-stopping moment passed before he realized what he was looking at. The distance was almost too great, the early morning sun not quite reaching street level below the trees yet. The lack of light made him wonder if what he saw was actually what he saw.

It was the infected, dozens of them. Brandt couldn't make out finer details, but he had no doubt it was the infected. They lurched down the street at varying speeds. Some shuffled like they didn't have enough control of their limbs to do anything but pitch forward in an effort to keep up with the others. The ones in the lead moved more quickly, nearly running as they made their way toward Brandt's position.

"We've got to go!" he called. He hit the Jeep's back door with his fist in frustration before skirting around to the front passenger door and throwing it open. He was pissed. There was no other word for it. He'd hoped they'd be able to stay there for more than a week, but the arrival of the two men he'd been so determined to save had sent the group into a tailspin again. He put a foot on the edge of the door to haul himself in but stopped short when he glimpsed Cade.

She stood halfway between the Jeep and Ethan's motorcycle, her eyes wide as she shook her head at Ethan. Her mouth moved as she said something he couldn't hear, but Ethan didn't reply, instead grabbing her by the upper arm and giving her a rough shove toward the Jeep.

"Get in the car, Cade," Ethan ordered, his voice barely audible over the noise coming from down the street. Brandt stood on the edge of the door to look over the roof, and he was surprised to see how much ground the infected had gained in the short amount of time the group had delayed. Ethan noticed this as well, because he added in a near-shout, "We don't have time for this! Get in!"

Cade still hesitated, torn between going with Ethan and going with Brandt and the other men. Ethan caught Brandt's eyes over her head. "Brandt," he said simply. The one word said everything Brandt needed to hear. He hopped down from his vantage point and went to Cade, grabbing her firmly by the arms and pulling her toward the Jeep.

"Come on, we've got to go," he said gently. "There's no time for this, unless you want all of us to die." He wrestled Cade to the back passenger door, fighting against her resistance the entire way, and with Theo's help, he hauled her into the backseat. He slammed the door behind her, hoping Theo would be able to keep her from jumping right back out, and looked at Ethan once more. The older man mounted his motorcycle and fastened the helmet he'd found in the bike's saddlebag firmly onto his head. He glanced back at Brandt and gave him a short nod.

"Good luck," Brandt called before climbing into the Jeep. As Gray backed out of the driveway, he watched in the side mirror as Ethan revved the motorcycle's engine and gunned it, tires spraying gravel as he sped into the street, away from the house and his fellow survivors.

Heaven knew Ethan could use all the luck he could get.

* * *

In Transit to Memphis, TN

The motorcycle's engine thrummed between Ethan's thighs as he raced the black-and-red bike toward the end of the block. The chilly early March air cut through his woefully inadequate jacket and stung his eyes and cheeks. Ethan didn't dare look behind him, where he knew that dozens of infected surged toward the house in which he, Cade, and Brandt had spent barely a week. He knew without looking that the infected continued to merge on their position, regardless of the flight of their prey.

He couldn't look back to make sure his friends had escaped safely. He had to trust that Gray had gotten the four of them clear and into the side streets heading south. For now, he had to focus on driving, watching his surroundings as he darted and wove between crookedly parked cars and emptied trash cans scattered in the street.

As Ethan took the turn at the end of the block, he let out a steadying breath. He hadn't driven a motorcycle in years, but it was coming back to him easily. He'd sold the bike he owned throughout his college years to pay for his and Anna's honeymoon. Anna hadn't wanted him to sell it, but he'd thought the trip was more important than the bike. He'd been right: their week in the mountains was an experience he wouldn't have traded for all the motorcycles in the world.

He swallowed hard as his thoughts lingered on Anna, and he forced his mind away from his wife. Contrary to Cade's insistence, he wasn't fooling himself about what he'd find when he returned to Memphis. He was well aware that the chances he'd find his wife alive were slim. But it was that slim chance that pushed him to go back, to return to her last known location, to try to find her. He couldn't give up on Anna until he knew for sure whether or not she still breathed.

It took Ethan over an hour to make it to Tupelo's northernmost city limits. By then, the sun shone high in the sky, lightning his way more brightly than before. He shivered almost violently. He slowed the motorcycle to a stop in the middle of the highway and braced his feet on the ground, examining his hands. His knuckles were an angry shade of red from the wind, and his fingers felt stiff when he flexed them. He rubbed his hands together to help restore the circulation and looked around cautiously.

The highway was oddly silent and still. Ethan shifted on the leather seat and checked the roadway behind him, his hand drifting down to rest on the butt of his pistol. His green eyes skimmed the highway, and he debated whether he should draw his weapon. There was no immediate sign of danger, though, so instead he retrieved Gray's maps from his bag.

This trip had the potential to be a logistical nightmare, he realized as he studied his maps. He'd wanted to go to Memphis alone; indeed, he'd *insisted* on it, despite Cade's protests. But now that he had succeeded in departing Tupelo alone, he felt wary and uneasy and unprepared. And exposed. That was the worst of all; it gave him a disconcerting tingling sensation between his shoulder blades and made him want to look behind him. He knew it was because he didn't have anyone to watch his back.

He was still too close to Tupelo for his personal comfort. He planned to get as close to Memphis as daylight and fuel would allow. The motorcycle had over three-quarters of a tank of gas; it would be more than enough for the journey to his city. Barring any delays, he estimated that he'd reach

Memphis well before sunset and perhaps even have time to start his search for Anna.

But Ethan would never get to Memphis if he continued sitting in the middle of the highway. He returned the maps to his bag and started the bike's engine again. As he began driving north, he figured it would be worth a short detour in the next town to search for a comfortable leather jacket to block the wind, since the denim one he'd scrounged up wasn't doing much to keep him warm.

Ethan had estimated the trip would take two hours, but the journey took closer to six. He arrived at the end of his street just after four in the afternoon. He cut the engine and rolled the bike to a stop as he took in the sight before him. Thankfully, he'd traveled unmolested to the trip to the city, but that streak of luck had come to an end.

The street wasn't overrun with infected, but it played host to more than just a few. Smoke hung heavily in the air, the stench threatening to make Ethan sneeze. On his approach to Memphis, he'd noticed numerous plumes of smoke towering above the city like the world's tallest skyscrapers, nearly brushing the clouds. The fires were uncomfortably close to the home he'd shared with Anna.

But at the moment, the fires were the last things on his mind. He studied the wandering infected on the street and weighed his options as he removed his helmet. He'd yet to be spotted, so at least his luck held out in that respect. The next task would be getting to his house unscathed.

Ethan dismounted the bike and let the kickstand down with a quiet click. His ears barely heard it, but it was loud enough to draw the attention of one of the infected. And one was all it took.

A dark-haired woman jerked her head around at the sound. He looked at her long enough to take in her bloodstained white blouse and dark skirt, her bare feet and shredded hose. But what captivated his attention wasn't her disheveled appearance but the expression on her features: a contortion of hatred and hunger, the predatory look he'd seen over and over on the infected he'd encountered during the prior month.

The woman snarled and bared her teeth. The animalistic noise drew the attention of more infected to Ethan. He drew his pistol and aimed it at the infected that started moving toward him, panic growing into a knot in his stomach, welling up in his throat. He swore and took a step back, glancing from left to right and back again.

The houses within a quick sprint's distance were boarded and shuttered. They didn't look safe enough to hide in *or* easy enough to get into with any degree of speed. Ethan barely had time to think; the woman who'd first spotted him was nearly within arm's reach. So he did the only thing he could do.

He ran.

He lunged right and dodged the woman's grasping hands, sprinting for the gap between two houses, nearly colliding with a mailbox as he sped across the sidewalk. The mob on the street behind him gave chase as he reached the end of the space between the houses and turned right.

Perhaps he could circle back around the block, get behind the frenzy of infected, and retrieve the motorcycle he'd so carelessly left on the street. It was a small hope, but it was worth trying. There was no way he could outrun the infected forever; he had to get a method of transportation, and his motorcycle was the closest. Not to mention that nearly all of his supplies were still strapped to it, save for the one small bag slung over his shoulder—which didn't contain enough to survive on for any extended length of time.

It took Ethan mere moments to reach the halfway point down the block, but to his burning lungs, it felt like hours. The thought of his pistol flitted through his mind, and he fumbled at the holster on his hip. He drew the weapon as he ran, his heart hammering against his ribcage.

A shock of blond hair caught Ethan's eye, and what he saw made him stumble in surprise. A tiny, slender girl stood on the porch of a house, beckoning to him frantically with both hands, looking between him and the approaching horde.

"Over here! This way! Hurry!" the girl shouted. She didn't wait for Ethan to respond. Instead, she vaulted over the porch railing with the grace of a gymnast, one hand braced against the wood, and disappeared along the side of the house.

Ethan clambered over the fence surrounding the house and sprinted along the path the girl had taken, his chest heaving as he looked around the dark space alongside the house. Where had the girl gone? Had he just run unwittingly into a trap?

"Here!" the girl's voice came again from Ethan's left. He looked over and down and spotted a cellar door jutting partway from the ground, masked in the dark shadows beside the house. The girl held the door above her head, watching the street in growing alarm as she waved her free hand wildly at him. "Get in! Come on!"

Ethan covered the ground between them in two steps. He glanced back and saw that in the span of time he'd been looking for the girl, the infected had caught up to him. They were clustered at the chain-link fence separating Ethan and the girl from their jagged teeth. Even as he watched, they grasped the fence and shook it, clawed at it with their bare hands, desperate to get to their next meal. He swore under his breath and slipped past the girl, stumbling down a short set of steps into the dank-smelling cellar, and the girl let go of the door. It fell shut with a heavy thud, swallowing them into darkness.

* * *

Tupelo, MS

Cade knelt on the backseat and peered out the window long after Gray had driven the Jeep out of Tupelo, gripping the back of the seat and watching for Ethan. She'd convinced herself that he would follow them, that he'd change his mind and turn around. But as Tupelo receded into the horizon behind them, her shoulders slumped. He wasn't going to show up.

The disappointment was overwhelming.

A hand pressed against her back. She didn't have to turn to know it was Theo attempting to offer her some level of comfort. She drew in a heavy, rattling breath and smiled gratefully. His touch was the catalyst that allowed her to loosen her grip on the seat and sink into it limply.

"Are you okay?" Theo asked.

Cade clenched her teeth, squared her shoulders, and sat up straighter in her seat. She refused to be seen as weak—it wasn't in her personality to allow weakness to crack the badass façade she'd spent years cultivating in the IDF to prove her worth. She would never allow that hard work to go to waste over a moment's grief.

"Yeah, I'm fine," she answered shortly. How many times had she said that in the past day alone?

She shifted her gaze to the dashboard and watched the flickering lights on the police scanner. No matter how many times she tried to focus on something other than thoughts of Ethan, her mind kept going right back to the way he'd looked at her when he'd told her he was leaving. It had been a look of disbelief, a look that said he couldn't wrap his mind around why she'd protested his departure. As she replayed their argument over again in her head, she only felt one emotion, one that threatened to overpower her: guilt.

Before Cade could pursue her analysis of her feelings any further, Brandt's voice broke in. "Cade! You still with us?" He snapped the words out, his tone hinting that he'd called her name more than once. "Stop moping. We've got shit to plan, and I don't need you zoned out while we're doing it."

Cade gritted her teeth and punched the back of his seat. He yelped in protest and turned in his seat to glare at her. "What the hell?" he demanded.

"Shut up, Brandt," she snarled, her irritation and lingering guilt overriding her normally collected exterior. She punched the back of his seat again, and he put his hands up defensively.

"What the hell did I do to you?" he asked in bewilderment. "You've been all punch-Brandt today, and while I like my women forceful, I can't say I'm particularly enjoying this all that much."

"You breathed my air," Cade said sarcastically. She fought the urge to punch his seat—or perhaps his face—again.

"Cut it out, both of you," Theo interjected. He put a hand between them to block her view of Brandt—as if she were a dog, easily distracted when her view was diverted. She gave Theo an ugly look and swatted his hand away. "We don't have time for this! We have plans to make, important ones.

You can bitch at each other all you want after we get where we're going, okay? But not in the Jeep."

"I second that motion," Gray said from the driver's seat.

"You would," Cade muttered. She glanced at him and saw he still watched the road intently, both hands gripping the steering wheel.

"We're officially declaring the Jeep a Bitch-Free Zone," he added. "No bitching, no whining, no exceptions."

Silence fell, broken only by the sound of the Jeep's tires on the highway. Cade looked out the side window as she struggled to rein in her emotions. As she'd done the month before, in the aftermath of her escape from Memphis with Ethan, she shoved the emotions to the back of her mind and buried them, fastening them down tightly so they wouldn't escape and wreak havoc again.

"So, ah, what's the plan?" she finally asked. She avoided Brandt's face as she looked instead at Gray. The man had begun digging in the green bag resting against the console between the front seats, searching frantically with one hand. "You *do* have a plan, right?"

"Well, I figure if we can make it to Meridian, we'll be okay for the night," he said. He jerked the wheel to avoid a stalled car in the middle of the road, and Cade's stomach lurched. He pulled a folded paper out of the bag and shook it wildly, trying to unfold it. Once he'd successfully rattled the paper loose—and Cade's nerves along with it—he attempted to look at it and the road at the same time.

"I figure if you'll keep your hands on the wheel and your eyes on the road, we'll be more likely to make it to Meridian," Cade said. Gray glanced at her in the rearview mirror in acknowledgment before passing the paper to Brandt. He put both hands on the wheel and relaxed back in his seat. "So what's the plan then?" she prompted again.

"I figure we should avoid getting out of the Jeep," Brandt spoke up. "Maybe we can find a house that looks secure enough, park in the garage, and sleep in here."

"Sleep *in* the Jeep?" Theo repeated. "Like...where? This isn't exactly the world's roomiest vehicle, you know."

"We'll manage," Cade said flippantly. "We can't run the engine to keep warm, though. It would use too much fuel. It *does* get pretty cold at night, you know."

Brandt nodded absently and flipped the page in his hands over, like he expected to find the secret of life doodled on the back. "Yeah, I know," he said. "As you say, we'll manage. There are blankets in the back somewhere, and we can leave the engine idling enough to get the temperature comfortable before turning it off. Will that work?"

Cade shrugged and brushed a hand through her hair, grimacing at how oily it felt. For just a second, she wished for a shower, preferably one with warm water. She was sure if she had a good, thorough bath, she'd start to feel a little more human again. Instead of dwelling on the idea, she took her dark hair down from its band and pulled it into a fresh ponytail so she wouldn't experience the grossness all over again. "If it has to work, it'll work," she said, snapping the band into place.

* * *

Memphis, TN

Ethan drew in a breath as the darkness descended on him and fought the urge to put his hands out as if to feel his way along a wall. The sound of rattling metal on metal drew his attention to the door, and the click that followed made him tense. He imagined the blonde girl had a gun on him and perhaps planned to rob him of what little supplies he had. Loss of supplies meant almost certain death. He tried not to panic as his imagination ran wild in the pitch-black darkness.

There were muffled, scuffing footsteps, and a camping lantern flickered to life. Ethan was looking right at it, and he quickly put up a hand to shield his eyes from the sudden brightness. Spots danced in his eyes as he finally saw the girl. She knelt beside the lantern, adjusting the brightness down, a chagrined look on her face.

"Sorry. I forgot how bright that was," the girl said. She stood and looked toward the door. Banging and scuffling could be heard on the other side. Ethan followed her gaze and saw the door was securely fastened by a chain and padlock. "I don't think they're going to get through that. They haven't managed yet, anyway," she said confidently, sounding almost cheerful, and he couldn't decide if he was amazed or appalled.

"Well, ah, thank you?" he tried. "For getting me out of that mess. I didn't think I'd get away for a minute there."

The girl flitted her hand through the air nonchalantly. "Hey, no big deal. I'd hope you would have done the same for me."

"Of course," Ethan said automatically. He crossed his arms and observed their surroundings. They were in some type of cellar—almost a crawlspace below the house, really, judging by how low the ceiling was. The floor was dirt, and it made the space smell damp, dank, and earthy. He shifted his hands to his front pockets and examined the girl who, in her turn, studied him.

Her blond hair lay tangled and messy over the shoulders of her dirty blue track jacket; her jeans were filthy from crawling in the dirt in the crawlspace. A smudge of brown decorated an otherwise fair face, and her blue eyes studied him with a wide-eyed, slightly frightened innocence that contradicted her feigned casualness. He tried to guess her age. She looked horribly young; he didn't think she was a day over sixteen.

"What's your name?" he asked.

The girl tucked both hands into her pockets and ventured a small smile. "Nikola," she answered. "Nikola Klein. And you are?"

"Ethan Bennett," he answered. "Formerly of the Memphis PD. Definitely not anymore."

Nikola let out an undignified snort. "No, I don't think so." She looked him over again and added, "I had you pegged for a cop when I first saw you out on the street."

Ethan raised his eyebrows. "You did? How so?"

Nikola shrugged and rocked on her heels. "Cops, they have a certain way of walking. Kind of like military guys? It's really noticeable." She hesitated, then said, "My dad was a state trooper. He walked the same way."

He glanced around the dark space again. "Where *is* your dad?"

"He's…he's not here," she said delicately. He recognized the downcast look on her face. It was then he understood; this girl had not just been through what every survivor had been through: the loss of someone she loved dearly. She'd lost everyone. She didn't bring up a mother or other relative, despite his questioning look, and he guessed it was because she had no one left. He cleared his throat uncomfortably before speaking again.

"How old are you?" he asked gently. "You don't look a day over sixteen."

"That's because I'm fourteen," Nikola confirmed. She scooped up a backpack from the dirt beside her camping lantern. "I turn fifteen this summer," she continued, unzipping the bag and rummaging through it. "You hungry? I don't have much, but I think it's enough to hold us over."

Ethan didn't answer. Instead, he stared incredulously at Nikola. Fourteen? She was only *fourteen*? How in the world had the young girl survived unassisted for a month in the horror movie the world had become? How did she gather supplies, feed herself, defend herself against the monsters outside when they threatened her sanctuary? Where had she *been* for the past month?

"Can I ask you a question?" Ethan asked. Nikola pulled a bag of beef jerky out of her backpack and offered it to him. He didn't take it; he just watched her face. "How in the hell are you still alive? How are you still even *here*?"

Nikola looked at him with an expression crossed between worry and annoyance. "What, you don't think I can take care of myself?" she asked. "I can handle it. I'm tougher than I look. Besides, isn't it just a matter of avoiding them? And I've got it covered if they get too close." She picked up an aluminum baseball bat resting beside her pack and twirled it with no small degree of skill. "Softball, three years. I've got a mean swing."

"I'm sure you do, but I don't know how effective whacking somebody with a baseball bat is going to be if they're intent on killing you," Ethan pointed out. "You haven't had to actually use it yet, have you?"

"No, but I figure that's a good thing." She gave him a halfhearted shrug and shouldered the bat. "It could be worse, right? I mean, I could try using a gun and end up shooting my foot off or whatever."

Ethan raised an eyebrow. "Your dad was a state trooper and you've never used a gun before?"

"He said they were too dangerous. He didn't want me to accidentally shoot myself," she explained. "He told me to never touch his guns, and so I didn't."

"We'll have to fix that," Ethan said. He sighed wearily and rubbed his face. "I don't know how I feel about you running around out here without a better weapon than a bat."

Nikola jumped at the sound of a particularly loud bang at the cellar door. They turned as one to look at the door. It lifted a few inches before falling shut again with another loud thud. The infected outside seemed more determined than ever to get in. Ethan swallowed nervously and gripped the holstered weapon at his side.

"We have to go," Nikola said suddenly. She scooped up her backpack, jammed the beef jerky back into it, and zipped the bag closed, slinging it over her shoulder so it rested securely against her back. "They'll get in sooner or later, and I don't want to be here when it happens."

"Agreed," Ethan said. He glanced around, searching for an escape route in the dark cellar. "How are we going to get out of here? They're blocking the door, and I don't like the idea of shooting my way through."

"Follow me." Nikola beckoned and grabbed the camping lantern, then went to the cellar wall opposite the door. She smoothed her free hand along the wall, then let out a triumphant yelp and set the lantern down, digging her fingers into the dirt wall and pulling at it. A square wooden door swung away from the wall, falling off into her hands, and she dropped the board onto the floor and set her lantern into the knee-high square left behind. "After you? Or do you want me to go first?" she asked.

"What's this?" Ethan asked, both impressed at Nikola's ingenuity and wary of the dark space. He looked into it and saw by the light of the camping lantern that it was cramped and dark. It smelled as dank and dirty as the rest of the cellar.

"It used to be one of those tunnels that runaway slaves used during the Civil War or whatever," she explained. "Well, I think it was, anyway. I just know it links to the cellar in the house next door."

Ethan shook off the creepy feeling the space gave him. "Thank God I'm not claustrophobic," he said. "You go first. I'll follow in case they make it through the door before we get to the other side."

"Fair enough," she agreed, scooping up the lantern and dropping to her knees. It took her only moments to disappear into the dirt tunnel.

Ethan glanced back at the cellar door one more time as it lifted and thudded closed again. Nikola was right; the infected were dangerously close to getting into the cellar. Even if they didn't get in right away, they'd keep trying until they did, because they knew Nikola and Ethan were in there. He shook his head and dropped to his knees to crawl in after Nikola, following the girl into parts unknown.

CHAPTER SIXTEEN

Biloxi, MS

Remy's eyes flew open, and she stared into the darkness, her hands gripping the sleeping bag she lay on with fearful desperation. Her heart raced, and her pulse was as fluttery as her breathing. She drew in a shuddering breath and struggled to calm her nerves as the echoes of her nightmare rang in her ears. She shook her head like she could rattle the dream free, then blinked and tried to orient herself. It took her long heartbeats to remember where she was: an abandoned house near Biloxi, Mississippi, once the home of a family of four that had fled on short notice.

She reached blindly for the camping lantern she'd foolishly turned off before falling asleep and, after fumbling at the switch, the luminous light flickered on, momentarily blinding her. She rolled from the bed and landed in a crouch beside it, the carpet absorbing the sound of her shoes. Taking a step toward the barricaded door, she listened carefully for sounds of intruders. The night before, she'd shoved a heavy dresser in front of the door right before slinging her sleeping bag across the master bed and collapsing onto it. The dresser hadn't moved an inch, which meant she'd slept the night away safely. She blew out a breath of relief and straightened, rolling her shoulders to loosen the muscles and scanning her eyes over the bedroom again. Then she angled her watch toward the lantern to check the time. It was dawn.

After cleaning up in the attached master bathroom—a liberal splashing of cold water across her face, a thorough hair brushing and tooth scrubbing—she dug out a couple of candy bars and a map she'd found in a looted convenience store the day before. She tore one of the candy bars open with her teeth and, as she ate, squinted at the map, trying to figure out what she was looking at. It was a hopeless waste of time, really. She'd never learned how to read a map. As a result, everything she'd done over the previous month had been close to guesswork.

Remy wasn't sure her mind was in the right place for making plans, especially ones requiring her shoddy map-reading skills. The nightmare had left her rattled; she couldn't get Maddie's screams and the bang of the gunshot out of her ears. Though she knew it wasn't real, she couldn't expel the stench of blood and gunpowder from her nose, tangy and metallic and haunting.

She shoved her map back into her backpack and braced her hands against the dresser blocking the door. As it dragged across the carpeted floor, she entered a meditative state, motivated by the burn in her biceps, focusing and centering herself on the immediate. Once the door was unlocked, she set about gathering her supplies to head out on foot.

Remy packed her supplies and pinned her long hair back from her face before gathering her backpack, the hunting rifle she'd found several houses back, and her bolo knife. She hadn't needed to use either yet, but she knew going outside would make those odds increase tenfold. As she slipped down the stairs, she wished, not for the first time, that she had real combat skills. She'd had numerous chances growing up to take all sorts of self-defense classes, but her laziness, coupled with her general resistance toward authority and organized education, prevented her from taking her mother up on the repeated offers.

The downstairs level was clear, much to her relief. Once satisfied that there were no impending dangers, she made a beeline for the kitchen to ransack the cabinets and fridge for food. She hauled useful supplies from the kitchen: emergency candles, a few cheap flashlights, a pack of spare batteries, a couple of dozen cans of food. Unfortunately, she couldn't take all the food with her without impeding her own mobility, especially since the only mode of transportation she had was the Harley Davidson Touring motorcycle she'd found in a parking garage on the outskirts of New Orleans, its owner lying dead nearby. She gathered everything she could carry and slipped out the door leading to the garage. She stuffed most of the food and flashlights into the saddlebags, though she made sure to keep some food in her backpack. She had no intention of being separated from that pack and figured it wise to keep necessary items in it just in case.

She wheeled the bike into the street and climbed onto it, starting the motor without difficulty. She revved the engine a couple of times, warming it up, then started east, heading into the heart of Biloxi.

Three hours later, she found herself at an impasse. The highway she traveled on was completely blocked, along with all the streets surrounding it, like someone had set up a road-block with vehicles. She came up on it suddenly and nearly laid the bike down on the road in an effort to stop quickly enough to avoid the leading edge of the mess. Bracing both feet against the pavement, she gripped the handlebars and panted like she'd run a marathon, staring at the crashed cars with wide eyes.

"Aw hell," she said out loud, cutting the engine and lowering the kickstand. She scanned the blockage, searching for a way through, then frowned. All of her potential options involved abandoning her bike and going on foot. There were no gaps that would allow her to roll the bike through.

Remy slid off the motorcycle, adjusted her backpack, and resisted the urge to kick the bike. Finding a clear route could take too much time and too many miles, and she didn't have either to spare. She needed to get to the other side of Biloxi and find a hiding place before dark, when the infected tended to be more active. Hoofing it was her only real option.

She rummaged through the bike's saddlebags, looking for anything useful. There wasn't much she could afford to take with her: a few granola bars and a bag of almonds she'd forgotten were in there and a couple of cans of warm Coke, plus a Swiss Army knife. She put the food and drink into her pack, stuffed the knife in her pocket, and secured her weapons before starting forward to climb over the mess in front of her and find a clear path on the other side.

She hiked over the first of the cars and stood on a vehicle's crumpled hood, looking out at the scenery beyond. Once she got a good look, her heart sank. Any thoughts she'd had about getting through this mess were immediately dashed into the dirt.

Cars and trucks of all types, crashed together, driven on sidewalks, told small parts of a larger story of human panic and terror during Biloxi's outbreak. Remy was thankful she hadn't had to endure this particular event; apparently, it had begun in New Orleans while she'd been in the holding cell at the police department. That didn't make the sight any less depressing, though.

She sighed and sat on the car's hood, propping a foot up to tighten her shoelaces. She caught a glimpse of movement out of the corner of her eye. She froze, her shoulders involuntarily tensing, and grasped the hilt of her bolo knife, but she didn't draw it, not yet. She didn't know if the movement had come from a sick person or a healthy one—not that it made much difference; she'd already had more than one run-in with healthy people, and those encounters had ranged from uncomfortable to dangerous. It was why she'd chosen to stay away from people and go it alone.

Regardless of her decision, she didn't want to pull a weapon on anyone if she didn't have to. She held fast, waiting, hoping it wouldn't be some innocent person who just happened to be nearby.

Movement to her left, in the opposite direction, cemented the fact she hadn't seen healthy people. She stood on the roof of the car for a better perspective.

"Oh, fucking hell," Remy murmured as she saw what was coming in her general direction: too many sick people, more than she could handle. She grabbed her rifle and jumped from the car to the ground. Her ankle turned as she landed, and a sharp pain ran up her leg, nearly sending her crashing to the ground. She gasped, startled by the sudden pain, and forced it aside, starting to run as fast as the tangled maze of vehicles would allow.

Remy's actions opened a set of unseen floodgates. As she skirted around the first few cars in the street, infected burst from the streets, alleys, and buildings around her, tripping over debris and each other in their haste to get to her. A whimper of fear tried to overcome her, but a surge of adrenaline beat back the terror, and she put on a bigger burst of speed. More sick people emerged from the side roads ahead, and she hoped she could run faster than them, get past them and get to safety.

Roughly a quarter mile ahead, sitting like a beached whale in the street, was a white RV, an older model with the cab built into the RV itself. Figuring that was as good a refuge as any, she ran toward it, hoping that the door was unlocked and there was no one inside.

Luck was with her. The driver's door was unlocked, and she flung it open and scrambled inside, falling onto the cushy driver's seat. Her rifle dug into the small of her back and her shoulder blade as she pushed herself up to pull the door closed. A group of sick people tried to shove in through the door after her, and she kicked at them frantically, unable to get to any of her weapons with the steering wheel and the back of the seat in her way. Shoving them out of the way and wrestling herself free at the same time, she yanked the door shut, hitting the lock at the same time. Then she slumped in the seat, panting, as the people outside threw themselves frantically at the door.

The sight of them whipped her into motion. She climbed out of the driver's seat to the passenger's and slammed her palm onto the lock, then ducked into the living area in the back of the RV. As soon as she was clear of the cab, she pulled her rifle off her shoulder and aimed it into the RV's darkened interior. Nothing moved, so she eased deeper into the cabin, checking to make sure the side door too was locked before finishing her search of the rest of its interior. Once she was sure no one lurked inside, she flopped onto one of the couches to catch her breath before digging out a flashlight from her backpack to examine her ankle.

It was already swelling, and she struggled to get her tennis shoe off without hurting herself. Once the shoe and sock were off her foot, she tugged her pant leg up and let out a low whistle. "Holy crap," she murmured. Bruises were already forming on her ankle, along with a large, swollen lump that bulged from the side of it. She prodded the lump gently with her fingers, afraid to press against it too hard. Maybe it was broken. She had no way to tell; she certainly wasn't a medical professional.

Remy lowered her foot to the floor and hauled herself to her feet, careful not to put too much weight on her injured ankle. She hobbled to the cabinets in the miniature kitchenette, searching them and finding a few bags of chips, some snack bars, and several bottles of water. She tossed it onto the couch, then looked around, wondering what else useful she could find.

That was when she spotted what she'd missed when she'd been in the cab: a CB radio.

"Oh, joyful day," she said, grasping the kitchen counter and using it as support to hobble her way to the cab again. She ignored the hands pounding on the doors and windows and picked up the microphone, twisting a few dials on the device. It didn't appear to be working; maybe it needed power.

She saw the keys in the ignition and decided to see what would happen, turning them enough to switch the battery on. The dash and the radio lit up like a Christmas tree, and she sent up a silent prayer of thanks before grabbing the mic and pressing the button on the side of it.

"Hello?" she called into the mic. "Hello, is anybody there?" She released the button, waited a moment, then tried again. "Hello, can anybody hear me?" After five minutes of trying and failing to get an answer, she gave up, cutting the RV back off and retreating into the cabin again.

For nine days, she kept trying randomly throughout the day to raise someone on the radio. On day four, she ran out of food, which only made her plight that much more urgent. And through it all, her ankle kept throbbing, pulsing with pain with each of her heartbeats, and she'd have given a finger for a bottle of ibuprofen.

On the ninth night, as she went through the motions of clicking the RV's battery on and picking up the mic, contemplating her current situation, she realized she'd given up hope. She was going to die here, starve to death because she had a busted ankle, was surrounded by sick people, and had no way out. She was resigned to this as she keyed up the mic and spoke into it for the third time that day.

"Hello? Is anyone there?"

There was a pop of static, then silence. She sighed and spoke into the mic again. "Hello? *Anybody?*"

Nothing.

Remy let out an exasperated groan and threw the mic down in frustration, resting her head against the steering wheel and fighting back a surge of tears.

That was when the CB radio crackled and came to life.

* * *

Meridian, MS

The Jeep was just shy of large enough for the four of them to sleep comfortably. Gray acknowledged this as readily as he acknowledged everything else with which he'd been confronted in the past month. Life had gotten as uncomfortable as the SUV in which he was now attempting to sleep, and he didn't have a choice but to put up with it.

Gray blew out a heavy breath and rubbed the heels of his hands over his eyes. He frowned and shifted once more in the driver's seat. It was reclined as far back as he could without crushing Cade in the seat behind him, but it still felt like it wasn't enough, and his back protested the incline at which he lay. He fought the urge to groan and closed his eyes again, shifting restlessly.

A light tap of a finger against his forehead made him open his eyes again. He blinked in the dim light and saw Cade leaning over him. She gave him a little smile and leaned in close.

"Can't sleep either, can you?" she murmured, her voice hushed. He shook his head, and she tilted her head to the side, indicating the door. "Come on, let's tell Brandt to get back in the car and we'll take guard duty."

Gray fought a yawn and opened the door. Theo stirred in the backseat but didn't wake. He made a face at his brother's sleeping form; he couldn't deny his jealousy over Theo's ability to sleep virtually anywhere, in any position. He slid out of the Jeep into the chilly garage, rubbing his hands over his bare arms and retrieving his jacket. Cade followed, and as she went to Brandt to send him to the Jeep, Gray tucked his hands into his pockets and looked around the building in which they'd hidden.

It was a two-car garage attached to a typical suburban family home on the southern end of Meridian, Mississippi. Gray had picked it because it was close to the outskirts of the city, and the home itself looked neat and undisturbed. He looked at the signs of suburban life that lined the shelves and cubbyholes and work benches around them: the pegboard full of tools, the cracked concrete floor, the weed eater and lawnmower shoved against a wall, the pile of old paint cans stacked beside them. He squeezed his hands into tight fists. The suburban routine that had brought this to life was gone, completely eradicated. The world would never again be the same.

"You look like you've got something on your mind," Cade said, emerging from the darkness of the garage. There was a thud behind them as Brandt climbed into the Jeep and shut the door. "Want to talk about it?"

Gray shrugged and accepted the pistol she offered, tucking it into the waistband of his jeans, even though he knew it went against every bit of gun safety his dad ever taught him. "I don't know," he answered. "I mean, I barely know you. I haven't even known you for forty-eight hours yet, and in that time, you've hardly talked to me."

"Which is why I asked." She examined her rifle nonchalantly. "I figure if we're going to be stuck in close proximity to each other, we might as well start the getting-to-know-you routine, you know?"

"I guess." Gray's voice was doubtful. He moved to the small door that accessed the street and peeked out the inset window, scanning the dark street warily. He couldn't see anything lurking nearby, so he returned to the Jeep. "What exactly do you want to know about me?"

Cade hummed and slid her hand down the barrel of her rifle. "I don't know. Just…whatever. Like, what'd you do before the world went to hell?"

He looked at her thoughtfully; she hadn't torn her gaze from her rifle as she spoke. "I was, ah, a mechanic," he said. "Did body work, mostly. Always been good at fixing shit."

"Yeah? That's useful," she said. She propped the rifle against her knee and pulled the bolt back. It made an ominous clicking sound that sent a disturbing chill down his spine, and the muscles in his back stiffened. "You should get some of the tools in here together and load 'em in the Jeep," she suggested. "Never know when we might need them."

Before he could respond, Brandt burst from the Jeep, nearly spilling onto the cracked concrete floor. Once he gained his footing, he slapped his hand against the vehicle's roof. An echoing thud rang out through the garage. "Get over here," he ordered. "We've got a situation."

"A situation?" Cade repeated. She straightened and looked at Brandt with a dark, unreadable expression, slinging her rifle over her shoulder and moving toward him. A wave of nervousness welled in Gray's gut. A situation? What sort of situation could have arisen in the Jeep when the only people in there were Theo and Brandt? The thought that something was wrong with Theo evoked a flutter of nausea.

"What sort of situation?" he asked.

"There's a girl on the scanner," Brandt said. "Says she needs help."

Intrigued by Brandt's words, Gray slung himself into the driver's seat. As he righted the seat, the radio crackled to life, and a young woman's voice rang out over the speaker. "*Hello? Are you still there?*"

Gray and Brandt fumbled for the mic at the same time. They wrestled over it for a moment before Gray successfully pulled it away and pressed the button on the side. "Yeah, we're here. Who's this?"

"*My name is Remy,*" the girl's voice came through. "*Who is this? You sound different than before.*"

"You were talking to Brandt then. This is Gray," he answered. "Brandt said you needed help?"

"*Yeah, I think I'm trapped,*" Remy said. He raised an eyebrow at her words. She *thought* she was trapped? Either she was or she wasn't. "*I might need a bit of help getting out of here,*" she continued.

Gray motioned to Brandt to give him the bag at his feet. The older man picked it up and opened it, and Gray snatched it from him to dig out the maps himself. "Where exactly is 'here'?" he asked, pulling out his atlas and starting to search for the map of Mississippi.

"*I'm stuck in an RV in Biloxi,*" she said. "*There are some of those...*things *outside. And I think I broke my ankle, but I'm not sure. It could just be a bad sprain. It's swollen like hell, and I can't really walk on it.*"

"Damn, that might complicate things," Brandt muttered. What in the world was Brandt talking about? Gray caught a glimpse of his eyes and fought back a groan. Brandt was planning something, probably a rescue mission. He didn't know if they had the resources or skills for something like that.

But Gray knew one thing above all else: they were going to have to try anyway.

He let out a steadying breath and keyed the mic again. "Hey, uh, Remy? Where exactly in Biloxi are you? We need the nearest intersection to your location."

As Remy spoke, Gray grabbed a pen from his bag and scribbled the information she gave him on the back of the map, across the state of Missouri. Cade leaned against the doorframe, watching intently.

"Are we going after her?" she asked as she leaned in to read what he'd written.

He paused and lowered the pen to look at his companions. Brandt looked determined, his jaw set in a tight clench as he slid out of the Jeep and went to the back. Cade looked almost excited, and he wondered if she felt a thrill at the idea of shooting something. Considering how attached she was to her rifle, he wouldn't have been surprised if that were the case.

The last person Gray turned to was Theo. His brother sat silently in the backseat; he hadn't spoken since Remy's voice had sparked the night's excitement. His eyes met Gray's, and he nodded to signal his agreement.

"Yeah, I guess we *are* going after her," Gray said. "Why shouldn't we, really? We're going in that direction anyway, right?"

"My thoughts exactly," Brandt said, reappearing in the open passenger door and dumping an armload of liquor bottles onto the seat. Gray frowned as he saw the multiple bottles of alcohol.

"What's all that for?" he demanded. "Planning on opening the first operating bar post-Michaluk?" Brandt ignored the question and sorted through bottles, counting under his breath. When he finally spoke again, it was to bark out orders.

"Theo, get up here in the front seat," he said, gathering the bottles and cradling them against his chest. "You're going to help Gray navigate for a bit while Cade and I take care of this."

Gray raised an eyebrow as Brandt shifted the bottles enough to open the back passenger door. "What exactly is the 'this' you and Cade are going to be taking care of?" he asked. A heavy sense of dread settled in his stomach.

Theo slid out of the backseat and gave Gray a smirk, scrambling into the front. "I'm not sure we want to know," he confided. "Especially if it involves all of that alcohol."

Gray bit back a snort of amusement as he realized Theo had practically read his mind. He twisted around in his seat to look at Brandt. The older man cracked open a bottle of Jameson and waved to Cade to get into the Jeep. "Wait, are we leaving *now*?" he asked incredulously.

"I don't see why not," Brandt said, giving the bottle in his hand a thoughtful look. Then he leaned out the door and began pouring the liquor onto the garage's concrete floor.

"What the hell are you doing?" Gray exclaimed as the amber liquid spilled from the bottle. "You're wasting that!"

"I'm making Molotovs," Brandt said mildly. The sound of the garage door opening drowned out his words. Cade stood by the open garage door, her rifle up on her shoulder, scanning the street outside before joining her companions.

"It's all clear," she announced, jumping into the backseat and pulling her door shut. "I'm ready whenever you guys are."

"Wait, wait, *wait*," Gray insisted. "Why are we leaving *now*? It's dark. It's dangerous. The last thing we should be doing is heading out after sunset."

Brandt rolled his eyes, which only made Gray clench his jaw in annoyance. Brandt capped the bottle in his hand and set it on the seat before leaning between the front seats and grabbing the scanner's mic again. "Remy, you still around?" he asked into it, glaring pointedly at Gray.

"*Yeah, I'm still here.*"

"What's your situation with food and water?" he asked.

"*I've got two bottles of water left, but I've been out of food for about five days now, I think,*" she said. The sheer exhaustion in her voice twisted a knot of concern in Gray's stomach. "*It might be four days. Somewhere around that, anyway.*"

"Shit," Theo breathed out. "She could go longer without the food, but with the way things are, I wouldn't recommend it. And she's dangerously close to running out of water. Two bottles won't last her long enough to stay adequately hydrated. She'll hit the point where she'll be too tired to run. If she hasn't already gotten there, that is."

"We shouldn't make her wait until morning before we help her," Cade said solemnly. The crack of a seal breaking on a bottle cap punctuated her sentence. "We need to get moving and give her whatever help we can lend."

As much as Gray wanted to help Remy, he wasn't comfortable traveling in the dark. There were too many unknown dangers, visibility was too low, and it was much easier to get jumped by the things that crept about in the night. But he also realized that, despite his discomfort at the idea, he was outvoted by the others, and if he didn't drive, someone else would. Regardless of his choice, Gray would be dragged along involuntarily, so he resolved himself to going along with the plan, turning the key in the ignition with a sigh.

* * *

Memphis, TN

Ethan followed Nikola through the dark tunnel, his fingers digging into the dirt as he shuffled along. He kept his eyes locked onto the teenager's thick, tangled blond hair, visible in the flickering blue halogen light of the lantern that she pushed along ahead of her. His stomach churned, and he clenched his teeth against a surge of queasiness. He didn't like the sinking feeling of the unknown.

Nikola disappeared from his view, and he reflexively jerked his head up to look for her. His head hit the dirt tunnel's ceiling, and he winced. He ducked lower and scrambled for the end, where Nikola's light still illuminated his way. He gained his feet and squinted into the cellar in which they now stood; it was as dark as the one they'd left, and the only light came from the lantern Nikola had lifted to shine across the cellar.

"So what's the plan?" he asked, rubbing at the sore spot on top of his head. "I'm assuming you have one?"

Nikola snorted and looked at him in disbelief. "Wait, you're asking a *fourteen-year-old girl* for a plan? My plan involved getting us here. That's as far as I got."

"Oh Lord," Ethan groaned, covering his face with a hand. "Grant me serenity, etcetera, etcetera." He blew out a breath and looked around, trying to decide what their first action should be. The sound of the other cellar's door cracking and groaning decided it for him. "Shit," he muttered. He glanced at Nikola; she watched the entrance to the tunnel with wide eyes. "We need to barricade this thing first, just to buy us extra time," he decided.

"With *what?*" Nikola asked, waving her hands around the empty cellar. "This place isn't exactly loaded down with stuff to shove in front of it."

Ethan squinted in the meager light, searching for anything with which to block the entryway, then swore under his breath and grabbed Nikola's arm, tugging her toward the exit that led outside. "We need to get out of here fast then. We don't have much time." He laid a hand against the door but hesitated and looked back at her. "You know where my bike is?"

"The motorcycle you rolled up on?" Nikola asked. "Should still be in the middle of the street where you left it."

His mind raced. "Okay, I think I might have a plan," he said. He tried to put the pieces together as the sound of cracking wood and beating hands echoed more frantically through the tunnel behind them. "We're going to make a run for my bike. First, though, we need to make a stop." He rattled off Cade's address, even as he pressed his ear to the slanted wooden door that opened to the outside world.

"I know where that is," she said. "But why do we need to go there?"

"I've got a few things to pick up that we could use," Ethan answered vaguely. He rested his hand against the scratched wooden surface; splinters threatened to poke through his skin. "If we get separated, go for that house. Hide in the basement if I'm not there. And if I don't show up within five minutes, make for the motorcycle and get out of here," he instructed. He paused and turned to look at her. "Do you know how to drive a motorcycle?"

"I don't even know how to drive," she admitted, her cheeks flushing. "I'm only fourteen, remember?"

"Shit," he muttered. "Well, I guess that means we can't get separated." He pressed his hand more firmly on the door as his other hand pulled his pistol from the holster on his hip. "When we get out of here, which way do we run? Left or right?"

"Left," Nikola confirmed. She set the lantern on the dirt beside her and tightened the straps on her backpack.

"Any obstructions between here and there?"

"There's a fence around the yard," she said. "The gate's blocked, so we're going to have to find a way over it."

"That's not a problem," Ethan said dismissively. "I can get us over that. What else?"

"The cars on the street," she continued. "They're pretty much bumper to bumper, shoved up against each other. We'll have to go over those."

"No way around?"

Nikola shook her head. "It would take too long."

"Good to know. Anything else?"

"Nothing I can think of. But I haven't studied the streets outside very carefully since I started hiding in people's basements," she admitted sheepishly.

"Hey, that's okay," Ethan said, motioning for her to join him. She brought the lantern with her, lighting her way. "You might have to ditch the lantern. You'll need both hands out there."

"Yeah, I know," Nikola said, sighing. "I just don't want to. It's been useful."

He patted her back. "Don't worry. We'll find you another one." He pushed gently against the door. "Ready?"

"As I can be." Her voice was cheerful, and he was surprised at how easily she'd fallen into a confident mindset. He wondered how she did it, how she could dismiss the horrors outside. A fleeting thought that maybe she didn't actually do so whipped through his mind faster than he could catch it, and he wondered what this girl dealt with on a daily basis, alone in the world with no one to rely on.

"Okay," Ethan finally said. Nikola set the lantern on the top step as he pushed the door open, using his shoulder to heave it up and to the side. The door fell with a bang against the ground. There was no way to prevent the noise, but he still winced at its volume.

He lifted his pistol and scrambled up the steps, sweeping the immediate area to make sure there weren't any infected waiting to grab them the moment they emerged from the cellar. With the coast clear, he hauled himself out and reached back to pull Nikola with him. Without another word, he ran left as she'd instructed, Nikola on his tail as they sprinted to the wire fence looming ahead.

Ethan grabbed the top of the fence and vaulted over it, narrowly avoiding the Romeo catchers. He grabbed Nikola and physically hauled her over the fence as she dug her feet into it and pushed herself along. She breathed a quick word of thanks and then ran, taking the lead as they made for the sidewalk and the line of cars blocking the path to Cade's house.

Ethan dashed madly for the street, his legs pumping and his breath picking up. Movement to the right caught his attention as he ran. One of the infected was making its way toward them. Nikola saw it, too; her step faltered, and she glanced back at him uncertainly.

"I've got it! Keep going!" he called, pointing his weapon at the oncoming enemy. The infected woman didn't break stride as he aimed, absorbed as she was in the acquisition of her next meal. Ethan gritted his teeth and squeezed the trigger. The shot struck her shoulder, but Ethan didn't stop to try shooting her again. Instead, he sped up to catch up with Nikola; she'd just barely reached the line of cars ahead of them.

"Go over them!" Ethan yelled, covering the last few feet between him and Nikola. He nearly slammed into a car as his shoes slipped on the gravel scattered on the sidewalk. He and Nikola scrambled across the car's hood, their feet finding purchase on the tires and bumper.

Ethan cleared the car first and turned to help Nikola over the last half of the hood. The infected woman had reached the other side of the car, and she grabbed for Nikola's shoe. Ethan grabbed Nikola's wrist and hauled her bodily across the hood, pushing her behind him and lifting his pistol once more.

It only took one shot. The woman's brains sprayed backward in a shower of blood and bone and gray matter. She fell back to the sidewalk, disappearing from view.

"Holy shit," Nikola squeaked. Ethan lowered the pistol and grabbed her hand, tugging her in the direction of Cade's house.

"Run! There's more coming!" he snapped. His angry tone broke through her frozen shock, and she ran with him for the house. Ethan dodged through a small gap between two cars, banging his knee against a bumper and ignoring the pain as he grabbed Nikola's hand. They stumbled up the front porch steps.

The front door still stood wide open, just the way Ethan and Cade had left it. Ethan didn't have time to wonder why that was. He grabbed the teenager again and nearly slung her into the house. He darted in behind her and slammed the door shut, throwing the locks as quickly as his shaking fingers would cooperate.

"Barricade that door!" Ethan ordered. But even as he said the words, the memory of a shattered patio door flashed through his mind, and he knew the effort would be wasted. He stopped Nikola, who was in the process of shoving a heavy table in front of the front door. "Never mind, not enough time," he said. "And it's pointless anyway. Upstairs, now."

"Why is it pointless?" she asked, following Ethan up the stairs.

"Because the back door is busted wide open," he said. "It happened last month, when the virus hit Memphis. Cade and I were here, and they came in."

"Cade?" Nikola asked, trying to keep up with his pace. "Who is he?"

"She," Ethan corrected absently. He reached the top of the stairs and stopped her just behind him. The stench of rot hit his nose. It was the distinctive smell of death, one he'd experienced several times in his line of work, and he drew up short. Looking around cautiously, he squinted into the darkness of the hallway and fumbled for a small flashlight in his bag, finding it and turning it on. It took him precious seconds that they could ill afford to spare to realize the smell came from Andrew's body. The man lay in a heap near the top of the stairs, exactly where he'd fallen when Ethan shot him the month before.

The sight of the body reminded him of the other one in the house somewhere. He breathed in slowly and glanced back at Nikola. He didn't want to worry her, so he continued speaking casually, picking up where he left off.

"Cade is my best friend. She's a marksman. Served in the Israel Defense Forces," he explained. He eased his way over Andrew's remains, one foot at a time. Nikola hesitated and glanced at the body, and Ethan wondered if her legs were long enough to step over. He handed his pistol to her and picked her up, physically lifting her over the body. "So basically, she's perfectly suited to survive this kind of thing," he continued. "Maybe you'll meet her sometime soon, if our luck holds out."

"I hope it does," Nikola admitted, her voice hushed. She stuck close to Ethan, right by his elbow, and he began moving toward Cade's room, one slow step at a time. "I haven't seen many people. You're the first in a long while." She slipped her backpack around and slid her aluminum baseball bat out of it like she was unsheathing a sword. "It gets old being by myself all the time."

"I can imagine," Ethan said. He paused in the doorway to Josie's room and forced himself to look inside. The late afternoon was passing by and early evening settling in, making everything more difficult to see. He clenched his teeth and resigned himself to stepping into the room to make sure no dangers lurked inside.

He startled when he felt a touch on his elbow. It was only Nikola, though, pressing closer to him in the dark hall. He shone his flashlight into the guest room; the beam of whitish-blue light illuminated the bloodstained bed. He struggled to not close his eyes as he remembered what had happened to Josie the month before.

The room was blessedly empty of movement. He breathed out in relief. "Come on, Nikola. We've got a few things to grab around here," he said, stepping away from the doorway to head to the master bedroom.

He'd managed two steps down the hall when a shriek behind him pulled him back around again. He froze in shock as a small, dark-haired girl pounced out of the shadows of the bathroom and slammed into Nikola, bowling her over to the hallway carpet, her small hands grasping desperately at the teenager's face.

CHAPTER SEVENTEEN

Biloxi, MS

As Gray slowed the Jeep to a stop, Cade leaned between the front seats to look at the street ahead. It had taken them the better part of the night to make the trip to Biloxi, and the ride had been refreshingly uneventful. Theo had spent most of his time in the front seat fiddling with the radio, changing from one station of static to the next like he'd discover something new by magic or sheer determination, at least until Brandt forced Gray to pull over so he could swap places with the medic. And now, as Gray put the Jeep into park, the interior of the vehicle fell into stunned silence as the occupants took in the sight before them.

The RV rested halfway down the street from the intersection Remy had given them, exactly where she'd said it would be. It sat like a beached white whale among the sea of smaller cars surrounding it, its metal siding illuminated dully by the moonlight overhead. And all around the RV and cars surrounding it were the infected, masses of them, all standing and staring at the vehicle like they sensed the uninfected person inside. Cade had no idea how they were supposed to get to the injured girl inside, not to mention get her *out*. Not with just the four of them against the dozens of infected.

"Fuck," Gray breathed, a tremor in his voice. "How are we supposed to do this?" He gripped the steering wheel tighter, his knuckles turning white. "It's…it's got to be impossible."

Cade's eyes flitted to the man in the passenger seat. Brandt sat with his eyes locked onto the street before them. There was an intensity in his gaze that she hadn't seen before. The look didn't do much to alleviate her nervousness, mainly because she knew what he was thinking: that they'd have to try at all costs. And "all costs" would probably mean they'd end up dead. That was how missions like that always turned out.

"We've got to do something," Brandt said, surprising no one. "We can't just leave her there. You heard her. Her ankle might be broken, and she's out of food and almost out of water. If we don't get her out of there, she's as good as dead."

"But *how* are we going to get her out?" Cade asked. She kept her voice low in the presence of the infected and realized the others were doing the same. Another silence fell over the Jeep's interior. She closed her eyes and tried to focus, to come up with an idea, any idea. But all she could hear was Brandt's quiet breathing in her right ear and Gray's fingers drumming on the steering wheel in her left.

"We need to get me in there," Theo said suddenly. Cade turned to him in amazement. He unzipped his medical bag and rifled through it as he continued. "She might have a broken ankle, right? That means it'll be difficult, if not impossible, for her to run. And if she can't run, then we have a problem right there."

"He's right," Brandt said, tearing his gaze from the street. "I think I have a plan, but I'm not sure how you're going to like it."

"I really hate when people start their plans like that," Cade muttered. "But that's way more than what I have to offer right now."

"Well, here's what I'm thinking," Brandt started. "Gray, you're going to stay with the Jeep and guard it. After we get out, you'll take it two blocks in the direction we came from and wait there. Theo, you'll take whatever you need with you. Cade and I will cover you and try to clear a path to the RV."

"And if one of us gets infected?" Theo asked solemnly. He was transferring supplies into a smaller bag, packing and discarding items as he saw fit.

"We'll cross that bridge if we come to it," Brandt said. "My plan isn't perfect. We'll have to make it as close to the RV as possible with as little noise and attention as we can manage. That will be easier said than done."

"If not impossible," Cade grumbled.

"The cars," Gray said. He nodded toward the street, where cars lined the sides of the road, jammed against curbs, shoved against each other, a few halfway onto the sidewalk itself, the very definition of bumper-to-bumper traffic. "I'm sure you could get reasonably close to the RV if you hide behind them."

"'Reasonably close' doesn't equal 'inside,'" Cade pointed out impatiently. "Besides, the moment we abandon cover, they'll see us. And when they see us, we'll have to shoot. And when we have to shoot..."

"...it'll bring even more right to us," Brandt finished for her. "But we've got to do something. We can't leave her there."

"You mean we *won't*," Gray corrected. Brandt glanced at him but didn't acknowledge the truth of his words.

"It's the best plan I've got," Brandt confessed. "We'll have to go with it. Unless someone else has a better idea?"

Silence fell once more. Cade shifted in her seat and sighed. "I think this is the point where, if Ethan were here, he'd kindly inform us that this is a suicide run," she said. Her eyes met Brandt's for a brief moment. "But I also think you're right," she conceded. "We have to try. We can't call ourselves decent people unless we do."

Brandt studied her, perhaps trying to assess how serious she was. But the spell was broken. He gave her a nod and drew his gun from its holster, topping off the ammunition in its magazine calmly, almost mechanically. "We should get moving. It's after midnight. We don't have much time before they notice we're here."

Nearly an hour later, Cade crouched behind a battered old Buick, her trusty Jericho pistol in her grip as she peered around the side of the vehicle. Her rifle rested reassuringly against her back. She touched the strap gently, as if drawing energy and strength from it. The coast appeared clear from her vantage point, but she wasn't going to move until Brandt signaled to her.

Speaking of Brandt...

Cade leaned forward another inch and spotted him kneeling behind a pickup truck, Theo crouched beside him. The sound of the infected surrounding the RV ahead masked the noise of Brandt digging in the bag over his shoulder. She wondered what in the world he was doing until he pulled out one of the glass bottles they'd carefully measured out. It was over half full of amber liquid. Brandt opened the bottle and crammed a rag into it, and a slow smile spread across Cade's face.

"Molotov," she breathed to herself. "Badass."

Brandt gave her the watched-for signal, beckoning her to join him and Theo. She ran to them in a low crouch, taking a knee beside Brandt and squinting at him in the darkness. "What's the plan?" she hissed.

"Molotov cocktail," he said. "It'll create a nice diversion when I smash it against that building over there." He pointed to a brick storefront about fifty yards away.

Cade measured the distance with her eyes, frowning at the numerous cars blocking the path. "Can you manage that far?"

"If I didn't know better, I'd think you didn't have any confidence in me," Brandt teased. He gave her what she could only define as a shit-eating grin and flipped open the silver lighter in his hand. He struck the wheel with his thumb, and a bright flame burst forth. Cade rolled her eyes and gritted her teeth in exasperation.

"That does *nothing* to answer my question," she snapped.

"Well, we'll just have to see, won't we?" Brandt replied. He touched the flame to the alcohol-soaked rag stuffed into the neck of the bottle and abruptly stood. He drew his arm back as if ready to throw a football, then snapped it forward; the bottle shot through the air in a perfect arc. Cade ducked reflexively, and her eyes followed the flaming missile as it struck the brick wall and shattered on impact. A wave of flame washed out over the stones and illuminated their path. The sound of breaking glass echoed across the street.

"Go!" Brandt ordered.

Cade wasted no time. She leaped to her feet and raised her pistol, pointing it toward the masses of infected as her free hand grabbed for Theo. Her fingers found the strap of his bag, and she used it to haul the paramedic to his feet even as she started running toward the RV as fast as her boots would carry her, dodging between cars and around luggage and other debris littering the street.

The infected swarmed forward in response to the presence of the three humans making their way through their ranks. Cade swore and aimed her pistol at the nearest of them—a woman in a shredded band t-shirt and the remains of khaki pants—and squeezed off a shot. The bullet struck the woman in the chest; she staggered and quickly recovered, resuming her chase. Cade didn't dare slow or stop to take another shot with more careful aim.

There was a flash of light in the corner of Cade's eye. Brandt had thrown another Molotov cocktail, and fire spread among the thickest group of infected merging on her position. She aimed her pistol into the burning mass, but before she could open fire, the group of infected began screaming. The unholy sound sent a horrific chill up her spine. She squeezed the trigger—once, twice, three times—and two of the infected fell, writhing and burning.

As Cade skirted a four-door sedan, Brandt appeared at her elbow. Distracted by his appearance, she nearly ran right into the sedan's open back door. She caught the edge of the door and swung around it as Brandt panted out, "Path should be clear enough to get to the RV."

"I really fucking hope so," Cade gasped out. She glanced back and saw Theo was barely keeping pace with them; he looked winded, and she could hear his panting, even with the several feet of distance separating them. "We're almost there!" she called to him, trying to give him motivation to keep moving. As if the infected all over the street weren't motivation enough.

Three more sprinting steps took Cade right to the RV's door. She beat her hands frantically against it to rouse the occupant's attention and grabbed Theo by his shirt, pulling him in close to her. The paramedic flattened against the side of the vehicle and watched the surge of infected coming toward them. Cade sucked in a breath and raised her pistol but froze as Brandt stepped protectively between her and the oncoming horde. He had another liquor bottle in his hand, and he lit the rag he'd stuffed into it.

The RV's door flew open and rammed Cade hard on the shoulder. She sidestepped away from it as a girl's voice came from the RV's interior. "Get in! Quick!"

Cade didn't have to be told twice. She grabbed the strap of Theo's bag again, and she swung him around and shoved him into the RV more roughly than she intended. She was sure he'd forgive her for any bruises he'd sustained. Then she turned back to Brandt. He'd lobbed his glass grenade, and it had shattered, sending flames spreading across the pavement. As the clothes of the infected caught aflame, the awful screams surged in volume, and Cade struggled to not clap both hands over her ears. The infected staggered into each other, their mouths wide and their hands clawing the air.

"Oh jeez, come on!" Cade shouted, grabbing Brandt's shirt and pulling him away from the infected. He whirled around and pushed her to the door, and they stumbled into the dark RV. Brandt slammed the door behind them, and in moments, he'd locked it and begun barricading it as a temporary measure of protection.

Cade slouched against the white Formica countertop in the RV's kitchenette, panting and trying to catch her breath. She closed her eyes for a moment as her chest heaved. When she opened them again, she looked around the RV's compact interior.

It was a stereotypical affair, on the cheap end of the spectrum, the type of RV a middle-class retired couple might purchase for a road trip. It was dark and cramped, especially with four people crammed into it. Empty food packages and water bottles littered the floor by the couch-like bench near the front of the RV. The bench itself showed signs of recent habitation; pillows were piled at one end, and a woolen blanket lay in a pile in the middle of it. And the presumed former occupant of the couch perched on the driver's seat at the front of the RV, turned sideways with her foot in Theo's hand. The paramedic had wasted no time beginning his examination of the woman's injured extremity.

"You must be Remy," Cade said, moving deeper into the RV to examine what little was there.

"Yeah. Remy Angellette," the woman said, her voice strained, her face pale. She held the steering wheel in a white-knuckled grip as Theo prodded her ankle. She looked like she was about to pass out—the perfect way to cap off the entire situation. "I'd say I'm pleased to meet you guys," she continued haltingly, "but considering the circumstances, I'm kind of not."

Cade chuckled at Remy's attempted humor, but a loud thud against the side of the RV interrupted any response she could have formulated. She jerked to attention, and Brandt rushed to look out the window above the bench.

"What's the story?" Cade asked, joining Brandt. She holstered her pistol and slung her rifle off her back, just in case they needed something with bigger firepower.

Brandt didn't answer right away. He nodded toward the window, and she climbed onto the bench to look out. Another bang shook the RV. She looked out at the street, and her eyes widened in shock. "We're surrounded," Brandt said tonelessly. He raised his voice as the infected outside threw their bodies against the RV. "And they're definitely aware we're in here."

Cade swore. Her nerves made her hands shake, and she tightened her grip on her rifle to hide the tremors. "Shit. How long do we have?" She took two steps across the narrow aisle to look out a window on the other side of the RV. If anything, more infected were massed on the passenger's side than on the driver's side, which was downright sparse in comparison.

"What's going on?" Theo called from the front. He wrapped Remy's ankle in an elastic bandage, looping it around and under her foot to immobilize it.

"We're surrounded," Cade announced. The thudding outside the RV increased, and the entire vehicle rocked with the impact. She hugged her rifle against her chest as her nerves threatened to get the better of her.

"We're...*fuck*," Theo breathed. He plunged a hand into his bag and began digging for Heaven only knew what.

"How are we going to get out of here?" Remy asked. "I mean, what's the plan?"

A silence fell over the RV. The only sound was the banging from outside and the faint rattling of dishes in kitchen cabinets. Cade and Theo exchanged a wary look before she turned her eyes to Brandt, who had yet to speak.

"Brandt?" Cade prompted, keeping her voice controlled. Brandt didn't look at her; he'd begun pawing through his own bag, all of his attention focused on its contents. She only gave half a thought to the question of what he might be searching for.

The RV rocked again, more forcefully than before.

"Brandt," Cade repeated, anger seeping into her voice, overriding her nervousness. She didn't care; it wasn't time to play nice and polite when infected were literally banging at the door.

Brandt muttered something under his breath that she couldn't hear.

The RV rocked still more violently.

Remy let out a startled cry and gripped the steering wheel tighter.

Cade's temper finally got the better of her. "Brandt!" she shouted.

"*What?*"

"Plan! What is it?" she demanded.

"I don't have one, okay?" he yelled.

Cade froze as his words registered. "What?" she gasped. "You dragged us out here, you got us *in* here, and you don't have a way to get us back *out* of here?"

"I didn't get that fucking far in my planning, okay?" he snarled. "I didn't have much time and—"

"And that's your excuse for half-assing the plan?" Cade exploded. She nearly dropped her rifle when she flailed her hands in anger. The RV rocked again and tipped dangerously on the wheels on one side. Cade stumbled and almost fell against Brandt, but she caught the edge of the kitchenette's counter and hooked her fingers into the sink. The RV rattled frighteningly before righting itself with a hard shudder. "So help me *God*," she continued once she'd steadied herself, "if we get out of this shit alive, I'm going to fucking kill you myself!"

"I don't think now's the time to bitch at me, Cade," Brandt said, not looking at her as he pawed through his bag again.

"Then please, Brandt," she hissed through clenched teeth. The RV began to tip again, and she gripped the sink tighter. "Tell me exactly *when* a great time to bitch at you gets here, because this sure as *hell* seems like a fantastic time for it to me!"

Brandt didn't have time to reply to her angry tirade. The RV had reached its tipping point and, to Cade's horror, was unable to right itself. Her feet left the floor, and she dropped her rifle, clinging to the sink with both hands as the pavement rushed into view behind Brandt.

The RV crashed to the ground, floundering on its side as the infected overwhelmed it.

* * *

Memphis, TN

Ethan remained frozen, his feet practically bolted to the floor as his eyes took in the sight before him. The little girl. Her dark hair. Her SpongeBob nightgown. Her bare feet and horribly maimed skin. It took Nikola's shriek to drag him from his trance.

"Get her off me!" Nikola screamed. She braced the heel of her hand against the girl's forehead and pushed, fighting off her clawing hands with the other as she struggled to keep her attacker's mouth away from her skin.

Ethan snapped out of it and grabbed the child by the back of her nightgown, lifting her off Nikola and slinging her several feet down the hall. The girl tumbled head over heels before coming to rest on the carpet, lying motionless in a heap.

"You okay?" Ethan asked, grasping Nikola's hand and pulling her to her feet.

"Yeah. She didn't bite me, thank God," Nikola breathed. She wasted no time retrieving her baseball bat and gripping it in both hands, glaring at the girl. "You need to shoot her," she declared.

"What? She's dead," Ethan protested. Truth be told, he was reluctant to consider desecrating Josie's body further than it already had been. He might have been able to shoot infected on the street like it was nothing, but this was *Josie.* "She's not—"

"Does she *look* dead to you?" Nikola snapped. "Shoot her!" Her gaze was still locked onto the small girl's body, and she took a step back, her eyes widening. "Ethan, she's getting back up."

Ethan turned to look for himself. As he watched, Josie stirred and maneuvered her thin arms underneath herself, pushing off the floor and regaining her feet. "Jesus," he breathed. Cade's bedroom was past Josie. He couldn't see them getting past her and keeping her at bay as they collected supplies. Not with the manic, hungry look in the girl's once-brown eyes.

Nikola was right, and he knew it. He would have to put Josie down. He should have done it the month before when he'd shot Andrew. He'd have to do it before she hurt them or anyone else. She didn't deserve to linger like that.

"Ethan," Nikola warned, ducking behind him, taking shelter behind his body. Her baseball bat nudged the small of his back, but he ignored it and lifted his pistol. Josie had gained her feet again and started toward them. Ethan took a careful step back, goading Nikola backward a step or two, and aimed for Josie's head. He squeezed the trigger.

Josie's body fell with a thud. Ethan closed his eyes as a surge of pain rocked through his chest. Ethan's hand shook as he remained in the center of the hall, shielding Nikola protectively. After a long silence, Nikola pushed against his arm, and he finally lowered the weapon.

"Thank you," Nikola said softly. She glanced at the body on the floor, then averted her eyes to him. "What exactly are we in here to get? Because whatever it is, I think we're going to have to hurry to get it. That noise is going to attract a bunch of them here, and I don't think we can kill them all."

Ethan hesitated, staring blankly at the small heap of person on the floor. His palms sweated, grossly damp against the grip of his pistol. He mechanically holstered the weapon before wiping his palms down the thighs of his jeans. He looked at Nikola in silence. He had to hold it together, at the very least for her. Falling apart from the horror of shooting Josie wouldn't do either of them any good. He was responsible for Nikola; he was the only one willing and able to protect the skinny, dirty teenager standing with him, trying valiantly to block his view of the girl's partially decomposed body.

Ethan blinked and straightened, squaring his shoulders. Partially decomposed? He nudged Nikola aside, and as much as it pained him to do so, he went to the small corpse on the floor and nudged her with his shoe. She didn't move, so he knelt and rolled her onto her back. He took care not to look at Josie's face. The thought alone was unbearable; he was sure actually doing so would make him lose it. Instead, he focused on her wounds, the ones she'd sustained the month prior at the hands of Cade's boyfriend, Andrew. A horrible thought formed in his mind.

Ethan was no doctor, but in his line of work, he'd witnessed quite a few crime scenes involving violent deaths. And in that time, he'd quickly learned there were certain types of injuries from which a person could not recover. While the resiliency of the human body sometimes astounded him, there were situations in which a person was toast without question. As his brain worked feverishly to disassociate the body in front of him from the little girl he'd known, he was forced to acknowledge the injuries Josie had suffered were ones from which she shouldn't have been able to recover. Especially not with the extreme loss of blood she'd experienced. Which meant...

"Jesus Christ," Ethan breathed.

Nikola stepped forward. "What? What is it?"

"They come back," Ethan said, looking up at her with wide eyes. "They come back after they're dead."

Nikola gaped at him like a fish. Her mouth opened and closed several times before she stammered, "What...wait, what? That's not even...I mean, is that *possible*? When you're dead, you're dead." She paused, her eyes on Ethan, and swallowed hard before asking uncertainly, "Right?"

"Honestly? I don't even know anymore," he admitted, standing and wiping his hands on his thighs again. "One month ago, this little girl was dead. But no more than thirty minutes after she died, she and that man there," he nodded to Andrew's body at the top of the stairs, "attacked me and Cade."

"What did you do?" Nikola asked.

"I shot him in the head," Ethan explained. "But I couldn't...I just couldn't shoot Josie. So I just left her. I didn't think..."

Nikola shook her head and moved toward him. "What are we in here for?" she asked. It was an obvious attempt to distract him, but he welcomed it.

Ethan shook himself from the grief welling inside him and moved toward Cade's bedroom. "This is Cade's house," he explained. "She has a thing for collecting knives and guns and all sorts of fun yet deadly things."

"And you're thinking maybe we can get a few more guns to protect ourselves with?" Nikola suggested, following him.

"Exactly. Assuming no one has been in here since we left, there should at least be some ammunition for my gun," he confirmed. He stepped into Cade's bedroom and looked around thoughtfully. A crash sounded downstairs, echoing up to meet them. "Shit. We've got to go faster. We're about to have company," he said, dropping to the floor and sliding halfway under the bed. To his relief, several empty pistols were wedged into the slats on the underside of the bed, presumably where Cade had stuffed them before Josie's visit the month before. He grabbed them and slid out from beneath the bed.

"Closet," Ethan said as he emerged from under the bed. The teenager gave him a confused look. "There's a safe inside. Combination 22-33-22." She darted to the closet door and opened it, letting out a surprised gasp.

"I wasn't expecting *this*," Nikola said as she beheld the tall gun safe inside. "I figured it'd be one of those little box safe deals." She spun the combination dial as Ethan went to the dresser and pulled open the large bottom drawer.

"Cade has all sorts of goodies hidden around here," he said, digging boxes of ammunition out of the drawer. "Unfortunately, we don't have time to hunt for it all, and I doubt we could carry it all anyway," he added regretfully. He tore into a box of bullets for the pistols, opening his shoulder bag and starting to stuff the bullets inside.

Nikola pulled the safe's heavy door open with both hands. "Yeah, but she's got the awesomest shotguns *ever* in here," she gushed.

"Don't touch them," he warned, adding shotgun shells to his bag. "I don't want you messing with any of the guns in here. You could get hurt."

"Yeah, and I could get my face munched on by one of those things out there," she pointed out. She went to the door and stepped halfway into the hall to look out. "They're definitely in the house. What's the plan to get out of here, anyway?"

Ethan went to the gun safe and pulled out a shotgun, looking it over before checking if it was loaded. It wasn't; Cade didn't generally keep loaded weapons in her house unless she'd been by herself for a while and had been having a particularly bad bout of paranoia or nightmares. Ethan grabbed another box of shotgun shells from the dresser drawer and dumped the box onto the dresser top. He started loading the shotgun, sliding the shells into place, as he watched the door.

"We'll shoot our way out if we have to," he finally said. He snapped the shotgun closed and chambered a round. The noise drew Nikola's attention, and she swallowed hard. "I prefer doing this a little more sneakily, to be honest. We need to get out of the house as quickly as possible."

Nikola averted her eyes to look past him. He followed her gaze to the window. "Window?" she suggested. "We can walk along the roof and climb down the big tree at the corner of the house."

"It's a thought, but I don't know what it looks like out there," he admitted. He fastened a shoulder strap from the gun safe to the shotgun and slung the weapon over his shoulder before going to the window, unlocking it and pushing it up. It looked large enough for him to fit through, and he nodded to Nikola as he put a leg out over the sill. "Stay here, close to the window, okay? I'm going to step out and see what the situation is out here."

Nikola nodded and hefted her baseball bat, moving closer to the window. Ethan gave her a reassuring smile before slipping onto the roof. His head barely cleared the window frame, and he grabbed it in one hand to keep from falling as he gained his footing on the sloped roof.

A cold wind blew across the trees and roof, a product of the slowly darkening day. Evening was falling swiftly, and the darkness would only make their attempt at evacuation more perilous. He forced out a breath to steady his nerves and eased away from the window, crouching low to the roof and making his way to the edge. Dropping to his knees, he leaned to look over the edge of the roof at the ground below, hands gripping the metal rain gutter lining the edge of the roof as he checked the yard around the house.

To his surprise, the front yard was virtually empty. There was activity around the back, but the yard was quiet and still. He supposed most of the infected had already made it inside or around to the patio doors, which would have been the path of least resistance. He edged to the side of the house and checked the base of the tree at the corner. Nothing was there, either.

He eased to his feet and looked down the street. His motorcycle lay half a block away, resting on its side in the middle of the street, the failing sunlight glinting dully off its red finish. It was the best bet they had to get out of there, he thought as he returned to the window, kneeling and beckoning to Nikola.

"It's clear on the front and side of the house where the tree is," he murmured. "I think we'll go with your idea to get out of the house. How do you feel about motorcycles?"

Nikola shrugged. "I've never been on one," she admitted. "My dad would've killed me if I'd even tried it."

"Well, you're going to have to learn real fast how to ride on the back of one, because I want my bike," he said, offering her his hand. "Come on, get out here. We've got a tree to climb down, and we'll have to do it quietly."

Nikola put a cautious hand in his, carefully climbing onto the roof with his help. He left her there for a moment to duck back into the bedroom, grabbing another shotgun and a large hunting knife off the dresser, figuring it was better to have extra firepower in case they needed it. Then he joined Nikola on the roof once more. Together, they stepped off the roof and into the tree's branches to climb down to the ground below.

* * *

Biloxi, MS

Cade opened her eyes and groaned. She stared at the RV's kitchenette, which was now on the ceiling above her. A heavy weight rested half on top of her. She blinked and focused on it, discovering it was Brandt, lying protectively over her. He pushed himself up onto his hands and knees, grimacing, and looked at her for a moment as if assessing her level of consciousness. Then he stood, glass crunching loudly under his boots.

"Everybody okay?" Brandt called, retrieving Cade's rifle. Cade scrambled to her knees and winced as a sharp pain shot through her right hand. A large shard of glass from broken dishes had embedded into her palm. She let out a string of colorful curses as she pulled the wedge of glass carefully from her flesh.

"Yeah, I think so," she muttered, gaining her feet. She clenched her hand and winced at the fresh wave of pain that rippled through the wound.

"I think your friend got knocked out," Remy called from the front of the RV. Cade accepted her rifle from Brandt and slung it over her shoulder where it belonged.

"Shit," Brandt muttered. He rubbed the side of his head and climbed toward the front of the RV, his boots crunching over shattered glass with every step. He reached the front of the RV quickly enough and hefted Theo off of Remy. He shifted the medic's unconscious form toward Cade, who caught him and slung his arm over her shoulder. "You need a hand?" he offered Remy. He didn't bother waiting for her reply; instead, he wrapped his free arm around her waist and lifted her easily from the driver's seat.

"Thanks," Remy said as he set her on her feet.

"You okay to stand?" Brandt asked.

"I think so. Just take care of Theo. I'll be fine."

Cade frowned and studied the woman's face. Despite Remy's assurances, she looked awful. She wobbled where she stood, and her hand darted out to grasp the edge of the driver's seat as the RV lurched sickeningly. The sound of metal squealing against stone reached Cade's ears, and when the first of the infected showed up in view of the windshield, she grabbed Remy by the upper arm and hauled her away from the window.

"Brandt! Brandt, get back," Cade urged. She dragged Theo with her and nearly tripped over the obstacles that the overturned RV had created. Brandt lunged forward to join her and Remy and the unconscious Theo in the back of the RV. He took the man's weight off Cade's shoulders, much to her relief, and settled him on the couch, slapping his cheeks.

"They're going to get through that windshield pretty quick," she warned Brandt.

"What do you suggest we do?" Remy asked. Theo groaned as she spoke, his head lolling to the side as he neared consciousness.

"We might have to shoot our way out of here," Cade said.

"No, we won't. I have a plan," Brandt announced.

She rolled her eyes and sighed. "It's about damned time."

He chose to ignore her comment and looked at the unbroken window above them. "You think I can fit through that?"

"Maybe?" Cade hazarded, frowning. "I can't say for sure. It's sort of small, and you're not exactly a little guy."

"I'm going to pretend I didn't hear that," Brandt said, the beginnings of a grin spreading across his face. Cade wondered if the adrenaline was getting to him. Maybe he actually *liked* being stuck in impossible situations. The thought was unsettling enough to make her shudder.

"Remy, do you think you can run?" he asked.

"If I have to," Remy answered. "Why? What's your idea?"

"Cade and I are going to create a diversion," he explained. Cade wrinkled her nose, and her frown deepened.

"Way to volunteer me," she muttered loudly enough for him to hear. He shot her a stern look but continued.

"You and Theo are going to run for the Jeep," Brandt told Remy. "Theo knows where it's at. You'll have to help each other. Go between the cars, and make sure you always keep something between you and the infected. If you do that, you'll be fine."

A thud sounded against the windshield. Cade's heart leaped into her throat. More infected had discovered the windshield. Once they figured out it was breakable, it would only be a matter of time before they damaged it enough to get inside. And then it would be dinner time. There was no way they could fight properly in such cramped quarters.

"What about us?" Cade asked.

"After Remy and Theo get a block away, we'll make a run for it," Brandt said. "We're probably going to have to shoot our way out, like you said."

"Great," she said, without any of the enthusiasm the word implied. If anything, she was downright nauseated.

"So when are we moving?" Remy asked. She helped Theo sit up while keeping a hand braced against the edge of the couch for balance.

"As soon as possible," Brandt said, looking at the window above him again. After a moment's contemplation, he reached up and unfastened the latch. "I have something to do first," he added, sliding the window open. "We'll have to be ready to move fast once I get back in, okay?" He climbed onto the edge of the bench seat and grasped the window frame.

"And *where* exactly are you going?" Cade demanded. "You're not actually going out *there*, are you?"

"I've got to. It's part of the plan," Brandt said. The last word was strained as he hauled himself up by the edge of the frame, the muscles in his biceps and forearms bulging. He managed to fit through the small window without too much trouble.

After his battered black combat boots disappeared through the RV's window, though, a nervous stirring settled deep in Cade's stomach. She squeezed her fist closed, using the pain from the cut in her palm to ground her and keep her calm. She felt less confident now that Brandt was out of sight, and she wasn't sure why. She shook her head and looked to Theo. The man had sat up on the couch, and he had his head in his hand as he probed gently at his scalp. "You okay?" she asked.

"Yeah, just whacked my head," Theo said. He pulled his fingers from his blond hair and checked them for traces of blood. "I think I hit it on the steering wheel when the RV turned over. I'll be fine." He shifted his eyes from his fingers to scrutinize Cade's face. "So what's the plan?"

"You and Remy are going to make a run for it," she explained. "Brandt and I will hold them off before breaking for the Jeep after you." The sound of thudding footsteps along the RV above them met her ears, and she looked up. "I have no idea what else he has planned, though," she admitted. "He thinks and acts so fast that he doesn't seem willing to stop and fill me in."

Theo nodded and grasped the edge of the couch. With Cade and Remy's assistance, he got to his feet and propped against the edge of the bench, pawing through his bag. He took out two Advil and swallowed them dry before nodding at Cade's hand. "You're hurt."

She looked down at her hand. The wound bled more profusely than she realized; it was dripping onto the broken glass beneath her boots. "I cut it when the RV turned over," she said, shrugging. "It's not a big deal."

"How about you let me be the judge of that?" Theo suggested, grabbing Cade's wrist and giving it a gentle squeeze. She relaxed her fingers and let him examine the wound, wincing as he prodded it gently. "It's a smooth cut, not a tear, which is good," he said. "You'll need stitches, though. I can sew you up, but it'll have to wait until we get out of here." He plunged his hand back into his bag and pulled out a roll of gauze, wrapping it expertly around her hand, looping it across her palm and making a few passes around the base of her thumb to secure it.

"Thanks," she said, flexing her hand to see how secure the bandage was. Thankfully, he hadn't wrapped it too tight, so she was still able to bend her fingers enough to move them easily, at least enough to squeeze the trigger on her rifle, which was enough for her satisfaction.

Brandt reappeared in the window above them and dropped into the RV with his gun already drawn, the remains of the window beneath him shattering with the impact of his boots. "Ready to rock?" he asked Cade almost enthusiastically. She was, amusingly, reminded of a man attempting to be a badass action star. She struggled to not laugh at the thought.

"As ready as I'll ever be," she answered. "What do you need me to do?"

"Shoot the windshield out, and do it fast," he ordered. "Use as few shots as possible. Theo, Remy, be ready to run." He glanced at the younger man and woman. "Theo, when you go, cut right. Unless it's closed since I got off the top of this thing, there's a decent-sized gap that way that you two could make it through."

"Thanks, man," Theo said. He gave Brandt and Cade each a reassuring squeeze on the shoulder. "Best of luck to you two."

"And to you," Cade replied, giving Theo a short nod before lifting her rifle and taking aim.

"Whenever you're ready, Cade," Brandt said.

Cade cleared her throat and rolled her head from side to side, trying to loosen the tense muscles in her neck and shoulders. "Cover your ears," she warned the others before squeezing the trigger.

The rifle leaped to life in her hands. Bullet holes appeared in the glass before her, but she felt reassured by Brandt's presence as he stood beside her, his hands clamped over his ears. The bullets tore through the glass and struck several of the infected clustered on the other side. Three of them fell to the ground, still.

Cade ceased fire once she believed the glass was weakened enough. She lifted her rifle to point the barrel at the ceiling, and Brandt darted to the windshield, kicking the glass hard with the heel of his boot. It cracked and gave way before collapsing in several large pieces onto the pavement beyond. Brandt lifted his pistol without hesitation and put bullets in the heads of two infected that lingered right against the group's exit.

"Theo, go!" Brandt shouted with a stiff wave of his arm.

Theo didn't have to be told twice. He grabbed Remy's forearm and pulled her forward. The injured woman kept her feet, clinging to Theo as she ran, limping painfully alongside the medic. Cade moved up behind them to support their break for freedom. As the two veered to the right per Brandt's instruction, Cade fired at the infected closest to her companions' retreating forms. To her left, Brandt did the same. Once Theo and Remy had disappeared into the darkness, she looked at Brandt, a worried expression marring her face.

"What's the plan, Brandt?" Cade asked, forcing herself to not back away from the broken window and the infected that were moving in on their position.

"We're gonna blow this fucker," Brandt said. Cade caught a glimpse of mischievousness in his dark eyes, and concern and even a tiny inkling of almost-fear welled up in her gut. She swallowed hard.

"Blow it?" she repeated. She paused long enough to shoot into a small knot of infected before continuing. "You mean blow it *up*?"

"What else would I mean?"

Her stomach clenched. Yeah, she definitely was going to puke. "And *how* exactly would you propose we blow up an RV?" she asked, dreading the answer more than any answer she'd waited for in her life.

Brandt dug into his bag with one hand and aimed his gun with the other, squeezing the trigger twice. Cade didn't bother seeing if his bullets struck anything; instead, she watched as he pulled another Molotov cocktail from his shoulder bag. "Last one," he informed her.

"That's so *not* going to blow up an entire RV," she protested. "I don't know what you have in mind, but if you're trying to use a Molotov to do it, it's not going to work."

"Just trust me, it'll work,' he said. He took his silver lighter out of his bag, stuck it between his teeth for easy access, and nodded to Cade. "Ready to run?" he asked, his voice muffled by the lighter.

"Do I fucking have a choice?" she bit out. She checked to make sure she had all her belongings and flexed her injured hand again, trying to loosen the gauze just enough to grant her that smidgeon of extra movement she was worried she'd need. "You're leading the way, Evans."

"Of course."

"And if I die, I'm *so* haunting the hell out of you."

"Fair enough." Brandt hefted the glass bottle in his hand, as if testing its weight. Then he darted out of the RV and sprinted across the pavement, weaving between cars in the direction in which Theo and Remy had disappeared. Cade swore and took off after him, her legs pumping, dashing to catch up to him.

"Brandt! I'm going to kick your ass!" Cade yelled once she was within shouting distance. As he approached the half-way point down the block, he slowed and pulled the lighter from his teeth as she met up with him.

"Ready?" Brandt asked. The glint was in his eyes again, and he was barely out of breath.

"For what?" she panted.

"When I say go, I want you to shoot, okay?"

She aimed her rifle back the way they'd come. "What am I aiming at?" she asked.

"When you see it, you'll know," he assured her. He lit the black rag hanging out of the bottle, and before Cade could reply—or object—to his vague orders, he pulled back his arm and threw the bottle. The flaming projectile arced through the air and crashed to the pavement below the back end of the RV, the bottle shattering, and fire spread rapidly across the pavement. The flames were brighter and larger than they should have been from a mere bottle of liquor. Before she could question it, Brandt shouted, "Cade! Now!"

Cade squinted into the flames and swore. She had no idea what in the world he intended for her to shoot. But then she spotted her target nestled directly in the center of the flames and clenched her jaw, taking aim. They were far too close to the RV to do this, but they didn't have much choice. There were too many infected, and if they could kill a bunch of them in this manner and give the others a chance to escape—even if it took them both out with it—then so be it.

Cade's shoulders tensed, and she flexed her finger against the trigger. She let out a slow breath and depressed it.

As the bullet made impact, Brandt's arm hooked around her waist. He dragged her to the pavement, slamming them facedown onto the street. The explosion from the propane tank attached to the back of the RV shook the night, sending shrapnel and flames roaring into the darkness.

* * *

"Jesus Christ!" Gray gasped, sitting up straight in his seat and grabbing the doorframe as he stumbled out of the Jeep. The bright flash two blocks away lit up the night sky, nearly blinding him as he looked right at it. He rubbed furiously at his eyes and scooped up the pistol his brother had left him, pointing it into the darkness. He blinked to clear his vision of the bright blue spots dancing madly in front of him and saw two figures staggering toward him. He tensed and swung the pistol in their direction. It was only a warning shot from one of the figures that prevented him from squeezing the trigger.

"Gray! It's me!" Theo's voice came from the darkness.

Gray lowered the pistol and ran toward Theo, his heart pounding in his chest. "Theo! Thank God. What the hell happened back there? What blew up?" A thin trickle of dark red blood oozed down the side of Theo's face. "And what the hell happened to you?"

"I got fucking hit by something rather hard," Theo grumbled, "right in the damned head. That's the second time tonight. I'm sick of it." He hoisted the second figure into a better position against his shoulder. Gray focused in on the woman who sagged limply against his brother.

"Shit, what's wrong with her?" Gray asked, taking the weight of the slender woman off Theo's shoulder. As he swung her up into his arms, he tried to get a glimpse of her face, but her dark hair hung loosely in the way, blocking his view.

"Like I said, we got hit," Theo said bluntly. He took Gray's pistol and began moving toward the Jeep. "She took the brunt of it. I didn't see it coming and couldn't get us out of the way."

"Where are Cade and Brandt?" Gray asked, squinting at Theo in the light from the fire two blocks away. The man looked awful. Whatever news he had probably wasn't good.

"I don't know," Theo said, collapsing onto the driver's seat. "They made us go first. They were…" He waved his hand around vaguely as he tried to come up with the right word, then rested his forehead in his hand. "Fuck, my head hurts. I can't think," he muttered. He blew out a breath and tried again. "They hung back. They were covering us while we made a run for the Jeep. The last time I saw them was at the RV. I don't know where they are now."

Gray nodded, concern growing as he thought on Cade and Brandt. He and Theo needed them. They couldn't go it alone, especially not with an injured girl on their hands. They needed people to strategize for them, to handle the defensive aspects of survival that they didn't know how to do for themselves. With Ethan gone, that job had fallen to Brandt and Cade. They couldn't be dead. They just couldn't be.

"What are we going to do?" Gray asked. He managed to get one of the back doors open and carefully slid the slender girl inside, climbing in after her and beginning to check her for life-threatening injuries.

"I don't know," Theo said. He sounded exhausted and slightly out of it. "Let's face it, Gray. We need them," he continued. "I mean, hell, we've only really know them for about two days, but I already feel like I can't handle this shit without their support."

"Yeah, me too," he agreed. He looked toward the fire still burning merrily down the street. "Should we wait? Or just leave them here?"

"I don't think they'd want us to wait," Theo said. "I think they'd want us to get the hell out of here as fast and as far as we can. But honestly, I'm all for doing the opposite. Let's give them ten minutes."

Gray nodded and climbed into the back of the Jeep, carefully maneuvering around the young woman's unconscious body. He retrieved a pistol from the large black duffel bag Cade had left in the back and loaded it mechanically, keeping his eyes on the scene of the fire before them.

Ten minutes ticked by. Remy stirred with a soft groan, and her return to consciousness gave Theo a distraction from his own hurting head as he tended to her wounds. Gray stood guard outside the driver's door, silent and tense. The ten minutes they had allotted to wait for Cade and Brandt slid by faster than he'd have liked.

Ten minutes passed, and still they didn't come.

CHAPTER EIGHTEEN

Memphis, TN

Ethan let the motorcycle roll to a slow stop, his hands working the brakes with practiced smoothness. He braced a foot against the cracked pavement and cut the engine; it shuddered and died in the otherwise quiet parking lot. He shifted on his seat and looked over his shoulder at Nikola. She had his waist in a vice-like grip, and her eyes were squeezed tightly shut, even though the motorcycle had stopped. He smiled at the girl's nervousness.

"Hey, Nikola?" he said, patting the back of her hand. "It's okay if you let go now. We've stopped."

Nikola hesitantly opened her eyes and looked around, releasing her grip from his waist. She laughed, though her voice still shook. "Where are we?" she asked, dislodging Ethan's helmet from her head.

"Methodist University Hospital," Ethan explained. "Or what's left of it." He waited for Nikola to slide off the bike before dismounting. "My wife works here. *Worked* here. I wanted to check and see…" He trailed off and reached under his leather jacket for his pistol. Even he realized just how stupid this idea was. What in the hell was he doing here? It wasn't a safe place. He began to wonder if Cade was right; maybe he'd have been better off sticking with the others. But as this crossed his mind, Nikola's voice interrupted his thoughts.

"You want to see if she's still here, don't you?" She bit her lip and studied the dark parking lot around them.

Ethan watched as she pulled her bat from the bag strapped to the motorcycle. *Nikola* was why he was here. If he hadn't decided to come back to Memphis, then there was no telling where she'd have been at that moment. Still struggling along on her own at best. Dead at worst. The thought didn't sit well with him.

Ethan didn't bother replying to her question. "Just stick close to me."

Nikola blew out a breath and nodded. He could tell it was a struggle for her to not grab him by the back of his jacket. He chose to not mention her obvious nervousness, instead looking at the burned-out husk of the ER where Anna had once worked. He couldn't see much in the falling evening, so he went back to the bike and retrieved a flashlight.

"Keep your noise down as much as possible," he instructed Nikola. "We don't know what we'll find. We don't know what might be here."

Nikola nodded obediently and mimed zipping her lips shut. He gave her a small smile, but as he turned his eyes back onto the remains of the ER, the expression disappeared from his face. He couldn't believe Anna might have been in there.

He swallowed hard and shoved back his feelings. He couldn't let his emotions take control of him. They would distract him from any approaching dangers, and a mere moment's distraction could cost them their lives. He strode purposefully to the ER doors. The remnants of the entrance loomed over him, and his shoes crunched over blackened tiles and broken glass. Nikola followed him, sticking close, her bat raised and prepared to hit anything that might come at her. He squeezed her shoulder reassuringly before continuing inside.

The ER was the very image of chaos. Stretchers lay overturned and burned, and the nurses' station was cluttered with leftover emergency supplies. As Ethan gawked at the blackened scene before him, he tripped over an IV stand on the floor. He stumbled and caught himself against the husk of the station counter. Chunks of it crumbled and flaked under his palms.

It was as he straightened that he caught sight of her. She lay slumped against a wall, directly below the main oxygen shut-off valves outside one of the major trauma rooms. Her head was bowed low, her shoulders rolled forward like she'd hunched over to protect herself from the flames. Her clothes and skin were blackened and cracked, and her dark hair was gone, but Ethan knew—he wasn't sure how, but he was certain—that it was her. It had to be her.

"Anna?" Ethan whispered.

He pushed away from the counter and slowly moved toward the damaged body. His feet felt like they were dragging along the tiles, scraping forward with all the reluctance he felt in his body. He completely forgot about Nikola's presence as he reached the woman. He dropped heavily to his knees, eyes wide, and his gun clattered to the tiles as he tilted his head to look into the woman's face.

Ethan wasn't one hundred percent positive that it was her. Not at first. Not from this angle and not with her skin so blackened and burned. He leaned farther down and braced his hand against the charred tile. Then he saw it. From this vantage point, there was no doubt in his mind that it was her.

"Oh fuck, Anna," he whispered, heartbroken, closing his eyes as the pain of certainty washed over him. He reached out as if to touch her face, but his hand stopped inches away from her and dropped to the tile floor. "Jesus, why couldn't you have just stayed home?" he asked, though he knew he wouldn't get an answer.

"Is this…this is Anna?" Nikola asked softly. He opened his eyes but didn't look at her as she knelt on Anna's other side. Her blue eyes were on him, and he could feel the worry and concern in them. He drew in a breath, coughing as soot tried to choke him. Then he nodded and rubbed his face.

"Yeah. Yeah, it's her," he confirmed.

"How can you tell?"

Ethan gave a helpless shrug. "It's hard to explain," he said. "I just know. I'm positive. It's her."

Nikola fell blessedly silent after that, and Ethan shot her a grateful look before turning his attention back to Anna. He wasn't sure what to do. He and Anna had discussed their final wishes with each other a year after they'd married. Anna had told him at the time that she wanted to be cremated. He'd been against it; his upbringing had always dictated a gravesite and monument, and the thought of his beautiful wife burned to ashes had always disturbed him. It had been a small source of contention between them for the better part of a week. How odd, Ethan reflected, that in death, she'd gotten almost exactly what she'd wanted.

"Maybe we should find something to cover her with," Nikola suggested. Ethan didn't answer right away. Instead, he shifted, putting one foot against the ground in preparation to stand.

As he rose, a faint glimpse of gold around Anna's neck shone in the light from his flashlight. He leaned in to get a closer look and realized it was the locket he'd given her for Christmas. It was partially melted and covered in soot and other things he didn't want to consider. But as his eyes landed on it, he decided that he had to take it with him. He glanced at Nikola as she started into the major trauma room next to them.

"Be careful," Ethan warned her. She nodded and waved a hand at him, and he leaned farther over Anna's body.

The locket's chain was partially melted, and he was forced to break it to get the jewelry off Anna's body. Once the locket was in his palm, he turned it over and studied it. He remembered the expression on his wife's face when she'd opened the box on Christmas morning. He blinked rapidly to clear his eyes of tears and used his thumb to wipe the dirt and ashes from the damaged gold before gripping it tightly in his fist.

"Here." Nikola reappeared at his elbow and offered him the edge of a torn white sheet that wasn't too badly burned. He accepted it with a grateful smile, and together, they shook the sheet out and laid it over Anna's remains.

Nikola stood beside him in silence as they stared at the white-shrouded figure lying against the wall. He gripped the flashlight tighter and rubbed his fingers over the locket in his hand. Everything was quiet and still. Thankfully, there were no signs of any infected nearby. Perhaps they'd moved on to other areas with more potential for prey.

He startled as a hand touched his arm. He looked over wildly before realizing it was just Nikola. The young girl squeezed his arm and asked, "Should we get out of here?"

"Yeah," Ethan said. "Yeah, we should. I told my friends I'd track them down in Biloxi before four days were up. They've been instructed to not wait for me if I'm not there by then." He tucked the locket into his pocket, securing it to one of his belt loops. "You're not planning to stay here in Memphis, are you?" he asked.

Nikola hoisted her backpack higher on her shoulder. "Depends. Are you willing to let me come along with you?"

"Nah, I figure I'll just leave you here," he said sarcastically. The conversation was doing wonders to distract him from his grief, and he plunged headlong into it with as much enthusiasm as he could muster. "Seems like a good idea, you know? I mean, you're fourteen. It's about time you went out and took care of yourself."

She looked at him with wide eyes, blinking in surprise and examining his face. He couldn't believe she was taking him seriously, but before he could express that, she let out a merry laugh. The sound was horribly out of place in the charred remains of the ER, and an involuntary smile spread across Ethan's face at the sound.

"That's just wrong," she said, punching him lightly on the bicep. "Come on, can we get out of here? This place is starting to creep me out."

He chuckled softly and nodded, offering her his hand, which she took. "This place feels like a tomb," he agreed. With one more backward glance at Anna's shrouded body, he led Nikola back into the parking lot where the motorcycle waited.

"Do we really have to take the bike?" Nikola asked. She stopped beside the red-and-black bike and eyed it warily, twirling her bat in her hand.

"What, you don't want to ride on it?" he teased. He straddled the bike and lifted the kickstand, then twisted to pat the seat behind him.

"That thing scares the shit out of me," she complained, shifting from one foot to the other. "Can we find a car or a truck or a…a tank? Anything? It might be more comfortable or something."

"Nikola, the roads between here and Biloxi are probably bad," he explained. "And if they are, it'll be easier to get a motorcycle through whatever we come across. I don't want to have to abandon whatever vehicle we're driving, and I don't want to walk." He grinned. "Besides, I don't know how to drive a tank."

Nikola giggled and visibly caved. "Fine, fine," she said, sighing in resignation before stuffing her bat into her backpack and sliding onto the seat behind Ethan. After jamming her helmet back onto her head, she locked her arms securely around his waist, grasping her left wrist with her right hand and making sure her position was secure. "No complaining if I squeeze your guts out through your mouth, okay?" she said once she was settled.

"The mental image that gives me is *disgusting*," he replied. "Makes me think of toothpaste tubes." He turned the key in the ignition, and the roar of the bike's engine as he revved it drowned out Nikola's laughter.

* * *

Biloxi, MS

The blast from the RV slammed Brandt to the ground even as he pulled Cade with him, hitting the pavement hard, his breath rushing out of his lungs with the impact. His pistol skittered away, and he gripped Cade tightly and attempted to shield her body with his own. A tremendous roar filled his ears, and he glanced behind him. Burning propane rushed out of the remains of the tank, the flames fueled further by the gas from the RV's punctured fuel line and the alcohol that had ignited it all. Above it all, though, he could hear the screams of infected as they burned. The awful sound sent chills down his spine. He gripped Cade tighter to him and wheezed for air, waiting for the debris to quit falling around them, then staggered to his feet. Danger still mounted, and he wasn't willing to wait any longer.

"Come on!" Brandt shouted. The loud roar drowned out his words, and he had to repeat himself twice before Cade responded. She pushed up onto her hands and scrambled forward a couple of feet in an odd, crab-like walk to retrieve her rifle. He groaned in impatience and grabbed her by a fistful of her jacket, hauling her onto her feet. Several of the infected—and some moderately injured by others without visible wounds—had taken notice of the prey nearby and, despite the chaos of the explosion and their compatriots burning in the street, began to give chase. "Fuck, Cade, let's go, let's go!" he yelled.

She gained her feet easily enough, but as she took a step forward to run, her right leg gave out, and she nearly toppled to the pavement again with a pained cry. He caught her around the waist to stop her fall. "You okay?" he asked.

"It's my knee!" Cade said over the noise. "I think I hurt it!"

Brandt didn't hesitate, just grabbed Cade's arm and slung it over his shoulder, then pulled her close and hooked his arm around her waist. "Come on! Lean against me and run as well as you can."

Brandt helped her along the street, her body heavy against his, her gasps of pain with every step stirring up guilt in his gut. He shouldn't have thrown her down to the ground like he had. But what was a painful knee compared to getting hit in the face with flying debris? It was no contest, really.

As they hobbled along, Brandt slowed by Cade's limping progress but never once thinking he should ditch her to save his own skin, he came to the realization that there was no way they'd make it the two blocks to the Jeep. Cade slowed as she slung her rifle over her shoulder and drew her pistol instead, scanning the street again.

"We won't make it that far," she said, breathless from the effort of trying to run on her injured limb. "Not with my knee fucked up like it is. We've got to find some place to hole up."

"Yeah, we'll catch up with the others soon. I know where they plan to go," Brandt said. He turned his eyes onto the nearby buildings, but gunshots suddenly rang out beside him. Several of the infected had drawn closer to them—too close. He swore and grabbed for his own weapon, keeping his grip tight on Cade as he too opened fire. He carefully lined up his shots even as he pulled Cade backward farther down the street. "Come on!"

Cade staggered after him, her grip on his shoulder tightening, her nails digging painfully into the muscles and tendons of his shoulder. He ignored the pain; being caught by the infected would hurt worse than anything Cade could inflict on him.

As they ran, Cade twisted around and fired into the mass of infected following them. Bullets slammed into shoulders and arms and torsos and whizzed past harmlessly. Brandt breathed out a curse and scanned the buildings around them again. There weren't many options available to them. Most of the buildings were one- and two-story affairs, and a large portion of their windows were broken. Those would do them no good; they could barricade the doors, but if the windows were broken, the attempt would be futile. Instead, he looked higher, and his eyes landed on a five-story building that might have been an office complex before the world went to hell. Many of the first-floor windows were broken, but the top four floors looked secure enough for their use.

"This way!" he shouted.

Cade followed without question, leaning against him more heavily than before. They veered right to cross the street, dodging and weaving between cars and bicycles and other debris blocking the roadway. Brandt tripped over the edge of the curb when they got to the other side of the street but recovered with Cade's help. He sent up a silent prayer of thanks as he reached the office complex's front door, grasping the handle on the front door and pulling.

It didn't budge.

"Shit!" he yelled, slapping his hand against the glass inset in the door. Cade pressed against the wall beside the door and fired twice more before shooting him a questioning glance. She sucked in a deep breath and ejected the magazine in her pistol to reload. "It's locked," he explained, pulling on the door again uselessly.

"Move!" Cade ordered, slamming a fresh magazine into her pistol. Brandt backpedaled as she aimed the pistol at the door's lock, and she fired three quick shots into it. The lock shattered, and he planted his boot against the door in a hard kick. It swung open, and as Cade turned her attention back to the mass of infected racing toward them, Brandt grabbed her arm and hauled her inside the darkened building.

Their footsteps echoed on the tile floor as they stumbled inside. Brandt pushed the door shut behind them. It wasn't going to hold for more than a moment or two, especially since Cade had done such a thorough job of breaking the door's lock. But even the false sense of momentary security it gave him was enough. He swept the lobby with his weapon, and out of the corner of his eye, he saw Cade do the same. When they were passably satisfied that the lobby was clear, he grabbed Cade's arm again and pulled her to a door labeled "STAIRS."

"Where are we going?" Cade asked breathlessly, limping as quickly as her injured knee allowed.

"Top floor. We'll barricade ourselves in," he said, pushing her ahead of him as they entered the stairwell. The door swung shut behind him with a clang. He fumbled at it, searching for a lock, but gave up and pulled a flashlight from his bag. He flipped it on, and the bluish LED flooded the stairwell with light. He followed Cade up the stairs, keeping his pistol in one hand and the flashlight in the other. His speed was halved by her slower pace, but he wasn't going to complain. "When we get someplace safe, we can figure out how to get in touch with Gray and Theo."

"They've probably left us," she replied, her words short and breathless as she pulled herself along by the stairwell's railing. When she made it to the top of the flight, she added, "I'd have left us, if you know what I mean."

"Uh huh," he said noncommittally. The sound of shattering glass downstairs reached his ears. He resisted the urge to turn back to look or to prod Cade to speed up.

"Think Theo and Remy made it back to the Jeep?" Cade asked. "Or do you think we're the only two left?"

"How about we *not* think about that?" he suggested. "It's too fucking depressing."

Cade fell silent as they ascended another flight of stairs. The only sounds were their boots and Cade's pained breathing. The noise in the lobby had blessedly abated. Brandt was about to send up a silent thank-you for small miracles to whatever deity was listening when Cade spoke again.

"Do you think Ethan will make it back?"

"Cade!" Brandt snapped, louder than he meant to. He winced as his voice echoed through the stairwell, and Cade froze, her back stiff. Even he stopped to listen, straining his ears for the slightest sound to warn him of impending danger. But there was none, so he relaxed. "You're depressing the hell out of me, Cade." He gently poked his finger into the small of her back to get her attention. "Go on. We'll stop at the next floor for a break. I'm sure your knee could use a rest."

"Oh God yes," Cade groaned, her shoulders sagging as she reached the next landing. "It hurts like a very painful hurting thing."

Brandt laughed softly and shook his head.

It took nearly thirty minutes to reach the final landing that opened up to fifth floor. As Cade panted and slumped against the stairwell railing, Brandt slipped past her to get to the door. He rested a hand against it for a moment and listened intently for noises on the other side. Not hearing anything, he pushed it open and eased into the hall. Cade followed, stopping inside the stairwell door with her pistol out and her eyes focused on the hallway. He acknowledged her with a nod before stepping away to ease down the hall. His heart pounded as he made his way halfway down the hall, but his nervousness was unwarranted; the hall was empty, as were the offices into which he peered as he passed them. He turned around and beckoned for Cade to join him.

"I take it it's safe?" Cade asked, bracing her hand against the wall for support. Brandt hesitated and wondered if she'd smack him if he offered his help in a non-life-threatening situation. He decided to risk it and gently took her elbow in his hand. She didn't resist or object as he led her to an office facing the street.

"It looks like it's about as safe as it's going to get," he said. "I don't think we could hope for much else."

An hour later, Cade and Brandt had settled into the office as comfortably as they could manage. Brandt had ceded the cushy black leather office chair to Cade and taken up residence on the mahogany desk. He reloaded all their weapons and took inventory of their supplies as Cade studied her knee. She'd pulled her pant leg free from her leather boot and hitched the fabric up above her knee. She poked at the injured area gently, kneading and prodding it, making faces as she felt for damage.

"How is it?" he asked, examining a bullet he held between two fingers. He squinted at it, closing an eye to bring it into focus, and Cade stifled a laugh at his facial expression.

"I think it's twisted," she said. Some of her hair had slipped out of her ponytail, and she pushed the loose strands back from her face and wrinkled her nose. "It hurts like hell, but that's to be expected."

Brandt flipped the bullet into the air like a coin, then caught it and snapped it into the magazine in his other hand. "How long before you think you can run on it?" he asked. He slid the magazine into its pistol and holstered the weapon at his side.

"I don't know. Maybe three days?" Cade guessed. "But we can't stay here that long. No water, no food. Minimal security. In a word, we're fucked."

"Indeed," Brandt agreed. He turned his attention to his bag and pushed its spare contents around, shoving aside a thick wrap of rope to get to the bottom of the bag. He checked for food again, peering beneath the rope, like something edible might magically appear where there had been nothing before. "However, the technical term is 'in the shit.'"

Cade chuckled and pulled her pant leg back down, tucking it into her boot again. "I do believe I've heard that one before, once or twice, when I was in Israel."

Brandt smiled and slid off the desk to go to the window, brushing the blinds aside to look at the street below. The fire from the RV's destruction had burned out half an hour before, so the street had fallen into darkness again. He squinted, trying to make out any finer details, but it was too dark. Most of his planning would have to wait until morning; what they did would be contingent on where the infected were, and if he tried to plan without knowing, he'd have to wing it. Again. And *that* hadn't worked so well last time.

"You're still pretty pissed at me, aren't you?" he asked suddenly. He'd noticed a frigid tinge to Cade's voice throughout their conversation, and it had begun to bother him. He hated people being angry with him if it was over something he could fix. He turned away from the window and dropped the blinds; they banged together before going still.

"I don't know, Brandt. What do you think?" she asked. Her voice was smooth and steady, but an undercurrent of anger lurked beneath her words. "I'm pretty ticked, yeah. But right now, I'm trying to not focus on that. We've got more important shit to deal with. Like how in the hell we're getting out of here."

Brandt nodded. "Exactly. I figure we'll have to wait until dawn before planning anything. It's too dark right now." She raised an eyebrow and propped the foot of her uninjured leg against the edge of the desk, rocking the chair slowly and staring at him in silence. He fought against the urge to fidget as he looked back at her; her expression made him feel like a five year old facing down a teacher after doing something bad. When she'd stared him down long enough, she averted her eyes to the dirtied bandage wrapped around her right hand.

"So. We need a plan," he said after the moment passed. He leaned against the wall beside the window and crossed his arms. "At least, we need a plan for right now, anyway. Got any ideas?"

"Hmm," Cade hummed, tilting her head back to look at the speckled white ceiling tiles. "How much ammo do we have?"

"Not enough for much of anything," he admitted ruefully. "Maybe enough to make a run for it, but I can't say for sure. We left all of our good stuff in the Jeep."

She hummed again, making no comment as she contemplated the ceiling, pushing off the desk with her foot to methodically rock her chair. When Brandt finally grew impatient, he demanded, "So what's the plan, Cade?"

Cade shrugged and hissed through her teeth. "Oh, I don't know. Why don't you give me all your guns and go out the front door as a distraction while I sneak out the back and get out of here?"

Brandt blinked. "Wow, you really *are* mad at me."

She slammed both feet to the floor and rocked her chair forward. She barely winced as the action jarred her twisted knee, but Brandt definitely flinched at the pen that flew at his head with surprisingly good aim. He raised an arm to block it before it put out an eye. "No, you *think*?" she snapped. "No wonder the fucking quarantine of Atlanta pissed all over itself if people remotely like *you* were in charge!"

A silence fell over the office as they stared at each other. Brandt didn't dare say a word. Whatever defense he could mount would be put down by Cade—if she didn't just shoot him first. He pressed his fingers to his temples and closed his eyes. He could feel a headache coming on, and his supply inventory had already told him there was no aspirin to be had. Finally, he repeated, "We need a plan."

"No shit, Sherlock. Got one?"

He pressed the heels of his hands against his temples, massaging in slow circles. He was sure that, within the hour, his skull would split open. "Jesus, just give me a minute. Let me think," he grumbled.

"Oh, for the love of God," Cade groaned, dropping her head back against the chair's headrest and covering her face with her hands. When she continued, her voice was muffled. "Please, please, *please* don't do that."

Brandt shot her a dirty look, but she didn't notice, hidden as her eyes were. He huffed out an irritated sigh and looked out the window again. "You're sort of right," he conceded.

Cade dropped her hands to her lap. "And you finally admit the obvious," she said with a pleased smile. She fell silent as Brandt attempted to study the street below, then she leaned forward, the chair creaking with the motion, to rest her elbows against her thighs. "What, exactly, am I sort of right about?"

"The whole distraction thing," he replied.

"The distraction thing? You mean you're actually going to run out the front door?" Her tone suggested she was joking, but only halfway. The other half just sounded incredulous.

Brandt laughed softly. "No, of course not. But I definitely think we need to figure out a way to draw their attention away from the doors long enough to get out of here."

"What we need is another RV," Cade muttered. She started to get up, but as she put weight on her leg, she seemed to think better of it and sank back into her chair. She massaged her knee through her jeans, gritting her teeth. "Shit, my knee hurts."

"There's no way you can run on that," Brandt said. "We can't even try to get out of here until your knee is better."

"We can't stay here," she argued. "We don't have any food or water, and we're not exactly swimming in time here." She fell silent and studied her bandage again, then added softly, "Ethan's supposed to be back soon. He's going to pitch such a fit when he finds out what happened to us." She traced her fingers along the gauze tied around her hand. "You think he'll make it back okay?"

Brandt's expression softened at her words. "I think he'll be fine," he said. It was all the reassurance he could offer. "I personally am more concerned about *us* at the moment." He scooped his bag off the desk and slung it onto his shoulder before starting toward the door.

Cade sat up straight as he moved away, her eyes wide. "Where are you going?" she demanded.

"I'm going to find some supplies. There's got to be a break room with some vending machines in this building. It's about time they got busted open already. You stay here. I'll be right back."

As he stepped into the hall, he heard Cade call out, "You know, in horror movies, the guy who says he'll be right back is usually the first to bite it!" He only laughed and shook his head before shutting the door firmly behind him and heading down the hall.

CHAPTER NINETEEN

Biloxi, MS

Theo looked up from his quiet, unfocused contemplation of the worn wooden floor of their latest hideout in Biloxi. His vision was blurred with exhaustion, and he rubbed at his eyes to clear them. He hadn't slept properly in the two days that had passed since Brandt and Cade had gone missing. The incessant paranoia that had always lurked in the back of his mind had grown since their disappearances, and it prevented him from doing anything but taking care of Remy and keeping watch on the street from the upstairs windows. He, Gray, and Remy had become so thoroughly ensconced in the old house that they'd begun to go stir crazy with worry and boredom.

"When are we going to get out of here?" Gray asked for what Theo could have sworn was the millionth time. Theo resisted the urge to snap at his younger brother, instead shaking his head wordlessly and focusing once more on Remy. She lay on the couch, half asleep, her injured ankle elevated on pillows. She'd spent the past two days dealing with an exceptional amount of pain and discomfort, but Theo didn't dare give her any pain medicine stronger than aspirin. He didn't know if and when they might have to make a sudden escape, and he didn't want Remy to be out of her mind on pain meds if the need for evacuation arose.

He massaged his forehead tiredly and sucked his bottom lip between his teeth. He'd never have guessed that medical care would prove so difficult in the world in which they now lived. His supplies were limited; there wasn't much he could do outside of immobilization for broken limbs and aspirin for headaches and pain. He didn't want to imagine what would happen in a more serious situation. The small amount of drugs he had wouldn't last forever; if he didn't run into a scenario that required their use, the meds would expire and lose some of their potency, potentially increasing the risks of overdosing his patients.

Theo had become a paramedic with his hands tied by necessity. The feeling of helplessness didn't sit well with him.

Theo stood slowly and pressed his hands against his lower back, bending backwards and feeling the joints crack and groan with stiffness. He'd sat too long, watching Remy discreetly for any sign of discomfort beyond the norm. The listlessness she'd shown over the past day concerned him, but Gray had suggested it was mere boredom. He was probably right. Theo, ever the over-reactor, stressed too much.

Theo looked at his brother. Gray watched him with obvious concern. He hadn't answered Gray's question, and the silence that hung between them was awkward. He cleared his throat and rubbed his hand over the hair at the back of his head.

"Sorry," he said. "I was thinking."

He could see the doubt in Gray's eyes from halfway across the room. "You're exhausted," Gray argued, moving closer to Theo, his voice low. "You haven't been sleeping again. This isn't going to be like the last time you decided to have insomnia, is it?"

It took Theo a moment to remember the "last time" to which Gray referred. It had been a week after Plantersville had fallen, when they'd been hiding in their parents' home. He'd gone an entire week without sleep and had nearly suffered a mental breakdown because of it. He'd been essentially useless until Gray had forced a sleeping pill down his throat and spent an entire night standing guard so he could rest. They did *not* need to be in that situation again.

"No, it won't be like that," he said in an attempt to reassure Gray. "I've been sleeping. Just not well." He glanced at the door and then Remy before returning his eyes to Gray's. "Any sign?"

"None," Gray said grimly.

"Are you sure they know where we are?" he asked. The thought had crossed his mind several times. But Gray merely shook his head and sighed.

"They knew. I'm sure of it. Brandt helped pick it himself."

"Well, shit. There goes that idea," Theo muttered. He shifted his weight from one leg to the other and tried to decide what to do.

As the oldest present and the one with the most knowledge of essential care and survival, Theo had become the *de facto* leader of the three—a position he'd neither requested nor cared to have. He'd considered the options and narrowed them to two. They could stay there, where it was reasonably safe for the moment and where they'd already taken steps to seal all the entrances to the building. They had enough supplies to last them several weeks if they were careful. That option would give them time to rest and give Remy time to heal. Their other option was leaving; they could try to find a better safe house farther from the city. But if they left, there would be no real way for Brandt and Cade and Ethan—if, in fact, any of them were still alive—to track them down. Not to mention it was always riskier to travel when not necessary, and he wasn't sure if it was in this case.

Theo knew they had another option, but it wasn't one he was prepared to consider: they could go back to the scene of Cade and Brandt's disappearance and try to find them. But with Remy hurt, it wasn't a real choice; they couldn't go back into the throat of danger when one of them couldn't even run. His and Remy's run for the Jeep two nights before had taken a lot out of the woman, but she'd done it without complaint. He wouldn't consider asking her to do it again.

And truth be told, if Cade and Brandt had succumbed to the Michaluk virus, Theo wasn't prepared to see them in the state in which the virus left its victims.

Gray still stared at him expectantly, still waited for him to offer a solution to all their problems. That was something he couldn't promise. It was a responsibility he didn't want. But rather than tell him that, he heaved a sigh and glanced at Remy again. She reclined against the sofa and watched them; the dark circles under her brown eyes made her appear pale. Looking at her cemented his decision.

"We're staying here," Theo announced. "There's no way we can manage travel, not with Remy's ankle. We need time to rest and recover."

Just hearing the words seemed to have alleviated Gray's worries; the deep crease in his forehead melted away. "Okay," he said. "Okay. So. What do we do now?"

"Well, you could start by getting me something to eat," Remy suggested from her perch on the couch. She gave Theo a small smile. "Just something light. I'm hungry enough to notice, but I don't want to eat too much. And maybe some water?"

"Of course," Gray said, abandoning his spot by the window and beelining for the supply bag that held their food and water. He rummaged through it and emerged successfully with a bottle of water and a can of sliced fruit.

"Good choice," Theo commented, eyeing the can of peaches. The syrup and fruit would help keep Remy's blood sugar up and prevent her from getting weak or dizzy. Despite the compliment, Gray ignored him and sat on the edge of the coffee table, offering the meager fare to Remy with a smile.

Theo's own smile spread across his face at the sight. Gray had become totally enraptured with Remy's very presence. He'd first noticed it as Gray had helped him get the woman out of the Jeep and into the safe house the night they'd rescued her. And in the two days since, Gray had nearly jumped through hoops not only to get Remy anything she asked for but to keep her attention on him; he talked endlessly about life before the outbreak, exchanging anecdotes, talking about movies and books and music and whatever else came to mind. Theo thought it was cute seeing his brother act like a bumbling teenager again.

The roar of a motorcycle outside the house distracted Theo from his thoughts. His heart jumped into his throat, and his ears focused on the sound. Gray and Remy had fallen silent. He swallowed hard before asking, "Did you guys hear that? Or was it just me imagining things?"

"It was definitely not your imagination," Gray confirmed. He stood and scooped up the pistol he'd laid beside him before joining Theo at the door. Both lurked by the door, listening intently. Judging by the sound of the engine, the bike idled just outside the house. Theo pressed his hand against one of the two boards holding the door shut and glanced at his brother.

"Maybe it's Ethan," Theo suggested. "I mean, we *did* plan where to meet up in case he actually came back."

"And he did leave on a motorcycle," Gray added.

"Who are you talking about?" Remy asked. She'd sat up on the couch, her dark eyes watching carefully as they stood by the door.

"Ethan," Theo answered simply, turning his attention back to the door. Gray took up the explanation where Theo left off.

"Ethan was sort of the leader of the group, I guess," Gray explained. "He seemed like he was in charge when we met him, anyway. He went back to Memphis to look for his wife. Said he'd come back in four days, max. We were just wondering if it was him."

"Won't know until we check, though," Theo said. He used a screwdriver to pry the boards away from the door; the nails groaned in protest. The door swung open as Gray stood guard by Theo, his gun gripped firmly in his hands. "Don't shoot that thing unless you absolutely have to," he warned. Gray nodded and eased his finger away from the trigger before stepping onto the porch.

And just like that, Gray's tense shoulders relaxed, and he let out an incredulous laugh.

"Jesus, you came back!" Gray called, hurrying down the steps toward the blond-haired man at the end of the walkway leading to the house. Ethan Bennett sat astride his red-and-black motorcycle, which still idled behind where they'd parked the Jeep. Theo walked out behind Gray but stayed at the top of the porch steps to observe the scene and keep watch.

"Don't call me Jesus," Ethan retorted, turning the key to cut the bike's engine. Even Theo stifled a laugh at the reply, and he leaned against the porch railing and looked the man over.

Ethan looked surprisingly good for someone who'd traveled so far so quickly. He was disheveled from the wind that had buffeted him, and his cheeks were flushed red. The ruddiness made him look younger and healthier. He'd acquired a brown leather jacket from somewhere. Theo would venture to say that Ethan looked better than he had before he'd left.

But the biggest surprise of all wasn't Ethan's appearance. It was the young girl who climbed shakily off the bike from behind him. She looked at her surroundings with a lost expression, like she couldn't believe where she was, even as she tugged the helmet from her head. Theo's previously neglected fatherly instincts kicked in when he saw the look in her wide blue eyes, and he abandoned his spot on the porch to hurry to her.

"Hey, sweetie. I'm Theo," he greeted her, putting an arm around her and squeezing. "Why don't you come inside with me? You look half frozen. What's your name?"

The young girl glanced back at Ethan uncertainly, but the man waved her on as he started collecting supplies from the bags tied to the motorcycle. "I'm Nikola," she answered, turning her eyes to Theo.

"Where are you from, Nikola?" he asked as he led her into the house.

Theo kept up the questions as he settled Nikola onto the edge of the coffee table and started checking her for injuries that might need tending to. He grilled the teen about her health and medical history and allergies. Ethan and Gray walked inside as he did so, Ethan actually laughing at something Gray had said, prompting Theo to nearly drop his stethoscope at the sound.

Ethan's good mood didn't last long, though. As he stepped inside and looked around, his laugh stopped as abruptly as it had started. His eyes scanned every face present, settling on Remy as a deep frown appeared on his face.

"Who is this?" he asked.

Remy sat up straighter and offered Ethan her hand. "Hi, I'm Remy. Remy Angellette," she said. "Your friends were nice enough to dig me out of a hole."

Ethan glanced at her hand but didn't take it. Instead, he looked around the room again and asked, "Where's Brandt?" He shifted his gaze across the room before settling it on Theo's face. Theo swallowed hard. "Where's Cade?" he asked, his voice growing several degrees colder. All signs of his good mood were gone.

"I...uhm..." Theo stammered, looking to Remy and then Gray. He tried to decide exactly what to say and, for that matter, *how* to say it.

"We lost them," Gray spoke up, releasing Theo from the need to find the words.

Ethan turned on Gray, his fists clenching at his sides, his jaw tightening. "You *lost* them?" he repeated incredulously. His voice nearly boiled with anger. "How the hell did you lose them? How the *fuck* do you *lose* two grown adults? And that better *not* be a euphemism for dead, or so help me God, I'm going to kill every single one of you."

"Honestly, we don't know if they're alive or dead," Theo interjected. "We got separated. There were infected everywhere, and they decided to create a diversion while Remy and I got out of there."

"Got out of *where*?" Ethan demanded.

"It's my fault," Remy said in a rush of breath. Every pair of eyes in the room turned toward her, and she shifted uncomfortably as she realized she'd put herself on the spot. "I was trapped in an RV, and they came to help," she said. "Things got really bad, and we made a run for it. We got separated, and there was an explosion—"

Ethan turned away at the word "explosion," and Remy's dialogue stopped abruptly. He started directly for Theo and backed him up against the nearest wall, slamming him against it with a thud before holding his hand out. "Keys. Now," he growled.

"What about our supplies?" Theo asked, even as he passed the keys to Ethan. He wasn't going to argue about the vehicle, but he didn't like the idea of being separated from the supplies.

"Fuck the supplies!" Ethan yelled, his face inches from Theo's. Theo resisted the urge to either flinch back from his anger or hit him in retaliation, but only barely. Ethan pushed away and grabbed his motorcycle bags before storming out the front door again. Theo hurried after him, watching as he threw the driver's door open and slammed the bags into the Jeep.

Theo continued watching Ethan for a moment, not tearing his eyes away as he spoke to Gray. "You're in charge," he said. "I'll be back. Get Nikola some food and keep an eye on those two for me, would you?" He scooped up his shoulder bag and stepped onto the porch.

"Where are you going?" Gray demanded.

Theo waved off Gray's question and nodded toward Ethan. "I'm going with him. I'll be back," he repeated. He gave Gray's shoulder a squeeze of reassurance and then headed down the sidewalk at a brisk pace to catch up with Ethan before he jumped into the Jeep and sped off.

Ethan barely looked at him as he reached the Jeep. "What do you want?" he asked shortly, sliding into the driver's seat without waiting for a reply.

"I'm going with you," Theo said. He circled the Jeep to the passenger side, his shoes crunching over the glass and gravel littering the road. He was already pulling the door open as Ethan voiced his objections.

"No, Theo. I'm going by myself. They might need you." He jabbed his thumb in the direction of the house. Theo scrambled into the passenger seat before he got the wise idea to drive off while he stood there.

"They'll be fine," Theo replied. "Gray knows basic first aid and CPR. None of them need me right now, anyway. *You*, on the other hand, will need help, and I'm offering it to you." Ethan stared at him, his jaw set in a hard line, and he stared right back. "You need to stop going off on your own, Bennett," Theo finally said. "It's not doing you any good. If we're all going to stick together, you need to get used to the idea of teamwork."

"I can work with a team just fine."

"Yeah, and you've done a shit job proving it," Theo argued. He pulled the door shut and buckled his seatbelt. "You're taking my help. At the very least, I can show you where we last saw them. At best, I can help you get them out of there, *if* they're still alive. And if they're injured, then you'll *really* need me."

Ethan pondered his words. Theo was grateful he was at least considering it. Not that he planned to give him a choice in the matter. Ethan had already taken off on his own once, and they were lucky he'd gotten back in one piece. Theo refused to let him run off again; he doubted even Ethan's luck would hold out twice.

Ethan sighed and started the Jeep's engine with a brutal twist of the key. "Fine then," he snapped, easing the Jeep out of its spot by the curb. "But if you fall behind, I'm not coming back after you. You're on your own. Got it?"

"Got it," Theo affirmed. He sat back in his seat and opened his bag to start an inventory of his medical supplies. Anticipation of the impending action built in his stomach, and he hoped he and Ethan were doing the right thing.

* * *

Cade's head shot off the mahogany desk as she sat up straight and looked around wildly. Her elbow knocked a half-empty bottle of water onto the floor, but she ignored the warm liquid that sloshed out and splashed against her boots. She blinked hazily and pushed her tangled hair away from her face, trying to remember where she was.

It was early evening, and she'd dozed off in the office chair. Everything was silent. It seemed like the sound of her breathing echoed through the room. She shook her hair back again and wondered where Brandt was. The idea that he'd wandered off while she slept made her stomach burn. She stood slowly and rubbed her stiff back with one hand as she felt for her rifle with the other. It was on top of the desk, and she rested her hand against it and squinted in the dim room.

It took her a moment to spot Brandt. He slouched in a chair directly across from the door, his eyes closed, his chin resting against his chest. A pistol lay against his thigh, held there by the tenuous grip of three fingers. His breathing was rhythmic and deep; he'd fallen asleep on watch. He hadn't heard her startled waking, by all appearances, which made her nervous. It meant he slept deeply enough that he wouldn't hear any noises warning of coming danger. Even if he heard them, he wouldn't react quickly enough.

She studied Brandt as she stretched her arms above her head and worked the kinks out of her shoulders and back. He looked younger when he slept, almost worry-free, and she was jealous of his seemingly easy sleep. She hadn't rested well in over a month, not since the Michaluk Virus had broken out across the southeast. Every night, every time she closed her eyes, it was one horrible nightmare after another. She'd only ever managed to sleep when she passed out from total exhaustion. It reminded her of the time she'd spent coping with her return from active duty in the battlefield, when she'd woken up screaming night after night for eight miserable months. Then, she'd been able to see a therapist to cope with her nightmares. Something told her a therapist would be hard to find in a post-Michaluk world.

Cade considered waking Brandt, but no, it was better to let him sleep while he could. She glanced at the dark window and nudged the chair back before taking a tentative step onto her injured leg. She put her weight on it cautiously, increasing it gradually until she bore a good portion of her weight on her leg. Her knee let out a pained twinge, but it wasn't as bad as it had been two days ago. She believed she could run on it again. Perhaps now she and Brandt could plan their escape in earnest.

She took the several steps to the office window without much issue, though her knee let out another twinge of pain three steps in. She shoved the soreness aside, tamping it down in the back of her mind, and hesitated as her fingers brushed the hanging blinds. She didn't know what she would see when she looked out. Brandt had barely let her get up from her chair over the past two days; he subscribed to the idea that the less weight she put on her knee, the faster it would heal. She sighed and pushed the blinds aside, squinting into the dimming sunlight. Everything on the street five floors below was as still and quiet as the office. She shivered as the cold radiated off the pane of glass in front of her, then leaned closer, resting her forehead against the glass. She looked straight down the side of the building, her eyes trailing along the base of the building and the sidewalk.

Much to her surprise, the infected that had spent the first day of their entrapment pressed against the building and flooding the first floor had dispersed. There were still infected below; some slumped against the side of the building, and others sat on the sidewalk or against cars or stood among the debris on the street. But there were nowhere near as many as there had been two days before. She wondered if the borderline panic she'd felt as she and Brandt ran from them had inflated their number in her mind. The thought that the RV's explosion had killed more than they'd suspected flitted through her mind, too. Either was a possibility.

Cade looked past the infected scattered below and scanned the street, back the way they'd come two nights before. The RV sat slumped in the street like a dead whale, a burned-out husk of metal. She imagined she could still see smoke, though she was sure that any flames had long burned out. A few crumpled bodies lay scattered near it, victims of the blast. Otherwise, the infected seemed to avoid the site.

A thump sounded behind her. She whirled around defensively, and relief flooded her veins when she saw it was only Brandt. He'd startled awake much in the same manner Cade had, and she smirked as he looked around, a delirious expression on his face.

"Welcome back to the land of the living," Cade joked. She walked to him and playfully batted him on the back of the head. He took a halfhearted swat at her and yawned.

"I see you're up and moving," he observed, rubbing his face and scratching a hand through his dark brown hair. "How's your knee?"

"It feels a *lot* better," she admitted. She rubbed the appendage in question, kneading it with her fingers, probing for pain. She didn't feel any. "I think I'll be okay to run if you want to get out of here."

Brandt dragged himself out of his chair and rolled his head from side to side to work the kinks out of his neck. "Are you sure?" he asked, slipping past her to look out the window.

"I'm sure."

"Absolutely sure?" he pressed, his eyebrows knitted together in a concerned frown. Cade resisted the urge to roll her eyes.

"*Yes*, Brandt. I'm sure," she said stubbornly.

They studied the street outside silently. Cade tried to make out a route that would get them out of there, but she couldn't conceive a path that wouldn't take them right past a large group of infected. Any plan requiring them to shoot was out of the question; the noise would only draw more infected to their location, and in their exhausted state, they'd both be toast. As she pondered the street, a low, deep rumble of thunder sounded over the city. She glanced at the sky with the faintest twinge of nervousness.

"What do you think?" she asked. She moved as if to pull her hair into a ponytail, then made a face as she realized the rubber band she kept around her wrist was missing. *So much for that*, she thought irritably, letting go of her hair.

"I think…" Brandt started. He drew the words out as he too looked up at the sky. A flicker of lightning greeted their upturned eyes, and he grinned. "I think it'd be a great idea to wait for that thunderstorm to get here," he said. "If it's loud enough, it could mask any sounds we make, and the rain could help cover our movements."

Cade brightened at his words. "It sounds like you've got a plan. So what is it?"

"You're actually asking me to make the plan?" he asked, raising his eyebrows.

"Why not?" she asked with a shrug. She dug into her bag and pulled out a fresh tank top, slinging it over her shoulder as Brandt replied.

"Well, considering the absolute mess I made of getting Remy out of the RV, I figured you wouldn't want me touching anything remotely resembling a plan," he admitted.

"I won't let you touch anything resembling an *emergency exit plan*," she teased. She slipped out of her leather jacket and draped it over the back of the office chair before unbuttoning her blue flannel shirt. "I figure we'll be okay if you don't make that half of the plan."

Brandt grinned. "Yeah, I don't have much practice with it anyway," he said, going along with the joke as she wiggled out of her flannel. She grabbed the bottom of her dirty white tank top to pull it off but paused as she realized he was watching her.

"Hey, mister, this isn't a striptease. Turn around," she ordered, laughing and twirling her finger in a circle in mid-air. It wasn't that she felt self-conscious changing in front of Brandt; far from it, really. The military had a way of beating bashfulness and modesty out of a person, and it had done a sufficient job of it with Cade. She wasn't squeamish about changing in front of him. But she certainly wasn't going to give him a free show, either. Especially not if it ran the risk of making group cooperation awkward.

Brandt laughed and shook his head but politely turned his back to her, studying the street below. Cade quickly donned the new tank top before he got the idea to turn around again, then pulled on her flannel shirt without buttoning it and shrugged on her leather jacket.

"So what's the plan then?" she finally asked again, joining him at the window.

He glanced at her and asked, "You always wear flannel shirts?"

"They're the only long-sleeved shirts I packed last month," Cade replied. "They're warm and not bulky, so I don't have to worry about them slowing me down." She glanced out the window and hummed thoughtfully before prompting again, "Plan?"

"Well, I figure we'll wait until the thunderstorm really gets going," he said. Another flicker of lightning brightened the street outside. It was much closer than before, and Cade's nerves felt like they were vibrating under her skin. "We stick close to the building, keeping to the side of it so they can't completely surround us. As long as we keep them away from us, we should be okay."

"And after that?" she asked, tucking a stray lock of hair behind her ear.

"After that, we get at least a block down the street and find a truck that's got the keys still in it and enough gas to get us to where Theo, Gray, and Remy should be hiding," he concluded. Cade raised an eyebrow at him. "It's the best I can do," he said defensively. "We don't have a whole lot of options."

"No, it's not that," she said. "It's a good plan. Best we can do under the circumstances. I just…what if they're not there?" she asked. "What if the others had to move? There's no way we can know where they went if they didn't leave a note or whatever, so…"

"So what then?" Brandt finished. "Just means you'd be stuck with me for months and months on end." The smirk on his face was devious, and Cade gave him a dirty look before letting out a melodramatic groan.

"Oh God, Heaven help me if that's the case," she said, pressing the back of her hand to her forehead and closing her eyes, mock-fainting. She opened her eyes a crack to peek out at Brandt, and she laughed at the hurt look on his face. "Oh, come on. I'm kidding!" she protested. "It wouldn't be so bad. I mean, your cooking skills are shit and mine aren't much better, so we'd probably starve to death eventually, but you're a damn good shot, and I couldn't ask for anything more."

Brandt smiled and tugged her hair. She laughed and swatted at him as she ducked away from his hand, and she looked out the window again. "So we're stuck here until the storm starts," she said, leaning against the black metal frame surrounding the large windowpane. "What should we do until then?"

"I don't know. Maybe…" Brandt tapped his finger against his chin and looked around the room thoughtfully. Then he shook his head in frustration. "There's absolutely nothing to do in here."

"*That* explains why I'm going nuts with boredom," Cade said cheerfully. "I've been so tempted to roll my chair over to the window and play target practice just to keep from going insane. If it wasn't for the fact it'd waste ammo, I'd be doing it right now."

He snorted and shook his head. "You know, sometimes you scare me," he said. He retreated to the desk and sat on the edge of it, propping his foot into the seat of the desk chair.

"Oh good. Mission accomplished," she said with a grin, turning away from the window.

Brandt laughed and patted the desk beside him. "Come on, have a seat. I want you to rest your knee as much as possible before we get moving."

Cade smiled and sidled over to the desk, climbing onto it and making herself comfortable before relaxing back against her hands. They sat in silence and watched the flicker of lightning and listened to the deep rumble of thunder as the storm approached, pushing them closer to their impending escape.

"So why exactly do you put up with him?" Brandt asked suddenly, breaking the silence between them.

Cade startled and blinked, glancing at Brandt. "Put up with who?" she asked. "What are you talking about?"

He shook his head and waved a dismissive hand. "No, never mind. Don't worry about it."

She punched his bicep lightly. "Come on, tell me what you're talking about," she urged. "You can't ask something like that and then be all, 'No, never mind.'" She dropped her voice and mimicked him, and he laughed softly.

"I just mean Ethan," he clarified. "How do you put up with him? And *why*? I wouldn't willingly put up with someone like that outside of the world we're living in now, and you've been friends with him for, what, seven years? How do you deal with his bad attitude?"

"Ethan doesn't have a bad attitude," she protested. "He's just…abrupt."

"Which is a polite way of saying someone is an asshole."

"Yeah, well," she said feebly. "He's *my* asshole, so don't go insulting him, okay?" She chuckled and examined the slice in her palm. "My family was from the United States. My mom and dad were born here, and so was my older brother, Caleb," she started to explain. She didn't dare look at Brandt as she quietly told the story. "My grandparents—my mom's parents—were from Israel. Before my sister and I were born, my parents decided to move back to Israel, where my grandparents were living again, so they could be closer to their parents. Lindsey and I were born in Israel. We were all in the IDF, Lindsey and Caleb for two years each. I'm the only one who liked it so much that I stayed in it."

When she fell silent, Brandt asked, "You have a brother? You've never mentioned a brother. Just Lindsey."

"I *had* a brother," Cade clarified. Her voice cracked, and she cleared her throat before adding, "He died when I was twenty-four. There was a bomber, and he was on the bus...." She broke off and shook her head.

"Oh," Brandt breathed, realization dawning. He lifted his hand and hesitated before rubbing her back in soothing circles. "I'm so sorry, Cade. That's…that's so…" He paused as he tried to find the right words.

"Senseless?" she suggested. "Most deaths in this world are. Hell, our world's becoming nothing *but* senseless. She pushed her bangs away from her eyes and breathed in deeply. "I should be used to senseless by now."

"I don't think anybody ever gets used to senseless," Brandt said.

Cade shook her head. "But you weren't asking me about my family. You were asking me about Ethan." She ran a hand through her thick hair and twisted a lock around her finger, desperately needing to keep her hands busy and her mind distracted. "It's because he acts like a replica of Caleb," she explained. "So much like him it's almost scary. And when I moved back to America when I was twenty-five, he was the first person to befriend me. He was there for me when my grandparents passed, when my mom and dad both passed, and now when the whole world has pretty much passed. We're like brother and sister because of all the shit we've been through. So that's why I deal with his asshole attitude."

Silence hovered as she finished her store, as short as it was and as little as she'd been willing to tell. A rumble of thunder in the distance hung between them. Brandt gave her shoulder a squeeze. "Shit, Cade," he murmured. "I'm so sorry."

"Don't be," Cade said, tracing the seam of her jeans with her finger. "It's just the way it is, you know? Nothing to be sorry about."

An hour later found them still sitting on the desk, still waiting on the storm to begin. Cade was disappointed; it was one of those typical winter thunderstorms that rolled through the south and dumped a ton of rain on whatever random spot it chose. She was growing concerned that the block of buildings where she and Brandt hid wouldn't be one of those random spots. "What if it doesn't storm?"

"Oh, it will," Brandt said, his eyes steely with determination.

"But what if it doesn't?" she persisted. She slid off the desk to look out the window. "What then?" she continued. "Does that mean we'll be stuck here until another storm comes around?"

Brandt didn't answer right away. Another rumble of thunder shook the windowpane, and Cade turned to him. Instead of watching her as she'd assumed, he had his eyes glued to the door behind them. One hand was raised in her general direction as if to preempt anything she might say. She frowned, watching him as he narrowed his eyes and shook his head. "What is it?" she asked.

"I heard something," he replied, glancing at her before leaving his perch on the desk and heading toward the office door.

Cade frowned and shook her head. "Brandt, you've been saying you've heard something for two days now. Are you sure you're not just being paranoid?"

But even as Cade voiced her question, the faint sound of banging and thudding coming from outside the office became more audible as she drew closer to the door. She paused mid-step behind Brandt and sucked in a breath, squeezing her eyes closed and focusing on the sound. Even as she struggled to listen, she knew exactly what she was hearing. Her eyes snapped open.

"Is it coming from our floor?" she asked in a rush of breath. "Have they made it up here?"

"Stay here. I'll go check," Brandt said. Cade opened her mouth to object, but the look he gave her warned her not to push it. Instead, she nodded and stood back to give him room to open the door. Brandt drew his pistol and stepped into the hall, leaving the door cracked; she watched his progress through the crack.

Brandt eased into the center of the carpeted hallway, his steps slow and measured as he worked his way to the end of the hall. The noise was loudest near the stairwell door. A nervous flutter worked its way into Cade's stomach, and she swallowed hard. She recognized the same feeling on Brandt's face as he rested his hand flat against the steel exit door. He hesitated and looked at Cade for a moment. Then he pushed it open slowly and disappeared into the dark stairwell.

Cade watched anxiously for Brandt to reappear. She bit her lip and grabbed for her pistol in case she needed to back him up. But it wasn't necessary. Brandt stumbled back into the hallway and pulled the door shut behind him, fumbling at it for a moment like he was seeking a lock before giving up and running back to her.

"They're in the stairwell, one floor down," Brandt said breathlessly. He slammed the office door shut and locked it before pushing one of the visitors' armchairs against it for good measure. "And on every floor below it. They're working their way up the stairs. They're slow, but they're going to be up here within twenty minutes, if we're lucky."

"Lucky?" she repeated. "Define lucky. Twenty minutes doesn't equal lucky in my world!"

"We'll be lucky if we get the full twenty minutes," he said, his eyes darting around the office frantically. "It'll probably be less. I'm giving us the max. Makes me feel better."

"Fuck," she breathed out, glancing at the door. "What are we going to do?"

"Well, I have an idea, but I'm pretty sure you're not going to like it," he said. He'd begun digging in his bag, knocking several packs of vending machine crackers out of it as he pulled out a long, thin coil of rope that Cade hadn't been aware he'd had.

"What's the rope for, Brandt?" she asked, making a face at the faint tremor in her voice.

"You ever go rappelling?" he asked.

"Rappelling," Cade repeated blankly.

"Yeah. The IDF covered that with you in training, right?" he prompted. He dumped the rope on the desk and unwound it, straightening it and shaking out the kinks.

"Of course, but…" Cade trailed off as the impact of his question hit her. "Brandt, you aren't *seriously* suggesting we rappel down the side of a building, are you?"

"What other choice do we have?" He began wrapping the rope in a loose loop from his wrist to his elbow.

"We don't even have any equipment!" she protested. "I mean, yeah, we got a rope. But there's no harness or anchor, and we definitely don't have a carabiner or anything! And you expect us to just…go down the side of the building?"

"Anchor," Brandt said simply, patting his hand against the mahogany desk. "And you're wearing a belt. We can make it work as a sort of harness if you're not brave enough to go without one."

"You can't really expect a belt to—"

"Cade. Shut up," Brandt ordered. He dropped the rope on the desk and braced both hands against it. "We don't have a choice, okay? Unless you *really* want to go out down the stairwell and end up dying when you run out of bullets."

"You're assuming we won't die rappelling down the side of the fucking building," Cade shot back, crossing her arms. Despite her protestations, though, she knew Brandt was right. It wasn't that she was scared of dying—far from it; she'd become accustomed to the idea of death during her first tour of duty. What *did* frighten her was the idea of throwing herself off the side of a building with nothing but a thin rope and five stories of air between her and the street.

It wouldn't be a pleasant way to die.

"Fuck," she grumbled in exasperation. "How are we going to do this then?"

"First, we've got to make a door," Brandt said. He pulled the blinds aside and let in the darkening evening light. Then he moved to stand directly across from the window and drew his pistol again. Cade followed his lead, pulling out her own pistol as he turned to point his directly at the plate glass before them. "On the count of three. Spread your fire out. We need to weaken it enough to break it," he instructed.

Cade rolled her eyes. "I know, I know."

He didn't reply as he flipped the safety off on his gun. "One," he began to count. "Two, *three.*"

On three, they squeezed their triggers and fired into the window. The kick of the pistol in Cade's hands as she shot bullet after bullet through the window was oddly comforting. The glass spidered from the holes they put into it. The gun gave her a feeling of confidence, made her feel better and more powerful, more in control of her fate.

When they finally ceased firing, the window was riddled with bullet holes, and it looked like it was one good kick away from shattering. Brandt nodded in satisfaction and turned his back to the window, grabbing the rope and beginning to wind it around one of the desk's legs and fastening it in a complicated knot.

Cade heard a noise in the hall and glanced at the door. "Brandt, I think maybe they've made it to the fifth floor," she said uneasily. Brandt yanked hard on the rope, his muscles bulging as he hauled back to tighten it.

"Yeah, I know," Brandt grunted. He released the rope and sat back to survey his work, rubbing his hands together and flexing his fingers. "We need gloves," he said. "You don't happen to have any, do you?"

"No, but…" Cade trailed off and pulled the dirty tank top back out of her bag, holding it up for his inspection. "It won't be perfect, but we can shred it and wrap our hands up."

"It'll have to do," Brandt said. He pulled a small, black-handled knife from his boot and offered it to her. She smirked and pulled out a much larger knife from the sheath she'd kept fastened to her belt for the past month.

"I'll use mine, thanks," she said. She set the shirt on the desk and stabbed it almost viciously, dragging the blade down the front of it, tearing it in half, and ripping and cutting it into strips. She tossed him several before sliding her knife back into its sheath and winding the cloth tightly around her hands, making sure she still had mobility around her fingers. The gauze on her hand shifted, and she winced as the cloth rubbed directly against the wound on her palm.

"Okay, what kind of rappel are we using?" Cade asked, holding her hands up for Brandt's inspection. He took her hands in his and looked them over, his calloused thumbs smoothing against the insides of her wrists. She suppressed a slight shiver at the feeling and watched him adjust the cloth.

"The Dulfersitz," he said. "The best we can do with no harnesses. You okay with me rigging you up?"

"Do I have a choice?" she asked. Brandt smirked, and she arched an eyebrow. "Don't you *dare* try to cop a feel on me, Evans, or I'll put you out of your misery right now."

Brandt chuckled and shook his head before kneeling in front of her with the rope in his hands. He looped the rope between Cade's legs and around one of her thighs to the front of her chest. She stood still as he crossed it over her left shoulder and along her back, and he ran his hand gently over the center of her back before continuing rigging the rope around her waist. Cade's eyes widened as his hand brushed against her hair, but her nerves over what she was about to do overrode any urge to punch him. Instead, she drew in several slow, deep breaths. Brandt straightened and moved back around to her front, looking down at her and giving her shoulder a gentle squeeze.

"You okay?" he asked. "Can you do this? We can figure out something else if you can't."

"What, you think I'm chicken?" Cade half joked. She scrunched up her nose as she heard the tremor in her voice.

"No, I don't think you're chicken, but you're scared out of your wits," he replied knowingly. Cade tried to shake her head, tried to deny the accusation. He gave her a soft look, and for a split second, as he stared at her, she wondered if he was going to kiss her. But instead, he wrapped his muscular arms around her and gave her a tight hug that nearly took her breath away. "It's okay. I am too," he admitted softly. Her eyebrows shot up in surprise, but before she could respond, he let go of her and looked at the door. The sounds in the hall were getting louder and closer. "Time to go, Cade," he announced. He grabbed the desk chair, positioned it, and gave it a hard kick. It rolled across the room and struck the cracked window before continuing straight through the glass.

Glass showered through the sky, flickering lightning glinting off the shards as the chair sailed through the air and tumbled to the street below. It landed with a crash that Cade was sure would draw the infected right to them, but it was too late to worry about that. Brandt was right. They didn't have much time.

"After you, my dear," Brandt offered with a gentlemanly wave of his hand. He pushed the heavy desk closer to the window and tossed the remainder of the rope out. It went slack far below, falling about ten feet short of the sidewalk, but the difference was manageable.

Cade drew in a slow, deep breath as a cold gust of air blew in against her. The scent of rain was on the wind, and she turned her gaze up to the clouds above. They were dark and ugly. Lightning flashed in them like strobe lights at a nightclub. Cade blew out the breath she'd drawn in and turned her back to the window. Brandt put a hand on her shoulder.

"You'll be fine," Brandt said again. Cade nodded and balanced at the edge of the window, bracing her feet against the metal bar and kicking away broken shards of glass as they stuck into the rubber soles of her boots. She looked behind her as she grasped the rope, and Brandt added, "Push off hard. Clear the building as best you can." He grabbed the rope to help steady it.

"Might as well get this over with, right?" she said with false confidence. She bent her knees and pushed off from the window frame before she could second-guess her decision. Her stomach somersaulted as she flew out into the empty air, and she clenched her teeth as nausea threatened to well up in her throat. The only sensations she could feel were the wind against her back and face and the rope sliding between her cloth-covered fingers. Then the rope caught tight as she grasped it firmly in hand, and she swung back toward the building like a pendulum. She stuck her feet out, and her boots slammed against the metal beams dividing the windowpanes with a thud.

The impact shook Cade's entire body. Before she could get a good foothold on the window frame, her boots slipped, and she was suddenly hanging free. The only things that held her up were her tenuous grip on the rope and the rope itself that cut into her right thigh and waist. She twisted her hands into the rope, looping it tightly. She gritted her teeth as it cut into her fingers and the wound in her palm. Blood stained the white cloth around her hand. She forced herself to relax as her body thumped against the windows.

"You okay?" Brandt called. Cade didn't dare look up as she rested her forehead against the cool glass. Her entire body trembled from the adrenaline and terror she'd felt at falling. She scrambled her feet against the glass and braced them on the pane once more as she recalled her training. She finally looked up and focused on Brandt's worried face as he watched her from the broken window above. She managed to give him a thumbs-up as she shifted and stared walking slowly backward down the glass, one careful step at a time. He gave her a reassuring smile that made her feel marginally better.

Cade made it to the bottom of the rope five nerve-wracking minutes later. She dropped the ten feet from the end of the rope to the sidewalk easily. As her feet touched the ground, she wanted nothing more than to drop to her knees and kiss the concrete beneath her feet. But she didn't have time for such ridiculousness. She drew her weapon from its holster and stepped aside to make room at the bottom of the rope, putting her back to the building and scanning the street around her for any infected. She was in a dangerous position, exposed and alone on the street in the falling darkness.

The street seemed reasonably clear, though; with the exception of a couple of infected on the sidewalk across the street that hadn't noticed her yet, there weren't any anywhere near her. She glanced at the sky as a couple of raindrops fell onto her shoulder and swore softly, her words covered by a rumble of thunder. Of all the times for the storm rolling in to choose to drop its rain, it had to be right then, when Brandt had a rope to climb down.

A loud crash and several gunshots burst out above her head. She froze. She swallowed hard and squinted at the broken window above her head as the rain came down more earnestly. She tightened her grip on her pistol as another three shots came from the office above.

Then suddenly, Brandt was there. He grabbed the rope and slid down it like a monkey on a vine, like it was second nature. He didn't bother to swing out from the building as he walked backward down the glass, his boots barely touching the surface in one step before taking another. Cade was impressed by his speed and his willingness to perform a borderline free fall from five stories up.

Brandt's boots hit the sidewalk beside her with bone-jarring force. Cade took a quick step back as he landed. "You okay? What happened up there?" she asked. Thunder boomed overhead and nearly took her words from her.

Brandt flexed his hands, then held them up to examine them in the darkening gloom. Angry red stripes scored his palms and fingers. Cade winced in sympathy pain at the thought of the rope grinding against bare skin. It didn't seem that her tank top idea worked very well when Brandt practically fell down the side of the building. "They got into the room about when you hit the ground," he said. He dropped his hands and fumbled for his pistol. His fingers didn't seem to be working right, so Cade pulled the weapon from its holster and handed it to him wordlessly. "They broke the fucking door right down. I didn't have time to get the rope around me before I had to go." He glanced up at the window and muttered, "Fuck, that hurt."

"Would have hurt worse if the rain had really started by the time you got down here," Cade said, even as the patter of rain intensified. Then it seemed like the bottom of the clouds opened up, and a sudden heavy downpour of water fell from the sky and soaked them through within seconds.

"Kind of like that?" Brandt called over the rain. He grabbed her wrist and tugged her down the street. "Come on, we've got to get going. A block or two this way and we'll start hunting for a car or truck or *something* with keys."

Cade followed him down the sidewalk. She did her best to keep her eyes on their surroundings, but the rain pouring into her face made it difficult. She wiped at her eyes and kept close to Brandt as he strode rapidly down the street. Her knee twinged in protest with every step she took, but she ignored the pain and pushed ahead.

They were a block and a half away from the office building within minutes, despite the rain still beating down on them and the erratic thunder crashing overhead. She swallowed hard and glanced at the sky before moving alongside and then ahead of Brandt. His adrenaline was running low, judging by the hunch of his shoulders and the bend of his back. Cade patted his shoulder as she moved past him to take point.

"Start looking for a car we can use," Brandt said. Cade shook her wet hair back from her face and nodded in acknowledgment. She went to the first car that looked easy enough to maneuver out of its tight spot. Brandt passed her his flashlight, and she shone it into the passenger compartment. There was no sign of keys in the ignition, so she shook her head and moved to the next likely candidate.

After Cade checked the fifth promising car on the street, Brandt making noises of exasperation as they were forced to pass it over like the last four, a bright light ahead drew her attention. She squinted as it moved closer and closer, accompanied by a low roar. She backed up a few steps, lifting her pistol and pointing it into the light. Brandt grabbed the back of her jacket and pulled her behind him to shield her body with his own. She realized, belatedly, that the blinding lights were headlights and the roar was the sound of an engine.

"Cade! Brandt! Come on, get in!" a familiar voice shouted from the other side of the light. Cade put up a hand to block the light and see who it was. As the voice called out her name again, she sucked in a shocked breath.

"Ethan?" Cade gasped. Joy flooded into her, and she stumbled past Brandt, hurriedly limping toward what she now knew was the Jeep, her knee aching and her wet hair falling into her face as she raced toward her best friend. When she reached him, she flung her arms around his shoulders as a desperate sob of relief welled up in her throat. Ethan gripped her in return, his fingers twisting into the leather of her jacket as he held her tightly.

"Fuck, you're a mess," Ethan said in her ear. He opened the Jeep's back door for her. "You okay? Are you hurt? Either of you?"

Cade clambered into the backseat. She knew they didn't have much time for happy reunions outside on the street in the rain, not with the infected close by. Brandt joined her from the other side of the Jeep a moment later, and she buckled her seatbelt as she answered. "My knee and hand, and maybe Brandt's hands too," she said.

Ethan shut his door and put the Jeep in reverse. He backed up with a squeal of tires before whipping the vehicle around and starting back the way he'd come. Cade looked at the passenger seat, and another grin split her face when she saw Theo there, twisted in his seat, watching her with concern. "Theo! You guys made it!" she exclaimed. "Where are the others?"

"They're at the house," Theo said. "Ethan showed up today, and we came back to get you two."

"Thank God you're all okay," Brandt said fervently. Cade nodded in agreement and turned around in her seat, looking back at the office building in which she and Brandt had spent the past three days. The time there hadn't been *too* bad; if it weren't for the lack of supplies, she wouldn't have minded staying longer. The company had been great—once she'd gotten over her irritation at him getting them stuck in the office building to begin with. She'd found a new friend in Brandt that she hadn't known lurked in him.

And now she trusted him with her life, completely, totally. He'd pulled her out of sticky situations twice, and he'd helped take care of her and she of him. People had to earn her trust, and Brandt had, twice over.

The office building receded into the distance and disappeared when Ethan took a left turn. Brandt laid a hand against her back as she watched, wide eyed. She turned to give him a soft, grateful smile.

As Cade looked into Brandt's dark brown eyes, she thought maybe they were going to be okay.

CHAPTER TWENTY

Biloxi, MS

The ride back to the safe house Theo and his brother had staked out was uneventful, save for a sticky moment where Ethan took a wrong turn and nearly drove them into a mess of infected gathered in the middle of the street. The skillful driving Ethan managed as he got them away from the crowd of infected had sent Brandt's heart leaping into his throat, but at the same time, he couldn't help admiring the way Ethan steered the Jeep around the debris and infected in the street.

But now they were finally in the safe house, hunkered down and trying to recover from the events of the previous three days, as Theo buzzed between his three patients to ensure their scuffs, cuts, bruises, and burns were healing appropriately. Brandt's hands still hurt; his palms had been scored by angry, red rope burns that had made curling his hands into fists virtually impossible—at least, not without a significant amount of stinging pain. It had been a bad idea to slide down the rope like he had, but it wasn't like he'd had a choice. The infected had gotten into the office he and Cade had been hiding in, had been staggering straight for him, their hands extended, and there had been no other way out besides the window. The burn on his right hand had been bad enough that it was probably going to scar, but between that and dying, he'd take the scar.

He was admittedly surprised that Ethan had made it out of Memphis in one piece. Or at all. It spoke to Ethan's resilience that he'd managed the feat, against all odds, and not only that, he'd brought someone back with him. Not his wife—Brandt hadn't expected Ethan to get that lucky; nobody in this world got *that* lucky. But he'd been lucky enough to stumble on Nikola Klein, had rescued her from a fate that Brandt didn't even want to imagine for a person so young.

"You hungry?" Brandt looked up, startled from his thoughts, to see Cade standing beside the couch he sat on, a plate in one hand and a bottle of water in the other. "It's nothing fancy," she added. "Just a bunch of stuff out of cans that Ethan threw together. I figured you'd be hungry since you haven't eaten today."

Brandt wasn't very hungry, but he took the plate from her anyway. "Thanks," he said, setting it carefully on his lap and taking the fork she offered him. The food on the plate wasn't particularly appetizing: canned vegetables and some sort of canned sausage. He wasn't a fan of anything canned— it always had a bland taste to it, like every bit of flavor in the food had been carefully wrung out before being sealed into the cans. He supposed he'd have to get used to it. It wasn't like he could just hop in a car and drive to the grocery store, pick up some chicken, and fry it on the stove.

Brandt carefully scooped up some of the canned green beans on his plate and lifted the fork to his mouth, though it was awkward business, as he couldn't grip his fork properly with his hands swathed in the light layer of gauze Theo had wrapped around his palms. "What's the plan?" he asked once he'd chewed and swallowed the beans. "What are we going to do once we get out of here?"

"I…don't know," Cade admitted, sitting on the empty coffee table in front of the sofa. "It's currently undecided."

"We can't stay here forever."

"Yeah, I know," Brandt said, poking at one of the little sausages on his plate. Someone had made an effort to render them more edible than they would be straight out of the can; that didn't mean they were any more appetizing. "That's why I was asking about a plan. We need to come up with something that will ensure our long-term survival as a group."

There was a thump somewhere upstairs, like someone had put their feet down on the floor too heavily in an effort to get up quickly. He glanced at the ceiling, raising an eyebrow, before giving Cade a questioning look. "Ethan found a ham radio or something in the attic. It's amazing how many people have stuff like that stored in their houses."

"Probably because they have no idea what the hell it is." He stabbed a sausage and chanced a bite. It wasn't horrible—but it wasn't good, either. He chewed as quickly as he could without looking like he was having a seizure localized in his jaw and swallowed. "Considering there's no power, how did he get it running?"

"Gray rigged up something with a car battery," she said. "It lets them run the radio for an hour or so before shutting it down."

"What the hell do they even need the radio for, anyway?" he asked. "It's not like there's anyone out there that can help us."

"No, but we might be able to help someone else," a voice said from the other side of the room. Brandt tore his eyes away from Cade to see Theo coming down the stairs, Gray and Ethan right behind him. Nikola and Remy were nowhere to be seen, presumably somewhere upstairs. "Seemed like it worked well last time we tried."

"Theo, we almost *died* last time," Brandt pointed out, waving a hand between himself and Cade. "I wouldn't call that 'working well.'"

"Touche," Theo acknowledged with a small smile.

"I'm assuming you came down here for a reason," Cade said.

"Actually, yeah," Ethan said. He slid past Theo to join her and Brandt by the couch, sitting on the coffee table beside her and resting his elbows against his thighs. "Something's come up, and we want to talk to you guys about it."

"What sort of something?" Brandt asked cautiously.

"We've been listening to the radio upstairs," Gray said, "mostly just trying to find out what's going on in the areas around us."

"And seeing if there are any updates on the virus in general," Ethan added.

"We've picked up a transmission from a group in west Alabama," Theo said. "They're begging for help. They said they're surrounded by a small horde of infected and don't have many weapons. They have mostly women, children, and several elderly with them and not enough able-bodied people to defend them if the worst comes to pass."

"So what are you proposing?" Brandt asked. "That we go help them?"

"We need to do something," Ethan said. "Cade's right about me—despite the way I've been acting like an asshole the past month, my natural instinct is to help people who need help. That's why I became a cop in the first place. I wanted to help people. I still do. But I can't do it as a cop anymore, so I need to find a new way to do it. I did it for Nikola in Memphis—well, she saved me more than I saved her, but the point still stands. And you guys did it for Remy. That tells me that it *can* be done. And I think we should do it. But I'm not going to *make* anyone do anything. The decision has to be unanimous. Either we all go or none of us goes."

"What have Nikola and Remy decided?" Brandt asked.

"We're not telling," Gray said. "We don't want any of our decisions to influence whatever choice you two make."

"So allow me to make sure I understand the details right," Brandt said. "You're asking if we'd be willing to drive to the middle of nowhere in Alabama, specifically to rescue a bunch of people who have managed to get themselves trapped by a horde of infected, for absolutely no other reason than because we can and because they need the help?"

"That's...pretty much the long and short of it, yes," Ethan replied.

Brandt looked up at Cade, who was already staring back at him, the look in her eyes making him think she was trying to read his mind. He had no idea what her answer was going to be, and he couldn't exactly ask her in front of the others in the room. Not when Ethan wanted them all to make the decision independently. His immediate instinct was to tell Ethan no, that they should stay where they were, maybe even take the time to find a place a little more secure, that they had no business going out attempting to play hero when they could barely take care of themselves.

But then he thought of Remy. If it hadn't been for them, she would be dead. There was no doubt in his mind about that. If they hadn't been there to get her out of that RV, to get her to a place where she could be treated for her injuries, then the infected would have eventually breached the RV's flimsy defenses and eaten her alive. Sure, the rescue effort had turned into a bit of a cock up, as the Brits liked to say, but in the end, it had all turned out fine: Remy had ended up in safe hands with Theo and Gray, and Ethan had returned and rescued him and Cade in the nick of time in a ridiculous *deux ex machina* moment that he was by no means ungrateful for. Maybe this was Ethan's way of pointing out that, so far, they'd had the best of luck under the circumstances and that it was time for them to consider paying it forward.

He looked up at Cade again, and she gave him the barest of nods, so slight it was almost imperceptible, and he would have doubted that he'd have even seen it if it wasn't for the serious look in her eyes. She was going to say yes. He was certain of it.

And suddenly, he wanted to say yes, too. He wanted to go with them, to help people, if only because he had no desire to let Cade out of his sight.

Brandt turned his eyes away from Cade, focusing them on Ethan again. The older man stood beside the couch, near his feet, his arms folded over his chest as he waited patiently for their answers. Brandt cleared his throat.

"Well, when do we start?"

ACKNOWLEDGMENTS

Acknowledgments are always the hardest things to write, because I'm always worried that I'm going to forget someone important. That said, if I forget anyone, I apologize!

I obviously have to begin by thanking my family. All of you have been so amazing and supportive, and I couldn't wish for anything more. I love you all!

Many thanks to the people at Permuted Press for giving this little book a chance to see the light of day in front of an audience that I don't think I would have been able to reach on my own. Without your willingness to entertain my sometimes oddball ideas for what to do with this series, I don't know where this book would be.

A huge thanks to all my readers and supporters. To name all of you would take pages, but I know who you all are. Thank you for all the times you've stopped by my tables at conventions, chatted with me online, liked a Facebook post, retweeted a Twitter post, and read and recommended my books. I seriously couldn't be doing this without each and every one of you.

ABOUT THE AUTHOR

Jessica Meigs is the author of *The Becoming*, a post-apoca-
lyptic thriller series that follows a group of people trying to
survive a massive viral outbreak in the southeastern United
States. After gaining notoriety for having written the series
on a variety of BlackBerry smartphones, she self-published
two novellas that now make up the first book in the series.
In April 2011, she accepted a deal with Permuted Press to
publish *The Becoming* as a series of novels. The first of the
series, *The Becoming*, was originally released in November
2011 and was named one of Barnes & Noble's Best Zombie
Fiction Releases of the Decade by reviewer Paul Goat Allen.
Five more novels and an assortment of novellas followed.

In 2013, she released *The Unnaturals*, a series of dark
fantasy novels that use the biblical Book of Revelation as
a springboard into a world where vampires, werewolves,
demons, and others creatures plague humanity and a group
of government-employed assassins must stop them before
they set the wheels of the Apocalypse into motion.

Jessica currently lives in semi-obscurity in Demopolis,
Alabama. When she's not writing, she works full time as
human resources for an ambulance service. She can be

found on Twitter @JessicaMeigs and on Facebook at face-book.com/JessicaMeigs. You can also visit her website at www.jessicameigs.com.

Jessica is represented by Sam Morgan of Foundry Literary + Media.

PERMUTED PRESS
needs **you** to help

SPREAD (THE) INFECTION

FOLLOW US!

𝑓 | Facebook.com/PermutedPress

🐦 | Twitter.com/PermutedPress

REVIEW US!

Wherever you buy our book, they can be reviewed! We want to know what you like!

GET INFECTED!

Sign up for our mailing list at PermutedPress.com

PERMUTED
PRESS

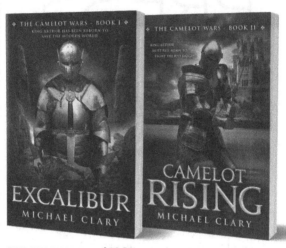

THE ULTIMATE PREPPER'S ADVENTURE.
THE JOURNEY BEGINS HERE!

EAN 9781682611654 $9.99   **EAN** 9781618687371 $9.99   **EAN** 9781618687395 $9.99

The long-predicted Coronal Mass Ejection has finally hit the Earth, virtually destroying civilization. Nathan Owens has been prepping for a disaster like this for years, but now he's a thousand miles away from his family and his refuge. He'll have to employ all his hard-won survivalist skills to save his current community, before he begins his long journey through doomsday to get back home.

THE MORNINGSTAR STRAIN HAS BEEN LET LOOSE—IS THERE ANY WAY TO STOP IT?

An industrial accident unleashes some of the Morningstar Strain. The

EAN 9781618686497 $16.00

doctor who discovered the strain and her assistant will have to fight their way through Sprinters and Shamblers to save themselves, the vaccine, and the base. Then they discover that it wasn't an accident at all—somebody inside the facility did it on purpose. The war with the RSA and the infected is far from over.

This is the fourth book in Z.A. Recht's The Morningstar Strain series, written by Brad Munson.

PERMUTED
PRESS

WE CAN'T GUARANTEE THIS GUIDE WILL SAVE YOUR LIFE. BUT WE CAN GUARANTEE IT WILL KEEP YOU SMILING WHILE THE LIVING DEAD ARE CHOWING DOWN ON YOU.

This is the only tool you need to survive the zombie apocalypse.

OK, that's not really true. But when the SHTF, you're going to want a survival guide that's not just geared toward day-to-day survival. You'll need one that addresses the essential skills for true nourishment of the human spirit. Living through the end of the world isn't worth a damn unless you can enjoy yourself in any way you want. (Except, of course, for anything having to do with abuse. We could never condone such things. At least the publisher's lawyers say we can't.)

PERMUTED
PRESS